SHOW ME .

D0533871

'Ted Allbeury's Cold War espionage novels have always been tightly plotted, tense and gripping. Here, in a more ambitious book, he tells the intriguing and extraordinary story of a double agent . . . A fascinating view emerges of the changing perceptions of the superpowers . . . Even more extraordinary is the fact that the novel is based on the experience of a real person.' *Books*

'Marvellously involving and thought-provoking read – the best book yet by Britain's master of the espionage novel.' *Woman and Home*

'Allbeury already has a deserved reputation as writer of novels on espionage and a large reader-ship – both can only increase with this gripping tale.' *Manchester Evening News*

'An extraordinary, powerful tale.' *Birmingham Sunday Mercury*

'One of the masters of espionage has come up with another winner . . . whether or not it's true, it's yet another example of Ted Allbeury's story-telling craftsmanship.' *Sunday Telegraph*

Show Me A Hero

___

Ted Allbeury

CORONET BOOKS
Hodder and Stoughton

Copyright © Ted Allbeury 1992

First published in Great Britain in 1992 by New English Library

Coronet edition 1993

Printed and bound in Great Britain for Hodder and Stoughton Paperbacks, a division of Hodder and Stoughton Ltd, Mill Road, Dunton Green, Sevenoaks, Kent TN13 2YA. (Editorial Office: 47 Bedford Square, London WC1B 3DP) by Clays Ltd, St Ives plc. Photoset by Rowland Phototypesetting Ltd, Bury St Edmunds, Suffolk.

British Library CIP

Allbeury, Ted
  Show me a hero
  I. Title
  823[F]

ISBN 0-340-58087-9

This is for Eleanor Wright – the pre-Raphaelite beauty of Tunbridge Wells – with love from us all.

Most espionage novels concentrate on the actions of an agent in some particular operation, usually involving guns and general mayhem. But in real life the operation of an espionage network is very different. In this novel I have tried to give an impression of the life of a man who runs a KGB network in the United States. With more emphasis on his life than the work that he did. The novel covers a long period and for clarity I have kept to the same name for the central character and ignored his obvious need for aliases.

Show me a hero and I will write you a tragedy.

F. Scott Fitzgerald – *The Crack-Up*, 1945

Vain hope, to make people happy by politics!

Thomas Carlyle, 1831

Man is a credulous animal, and must believe something; in the absence of good grounds for belief, he will be satisfied with bad ones.

Bertrand Russell, 'An Outline of Intellectual Rubbish', Unpopular Essays, 1950

1

Mary Taylor wondered why they had banned the TV crews and limited the press conference to journalists and radio. Even still-photographers had been excluded. Most press conferences at Camp David had three or four network crews. It couldn't be a security problem. Maybe he just wanted to limit the time he gave them. The TV people always used their weight and dragged things out.

They were still testing the microphones and recorder when he walked over to the dais. Blue shirt, no tie, grey slacks and Reebok trainers that looked as though they actually did some work. The wispy hair was lifting in the slight breeze and already that rather attractive lop-sided smile, as somebody moved the main mike. She'd always liked him even in the old days before he was Vice-President. He was really nothing like Reagan but in some ways they seemed much the same. Likeable All-American boys. But Bush was different because he had his hands on the levers and he not only did his homework but he understood it. His stint as boss of the CIA had seen to that. And he wasn't likely to confuse Bolivia with Brazil. Not that Ronald Reagan lost votes because of gaffes like that. Most Americans couldn't put their finger on Czechoslovakia on a map of the world. Reagan made voters feel that they really could be President of the USA if they wanted to.

There were all the usual questions about arms reduction and Star Wars, as SDI had been christened by the press. The features girl from the *Post* tried to hassle him about abortion but he gave her the smile and pointed to the man from *The Times* of London.

'Yes, Mr Long.'

'Mr President, there are some in Europe, and I understand in the USA too, who wonder if the White House isn't dragging its feet now that *glasnost* and *perestroika* have changed the international climate. Are they right, Mr President?'

'Well now – we've made considerable progress in our negotiations with the Soviets on arms reduction, the outlawing of chemical warfare weapons and troop reductions. I wouldn't call that dragging our feet.'

'Mr President, I was thinking more of the psychological aspects of *glasnost*. The world sees the Soviets stretching out the hand of peace and the US government taking a rather aloof attitude. Not ready to accept the end of the Cold War.'

The President smiled. 'I'm delighted that the press are giving so much space to good news for a change. But let me make clear that this administration is responsible, as all administrations are, for the security of the United States and its people. We have had nearly forty years of Cold War – not, I hasten to add, of our making. We welcome wholeheartedly the changes in the countries of the Soviet bloc and in the Soviet Union itself – and we shall be only too ready to assist that progress to democracy. But in those countries you cannot go overnight from overbearing dictatorships to democracies – there are no organised political parties that are capable of ensuring that democracy prevails – it takes time and we must give them time – not rush in in a state of euphoria at the risk of being considered a de-stabilising influence. Yes . . .' The President nodded towards a man in the back row. '. . . Yes, Ted.'

'Mr President. With the new climate between the two super-powers is the administration aware that many Americans feel that it is time to end our commitment of troops and weapons to NATO?'

2

He got the old smile as the President said, 'When we have made progress on the main issues, the question of NATO and Warsaw Pact forces will undoubtedly be discussed. We have to find out what the other side have in mind.'

One of the old China hands from PA-Reuters stood up.

'Mr President, doesn't your use of the term "the other side" show that the administration is reluctant to abandon its adversarial stance towards the Soviet Union?'

'Mr Olson – it is Mr Olson, isn't it? – right. Mr Olson, when two lawyers appear in court, one defending, the other prosecuting, they both refer to "the other side" and they each assemble the facts of the matter in court to suit their different cases. However – it is not unusual for the two of them to play golf together on Saturday afternoons.' He grinned. 'I suppose the diplomatic equivalent is making one's points in arms reductions talks and then going for a walk in the woods together.'

There were a number of shouted questions but the President said, 'I'm sorry, ladies and gentlemen, but I have meetings scheduled. Thank you for your time and your questions.'

She saw O'Brien walking towards her. He was the President's Press Secretary but she had known him way back when she was with NBC and O'Brien had been on Madison Avenue.

He pulled up one of the empty chairs and sat beside her. 'Glad to see you, Mary. It's been a long time.'

'Will he see me?'

'What's your piece for?'

'Nobody yet. I'm free-lance now but it could end up in one of the nationals.'

'News or think-piece?'

'Think-piece.'

'OK. I can get you in in about ten minutes. He's making some calls right now. But a couple of conditions.'

'Like what?'

3

'Only fifteen minutes and no direct quotes. Background for you and not repeat not an interview.'

'I'm flattered.'

O'Brien looked surprised. 'Oh, I thought you would be huffy. How come you're flattered?'

'Flattered that he'd talk with me off the record and trust me not to abuse it.'

He smiled. 'You've got a good track-record, honey. How's the small boy?'

She laughed. 'The small boy's at Yale doing law.'

O'Brien looked at his watch. 'I think we could wander in now.'

The President smiled as he took her hand. 'Nice to see you, Mary. I guess Sean already told you the ground rules. They OK with you?'

'Of course, Mr President. I'm grateful for the time.'

'Sit down, make yourself comfortable.'

When she was seated he leaned back in his chair.

'Fire away.'

'The so-called Eastern bloc countries and the lurch to democracy. What's going to happen in the end?'

'In the GDR there's a chance that they could form new parties based on the political parties in the Federal Republic. And having the FRG alongside them and the possibility of economic and financial help from Bonn will help. But the Communists aren't going to give up without a struggle. Not right away but maybe in a year or two's time. Euphoria doesn't last and if the new leaders don't improve living standards people will be disillusioned. And in Czechoslovakia and Hungary they've got to go all the way back to square one. And that ain't gonna be easy.'

'And re-unification?'

'Bonn want that and they'll work hard to get it. But there are long memories in Europe. Whatever they say in public the French won't like it, neither will the Poles and the Italians. Maybe in ten years' time when the East

4

Germans have worked their passage. If they rush into it it could turn out to be a real can of worms.'

'What about NATO and withdrawing our armed forces in Europe?'

'Moscow are already doing a great PR job about reducing numbers on both sides but it depends on what they mean. Just pulling out numbers equally isn't on for us. It's got to be the number of troops and weapons that are left. They've got far more of everything than NATO at the moment.

'And you've got to remember that if things went wrong they've only got to roll across Poland or East Germany and they're on the way to the Rhine. We'd have to send troops from the States. Could be over before we get there.'

'Do you think that Gorbachev really means it?'

'Oh, he means it all right. He doesn't have any choice. The Soviet economy is crumbling to dust because of its corruption and inefficiency. You've got to remember that *glasnost* and *perestroika* didn't start with Gorby. It started way back with Khrushchev when he denounced Stalin at the Twentieth Congress – in 1956 if I remember correctly. But the time wasn't right. And Gorbachev has got problems beyond the economy. The new upsurge of nationalism is just as big a problem.'

'What about the suggestion that we're dragging our feet in ending the Cold War?'

'They created the Cold War, Mary. Not us. And now they want to end it. That doesn't mean they've necessarily given up their aim of sustaining subversion and expansion wherever they can. They've got a chaotic situation on their hands and I've got no intention of rushing in and ending up taking or sharing the blame when they make a mess of it – as they probably will.

'The Western public have been the target of a superb PR exercise from Secretary General Gorbachev. What most of them don't realise is that in all his public statements about *glasnost* he has at no time ever suggested, or even hinted, a set of reforms that would turn the Soviet Union into a pluralist society, nor has there been the slightest questioning of the supreme authority of the Communist Party. He's a communist, Mary. Don't ever forget that. And don't let the public forget it either. Deeds not words are what they should go by.'

'And what about Star Wars? They seem fanatical about us giving up that whole project.'

For long moments he looked at her then he leaned forward towards her and said, 'No quote, no hint, not even a vague reference to what I tell you. OK?'

'Of course, Mr President.'

'They're far ahead of us on SDI. They've already got it. It's that kind of deceit and hypocrisy that I have to bear in mind when I hear the words *glasnost* and *perestroika*.' He stood up. 'I'll have to go, Mary. It was good to see you. Stay and have a drink with Sean.'

Camp David had been cleared that night of everyone except Marines and Secret Service agents. Not even White House staff were allowed to stay.

The President dined that night with his wife and the old man. When it was time for the old man to leave the President walked with him to the door. He remembered what Malloy had told him about the old man's arthritic hands and he took the old man's hand very gently as he said, 'You've helped clear my mind and I'm truly grateful.' Then he smiled and said, '*Da svedahnya a spasibo.*'

The old man smiled. '*Da svedahnya.*'

Bill Malloy drove the Lincoln to the servants' section of the main building and helped the old man into the passenger seat. They took the service road to the main road and then Malloy headed for the airstrip.

They sat in the car as the plane was checked over and Malloy said, 'You don't want to change your mind?'

'No. I called it a day long ago.' He smiled. 'I hope we'll still see you from time to time. Both of you.'

6

'You will. I wish we could tell the world how much we owe to you – the man who won the Cold War.'

The old man shook his head. 'Not *won* it, my friend. Just helped you people in a small way to make sure it didn't become a real war. And that's all that matters.' He turned his head to look at Malloy. 'You people have got a lot of things to work out, my friend. When you look at the new democracies remember what Bertrand Russell said.'

'What's that?'

'If one man offers you democracy and another offers you a bag of grain, at what stage of starvation will you prefer the grain to the vote?'

Then they were signalling that the plane was ready for take-off. Malloy walked with him to the steps and waved back when he had climbed up to the entrance.

Malloy stood there long after the plane had taken off. It was probably the last time he would see him and he felt both guilty and sad about the old man. Despite all that he had done to help them it had been a wasted life. So lonely, even when he was with people. The mind that was so shrewd and yet so innocent. The heart that bled for all humanity but found no solace from individuals. Loved but not loving. A man to respect but not admire. He took consolation from knowing that although they had used him they had not abused his dedication. Jack Kennedy had said – 'We will pay any price . . .' and the old man had been part of that price. But it was Moscow who had drained the soul out of him for a cause that was crumbling to dust all over the world.

Malloy walked slowly back to the car. At least the old man had Tania who saw him as a saint and had love enough for both of them.

2

As the train made its way over the snow-covered plains of Poland he wondered if he had done the right thing. It had been bad enough when Rosa was alive, the chaos of Moscow: that mad monk in the Palace, the third Duma as ineffective as its predecessors and the evidence from every quarter that the Jews were going to be the next target. He had been warned that he should get out and take the family with him. The army would kill Jews just as ruthlessly as they had shot the workers. And then the news from the doctor that Rosa had only a few weeks to live. In fact she had struggled on for nearly six months. The police had stopped him as he left the synagogue. Checking through his papers, shouting question after question until Lensky had intervened. Lensky was a lawyer and a wealthy man with influence everywhere. But it had been the final warning that they had to go.

He looked at the children asleep on the opposite seat. He wondered what would become of them all. Andrei the five year old, Anna just four and Ivan the baby, only a year old. For years he had worked for the Party in his free time. Waiting for the day when the workers would rise and the Party would take over. There had been uprisings but they had all been put down by the Tsar's soldiers. It seemed unbelievable, Russian soldiers shooting down Russian workers. He sighed and shook his head. One day it would happen but he wouldn't see it. He wasn't escaping because he was a communist but because he was a Jew. Not a good Jew, just a Jew, and that was enough. When he had talked to Lensky about going underground Lensky had pointed out that he had three young children to care for. And somehow he felt that Lensky was also telling him that being a Jew, even after the revolution, he wouldn't survive. There were big men in the Party who were Jews. He wondered how they would survive. Lensky was a Jew but he was a rich man who knew influential people, not only in Moscow but all over the world. God knows what would have happened to him and the children if it hadn't been for Lensky. But there would be work to be done for the Party in Paris. Maybe Andrei would be the one to see the dream come true. He'd teach him what it was all about. He was a good boy and quick to learn. Lensky had given him the tickets to Paris and enough money to live on until he found work. He'd heard that gloves were much in demand in Paris, and there were other things he could turn his hand to if he had to. Mikhail was going to sell their few belongings in Moscow and send the money to him when he had an address in Paris. The only things he had brought with them were clothes and his Party pamphlets and one book – the fourth German edition with Engel's preface of Marx's *Das Kapital*. There were pamphlets in Russian of translations of *Value, Price and Profit* and *The Class Struggles in France*.

They had left Moscow on February the 13th, 1913.

A woman Party member, a refugee from Latvia, had met them off the train and had taken them to a house in Montmartre. They had been given two attic rooms in an old house, thanks to Lensky's influence. The woman apologised for the limited accommodation and Grigor Aarons had been quietly amused. They had had one room for the six of them in Moscow and the two large rooms they had been given were luxurious in comparison. And to add to his relief the woman's daughter would look after the children while he was at work, and there was already a job for him in a small but stylish glove-maker's workshop at the back of a fashion shop in Faubourg St Honoré. He tried hard not to think of how happy Rosa would have been in such circumstances. His efforts must be for the children now. And for the Party. Their day would come. It might take years but it was inevitable.

The children sat around the battered, folding table of the kind that rich people used for playing cards. He had done them a chicken soup with pumpernickel bread and he sat on the chair by the window as they ate, chattering and laughing about their poor friends at school who couldn't speak Russian. There were two apples between them and as Grigor cut them in half and gave them each a piece it was Anna who turned towards him and said, 'Anne-Marie at school asked me why we are here, Papa. Why are we here?'

It was Andrei who answered. 'Because we're Jews.'

'We're not Jews, we're Russians.' Anna looked at her father. 'Isn't that so, Papa?'

'We're both, little one. Now get on with your apple. And 'van, it's your turn to wash up and fix the bed for tonight.'

With three young children to care for Grigor Aarons had not been called up to the French army when the war started and the shortage of able-bodied men had meant that he was put in charge of the workshop which was now making canvas belts and leggings for the navy and the army.

Eventually the war ended. Andrei and Anna were doing well at school and Grigor Aarons was now a junior partner in the glove business. The wonderful news of the October Revolution in October 1917 had been celebrated discreetly, but although the children had been told about the events in Moscow they were too young to understand what all the fuss was about, although they were used to hearing long arguments and discussions in the living room as they lay in bed. At home they spoke both Russian and French.

Russian at meal-times and French when they told their father about school.

By the time Andrei was twelve years old his father talked to him every day about the struggle in Russia, telling him the names of all the important people involved. He learned about the struggle between the Bolsheviks and Mensheviks and the opposition of men like Trotsky, Zinoviev and Bukharin. And he heard about the Comintern who would bring Communism to all the workers in the world and help them in their struggles against the capitalists. Although his father never said so Andrei knew that these were things that should never be discussed with outsiders.

They were good years. France was beginning to recover from the war, and his father was doing well at his work. There were titled ladies and wives of government ministers who would only have gloves made personally for them by Grigor Aarons.

By the time Andrei was sixteen years old he was working for his father who had been made an equal partner in the glove business. In the evenings he spent his time with the young communists who sat in cheap cafés putting the world to rights and speculating on the outcome of the revolution in Moscow. He spoke reasonable French now but most of his companions were refugees from the Baltic States – Lithuania, Latvia and Estonia. With a few French students from the Sorbonne and Italians who worked in restaurants and hotels. But his closest friend was Igor Serov. Not that either of them was much given to outward expressions of friendship but Serov seemed impressed by Andrei's ability to convince wavering Party members that all was well with both the theory and practice of Communism. He never knew how Serov earned his living but he guessed it was some sort of administrative job. One didn't probe too deeply in a community where forged papers and new identities were the means of survival. But there was no doubt that Serov knew far more about what was going on in Moscow than could be learned from the newspapers.

11

In 1928 the Party in Paris was shaken by the news that thirty senior Party members, including Trotsky, Zinoviev and Kamensky, had been banished from the Soviet Union and were living in exile. The official announcement had named no names, it was Serov who had told Andrei, whose father wouldn't believe it, saying it was revisionist propaganda.

Grigor Aarons died in 1929, a week before Andrei's twentieth birthday. An epidemic of 'flu had swept through Paris and taken a heavy toll. Andrei became the head of the family and he took to his new responsibilities conscientiously. The other two had jobs now. Ivan as a bell-boy at one of the big hotels and Anna as an assistant in a large department store. They all got on well together despite their different temperaments and Andrei was loved and admired by the two of them. Even Ivan, who had grown up to be rather independent and cheeky, did what he was told. Andrei was nearly twenty-one when his life changed dramatically. It was Serov who changed it as if it had all been planned long before.

They were sitting at a table in a small café not far from Andrei's place.

'Why do you always have hot chocolate, Andrei? Why not coffee?'

'Coffee is for dilettantes. It's just a stimulant. Hot chocolate is a food. I don't need stimulants but I do need food.' He smiled. 'Anyway I like it better than coffee.'

'Are you still at that dreary job in the glove workshop?'

'If you want to put it that way – yes.'

'I've been asked to talk to you about something more important.'

'Oh. What is it?'

'The Party want you to work for them full-time.'

'Who in the Party said this?'

'Somebody high up. You wouldn't know his name.'

'How do they know about me?'

'I've told them about you.'

'And what do they want me to do?'

'They want you to go back to Moscow to a training centre for a few months.'

Andrei shook his head. 'I couldn't leave the family. They need me.'

'The Party needs you too.' Serov lit a cigarette. 'I'll look after the family while you're away.'

'What sort of training?'

'You've heard of the Comintern?'

'Of course.'

'The Politburo run the Comintern and they're having a big shake-up. A restructuring. They want Party members to instruct foreign Parties on how to go about organising the revolution in their own countries.' He paused. 'They see you as covering a number of countries. At least France, Spain, Italy and Germany.'

'Surely I'm too young for anybody to take any notice of what I say?'

Serov smiled. 'I've heard you at work here, Andrei. You've got a wonderful way with the doubters.' Serov laughed. 'You actually listen to what they say, and most Party zealots never listen. And then you've got such confidence in persuading them with your own views. It's young people we have to convince now, Andrei. The old Party sweats are worn out. They've always just taken the Party line from Moscow and that's it. They never argued – they just accepted it. That's not enough these days.'

'How long would I be away?'

'Four months – maybe six. And you would be paid and the money would be transferred here to your family.'

'Tell me who this high-up Party man is, even if I wouldn't know his name.'

'If I tell you, will you go for the training?'

'Tell me.'

'It's an old friend of your father. Jakob Lensky. He's a member of the Politburo now.'

'But he's a Jew and . . .'

'So are half the intellectuals who are running the Party now. Anyway you'll be Lensky's protégé.'

'And you'll visit the family every day?'

'I can't promise that but I'll be available whenever they want me. They won't be a problem, Andrei, you've trained them well.'

'I'm thinking about little 'van.'

Serov laughed. 'Little 'van is sixteen or seventeen now and he's quite capable of looking after himself. So is Anna. Don't worry, I'll keep an eye on them. You'll never have another chance like this to serve the Party.'

It had taken three days for the train to get to Moscow. The high arches of the Byelorussky terminal were hung with clouds of steam and fog. Lensky was waiting for him by the ticket office. As always, looking prosperous and important.

Lensky took him to an apartment on Tverskaye Street where they had eaten *blinys* and *pirozhky*. Lensky had offered him vodka as he waved Andrei to a comfortable leather chair and had smiled when Andrei asked for tea instead.

'Your friend Serov has told me all about your excellent work in Paris. Your father would have been very proud of you. I wish he had lived to come back and see the Party in action.' He made a sweeping gesture with his arm. 'Turbulence, yes. Maybe even errors of judgment. But above all enthusiasm and dedication to what we believe in. But the revolution is for export. All over the world. And young men like you – with talent and with training – will show our comrades in other countries how to achieve our goals.'

'I'm not sure that I am as talented as you seem to think, comrade Lensky.'

Lensky smiled. 'Leave it to us to judge that, my friend.'

'Where do I have the training?'

'Moscow Centre have taken over the old Kuskovo estate. It's about ten kilometres outside the city. Rather

14

primitive conditions but the training is excellent. Only the most promising are sent there. You've been nominated by me so I want you to do your best.' He smiled. 'I'm sure you will.'

Kuskovo Palace and its vast park had been the summer home of the Sheremetiev family, one of the oldest Russian noble families of statesmen and soldiers. But now it was surrounded by a six foot high fence covered with barbed wire. An ancient car had taken Andrei to the gate which was flanked by two armed soldiers. In the guardhouse a man asked him his name.

'Aarons. Andrei Grigorovich.'

The man checked a list of names and then reached for a row of tags on hooks, taking one down and handing it to Andrei.

'We don't use names here. Your number's three nine. Thirty-nine. You'll be in the Dutch house, comrade.' He pointed through the barred window. 'It's quite a walk. The first house is the Hermitage, then the grotto and then your place.'

As he walked across the parkland towards the buildings he thought of what the taxi driver had said as they stopped at the gates. 'You know what this place is, comrade? It's where they teach the bloody niggers how to make revolutions. All the money they want but not a bloody kopek for the likes of me.'

The man at the podium looked like an academic, and he was. Lank hair, a pale face and heavy glasses. He held up some pamphlets as he looked at the students.

'You must read and absorb these thoroughly.' He pointed at the titles one by one. *The rôle of the Marxist-Leninist party in the revolutionary process. The struggle for the unity of the world communist revolution* and *Party members and the struggle for national and social liberation.* He looked across at them. 'This is going to be your task

15

in your own countries, comrades. You never deviate from the principles laid down in Moscow.

'You will have instruction in motivating local Communist Parties, trades unions, students, workers and in using radio and newspapers to create a sympathetic attitude towards the Soviet Union. There is much to be done and you are the men and women who have been chosen to do it.'

Two of the thirty students, and one of them was Andrei, were to get additional training, but this was training by the intelligence service in Moscow. But they, like the other students, had been told that Comintern members would never be used for intelligence work.

The days of the extra training were long and exhausting. Walking the streets of Moscow in the rain and snow learning how to throw off somebody who was following him. Learning the use of codes and identifying places where signs and messages could be left. How to use signs so that they could only be recognised by the contact and how to use cut-outs so that nobody but the agent in control would know who was in the network and what they did. Then there was the system of messages broadcast on Radio Moscow on long-wave, disguised as letters from listeners. Words emphasised when giving the titles of songs requested by overseas listeners.

Finally there was instruction on the short-wave transceiver that could operate as far as Moscow from Paris or Berlin for urgent messages and instructions. Somebody who could use a Morse-key and service the radio would be available wherever he operated.

There was a week at the Moscow Film Centre where he was taught how to use a small camera and light-stand for copying documents. He was taught how to develop film but was told that unless there were specific orders exposed film would be passed on without being developed.

A specialist officer showed him how to pick simple locks and how to immobilise motor vehicles.

Like everything that he was taught Andrei absorbed it

conscientiously. Time and money were being spent on him by the Party and he had to make sure that it wasn't wasted. He didn't see an immediate use for the spy training in doing his Comintern job but if people above thought it was necessary they would have good reasons.

Although he had vague dream-like memories of Moscow from when he was a child, the six months he spent there had been a wonderful opportunity to look at all the places his father had talked about. When his day's training was over he'd walk around the city, admiring the beautiful old buildings and talking with men like his father working on the roads and building sites. But when he talked about the changes since the Revolution he found them suspicious and reluctant to talk. When he had mentioned this to Lensky he was surprised when he had warned him not to talk to strangers. And there was even a hint that he shouldn't discuss politics with the people who were training with him.

On his walks at night he always came back to Red Square to stand looking at the light on the flag on the Kremlin building. That deep red flag with its hammer and sickle always moved him as it streamed out in the wind against the dark sky. It was like a beacon for all the peoples of the world.

The other student who was given the special training was a girl, a Spanish girl. They shared accommodation with an instructor in an old house near Manège Square. She was in her early twenties and although she was very attractive he found her too extrovert for his taste. Seemingly ready to take risks when caution would be more successful. She told him he was too cautious and too aloof. She obviously liked him and he found her company strangely comforting. Her optimism a counter to his caution. She was obviously well thought of in Moscow and knew people of influence and it was she who told him about Lensky.

They were drinking tea and reading their notes in the

17

apartment one evening when she looked over at him and
said, 'Are you going to be Comintern or intelligence?'

'Comintern.'

'But you were sponsored by Lensky.'

'So?'

'Lensky is intelligence.'

'I don't believe it. He's a lawyer.'

She laughed. 'You're really rather an innocent in some
ways, Andrei.'

'In what ways?'

'About what goes on inside the top layers of the Party.
The struggles for power. Lensky for instance. Being a
lawyer doesn't stop him from being a spy.'

'And you. Will you be Comintern or intelligence?'

She smiled and shrugged. 'The same as you.'

'What's that mean?'

'Haven't you worked it out yet?'

'No.'

'The spies don't trust even Comintern members. Especially non-Russians. They want you to tell them if you come
across doubtful members. They trust you for several
reasons. Firstly because Lensky trusts you, and secondly
because you were the most intelligent arguer of the Party
line on the instruction course. And they trust you because
you're a Russian.' She laughed. 'And they trust me
because they desperately need someone who speaks
Spanish and who will take some risks in the cause.' She
paused. 'You'd better be aware, Andrei, that despite the
revolution the big boys are still struggling to see who holds
the reins.'

'That's nothing to do with me.'

'It may be one day, sweetheart.' She laughed. 'Ask Lensky if you don't believe me. Whoever wins Lensky will be
up there at the top.'

Lensky was standing by the window looking at the lights
of the city as the snow fell steadily in big soft flakes. He
didn't turn as he said, 'There's a man I want you to meet

tomorrow before you leave. His name's Spassky. Gene Spassky. He's only about five years older than you but he's going to be very important. He knows about you. Later on when you've settled into the work he'll be your controller.'

'Is he a spy?'

'No.' Lensky hesitated. 'Well, let's say he has intelligence connections. He is a senior man in the Party and his work straddles the security service and the Comintern. You can trust him. If you've got any problems he can deal with them.' He waved his hand towards the low table where Andrei was sitting. 'The two packets on the table are for Anna and Ivan. Give them my love.'

It was the man named Spassky who had carried his canvas bag for him as they walked to the station. He had asked about Anna and Ivan. Would they be willing to be part of his team in Paris? Were they committed? Had he mastered the code they would use to him when they wrote to him? How well did he know Serov? Spassky didn't seem particularly interested in his answers as they trudged through the snow. And his last question, just before the train pulled out was how he was going to convert the gold into francs. He seemed satisfied with the answer. Spassky neither waved nor said any farewell as the train started its long journey.

3

Serov met him in from the train and insisted that they went to a café before he went home.

Over coffee Serov had broken the news that in the next few days there would be reports in at least two French newspapers that five million Russian farmers had not only had their land confiscated but had been sent into exile in the remote areas of the Soviet Union. A German newspaper was to claim that at least a million farmers had been murdered.

Andrei said, 'Is it true?'

Serov shrugged. 'More or less. The figure I heard was not five million but seven million. It will mean almost no harvest for two years.' He smiled. 'I can't see the Moscow bureaucrats sowing and reaping, can you? And the farm labourers who helped slaughter the farmers won't expect to be working hard for whoever their new masters turn out to be.'

'Why didn't Lensky warn me?'

'He wouldn't know about the newspaper articles and the purge of the *kulaks* was last year.'

'How the hell do I explain this to the Party members here?'

Serov smiled. 'I don't know but I'll be interested to hear what you tell them.'

'Do they know already?'

'There was a piece in the newspapers today. Just a few paragraphs. Possible famine in Russia and all that sort of stuff.' He paused. 'I've arranged a local Party meeting for this evening. You'd better explain it to them.'

'Why don't you do it?'

'Lensky wants you to do it. He wants you to go to Marseilles as well. They're feuding amongst themselves. He wants you to sort them out.'

'I want a couple of days with the family before I go anywhere. I've been away six months.'

'Lensky says he wants you to get a bigger place. I've got one for you to see.'

'Where is it?'

'In the Batignolles. Rue Legrande. Anna and Ivan have seen it. They love it.'

'Why does Lensky want us to move?'

'So's you've got enough room if we ever need it for one of our people on the run. Just for a night while we sort things out for them.'

They moved to the new place the next day and the family were delighted. But Andrei vaguely resented Serov's interference in his family life. Nobody in Moscow had ever told him that Serov was in some way his superior, but because Serov seemed to be in constant touch with Lensky he accepted the situation.

The Party members in Paris and Marseilles had accepted his explanation of the purge of the *kulaks*. Attempts to split the Party's loyalties and to try and change its methods and objectives were considered disloyal by any standards. The same strict retribution had to be meted out to the *kulaks* as had been applied to the traitors like Trotsky and Zinoviev.

His next trip had been to Berlin where the Party was in danger of splitting on the same lines as the Party in Moscow. Andrei had realised that Stalin had to be shown as the only man who had the will and the strength to carry through the Politburo's programme. And if there had to be old comrades who were sacrificed because of their disruption and opposition, then so be it.

When Andrei returned from a brief visit to Spain on Moscow's orders there was the first of the fugitives installed in the apartment. She was a young French girl, Chantal Lefevre. She was wanted by the French police for 'acts of subversion against the security of the State'. Not only had she been active and successful in helping to organise a militant trades union representing workers in the clothing trade but had played a substantial role in producing an underground Marxist-Leninist newssheet which gave details of bribery and corruption of politicians by arms manufacturers who she had referred to as 'The Merchants of Death'.

Andrei fell in love with her the first moment he saw her. She had long black hair and big brown eyes and could have been taken as Jewish, but she wasn't Jewish. Her family ran a hotel in Lyon and she had grown up in an ambiance of toleration and faint scepticism about the people who governed France in a time of uncertainty and tensions in French society.

Her parents had always tolerated the activities of their only child, Chantal. Admired her courage and tenacity but had doubts about whether her chosen cause deserved such sacrifice and loyalty. Anna had already made her feel part of the family.

It was Chantal who persuaded him to explore the area where they lived and to spend some time away from his meetings and arguments with the refugees from the East. To him, where they lived was of no interest. It was just a base for his work.

She took him up to the area around the rue de Rome where the shops served the students of the Paris Conservatoire. Shops where lutes and violins were made and sold, sheet-music and guitars.

The Batignolles was an area of calm between the sleazy Place de Clichy and the Gare St Lazare.

She had taken him to a small café where she was obviously well-known and liked and as they sat at a pavement table she said, 'If you don't get away from it you'll get like all the others.'

He smiled. 'What's that mean?'

'They become fanatics. They aren't interested in people any more or what's going on in people's lives. People are just targets. For them it's still 1917. They don't realise that ordinary people, however committed to the Party they are, have to live their lives. They fall in love, they have tragedies, deaths and illnesses, problems in their work, debts and so on.' She smiled. 'You're too special to be allowed to become a Party hack. We need people with imagination like you to lead us or we end up with nothing to show for the revolution but discussion groups and agitators.'

'What makes you think I'm so special?'

She looked away for a moment at the people passing by on the pavement, and then back at him.

'Tell me. Would you be prepared to tell a lie to make a Party point, knowing it was a lie and knowing that the person or persons you were lying to would believe it because it was you who was saying it?' She laughed. 'Not very clearly explained. But you know what I mean.'

He smiled. 'The answer's – no. I wouldn't knowingly tell a lie to make a Party point. But that would be because when the people in Moscow do something that seems contrary to Party thinking it's because they have a good reason for doing whatever it is.'

She laughed. 'You should have been a teacher, Andrei. Or maybe a priest.'

He shrugged. 'Maybe I could do more for the Party as a teacher or a priest.'

'Serov says you're already marked down as a top man in the Party.'

'Tell me about Serov. How well do you know him?'

'He's got a sort of watching brief for Moscow. Reports on people. Speaks French perfectly. His mother was French. He's very shrewd. Spends a lot of time with the unions. Covers all of France and Belgium for Moscow Centre.'

'Is he Comintern?'

'That's what he says.'

'What do you think?'

'I think he's a spy.' She smiled. 'You are too, aren't you.'

'I'm not sure. My orders were that I was Comintern.'

'But you had intelligence training, didn't you?'

'Who told you that?'

'Serov.'

'He talks too much.'

She laughed. 'He's a sucker for pretty girls. Wants to impress.'

'Did he impress you?'

'No. He's not my type.'

'What's your type?'

She grinned. 'Like in American films – I plead the Fifth and don't answer.'

He opened his mouth to speak and then closed it and said nothing.

'What were you going to say?'

'It doesn't matter.'

'Tell me.'

'Let's leave it.'

'I know what you were going to say so you might as well say it.'

'What was I going to say?'

'You were going to say that you like me.'

'How did you know?'

She smiled. 'You're really rather an innocent, Andrei Aarons. I know you like me. And I like you too.'

'Why do you like me?'

'Because you're a nice man. And a modest man. You've got great talents but you don't realise it. I feel safe with you.'

'I don't just like you, Chantal. I love you. I loved you the first time I saw you. And I've loved you more every day that's gone by. I feel safe with you too.'

24

Despite dire warnings from Serov that it would dilute his efforts as a Comintern organiser they had married two months later. Andrei had been surprised at the large number of people who crowded into the *mairie* to see them married and even more surprised that there was a telegram of congratulations from Lensky in Moscow.

In September 1937 he had a message from Moscow instructing him to go to Berlin for a discussion with Lensky.

They had met in a small hotel on Kantstrasse and Lensky had brought a silver-framed mirror for Anna and a watch for Ivan. Then he settled back in his chair and looked at Andrei.

'Our people in Spain and here in Berlin said that you were so convincing about the need for Trotsky and the others to be exiled that the waverers were completely satisfied. How long did it take you to decide what to say?'

'I had already had to do the same thing in Paris the day I got back from Moscow so I was used to the questions and the arguments.'

'Yes, but how did you work out what to say?'

Andrei shrugged. 'I didn't have to work anything out. If a man, no matter how important he is, wants to divert away from the Party's commitments then he must be stopped. We haven't the time or the energy for polemics and dilettante discussions of alternatives. We have decided what our aims are and how to achieve them, and those who want to deviate are enemies of the people.' He paused. 'I consider that sending them into exile was the least that could be done.'

'You never have doubts?'

'No. Never. The time for doubters is long gone. We want action now, to make a dream come true. Not only for us but for the whole world. Nothing matters but that.'

'I wish we had a thousand like you, Andrei.'

'They are there, Comrade Lensky. They only need to be trained. Lenin and Marx laid down the pattern to revolutionise the world. Comrade Stalin is making it happen.'

'Does your Chantal share your views?'

'Of course. The whole family do.'

Lensky looked towards the window and then back at Andrei. 'What I am going to tell you is only between you and me. Is that understood?'

'Of course.'

'We want you to move. You and the family. We want you to move to the United States. And we want you to move in the next two months.' He sighed. 'There is very clear evidence now that the Nazis intend harassing all Jews. That's why we sent you the false passport. In some places it has already started. Jews are being publicly humiliated and in some cases murdered.'

'But I'm usually in Paris, comrade. I'm only here in Germany for one or two days at a time.'

'I know. I know.'

Lensky stood up and walked to the window, looking out for long moments before he turned to look back at Andrei.

'The confidential part of our talk is that I want to tell you that there is mounting and irrefutable evidence that Hitler intends a war. He intends to take over the whole of Europe. Jews will not be safe anywhere in Europe. We can't afford to lose you. You have talents and characteristics that are rare and valuable. We have already lost two key men, one here in Berlin and one in the Ruhr. They were arrested in the middle of the night by the Gestapo and nobody knows what has happened to them. The police and the Gestapo deny all knowledge of their arrests. We have an informant in the Kripo. He tells us they were arrested because they were classed as Jewish agitators. The SA are hounding Jews in the streets, smashing up their shops and their homes. The Nazis fear nobody. Not the British nor the French. The Civil War in Spain is just a trial run for the Luftwaffe. They will have their war, believe me. And the signs are that they'll win.' He sighed. 'I'm sorry to be the bearer of such bad news.' He shrugged. 'But that's how it is. Not just my opinion but Moscow's own analysis of what will happen. When – we don't know. But not long now, I'm afraid. We need to look to our defences. We need your help.'

For several minutes Andrei sat in silence and then he said, 'What do you want me to do in America?'

'Influence people. Organise our own people there to see Moscow as an ally. A nation wanting peace. To most Americans we are the enemy. Put our good points over. Make them like us in case our turn comes.'

'What do you mean – our turn?'

'When Hitler has conquered Europe he will turn on us. The Americans will want to keep out of any wars in Europe. Make them at least sympathetic to our own efforts to avoid war.'

'And the people in intelligence in Moscow?'

'Nothing for them. If the Nazis attack in Europe we want no sign that we are spying on the Americans. We shall order our people to stop all espionage activities.'

'You know I don't speak English. None of us does.'

'So start learning. Leave France to Serov. He's not a Jew. He can survive.'

'There will be immigration problems.'

'No. We shall arrange all that. You will all travel on German passports in your own names. They are sympathetic to Jewish refugees in America. We have people there who can get you in without a problem. And in the course of time you take out American citizenship.'

'That means we stay there for a long time?'

'Permanently, Andrei. Settle down and be an American family. You will have funds to do what you need.'

It was February 1938 before they moved to the USA. Andrei went first, alone. With advice from other Russian Jews he decided that they would live in the Brighton Beach area where there were so many immigrant Jews from Russia and Poland that one more Russian-speaking family would go virtually unnoticed.

It was a poor district, a few stops on the elevated before Coney Island, but living conditions were far better than in Moscow. The shops, the food, the whole atmosphere made him feel at home. He could speak Russian without seeming to be anything other than an American and he was sure that the family would settle in easily.

In the two months before the family were due to arrive he found that he missed Chantal more than he had expected. He kept himself busy, finding them a quite roomy apartment over an empty shop, checking out the shops and the possibility of jobs for all of them. It obviously wasn't going to be easy to get jobs locally but it was only ten cents on the elevated to Manhattan and he heard that there were jobs for girls in Sheepshead Bay and further north in the Prospect Park area, without having to cross the bridge to Manhattan.

By the end of the first month he had made contact with several of the leading local communists and had talked at private meetings about Moscow's policies. He was listened to with respect and they assumed that he was a Comintern agent without him ever saying so. They were used to hiding their allegiances but there were plenty of ordinary Party members who quite openly advocated communism. He was made welcome by several families who helped him buy used furniture and kitchen things for the apartment. And he spent at least two hours a day improving his English.

When Lensky had told him of their move to New York it seemed just part of the routine of his work for Moscow, but now he was actually in New York he was full of doubts. He realised that because of his broken English he was avoiding going into Manhattan. He had gone in twice and had found the crowds and its busyness overwhelming. It seemed preposterous that he was expected to not only survive but to influence these people.

He had a natural skill for learning and absorbing foreign languages but what you needed for shopping or talking to

28

neighbours wasn't enough for what he was expected to do. But if that was what the Party wanted he had to prepare himself to do his best. For the first time in his life he doubted his ability to do what they wanted. Why should these lively people give a damn about his views on how they should live their lives? Suddenly his life in Paris that had seemed so full of activity seemed to have been too casual, too easy-going. And he wished he was back there in his old routine. Sometimes when he was lonely he got near to accepting that he was scared. Scared of the task he'd been given. Unsure of how to go about it. And scared of failing miserably.

He ate alone, one meal a day, in the evenings, and then walked along the Boardwalk to Coney Island and then back to his books. It was in the evenings that he most missed Chantal. There was so much that he wanted to tell her and so much that he wanted to show her. He wired the address to her and several times he wrote letters to her but didn't send them. Written things, however innocent, could be dangerous.

At last he got a cable from Serov saying that they had left on a Latvian boat from Le Havre and would be about three weeks at sea. At the start of the third week he phoned the shipping office every day and on the Friday the boat was due to tie up the next day.

He was at the docks as the crew threw out the ropes to the longshoremen. And an hour later he saw them coming down the rickety gangway, staggering under bags and bundles despite him telling them to bring only personal essentials. They were smiling and waving as they caught sight of him as they walked across to the Immigration shack.

It was over an hour before they came through. Chantal rushing towards him, arms outstretched, her long black hair like a horse's mane in the wind. And then, with their arms around each other and Anna and Ivan grinning as they watched, Andrei had the feeling that everything was going to work out all right.

4

They had settled down slowly into the life of Brighton
Beach whose inhabitants amiably christened it 'Odessa by
the Sea'. Except for Chantal it was just like being in
Russia. Hearing people speaking Yiddish and Russian and
Polish made them feel more at home than when they were
in Paris.

In the first few weeks he had taken them to see the
places they had seen in pictures in magazines or in the
cinema. Central Park, Times Square, Fifth Avenue and
Park Avenue.

He had taken them too to the Brooklyn Museum and
Prospect Park. They all thought that Prospect Park was
better than Central Park. At weekends they went to
Coney Island and sat on the beach with thousands of
others, working-class New Yorkers enjoying the sea, the
fresh air and the amusement park. And like the others
they queued at Nathan's hot-dog stand.

They always walked there and back and sometimes they
had a *knish* at Mrs Stahl's Knishes. But their favourite
place for a meal was one of the small Russian restaurants
on Brighton Beach Avenue underneath the El.

But the coded instructions he had got from Moscow in
the letter post-marked Mexico City meant some changes
in their lives. Not just his but the others too. The administrative rivalry in Moscow meant that rather than working
for the Comintern or intelligence, he would now have to
work for both. Only he could cope with the demanding
Comintern work and he would have to organise the others

there to handle the routine work that the intelligence people wanted. They would not be involved in intelligence work themselves but they had to be able to run a network that could act as couriers and cut-outs for the Soviet agents who operated in New York. At least those in Brooklyn and some in Manhattan. They wanted new 'dead-letter boxes', new routines and at least half a dozen safe-houses for agents on the run.

It suddenly seemed as if Moscow's policies of strict neutrality in the United States had been changed violently, as if Moscow was anticipating that the USA might become hostile to the Soviet Union for some reason. He had probed to try and get some indication of how this could come about but his questions had been ignored. Hitler and Mussolini had just signed a political and economic pact committing them to supporting each other in time of war with all military forces. But in Aarons' thinking such a pact was meaningless. Mussolini wasn't going to risk his new African empire for the sake of Adolf Hitler and his Nazis. The two were rivals not allies. Each one vying for the leadership of Fascism.

Andrei heard the clatter of the shoes on the wooden stairs and then Chantal and Anna burst into the room laughing and giggling so much that they couldn't speak. And then Chantal burst out, 'We've just seen you in a film at the cinema.'

Seeing the shock and confusion on her brother's face Anna said, 'Not really. But the star was exactly like you. It was fantastic.'

With his relief obvious Andrei smiled and said, 'I hope he speaks better English than I do. What was the film?'

'The man was called James Stewart and the film was called . . .' she turned to Chantal '. . . what was it called, Chantal?'

'It was called *Mr Smith Goes to Washington*.' She laughed. 'And he didn't speak better English than you. We could hardly understand what he was saying. But like you he was sticking up for ordinary people against the politicians.'

'Where's Ivan? Anyone know?'

'What's he done?'

'Who said he'd done something?'

'You always call him Ivan instead of 'van when he's been up to something.'

Andrei smiled. 'I want a family meeting after supper, that's all.'

When they had eaten and the girls had cleared the table he looked at each one in turn before he spoke.

'We've got to make some changes. First of all I've made arrangements to rent the shop downstairs. We're going to open a bookshop. Russian, Polish, Jewish books. I want you and Anna to look after the shop, 'van.'

Ivan frowned. 'Why the hell do we want a bookshop?'

'I want us to have the whole building and I want a place where people come in and out and that certain people can use to leave things or pass on messages. And Ivan, I want you to do some special things. I'll talk to you about them later.'

'Is something going to happen?' It was Ivan who asked the question.

'I don't know, Ivan. Why did you ask?'

'Somebody told me that Moscow were going to make a pact with the British and the French.'

'Who told you that?'

'Your friend at Café Arbat on the Avenue. The one who pretends to be a waiter and slops the soup all over the table.'

'He wouldn't know anything, Ivan.'

'He's a paid-up Party member. He showed me his card.'

'Then he's a fool. I'll talk to him.' He looked at Chantal. 'You got any of the good coffee, honey?'

She laughed. 'You're a real American calling me honey. I like that. Yes. I'll get us all some coffee.'

5

Bill Malloy took one last look at St John's Law School and then turned back to look at the traffic on Clinton Avenue. He half raised his hand to flag down a cab and then changed his mind. Walking would help him sort out in his mind what he was going to say to his father. The man whose sole ambition since the death of his wife was for his son to be a lawyer. To Patrick Malloy, being a lawyer meant that you were secure for the rest of your life. Not dependent on the whims of a ruthless employer. It had been a shrewd union lawyer who had got Patrick Malloy the insurance money when he had lost his arm when the brakes on the train he was driving had failed. They had tried to avoid paying any compensation and had then offered a sum that Malloy would have gladly accepted, but the smart young lawyer had advised him not to settle, and he'd finally been paid enough to buy a house on the outskirts of Jackson Heights. A three-storey house where they lived on the top floor and rented out the other two for enough to keep them all in what seemed to Patrick Malloy to be luxury after the three rooms in Astoria. Overnight they had gone from working-class to lower middle-class but Patrick Malloy never abandoned his Irish working-class standards. You didn't owe anyone a cent, you stuck by your fellow-workers and you went to Mass on Sunday without fail.

As Malloy walked back towards his house he knew that his father would be pressing him to take the job at his union – the Brotherhood of Railway Clerks – the union who had given his father a job after he lost his arm. Two grim years of unemployment while the compensation was being fought for and then the stability of the union job. The savings of a life-time had gone five years earlier in a vain attempt to find a cure for his mother's terminal illness. Since her death his father had concentrated all his hopes and affection on him. He had done his best to respond. His own ambition to be a professional ball-player had been put aside. He had gone along willingly enough with his father's wish for him to become a lawyer but he didn't share his father's devotion to unions. He understood all too well the problems of working people and their exploitation. But he found the union organisers in his father's union to be too rigid in their attitudes, still fighting long-lost old battles, with long debates on whether Stalin was their man or Roosevelt. Instead of which they should have been making up their minds about what their members really wanted from employers instead of going into meetings with a two-page shopping list of grievances. Lists that made it easy for employers to pick out a couple of worthless concessions that the union men could call a victory. And all the abuses and insecurities left unchanged.

Then there would be the sincere but annoying warnings about marriage to a non-Catholic. His father could point to three or four mixed marriages that hadn't worked out although he was well aware that none of them had failed because of religion. Maybe the theory applied in Ireland or Italy, Catholic dominated countries, but it didn't apply in the United States. His father had challenged him to give just two mixed marriages that had been successful and all he could say was that he never asked people what religion they had. He didn't have friends or acquaintances because of their religion.

But there was a debt to be paid to that humble, good-natured man who had struggled all his life to provide a home for his wife and son. No hobbies because they could tempt you to spend money. No trips to the ball-game, no booze, no luxuries, just books from the local free library and a bicycle to get to work until he had lost his arm. And then you walked. It had only been since he was at law school that he realised that all the homilies were because a disabled man was trying to be a mother as well as a father. And that his father's caution came from insecurity. A fear of not surviving in a tough, hostile world. But now there was the piece of paper in the envelope, confirming that he was entitled to practise law in the State of New York.

The old man was waiting for him, the tea already made and the cups and saucers prepared with milk and sugar. He still wore woollen shirts with separate collars attached with studs front and back. And that day he wore a tie. There was a white cloth on the table and a brown paper bag alongside the teapot.

He could see his father's eyes on the cardboard tube that held his certificate and he smiled as he handed it over. The old man pulled out the certificate and flattened it with his hand. And Bill Malloy thought for a moment that it was symbolic in a way. That big, gnarled hand gently stroking the piece of paper that represented so many sacrifices and so much effort.

Then his father tore open the paper bag and pulled out a picture frame, taking off the cardboard back and sliding the certificate into place before pressing the clips that held the glass.

'How did you know what size it would be, dad?'

The old man grinned. 'I phoned 'em. The office – Miss Levinski. She measured one up for me.'

'Did you tell her who you were?'

'Of course I did.'

'My God. I hope she doesn't tell anybody else.'

'Sit down. You want a cake? I bought a couple of those you like. Eclairs, ain't it?'

Bill Malloy smiled. 'You're a marvel. You really are.'

'Maybe. Anyway McGinty asked when you'd be starting at the office. I told him not until Monday. That OK?'

'I guess so.'

'It's a start, boy. Learning from books and teachers is one thing. Doing it for real's different.'

'For two years, dad. And then I do it my way.'

'If that's how you want it then so be it. Maybe you'll change your mind when it comes to it.'

'Dad, I can earn at least twice as much in a law firm. You know that.'

'Money's not everything. There's more to life than that.'

'Dad. Kathy and I are going to be married in two weeks' time.'

He saw his father open his mouth to speak and then close it as he stood up slowly and walked over to the corner cupboard. He opened the door and reached inside. There was an envelope in his hand as he walked back to the table. As he put the envelope down in front of Bill the old man said, 'I wish you both every happiness in the world. There's two hundred dollars in there to help you get started.'

Bill looked at his father and reached out to touch his hand where it rested on the table.

'I love you, dad. Thanks.' And he kissed the old man's cheek.

As Bill Malloy showered and changed for his date with Kathy he went over in his mind his talk with his father. He'd do two years at the union, but after that he would find himself a job with a law firm. He'd wondered why the old man went along with it so easily as if he wanted to get it over. Looking at that piece of parchment again and again. He smiled when he realised why the old man was so cooperative. He couldn't wait to put it in the frame so that it could be hung on the wall of the living room along-side the photograph of his father shaking hands with his other hero, Harrison, his union's boss at the annual conference. Bill Malloy didn't believe in hero-worshipping.

Experience told him that heroes all too often had feet of clay. Better admire a man for his talents and leave it at that.

They ate at Nico's place, pasta and cassata ice-cream and a glass each of the house red. And Bill Malloy suddenly felt young again. Young and optimistic. He reached out for her hand on the table, smiling as he said, 'You haven't changed your mind?'

She smiled back. 'About what?'

'You know about what.'

'So say it.'

'Will you still marry me?'

'I said I would two months ago.'

'So when?'

'What about your father?'

'Forget him. This is just you and me.'

'That wouldn't be a good start for us, Bill. He's a good man and he cares about you. We don't want to hurt his feelings.'

'I spoke to him this evening. I told him we were going to be married in a matter of weeks.' He paused. 'I also told him that I would only work as the union's legal adviser for two years.'

'What did he say?'

'He accepted it. Wished us luck.' He smiled. 'He's a great fan of yours underneath all that bigotry about non-Catholics. And he'd saved up two hundred dollars that he gave us as a wedding present.'

'He's a great old guy but he'll be very lonely without you there.'

'We'll see him as often as we can. I'll see him every day anyway at the union offices.'

'Can I make a suggestion?'

'Sure. What is it?'

'You said that the O'Haras were moving at the end of the month. Why don't we rent the floor from your father until we actually need a separate place.'

'D'you really mean that?'

'Of course I do.'

The pleasure and relief on his face was all the reward she needed.

'My God. He'll be so pleased.' He looked at her fondly. 'I love you so much, Kathy. I'm so lucky. I can't believe it.'

Two months later, a Wednesday, Moscow and Berlin announced that they had signed a non-aggression pact. It was the 23rd of August 1939 and Bill Malloy and Katharine Sarah Lane were married the following day.

In the White House the President and his senior advisors knew that a red light was flashing in Europe, and its light was visible across the Atlantic. At a meeting in the oval study Roosevelt reviewed the possible consequences with the leaders of Capitol Hill.

The President, in reviewing the likely outcome, concluded that the Allies had only a fifty-fifty chance of surviving. He suggested that it might prevent the outbreak of war in Europe if the United States revoked the neutrality law which required the USA to withhold sales of arms to aggressors and victims alike. The revision alone might act as a deterrent.

The man he needed to influence was Borah who could have carried the Senate. Borah refused. 'There is not going to be any war this year,' he claimed. 'All this hysteria is manufactured and artificial.'

When Hull from State said despairingly, 'I wish the senator would come down to my office and read the cables,' Borah said arrogantly, 'I have sources of information in Europe that I regard as more reliable than those of the State Department.'

Roosevelt looked at the men around the table after a poll had gone against his proposal and said quietly, 'Well, gentlemen. The responsibility is yours. I bid you good evening.'

For Party members all over the world the pact seemed incredible. A pact with the Nazis. But for the American public it was of no great interest. If they even noticed the event it was just one more example of the mess that was Europe.

6

For Andrei the signing of the German–Soviet Pact was almost incredible. He had got a message from Lensky explaining why it had been necessary and he was told to explain the situation to the Party leaders in New York, San Francisco, Chicago and Los Angeles.

It took him three weeks to make all the contacts and explain that Moscow had appealed to the British and the French for an alliance but they had sent junior officials with no powers to negotiate let alone sign an agreement.

There was bitterness everywhere and disillusion, and at his meeting in New York which he had left to the last there was open rejection of his explanation. A man named Herz had been the dissidents' spokesman.

'If it is true that those people were only juniors what was to stop Moscow sending a senior member of the Politburo to London?'

'It was a question of time, comrade. The whole matter was desperately urgent.'

'But they found time for Molotov to negotiate with Ribbentrop.'

'By then we had no choice. All other attempts had failed.'

'So we have guaranteed not to attack the Nazis when they invade Poland. What do we get in return?'

'A guarantee that Germany will not attack the Soviet Union.'

There was a clamour of voices dissenting and Herz shouted, 'So all those speeches by Stalin about the infamous Nazis were wrong, yes? The great leader was wrong. And now they are our allies and we share their guilt. And all over the world, those of us who have worked so hard for the Party are given the choice of looking like fools or criminals.' He was jabbing his finger at Andrei. 'You tell your friends in Moscow that we no longer believe them. They are traitors to the Party. Traitors to the working man all over Europe.'

'On what grounds do you say that, Comrade Herz?'

Saliva was erupting from the man's mouth as his anger took over. 'Because what Moscow has done is to tell the Nazis that they can take over Europe without fear of retaliation from the Soviet Union. We are not so naive as to not be aware of what this so-called non-aggression pact means. It means the workers of Europe have been handed over to the Nazi thugs.'

There was a clamour of agreement from most of the people assembled in the small hall. Most of them were seated but Herz was still standing, his face flushed with anger.

Andrei said quietly, 'Do you play chess, Comrade Herz?'

'Yes.'

There was a sudden silence in the room.

'Have you ever sacrificed a piece for the sake of a tactical move?'

'Of course.'

'I'd be most grateful if you would let me offer you an explanation of what happened in Moscow. I'm not saying that my reasoning is their reasoning but I believe that if I can analyse the situation then they can too. And with more information than I have. Will you give me a few moments of your time?'

Herz sat down and Andrei knew that at least the people were listening now.

'Hitler has said in public speeches many times that Moscow is his real enemy. The Bolsheviks. The Reds. The day would come when he would settle the matter once and for

41

all. We all know what that means. It means war. The invasion of the Soviet Union.

'But so far Herr Hitler has not invaded any country. But if he does, or when he does then non-aggression pacts don't necessarily apply. A pact made to persuade a potential aggressor to find a peaceful solution to some problem is not a pact made to stand aside and allow your ally to invade your neighbours.

'What if Moscow are only sacrificing their pride in the hope that it could contribute to peace?'

Herz stood up and Andrei nodded to him, giving way. 'Carry on, Comrade Herz.'

'And what if instead of ensuring peace it makes war more certain. Do we trust the Nazis to have changed their spots?'

Andrei nodded. 'Forgive me for not saying more in even this private meeting but I have faith enough in our cause and our leaders to be sure that when all this tension in Europe comes to an end the Soviet Union will not have ended up fighting with the Nazis to conquer Europe.' He half-smiled and said, 'We want to conquer the world with our hopes and our philosophy not with guns.'

There was a smattering of applause and a woman stood up.

'So when, comrade, do we fight on the side of our real friends?'

Andrei said quietly, 'We were doing that in Spain until Madrid surrendered to Franco, comrade.'

Then the applause was substantial and Andrei was relieved. Two senior Party members walked with him to the subway and he was back with the family just before midnight.

It was a warm night and after a bowl of chicken soup he took Chantal for a walk to the beach. A number of people smiled or nodded to them as they made their way round the small square with its trees and flowers.

Sitting in the quiet of the beach they could just hear the

faint waves of music from Coney Island, above the roll and swirl of the Atlantic waves.

He put his arm around her shoulder. 'How've you been, honey?'

'I was lonely without you. I hate it when you're away.'

'So do I. But most of the time I was on trains and buses. Trying to sleep.'

'Did they give you a rough time?'

'I did my best. How about you and Anna and Ivan?'

'Anna's always a great help. Always calm and full of common sense.' She paused. 'I had a letter from my parents. They seem worried that there's going to be a war with the Germans. Do you think there will be?'

'It's possible. How about Ivan? I've got a feeling you've left him to last for a good reason.'

She laughed. 'You're right. Two small problems. First of all a visit from a Mr Henschel who just walked in and said that if 'van doesn't keep away from his daughter he'll either go to the police or crack Ivan's head open.'

'Why should he do that? Is she pregnant or something?'

'No. But she's under age.'

'Like what?'

'Like only just fifteen. But she looks older.'

'What did you do with 'van?'

'I told him not to see her until you came back. He promised he wouldn't.'

'He's an idiot.'

'I think he's really gone on her. Wants to marry her as soon as she's of age.'

'What else was there? The second problem.'

'A man came with a packet for you. He said to hand it to you personally. He said if you've got any more he'll buy them but he'd prefer smaller ones.' She paused. 'I was worried and I opened the packet. I hope you're not cross.'

'What was in it?'

'Money. A lot of money. I didn't count it but it was in

43

tens and twenties. It must have been at least a thousand dollars.'

'Where'd you put it?'

'In your box under our bed.'

'That's OK. Don't worry.'

'What is it for, Andrei, the money?'

'The Party gave me some diamonds that I could sell for Party funds. They don't take up as much space as actual money. And they're more portable. And they've got a value whatever country you're in. Just forget about it. It's not a problem. What about the stocks for the shop?'

'The Polish girl at the main library has been a great help. Given me names and addresses where I can buy cheap and good stuff – classics mainly. She'll go with me on her time off. She thinks the shop's just what the district needs.'

'Do you feel settled here now?'

'As long as I've got you I'm OK anywhere.'

'You've got me for always, my love.' He smiled. 'What did that French priest say – *"Meilleur ou pire"*. For better or worse.'

Andrei was helping them place the books on the extra shelves that Ivan had constructed. Most of the books were second-hand but in good condition and there wasn't time to put them in categories or even to sort them by language. There was only one row of books in English, mainly histories of Europe and the biographies of Americans. And there were dictionaries of every European language and Russian, Latvian and Estonian. All the classic Russian writers were well-represented along with two shelves of romances.

Andrei was sorting out a cardboard box of rejects from the Brooklyn Library when he looked up and saw the man on the other side of the counter.

He smiled. 'I'm afraid we don't open until tomorrow.' He waved at the stacks of books on the counter. 'We're still in a bit of a mess . . .' And then he realised who the man was. He'd carried his canvas bag for him to the station in Moscow after the training course and he was returning to Paris. Lensky had said he was Gene Spassky.

Spassky was dressed like a seaman in a dark blue roll-neck sweater, grey flannel trousers and well-worn boots. He smiled as he saw recognition dawn on Andrei's face. He held out his hand.

'*Dobry djehn, tovarich.*'

'*Dobry djehn . . . kahk djela.*'

'*Spasebo kharasho,*' and then he said quietly, 'Where can we talk?'

'Upstairs. Follow me.'

Andrei took Spassky into the bedroom. There were no chairs so they sat side by side on the edge of the double bed.

'I can't stay long, Aarons. I've got to get back to New York to my ship. But Lensky wanted to warn you in advance of something that's going to happen.'

'What is it?'

'We heard in Moscow that you made a good case for that wretched pact with the Nazis.' He smiled. 'Another good mark, comrade. But there's worse to come I'm afraid.'

'What?'

'The Germans are going to attack Poland in a matter of days.'

'Well at least that lets us out from the Pact.'

'I'm afraid not. On the third day of the Nazi invasion we announce that we have to defend our borders and we go in from the east and take over about a third of Poland.'

Andrei was silent for several minutes and then he looked at Spassky. 'The world will say it was planned from the start. The Germans go in and then we play jackals to the Nazis.'

'And the world will be right, my friend.' Spassky paused. 'How are you going to defend that little scenario?'

'Tell me why Moscow needed to do it?'

45

'It won't help you. You'll understand, but outsiders won't.'

'Tell me all the same.'

'Put crudely, Moscow's buying time. When Hitler's finished with Europe he'll be ready to attack us. Every month will give us more time to be ready for them.'

'Are we so weak that we need the time? And how much time?'

'The answer to the first question is yes. We need every day we can get. We reckon that it will take Hitler about a year before he's conquered Europe. A few months longer if the British hold out.'

'And what do they want me to do?'

'First of all do your best to stop an internal split in the Party here in the USA and then hand-pick members who can put over our point of view. Not Party hacks but the intellectuals. People who can influence public opinion. If you need help or funds or anything, go to our embassies in either Mexico City or Toronto. Not Washington. I've brought Soviet passports and US passports for all your family. Use them with discretion. The US passports are in the name of Levin. Moscow have arranged to fund six bank accounts in that name. Two here in New York. One in Washington. One in Los Angeles, one in Mexico City and one in Toronto.' He reached under his sweater and handed over a packet. 'All the stuff is in here. Including addresses of banks and account numbers.' He shrugged. 'Moscow said that money is no object. Spend as freely as you need.' He stood up and held out his hand. 'They won't forget the good work you've done for the Party. A lot of people know your name.' He shrugged. 'I must get on my way.'

'Do you want a meal or anything?'

'No. I'll eat on board.'

Three days later the Germans invaded Poland. Friday the 1st of September, 1939. On the 3rd of September the British and the French declared war on the Germans. On the 17th, a Sunday, Russian troops swept in from the east and by the end of the month 60,000 Poles had died and the State of Poland no longer existed. The Soviet Union was expelled from the League of Nations.

7

Bill Malloy's first few weeks at the union had been fruitful. There were over a hundred compensation cases outstanding and he had dictated letters by the dozen to the employers concerned. A week later he followed up with telephone calls. Most of the responses were both negative and offensive but in a dozen or so cases he was listened to and meetings were arranged which led to settlements. The amounts of compensation achieved were at least double what the union had expected.

He got the agreement of most of the recipients to leaving 25 per cent of the total amount in a fighting fund. The balance to be paid after a year with interest added at 6 per cent. He then picked out six claims against large companies that he was satisfied he had a good chance of winning. He went to the two district courts concerned and then to the local papers, giving them details of the claims and a timetable of the evasions by the companies concerned. The companies all made products used by most families and some claims had been in action for two years. They were all for injuries so serious that the member concerned would not be able to work again. Four of them involved accidents incurred when driving fork-lift trucks or in two cases light locomotives on a works siding.

His efforts led to no press headlines but the claims and delays were publicised with a brief editorial giving details of enormous profits earned by four of the companies concerned.

The first meeting he was asked to attend was at a company that made cookers and ice-boxes with a household name.

The offices were palatial and the other side were represented by a well-known lawyer and their production director.

It was the lawyer who did the talking when they were sitting around the big table.

'My name's Hancox, Mr Malloy. My firm's offices are on Madison. I thought it might be equitable if we met here at my client's offices.'

'It suits me, Mr Hancox. I'm pleased to meet you. I've seen your name in the papers.'

'How long have you been out of law school, Mr Malloy?'

'About six months.'

'And you're full-time with the union I understand.'

'Yes.'

'Now this claim.' He smiled. A smile as between knowing friends. 'Fifty thousand dollars and a pension for life.' He paused. 'What do you base that on?'

'I've got medical certificates from the family doctor and two specialists that confirm that he won't ever work again. The claim has been ignored for two years by your client. Not even an acknowledgement of the letters the man wrote to your client. The State Statistics Office quotes 40,000 dollars as typical settlement in similar cases. The extra 10,000 are for aggravated damages caused by your client's unwillingness to negotiate a settlement.'

Hancox nodded. 'Of course you'll understand that other medical experts might query your medical offerings.'

'The court can judge for itself. The man is permanently in a wheelchair.'

'And the pension. How is that arrived at?'

'He was earning four thousand dollars a year when he worked. His only income now is ten dollars a week from the union and five dollars a week from the Brooklyn social services fund. I think he should get 75 per cent of his working wage.'

49

'I see. I noticed that a local paper printed a quite scurri-lous attack on my client. Was that your doing?'

'I gave all the local papers the facts. No opinion. Just the facts.'

'I think I ought to warn you that we are taking legal action against the paper concerned.'

'The court won't like that, Mr Hancox. They'll see it as an attempt to stifle the facts. It could be construed as harassment even.'

'But you agree that our conversation today is confi-dential?'

'No way. You didn't stipulate that and as far as I'm concerned it doesn't apply.'

'Is this the first compensation claim you've handled, Mr Malloy?'

'No. It's the first that I've had to go to court about.'

'And the others?' He smiled. 'They just caved in?'

'No. We established the facts and they accepted their responsibility.'

'You realise that the legal costs of these sorts of cases can be very heavy. Especially for the losing party.'

Malloy smiled. 'The union's established a legal fund. It's quite capable of coping with this claim.'

'I'm assuming that you set great store on winning this claim so that it creates a precedent for your claims on other large companies.'

'You're absolutely right.'

'Why did you pick on my client?'

'There're five others in your client's league so I went through them all in great detail. I also consulted a legal specialist on workman's compensation. The case against your client looked to be a winner. Also the length of time in which you ignored the claim will not go unnoticed.'

'And if you lose the case?'

'We'd go to appeal. But we won't lose it, Mr Hancox. You know that as well as I do.'

'And if you win. What's the first thing you'd do?'

50

Malloy hesitated for a moment and then smiled. 'I'd probably go out and get smashed.'

Hancox smiled but only faintly. 'Would you mind having a cup of coffee in the secretary's office while I discuss this with my client?'

'Not at all.'

As Malloy waited in the secretary's office he was sure that he would get an offer and that would be the basis for further negotiation. They had obviously intended to scare him with a name like Hancox but in fact it helped him. Hancox had a good reputation for doing his homework and Malloy had worked hard on assembling his case. Hancox would recognise that it was a sound case whereas some in-house lawyer would have to stick to his instructions to fight all the way. Good lawyers kept clients out of courts wherever possible. Hancox hadn't questioned the evidence on negligence because Malloy had discovered that a factory inspector had previously condemned the truck as dangerous through lack of maintenance. Given that point the rest of it was just a presentation of damage. The only area of dispute could be *quantum*, or how much.

When he was called back into the office Hancox was alone. The file of documents closed and pushed to one side.

'Do sit down, Mr Malloy.' When Malloy was seated Hancox said, 'I'm afraid I'm going to disappoint you, Mr Malloy.'

Hancox waited for a response but Malloy didn't speak.

'It's my impression that newly-fledged young lawyers are always looking for a good fight in court.' He paused and looked at Malloy. 'My client has considered this claim very carefully. As you will know there are points on which we could argue. However my client has agreed with your claim.' He handed over a typed sheet. 'That is a signed agreement and a cheque for the sum in damages is being prepared now for you to take with you. The pension arrangements are detailed in the agreement there.'

'Thank you, sir.'

'Can I suggest that you might like to acknowledge my client's good will by mentioning the settlement to those same newspapers. I think that would be fair, don't you?'

'I'll do that, Mr Hancox. I'd like to go further if your client agreed.'

'Go on.'

'I'm sure the press would like photographs of the cheque being handed over to their ex-employee by, say, a vice-president.'

Hancox smiled. 'And then you can send nice photo-copies of the item to your other potential opponents.'

'It could help, sir.'

'I'll see what my client says. I'll contact you in a couple of days.'

Two days later Malloy got the phone call from Hancox.

'I'm sorry, Mr Malloy, but my client would not agree to the publicity for handing over the cheque. I must confess I advised them against it. Not on legal grounds but because I thought it would be in bad taste. After all we're dealing with a man who is never going to work again.'

'On reflection I think you're right, sir. Not a bright idea on my part.'

'I'm sure you had the best of intentions. Anyway, I'm glad the matter was settled amicably.' He paused. 'If ever you fancy trying your talents away from union work I'd like you to give me a ring – and I mean that, it's not a gesture.'

'Thanks. I'll remember that.'

8

Aarons always had open invitations to stay with devoted Party members when he was on his tours but he always refused as gracefully as he could. It was vital to his role that he was never openly identified with the Party.

He sat in his room that night in the shabby motel just off the road from Los Angeles to Las Vegas. He looked at his watch. The man who was driving him to the meeting was already half an hour late. Then he heard the knock on the door and the man came in and Aarons knew that something was wrong.

'What is it?'

'There's a bunch of thugs from the town have gone to the camp and they mean trouble, Andrei. We'll have to call off the meeting for tonight.'

'Do our people need help?'

'We've phoned around and there are car-loads of people on the way.' He paused. 'We spotted two FBI men in the crowd who were watching. They weren't doing anything. Just watching while the local hooligans were screaming 'Commie bastards' and 'Jew-boys' and 'Free-love bitches'. It's best you don't go near the place.'

'I need to have the meeting. It's important.'

'How about I arrange a meeting for two days' time at a different site and we only have heads of local Parties. That way you could cover the whole of California in one go.'

'Can you do that?'

'Yeah.'

'I guess that's the best we can do. Why the thugs?'

'They know we've been holding the Summer School for junior leaders and there's a lot of bad feeling from the locals. They've threatened to smash up the school but they've never actually done anything before.'

'I'll wait to hear from you then.'

'You're sure you want to carry on? There'll be a lot of hostility from our people against you and Moscow.'

Aarons smiled. 'I'm used to it, comrade. And that's why I'm here.'

It had taken three days to get the group together and Aarons had been driven out to the hunting lodge that had been borrowed for the meeting.

There were twelve people around the plain wooden table and Aarons was aware of the hubbub of raised voices that went suddenly quiet when he walked into the room with the man who had driven him there. He looked around at their faces as the door closed behind him and he said quietly, 'Shall we sit down and chat.'

When they were all sitting he said, 'I'd be grateful if you would each give me your name and who you represent.'

There were two women and eleven men apart from himself and they each gave their names and the group they represented. And Andrei knew which one would be the trouble-maker. A man named Kaufman. Bald-headed, in his forties, wearing a blue and white striped shirt with short sleeves and smoking a thin cigar. There was always a Kaufman wherever he'd been. They were never convinced because their lives were devoted to dissension. They seemed to be against all forms of law and authority. They often referred to themselves as citizens of the world to cover their antipathy not only to their own country but to the Soviet Union as well. They didn't discuss, they argued, angrily, as if they were defending the Party single-handed. The fact that they were tearing it to pieces was just proof of their sincerity. But by now he'd met a lot of Kaufmans and he knew how to deal with them. The Kaufmans were quite useful because they were so offensive and aggressive that even their companions found them objectionable.

'Perhaps I could explain Moscow's reasoning on current events. There are . . .'

'Let's cut out the bullshit, comrade. There's no excuse we will accept for what Moscow has done.' There was perspiration on Kaufman's bald dome.

Andrei looked around the table inviting other comments but Kaufman interjected, 'I'm speaking for everybody round this table.'

The Kaufmans always made that mistake and Andrei was aware of the dissent on the faces of the two women.

Andrei looked around the table. 'Does that mean that everybody wants to end the meeting right now?'

There were a lot of dissenting voices and one of the women shouted. 'I've come three hundred miles to this meeting. I want to hear what you've got to say.'

Andrei nodded. 'Is that the majority view?'

Only two people didn't put their hands up.

For a moment Andrei closed his eyes, then opened them and started speaking.

'There is no denying the fact that Moscow's pact with the Nazis has made them outcasts in the eyes of the world. What we have to decide is whether we too consider their actions so irrational and duplicitous that we too consider them outcasts.

'So do we have to decide that the men and women who struggled so hard, with so many sacrifices to establish the first Marxist-Leninist State were either hypocrites or traitors? Because if we do we are abandoning everything we believe in. So what is the alternative? That the leaders of the Soviet Union are cowards perhaps?' He paused. 'None of these conclusions can give us much comfort. It means that we go back to our homes and accept that capitalism and Fascism are the real way.

'I'd like to ask you to take your minds back to September 30th, 1938. On that day Chamberlain and Daladier signed an agreement that handed over Czechoslovakia to

Hitler. The Soviet Union had informed both the British and the French that they would join in any attempt by the two powers to defend the Czechs. And the Czechs themselves had the strongest army in Europe. The offer wasn't even refused. It was ignored.

'Why did the British and the French surrender the Czechs to Hitler?' He paused. 'They needed time. Time to make plans and guns for the inevitable war with Germany. They were vilified for what they did. Vilified by countries who would not be affected by a war in Europe.

'You might ask why the British and French were not already strong enough to go to war.' He took a deep breath. 'It was because it is more difficult for a nation that wants peace, and talks peace, to re-arm in a hurry. They didn't want war with Germany. But the Nazis wanted it. And it only takes one army to make a war.

'So the British and the French gave away the Czechs to buy time to get ready for when they too were at war with the Nazis. They bought a year. I hope that Moscow has made as good a bargain.'

He reached for the glass of water on the table and there was a smattering of applause.

'Do you have any questions?'

An old man stood up. 'Does this mean, comrade, that Moscow will attack the Nazis this time next year?'

Andrei smiled. 'The other way round. The Nazis will attack us. It's just a question of when. It may be less or more than a year. I don't know. That it will happen is certain.'

A younger man stood up. 'Can we tell our people what you have told us?'

'Yes. I want you to tell them. But don't expect that the world outside will understand. The thugs who attacked the Summer Camp a few nights ago will always be with us. And others, who are not vicious, will not see it our way. Be patient with them. Time will prove you right.'

Andrei noticed Kaufman get up from his place and walk

56

out of the room. There were some smiles as the door crashed to behind him.

Andrei said, 'Accept that he cares. But his anger will always control his thinking. Such people can play a part. We must not dismiss them.'

He had stayed for another hour talking to small groups whose questions and enthusiasm showed that they had grasped the logic of his explanations.

The whole trip had taken him longer than he expected and he decided that his funds could allow him the luxury of a flight back to New York. Two of them drove him to the airport and waited with him until his flight was called.

Relaxed in his seat he closed his eyes and thought about the people he had met. They were strange people, the Americans. Unless they were recent immigrants they seemed to know so little about the rest of the world. And those who had recently come over combined a deep hatred of their original countries with a homesickness for the places they grew up in that made them defend the very countries they had fled from. The second and third generation Americans had long ceased caring about the world of Europe and its rivalries. And oddly enough it was the Jews, the victims of pogroms and harassment, who seemed to keep the European connection alive.

He had bought a cheap edition of Steinbeck's *The Grapes of Wrath* at the airport and as he reached for it in his canvas bag he remembered the newspaper he'd bought with the book. He would read that first before starting the novel.

It seemed that the British really were fighting on. The headline called it 'The Battle of Britain' and the text said that the RAF had shot down 180 Luftwaffe planes two days ago. His eyes went to the foot of the page and he saw the smaller headline. It was like a physical blow as he saw the headline and the photograph of Leon Trotsky who had been assassinated that day in Mexico City. His head smashed in by an ice-pick. The item went on to say that Trotsky had been sentenced to death in his absence, by one of the Moscow treason trials. He was reported to have been writing a biography exposing Stalin as being responsible for the deaths of over a million Soviet citizens. He closed his eyes and was aware of his heart-beats. They made it so hard, those people in Moscow. It was as if they were testing the believers with one blow after another. It wouldn't be hard to explain. Trotsky had been a dissident involved in a struggle for power. And he'd lost. But outsiders would neither understand nor accept the explanation. He slept for most of the flight and dreamed that he was walking again in the rain in Moscow with his father, the old man pointing out the masons chipping the names of the Tsars off the obelisk in Alexandrovsky Gardens beside the Kremlin walls.

9

The 22nd of June 1941 was a Sunday and that was the day that the Germans invaded Russia. The following day Malloy was surprised to get a phone call from Hancox.

'Mr Malloy, I wonder if you could spare me a few minutes of your time this afternoon. We could meet somewhere to suit you, but it would help me a lot if it could be somewhere in Manhattan.'

'My wife and I are going to the cinema to see *Citizen Kane* this evening. The second showing starts at 8.30. Just off Times Square.'

'How about we meet at six in the bar at the Waldorf. Would you mind if I asked if I could have half an hour with you in private?'

'I guess that'll suit Kathy. OK, six o'clock in the bar.'

Hancox was waiting for him and waved to a waiter as Malloy sat down. 'What'll you have?'

'A scotch on the rocks, please.'

'Two.' Hancox said to the waiter.

'Are you busy at the union?'

'I'm beginning to get on top of it but there's always plenty to do.'

The waiter brought the drinks and Hancox reached for the tab. When he'd paid he said, 'How do you feel about the war in Europe?'

Malloy shrugged. 'I guess it could go either way. I just hope Roosevelt doesn't get us into it.'

'Why?'

'It's not our war.'

'Not even if the Nazis win?'

Malloy frowned but smiled at the same time. 'What is this? You're trying me out about something.'

'We're going to be in the war whether we like it or not, Malloy. That's why I wanted to talk with you.' He paused. 'Can this chat be confidential between you and me? Nobody else. Not even your wife.'

'Sure.'

'D'you know Washington at all?'

'Not really.' Malloy smiled. 'A school visit and a couple of days doing research in the Congress building.'

'What kind of research?'

'I was checking out average pay for DAs in every State.'

Hancox smiled briefly. 'You ever heard of an outfit called the COI?'

Malloy shook his head. 'No.'

'The CIP?'

'No.'

'Are you bored with that union job yet?'

'In a way. It's kinda repetitious. I promised my old man I'd do two years and then I'd do it my way and go to a law firm.'

'How long do you have before you finish?'

Malloy laughed. 'Two months, three days.'

'How'd you like to join a special government organisation?'

'A law job?'

'No. The law's good background but that's all.'

'So why me?'

'I'll tell you later.'

'What is it? Why the mystery?'

'I'm not entitled to tell you. All I can say is that it's very hush-hush and it's an honour to be asked to join it.'

'Do you belong to it?'

'No. They asked me to find somebody suitable for interviewing. I put up your name. They looked into your back-

60

ground and they'd like to talk to you. Put you through some tests.'

'Sounds like some sort of intelligence job.'

'It would take three days – the interviews.' Hancox paused. 'D'you want to think about it?'

Malloy shook his head. 'No. When do you want me to go to Washington?'

'I'll phone you at your home number. It'll be next week. All your expenses will be paid. What will you tell your wife?'

'The truth. Just that I'm going to Washington.'

'Thanks for your time. I think you won't have wasted it.'

'You didn't tell me why me?'

Hancox smiled. 'Two reasons. First of all the answer you gave me when I asked you what you'd do if you won the compensation case. You said you'd go out and get smashed. I'm sure you didn't but it was a good answer. Both naive and refreshing.'

'The other reason.'

'If you'd said you needed time to think this over I'd have known I'd made a mistake.' Hancox stood up and held out his hand. 'Good luck.'

A car picked up Malloy from the small Washington hotel where they had put him up, and took him to a house just off Connecticut Avenue. The guard at the door checked who he was and dialled a couple of numbers on the internal phone. A few minutes later Malloy was being welcomed by two men. Malloy guessed they were only a few years older than him and they were well-dressed and typical ex-college types. They introduced themselves as Jack and Homer. Homer was the fair one.

They chatted about the journey, his hotel, New York and would Ted Williams be the American League Home Run champion that year. Then they settled down around the table, Malloy on one side, the other two facing him.

They asked a lot of questions about his background but

61

he sensed that they already knew the answers. And then Homer said, 'How about religion?'

Malloy smiled. 'How about it?'

'I guess you must be Catholic.'

'Why?'

'Irish. Father Catholic and Irish.'

'My father's American.'

Homer smiled. 'OK. Irish-American.'

'No. Not OK. He's American-American and so am I. I've never even been to Ireland.'

It was Jack's turn. 'You ever seen a dead body, Bill?'

'Yes.'

'How'd it affect you?'

'It made me sad.'

'Why?'

'It was my mother's body.'

'Would you kill somebody if otherwise he'd kill you?'

'I've never thought about it.'

'So think about it now.'

For a moment Malloy hesitated, then shrugging, he said, 'I guess I would.'

'What kind of people do you hate?'

'You mean actually hate or just dislike?'

'I meant what I said.'

'I hate bullies.'

They both laughed and Jack said, 'OK. We got the point – How's your marriage?'

'Fine so far as I know.'

'You happy with it?'

'Yeah.'

'Ever heard of the COI?'

'Mr Hancox mentioned it but he didn't say what it is.'

'What do you think it is?'

'In view of all the fandango I'm going through I assume it's some kind of intelligence set-up.'

Homer looked at Jack who shrugged and nodded and then Homer said, 'You'll be meeting a number of specialists while you're here and if it's appropriate you'll be given a full explanation of what COI does.'

'I'm assuming that whatever it is it's a genuine government agency?'

Homer smiled. 'Yeah. But it's not, repeat not, a bureaucracy.'

For the rest of that day and the whole of the next day Malloy was interviewed separately by two psychologists, given a series of multi-choice test papers and a physical check-up. On the third and final day there was just one interview with a man who was obviously very senior to all the others. He was introduced as Lieutenant Colonel Williams. Malloy guessed that the man was in his mid-forties. He was wearing a khaki shirt and no tie and a pair of grey slacks.

As he waved Malloy to one of the two armchairs he waited until Malloy was seated and then said, 'Well, Malloy, how're you making out?'

Malloy laughed. 'I've no idea, sir.'

'Did you understand what the tests were all about?'

'I had a good idea about most of them but I never grasped what the first interview with Jack and Homer was all about.'

'Why not?'

'There was no theme to the questions.'

Williams smiled. 'They were just running over your frustration tolerance levels. Checking out how you'd react in "no-win" situations.' He paused. 'What did they tell you about the COI?'

'Nothing.'

'Good. Then let me put you in the picture. COI stands for Co-ordinator of Information – which don't mean a damn thing to anybody – and isn't meant to. And sooner or later it's going to become OSS. Office of Strategic Services.' He shrugged. 'And that doesn't tell much either. The thing is – those who know the lie of the land are pretty sure that we're gonna get involved in the war. We don't

63

want it – but we're gonna be in it like it or not. And we're putting together a body of individuals who are going to help us win it. Not so much with guns as with their brains. The British have got an intelligence outfit – been in the business for decades. The Germans have got the Gestapo, the *Abwehr* and a thing called the *Sicherheitsdienst*. And the Russians have got two set-ups, their secret service and their military intelligence. But up to now we've had nothing. The Pentagon does a bit, State does a bit, and neither of 'em agrees on any damn thing. OSS is going to be ready to find out what's really going on.' He held up his hand. 'But not until the balloon goes up. It doesn't even officially exist as yet. We may be fishing around a bit right now but that's only to keep our hands in. When the signal goes we will be ready to establish the OSS and get going. So we're looking for people right now.

'What kind of people? Well, all sorts of people. Old, young, academics, lawyers, specialists of all kinds. And they'll all have one thing in common. They'll be men and women who'll have a go at anything. People who never say no. When they're asked to do something that's obviously impossible they think about it and then they do it. They don't think like bureaucrats, not even like soldiers and they don't think in straight lines. We want people with flair and moral courage.' He paused. 'Are you interested?'

'Am I being offered a place?'

'Yes.'

'Then I accept.'

'Good. Now let's go over some mundane details. I understand you've still got two months' obligations to your employers.'

'That's correct.'

'OK. Work out your obligation then you join us with the rank and pay of a captain. You'll have a couple of months of training and then we'll give you some permanent posting.'

'This means moving from New York?'

64

'Yes. Here in Washington in the first place, then . . .' he shrugged '. . . who knows?'

'Is there anything against wives moving along with husbands?'

'Is that what you want?'

'If it's possible.'

'Is she trained for anything?'

'She's a secretary at a local company.'

'We could find her a job while you're in Washington. But if the worst happens and we are in a war then you'd have to go wherever you were needed. Probably overseas. But your wife would get a marriage allowance and a quartering allowance and carry on with her job.'

'Can I tell her about all this?'

'Yes. But warn her that she must not talk about it to anyone else. Not even her parents if she has parents.'

'Thanks.'

Williams stood up, smiling as he held out his hand. 'Glad to have you aboard, Malloy. I think you're going to be a real asset.'

10

Andrei was stretched out on the bed, his eyes closed, and Chantal sat beside him, looking at his face and holding his hand.

'Anna's made you some chicken soup with noodles, would you like some?'

'I've got to go and see old man Henschel about Ivan.'

'That can wait, my love. You need some rest.'

He opened his eyes and looked at her. 'I'm not much of a husband to you, am I?'

'You're all I want.' She paused. 'Is there anything I can do to help you?'

'You do it already. You're my rock. My hiding place.'

'Hiding place from what?'

'The world. People. Questions, arguments, misunderstanding, quarrels. Families split by differences, marriages floundering, life-time friendships destroyed. Old ideas against new ones. The terrible jargon the Party seems to have established. Working men arguing about whether we should have "proletarian dictatorship" or "social democratic parliamentarism". All those long words and half the time they've no idea what they mean. But people give up their work or their families, their friends, almost their lives as if they've been infected with some terrible fever.' He smiled. 'I'm OK, my love. Sometimes they wear me out. That's all.'

They shared a bowl of soup together and then Andrei took Ivan into his bedroom. He pointed at the solitary chair and sat on the edge of the bed.

'Now, *mensch*, tell me what you want me to do.' He smiled. 'First of all what's her name?'

'Rachel. Rachel Henschel.'

'Is that the silversmith?'

'Yeah.'

'How old is she? The truth.'

'Seventeen next month.'

'Go on.'

'We want to get married when she's eighteen and to wear a ring until then.'

'You been to bed with her?'

'No.' Ivan shrugged. 'Not all the way.'

'And you want to marry her so you can bed her.'

'Well, I guess . . . no, it's we like one another. She likes me and I like her.'

'Like or love?'

'Hard to say. But I know she's the one for me.'

'And what does the old man say?'

'He says I'm a no-good. After his money.' He shrugged. 'The usual stuff fathers say.'

'You've had a lot of girl-friends since we've been here. What's so different about Rachel?'

'She don't want to change me. She likes me as I am. The others all want some fellow with a car and money to spend on them. Rachel doesn't care about all that.'

'OK. I'll see what I can do.'

'Thanks.'

The man the family all referred to as 'old man Henschel' was, in fact, just short of his fortieth birthday and was about to close for the night when Andrei tried the door. It was locked already but when Henschel saw who it was he slid back the top and bottom bolts and then unlocked the door, opening it cautiously.

'Mr Henschel. My name's Aarons. Could I have a word with you?'

For a moment the man hesitated and then he opened the door, locking it again when Andrei was inside. They both stood by the counter where some small pieces of silver-ware were on display under the glass cover.

'I came to speak on behalf of my brother, Ivan, Mr Henschel.'

'You're wasting your time, mister. Not him nor anyone else is gonna turn my little gal into his *tsatske*.'

Andrei smiled. 'I don't think that's what he has in mind. He wants to marry her when she is old enough. And he wants to do it with your blessing and mine.'

'He should live so long. He don't need anyone to speak for him, he's got *chutzpah* for ten, that fellow.'

'That attitude could give us both problems, Mr Henschel.'

The man shrugged. 'So I got problems. Who cares?'

'Maybe you could tell me your objection to him?'

'He's got no regular job. He's had a dozen girls before my Rachel. Who needs a guy like him?'

'He has got a regular job. He works for me.'

'Doing what?'

'He works at the bookshop I own and he helps me in many directions.'

'It's you with the bookshop then?'

'Yes.'

'A bookshop in this place? How to throw away money.'

'We already make a small profit and we're building up.' Andrei hoped that the exaggeration was excused in the circumstances.

Henschel said, 'Let's go in the back.'

Andrei followed him into a small workshop crowded with cupboards and work-tables. Henschel pulled out a chair for him and perched himself on the edge of the main work-bench.

'How much he make, your Ivan?'

'Just over twenty dollars a week. He'll get more when he's a married man.'

'All the time she wants to go dancing with him. Not here in Brighton Beach but up there in the city. And her not yet seventeen.'

'There's nowhere to dance in Brighton Beach but they could certainly go to Coney if you think that would be more acceptable.'

'They do what they want, not what I want.'

'I think if they felt you would be on their side then they'd do what you want.' Andrei smiled. 'I think Ivan would do anything to get your approval. He's quite genuine about Rachel.'

'So why don't he do it now?'

'I guess because he thinks you're against their friendship.' Andrei paused. 'It becomes a struggle for the girl between you and him. That's bad for both of you. And for Rachel too.'

'So what instead?'

'Let him give her a ring. Let him be part of your family and Rachel part of mine. My wife and my sister would make her very welcome.'

For long moments Henschel stared at the grimy back window then he said, 'OK. We try it, my friend. See how it goes.'

The night of 29th of December 1940 the skies over London were red with the flames of burning buildings as the Luftwaffe set about fire-bombing the almost defenceless city. From the docks, through the banking area to the West End, London was burning, and centuries old buildings were collapsing into heaps of rubble.

At the same time President Roosevelt was giving one of his fire-side chats to the American public. He was describing in every-day language the essence of what Washington insiders designated HR1776 which was officially described as *A Bill to Further Promote the Defense of the United States, and for other purposes*. One clause in the Bill provided for aid to 'any country whose defense the President deems vital to the defense of the United States'. In his chat he also renewed his pledge to keep America out of the war.

In the next few days the polls reported that 71 per cent

of the people backed him and 54 per cent wanted lend-lease to start immediately. The Bill became law three months later and Roosevelt asked Congress for nine billion dollars, and got it.

American shipyards were opened to damaged British ships and US warships were providing an escort service to British merchant ships in what was called 'the chastity belt', roughly 1000 miles of the Atlantic. Under great secrecy the US Navy was ordered to keep aggressors from operating west of the 1000 mile line.

The First Brigade of the US Marine Corps relieved the British troops in Iceland and were ordered to ready themselves for unspecified operations.

All this was as far as the President was prepared to go. The US was almost certainly going to be involved in the war against Hitler but he was aware that the first blow would have to come from the other side. The loss of an American warship was the least it would take.

In Berlin Adolf Hitler recognised the trap and despite the protests of Admiral Raeder he gave orders that every precaution would be taken to avoid attacking an American ship. Only the most senior officers of the *Oberkommando der Wehrmacht* knew that in a few months' time Operation Barbarossa, the attack on the Soviet Union, would be launched. Nothing must jeopardise that.

When Andrei heard the news on the radio that the Nazis had invaded the Soviet Union he felt a momentary relief that they were no longer linked with the Germans and that all his forecasts had been justified. But as the German armies drove deep into Russia he was sickened at the thought of what must be happening. That week the shop sold over a hundred wall-maps of Europe and the USSR for people to mark up where the battles were being fought. He listened to the broadcasts from Moscow and even there they made no attempt to hide the fact that the Red Army was being pushed back with terrible losses. The thought of what would be happening to the civilians in the

German-occupied territories was unbearable. But it had changed the attitude of the Americans overnight. Russians were no longer the Nazis' allies. There was a tension in the air as if more and worse was to come.

By the middle of July the Germans had taken Minsk, Smolensk and Tallin; by September they had taken Kiev and were in the outskirts of Leningrad. In October they took Orel and Odessa and were only fifty miles from Moscow. Kharkov fell in the last week of October.

There were reports of the Red Army taking back towns from the Germans and Moscow was still holding out against massive artillery attacks. But there was still a lot to be done to swing American public opinion behind the Soviet struggle. It wasn't their war and they didn't want any part of it.

Bill and Kathy Malloy had gone over to New York to spend the weekend with Bill's father. They had got up late on the Sunday morning and Kathy had cooked them the old man's favourite steak and kidney pie for a late lunch.

After they had eaten she took the portable radio into the kitchen. She was going to give the place a good clean-up and she could listen to the radio as she worked. She switched on the radio and the voice said, 'And now – *Gangbusters* – The only national programme to bring you authentic police histories. America's crusade against crime.' She switched over to a sweet music station playing Bing Crosby records.

In the cosy living room the two men were chatting. Bill Malloy smiling as his father launched into his standard diatribe about the men in the White House. No complaints about the President himself. The villains were the politicians, the Congressmen and Senators who wouldn't go along with what FDR wanted for the people.

'It's no good you smiling, boy. You need to know some of the facts of life.' He pointed his unlit pipe at his son. 'A quarter of the population lives on farms. You know what the average farmer made last year?'

'No idea, Dad. Tell me.'

'A thousand dollars for a year's hard work. And we've got unskilled workers laying the foundations for the new road – East River Drive they call it. Those men are on 832 dollars a year.'

'That's terrible. How do they manage?'

The old man swung his arm, sweeping aside the question. 'Three out of four farms are still lit by kerosene lamps. A quarter of the houses in this country don't have running water and a third don't have flush toilets.'

In the kitchen Kathy was cleaning the cooking stove and singing along with Bing.

Thanks for the memory – of sentimental verse, nothing in my purse and chuckles when the preacher said for better or for worse. How lovely it was.

And then the music stopped. She thought at first that the battery had gone but then there were a few seconds of the carrier wave. A few seconds later a voice announced breathlessly that the Japanese were bombing the US naval base at Pearl Harbor.

For a moment she stood there paralysed, a dishcloth clutched in her hand. Then she rushed into the living room and told them what she had heard. The radio was still on, still playing Crosby records and then the news-flash was repeated.

Bill Malloy stood up and said quietly, 'I'll have to get back to Washington, Dad.' He had not told his father anything about his work or OSS. He saw his father swallow and then nod. 'I understand, boy. Whatever you think best. Keep in touch.'

'I will, Dad. I will.'

In the White House the President sat at his desk dictating his first war bulletin.

'Yesterday comma December seventh comma nineteen forty-one dash a date that will live in infamy dash the United

72

States of America was suddenly and deliberately attacked by naval and air forces of the Empire of Japan period. Paragraph. The United States was at peace with that nation and comma at the solicitation of Japan comma was still in conversation with that government and its Emperor looking toward the maintenance of peace . . .'

He broke off and kept pounding his fist on the desk. 'Our planes were destroyed on the ground.' He said it again and again.

11

In the first few days after the declaration of war against the Axis the situation in OSS was chaotic despite all the pre-planning that had gone on for months. It was almost two weeks later when Malloy was told to report to Lieutenant Colonel Williams. The interview took place in a suite of rooms in a hotel that had been taken over by OSS for the sections in charge of operations in Europe, until a larger and more suitable building could be allotted.

There was no proper desk, just a plain wooden folding table of the kind that decorators use for pasting wallpaper. The colonel shook Malloy's hand and waved him to one of the several leather armchairs.

'Make yourself comfortable, Malloy.' He waited until Malloy was seated and then went on. 'I see from your records that you took French as a subsidiary subject at college. What's it like now?'

Malloy smiled and shrugged. 'I only scraped through the exam and I've not kept it up since leaving law school.'

'Fair enough. What do you know about a Brit outfit called Special Operations Executive?'

'I've read the OSS summary about them but that's about all. Just that they send people into the occupied countries in Europe on sabotage missions.'

'OK. And what do you know about railways?'

Malloy looked surprised. 'Nothing at all beyond what anybody knows.' Then he paused and smiled. 'I guess that's not true. My father was a locomotive driver and I must have absorbed quite a lot from hearing him talk about the railways. The routes and procedures, schedules and that sort of thing.'

'And the unions?'

Malloy laughed. 'Of course. He was a strong union man.'

'And you. Are you a union supporter? You worked for a small union, didn't you.'

'Yes. But I was never a member of a union.'

'Why not?'

'They were too simplistic for my taste. They just made it worker versus employer. And that way the worker is always the loser. They should have spent more effort on analysing what they wanted, money, improved conditions or job security. There were employers who were willing to talk but they were treated as if they were like the worst employers. Too much politics and not enough hard facts.'

Williams raised his eyebrows. 'Interesting. Well, let's get down to business. We're sending you to London. You'll be temporarily seconded to SOE for training. But before you go you'll spend some weeks under a top man at one of our main rail companies. In the course of your SOE training you'll get parachute training and weapons training. And you'll learn how SOE networks are organised.

'When that's finished you'll be briefed on what you'll be doing in France. Understood?'

'Shall I be under command of SOE or OSS?'

'Both. You'll be controlled by our London office but in the field we'll want you to take your time from the network you'll be attached to. They'll be responsible for funding you, your security and your facilities like radio.'

'What's SOE got to do with trains?'

Williams hesitated for a moment then said, 'OK. Let me explain.' He paused. 'Sooner or later we'll have to land in Europe. Hundreds of thousands of men. It will take time to assemble such a force and its weapons. Could be a couple of years before we launch. Rail and road communications will be of vital importance to stop the

Germans moving their troops and supplies to foil our attack. It will be your job to brief us on every aspect of the railway system in France. Track, signalling, repair shops, bridges, timetables, how the Germans operate. And most important of all – the places where sabotage will do most good. The network can put you in touch with French railway unions and railway men who are sympathetic to the Resistance. So . . .' he smiled, '. . . you'll be a very busy man.'

'How do I get all this stuff back to London?'

'You'll be told how on your training course with SOE.' He looked at his watch and stood up. 'I'm afraid I'll have to chuck you out. I've got another meeting. And – best of luck. Should be very interesting.'

'I need to explain to my wife what's coming up.'

'What have you told her so far?'

'Just that I'm employed on confidential work for the government.'

'What does she do?'

'She's with me here in Washington. She's a secretary to a hotel manager.'

'Would she be prepared to make a move? OSS need good secretaries. Ones who don't talk.'

'I'll ask her. I'm sure she'll say yes.'

'Let me know what she says.'

Andrei walked slowly along 20th and stopped at the row of small shops opposite the Flatiron Building. The third shop in the row was the shoe shop and as he moved slowly past it he saw that the pair of red shoes in the row at the front of the window were the wrong way round. The shoes were reversed, the right one where the left one should be. He walked on, crossed the street at the lights and strolled back to the Flatiron Building. His small office was on the tenth floor. A floor of single and two-roomed offices that were let on a monthly rental. He unlocked his door and hung his coat on a hook behind the door.

There were piles of books on the floor and on a table

against the wall and a front page from *Saturday Evening Post* tacked on the wall alongside the door. A Norman Rockwell painting showing a typical American farm family looking at a new baby in a home-made cradle with rockers.

Andrei opened his post. Half a dozen offers from out-of-town booksellers and a couple of enquiries. One for a first edition of *Collected Poems* by Robert Frost and one for a first edition of Pearl Buck's *The Good Earth*.

He looked at his watch after he had made a couple of telephone calls, put on his coat, locked the office and took the elevator down to street level. He crossed the street and as he passed the shoe shop window he saw that the red shoes were no longer there.

He walked down Broadway towards Union Square, his collar turned up against the biting wind. Five minutes later he turned into East 17th Street and headed for the coffee shop next to the pharmacy. He took a seat at a table in the far corner and ordered a coffee and a beef sandwich. A man came out from the kitchen a few minutes later, he was carrying a copy of the *New York Times* which he put down on the table with the bill. He talked with Andrei for a moment, took his money and gave him change before leaving for the kitchen. The newspaper was left lying on the table and Andrei slid it into his coat pocket as he stood up.

Back in his office he reached for the copy of Steinbeck's *Of Mice and Men* and slowly and carefully deciphered the message. When he had finished he read the message several times before burning it in the handbasin and flushing it away.

In the end Malloy had gone down to Chicago to the HQ of the American Railways Supervisors Association where a retired senior railwayman was to be his tutor for the next two weeks.

Malloy had never realised that operating a railway was so complex. To him a railroad was just some track, loco-motives and coaches. He was quickly disabused of those thoughts on the first day. Hector Maclean had been vice-president in charge of all three of the major operational divisions – the operating department, maintenance of way and mechanical.

Even putting in twelve hours a day of concentrated instruction it still meant that there was no time to cover the legal, personnel and accounting departments.

But at the end of the two weeks he knew where a railroad was most vulnerable to disruption, how to put a locomotive out of action with minimal explosive and how to derail a freight train by remote control. He also knew how to give instruction on logging the loads and destinations of both freight and passenger trains being used by the Germans. Part of his training at SOE was to be identification of German units in transit.

When he went back to Washington his mind was still crammed with details of arch tubes, circulators, automatic oilers, flues, valves, pistons, cylinders and the vulnerability of welded boilers.

Aarons was exhausted as he sat on the bench nearest the entrance to the zoo at Chapultepec Park. There were thousands of people eating picnic lunches, playing with their children or just strolling through the park. It seemed as if everyone in Mexico City had decided to spend Sunday in Chapultepec. Despite the urgency in the note he had avoided the most direct route to Mexico and it had taken him five days to get there. The message told him where the meeting place would be. It had to be on a Sunday and the person who contacted him would be somebody he already knew. He had only arrived at the bus station two hours earlier.

In the distance he could see the sickeningly high curve of the roller-coaster in the amusement park and a cluster of signs indicated the direction of the museums, the boating lake and the restaurants. The guide book said that the park had originally been the royal hunting grounds of the Aztecs.

Twice, as he sat in the sunshine his eyes had closed and only the noise of people laughing had woken him up. But in the end he had slept, his worn canvas bag on his lap, his hand through the leather handles. When he awoke there was a woman sitting on the bench beside him. Not somebody he recognised and he rubbed the sleep from his eyes and looked at his watch. He had been asleep for nearly an hour.

There were two paths down which his contact could come and he watched them both carefully. He had watched for ten minutes when a voice said in Russian, 'Welcome to Mexico City, comrade Aarons. We expected you last Sunday.'

He turned to look at the woman beside him but he didn't recognise her. She smiled and said, 'You don't remember me, do you, Andrei?'

He shook his head. 'I'm afraid I don't.'

'Well it was a long time ago, my friend.' She smiled and said quietly, 'Kuskovo Palace – the training school – and afterwards the special training at the apartment in Moscow. And you didn't know whether you were to be Comintern or a spy.'

'You're the Spanish girl. I remember now.'

She laughed. 'Not a girl any longer, Andrei.'

'What are you doing here?'

She shrugged. 'I'm Spanish.' She smiled. 'They find me useful. And you? What are you doing?'

He smiled. 'Like you I don't ever answer such questions.'

'You'll be staying with me while you're here. Sounds like you'll be here for a week.' She turned her head to look at him. 'Your old friend Lensky's here. Specially to see you. Quite an honour these days, believe me.'

'How long have you been here in Mexico?'

She sighed. 'A long time.'

'When do they want to see me?'

'Tonight about ten. There'll be time for you to have a

79

sleep at my place if you want.' She stood up. 'We'd better go.'

She walked him to a broad avenue and waved down a white taxi with a yellow stripe. As they got in the taxi she gave instructions to the driver in Spanish and then changed to English as she said, 'The taxis with orange-red stripes are *sitio* cabs and they don't cruise. And they're twice the price. No meters.'

As he looked out of the window he said, 'I've never seen so many flowers in a town before.'

'There are flowers in every street and every avenue. They love them. So do I.'

'Must be happy people.'

She shrugged. 'They are, but not because of the flowers. They live in tin shacks with no sewage disposal, no medicines and no jobs.'

'How do they get by?'

'They've got guts. They don't get by, they survive. The kids die while they're still kids. The girls go on the streets and the men into thieving, if they're lucky.'

The cab pulled up at an apartment block and when she'd paid the fare she took him up to her apartment on the fifth floor. It was small and well cared for and no traces of a man. As she locked the door she said, 'The couch by the window is yours for the night. I've got an air-bed coming tomorrow.' She brushed back her hair. 'You look tired. Do you want a sleep?'

'Do you mind if I do? Just an hour would do me.'

'Go ahead. I'll wake you in an hour. I'll let them know you're here.'

He was deep asleep when she shook his shoulder to wake him and as he opened his eyes he couldn't remember where he was. He seemed to spend his life waking up not knowing where he was. And then he saw her looking down at him. 'There's a coffee on the table for you. You've got an hour before we need to leave. The bathroom's over there.' He followed her over to the open door of the bathroom.

When he had washed and shaved he went back into the living room. She was sitting at the small table drinking her coffee and she pointed to the cup she had left for him. There was a sandwich on a plate beside the cup. Cheese and tomato.

'Tell me about your family, Andrei. I heard that you had married a very pretty French girl. Are you still married?'

He laughed. 'Yes. Why are you so surprised?'

She shrugged. 'The comrades don't make very good husbands. Especially the Russians.'

'What's wrong with Russians?'

'They may be OK in Russia but once they get to America they get the itch for some smart little chick and they're off.'

'Have you met many like that?'

'Too many. Like Spanish wine you Russians don't travel well.'

'And you? Are you married?'

'I was. I got a divorce as soon as I came over here.' She paused. 'Do you have children?'

'No.'

She smiled. 'No hostages to fortune, eh?'

'Exactly.'

'You've got brothers and sisters, haven't you?'

'One brother, one sister.'

'Do you see them at all?'

He smiled. 'Every day. We live in the same house.'

'Do they work for the Party?'

'Let's say they do anything I ask them to do.'

'They don't want you to go to the embassy. It's under constant surveillance by FBI agents.'

'Where do they want me to go?'

'It's a house not far from here, at the other end of the street market.' She stood up. 'We can walk there and you can see the market. It's for locals, not for tourists.'

The Mercado de Sonora in Calle San Nicolas was known locally as 'the Witches Market' because it sold those strange things that were supposed to have magic powers.

She pointed out items on the stalls as Aarons stopped and asked her what various things were for.

'The bunches of garlic are to protect your home from envy.'

'And those dead birds?'

She smiled. 'They're dried humming-birds to make a man successful with women. And the candles beside them are good-luck or bad-luck candles. The soap in the basket there is to make you rich.'

'And those live animals in the cages at the back?'

'They're for sacrifices.'

'My God, these people must be crazy.'

'Everybody's crazy, Andrei. Haven't you learned that? What about all those Russian peasants and their icons and my people who think that killing bulls in public is entertainment.'

He stopped and looked at her. 'You know, I don't even know your name.'

She shrugged. 'It's Maria. Maria Consuela Garcia.'

'What made you change?'

'Change what?'

'You were so enthusiastic in Moscow and now you sound cynical.'

'Maybe I am. Maybe I've learned a few lessons as the years went by.'

'What lessons did you learn?'

She sighed, looking away at the people at the market stalls. And then she looked back at him. 'I've learned that no religion and no political credo can work.'

'Why not?'

She shrugged and smiled. 'Because people are people. They want to live their lives their own way.'

'Even if it makes their lives worse?'

'Yes. Even if it makes their lives worse. They don't

think it does. And I'm inclined to agree with them.'

'Have you said this to our people?'

'Of course not. Or I shouldn't be here, I'd be in some labour camp. And what kind of Party is it where a Party member can't speak his mind?'

For a moment Aarons was silent, then he touched her shoulder gently for a moment as he said, 'As far as I'm concerned I haven't heard what you said.' He shook his head slowly and said quietly, 'The Nazis are killing our people – tens of thousands every day. We can't desert them now.'

She opened her mouth to say something then closed it and took his arm, leading him into the narrow alley that led to the avenue.

The medium-sized villa was surrounded by a white-washed wall and there was a gardener spraying the flower-beds from a hose. The Mexican didn't look at them as the girl led Aarons up the stone steps. The door of the house was open and gave onto a hall with a marble floor.

Lensky smiled as he held out his hand before kissing him Russian fashion on each cheek as he hugged Aarons before standing back and looking at him. He looked as if he were about to say something and then changed his mind.

'There's a room upstairs. Let's go up.'

The room was quite small but expensively furnished. The two armchairs were made of cane with thick soft cushions on the seat and back.

As he sat down Lensky said, 'Any idea why we wanted to see you?'

'No. I just got the message to come here to Mexico City.'

'We seem to have a problem, Andrei.'

'What problem is that?'

'You know Melnikov at our Washington embassy?'

'I've heard of him but I've never met him. My orders

were to avoid any contact with the embassy unless it was absolutely vital.'

'He provides the political situation reports to Moscow. Your reports and his reports don't agree.'

'About what?'

'The American attitude to the Soviet Union and the war.'

'What's his opinion?'

'He thinks the Americans are dragging their feet so that the Germans can go on slaughtering Russians.'

'I think he's wrong but it's a legitimate point of view. I've told local parties to agitate for a more urgent response. But the Americans have only been in the war for a few months. They're calling up tens of thousands of men, the factories are working day and night to make tanks, planes and ships.'

'Moscow prefer his view.'

Aarons frowned. 'It doesn't matter whose view it is. What matters is the truth – the reality.'

Lensky smiled. 'Don't be naive, Andrei. It suits Moscow to think that way. Great sacrifices are being made. They need a . . .' he paused.

Aarons said, 'A scapegoat maybe.'

'Don't spoil your record, Andrei. Everybody in Moscow admires your work. You've got a wonderful record. Why spoil it?'

'You mean they don't want the truth if it doesn't suit them?'

'That's for Moscow to decide.'

'So what do you want me to do?'

'Moscow accepts that you did an incredible job here in America before the war started. Many of the arguments that you deployed to defend the Party are now part of our history. Your role is fully acknowledged. But we are in a new phase now. There is a world war and we need new duties from our proven workers. That means a new role for you.'

Lensky waited for a response but Aarons stayed silent

and Lensky went on. 'From now on you'll be full-time intelligence with overall control of three of our New York networks. There are things going on that we must know about. I've got two specialists here to brief you on everything. And I've got a man who'll show you how to use a new radio. A radio that can give you instant contact with Moscow, direct or through Canada.' Lensky smiled. 'You've been promoted, Andrei. Your rank now is lieutenant-colonel with direct access to the Director of the First Chief Directorate, to me in the Kremlin and to Comrade Tokarov in the Politburo. You out-rank all other intelligence agents in the USA.'

'Do the other network leaders know about this?'

'They will do when you and I have finished here.'

'Who funds the networks I'll be controlling?'

'The existing channels will operate but we shall double or treble the funds. You'll have your own funds for special operations. You'll be getting 150,000 dollars a month funded through several accounts in different names. We'll be going through all that in the next couple of days.'

'Who am I responsible to in the States?'

'To nobody. You'll be under direct control of Moscow.'

'And you want no reports from me on the political situation in the States?'

'Not unless you're asked for them. There will be times when we want your opinion but it's not a formal responsibility.'

'And I can say what I really think?'

Lensky sighed. 'Yes.' He paused. 'Come here tomorrow at ten and we'll get started.' As Aarons stood up Lensky said, 'How do you get on with Comrade Garcia?'

'I've been asleep most of the time. She doesn't talk much.'

Lensky grimaced. 'Glad to hear it.'

As they walked back to her house she said, 'Did you solve the problem?'

'Who said there was a problem?'

She laughed softly, 'I've been around these things a long time, Andrei. I can smell it in the air. It's a kind of ritual dance, a ballet. The *pas de deux* with the steps all rehearsed and then the beautiful swirling music when all comes right. Or, of course – just an echo in the silence as an iron door closes.'

'And what kind of music do you hear tonight?'

'I don't recognise it, that's why I asked.'

'I'd better buy you a set of those tarot cards we saw in the market this evening.'

She laughed. 'Why not?'

The meetings had gone on for four days, the last day spent with Lensky alone. And Lensky now seemed more relaxed, telling him of the problems that the Soviets found in waging war against the Germans while trying to produce armour, planes, weapons and food to keep the country alive. They had eaten a meal together in the early evening and as they drank their coffee Lensky said, 'Do you miss Moscow at all, Andrei?'

Aarons shrugged. 'I never really knew it. I was a child when we left. All I knew about Moscow and Russia was the months when I was being trained and what my father told me. He missed it very much.'

'As soon as this war is over you must come to Moscow. Meet the people who matter and enjoy the respect that so many feel for what you've done.' He paused. 'Tell me about the family.'

'My brother is to be married shortly. A local girl. He works for me in the cause.'

'What kind of work?'

'As a courier. Anything I tell him to do he does. My wife Chantal and Anna run the bookshop. We make enough money to live on.' He smiled briefly. 'We get by.'

'As I said, when this is all over it will be a time for rewarding all those who have played a part in the nation's survival. Nobody will be forgotten.'

'How is your life?'

Lensky sighed. 'Not easy. The Party uses me as a trouble-shooter so I go from one problem to another. Big personalities clashing, criticisms of policies, rivalries even in wartime.'

'Is there still anti-semitism?'

Lensky was silent for a few seconds and then he said quietly, 'Not that affects me. Nor you.'

Influence had been used to get Aarons a seat on a plane to San Diego and Maria Consuela had gone with him to the airport and waited with him until his flight was called. Two days later he had got on a flight to Boston where he took the train to New York, and then he took the subway to Brighton Beach.

12

Malloy had been given four days' embarkation leave and he and Kathy had spent it in New York. With a little help from Washington they had got a special deal at the Waldorf.

The last day was a Sunday and they got up early, had breakfast and then walked up the Avenue to Central Park. There were few people about despite the fine weather that gave promise of an early spring.

They walked as far as the lake and sat on the bench watching a father row his two children back towards the boathouse.

Malloy was wearing his uniform with captain's double bars but no unit insignia and Kathy was aware that these would be their last few hours together for a long time. They had spent a day with his father who was obviously proud of his son in uniform, insisting that they stroll up to the cemetery and back so that his father's cronies could see them.

She had gone along with the move to Washington but she missed New York and coming back had emphasised it.

'Shall we be coming back to New York when this is all over?'

He looked at her, smiling. 'I hope so. You miss it, don't you?'

'Yes. Do you?'

'I hadn't realised how much I missed it until these last few days.'

'What do you miss?'

'Everything. The lights, Rockefeller Center, the Chrysler building, Pan Am . . .' he laughed, '. . . there's no other place. Like Jimmy Walker said – better be a lamp-post in New York than Mayor of Chicago.'

She laughed. 'For me it's Horn and Hardart Automats, Tiffany's, and Radio City Music Hall and the Rockettes.' She looked at his face. 'Are you scared at all, Bill?'

He frowned. 'Scared of what?'

'Of what you'll be doing overseas.'

'No. It's not dangerous, if you're properly trained.'

'Colonel Williams said he'd contact me from time to time because the mails are so bad.'

'I'll keep in touch myself, kid.' He smiled. 'Don't worry about me. I'll be OK.'

'What time do you have to leave tonight?'

'About eight. They're sending a car for me to take me to the airfield.' He smiled. 'I thought we'd have lunch back at the hotel and then there's a Bing Crosby film – *Holiday Inn* – how about we go and see that?'

'Can I see you off at the airport?'

'I'm not going from the airport, it's an army flight from an airfield.' He took her hand. 'I'd rather see you off at the bus terminal about seven and you'll be home by the time I take-off. OK?'

She nodded and shrugged. 'I'm going to miss you terribly.'

'I'll miss you too, honey. But the sooner we get on with it the sooner it'll be over.'

'Just come back in one piece. That's all that matters to me.'

He stood up. 'Let's go, honey. We've got time to walk back down the Avenue.'

They took a cab to the Port Authority Bus Terminal and Malloy had timed it so there was little time before the bus left. She bought a couple of magazines, kissed him good-bye and then took her seat on the bus, sitting in the window seat so that she could see him at least until the bus left.

As she looked at him she thought that he looked too young to be part of a war. In his uniform he looked even younger. She had always been doubtful about his joining OSS and now that she worked for them she was even more concerned. They had a recklessness that frightened her because they seemed to see war as some kind of game. And she knew from the reports that she was typing that it was no game. As the bus moved off she waved to him, holding up the teddy-bear that he had bought for her at one of the stores near Times Square. She watched him smiling and waving until the bus turned onto 42nd Street.

It was three days before Malloy landed at the RAF airfield in Scotland. He was taken across to the Officers' Mess and given a bunk-bed for the night. It seemed that he wasn't expected. Nobody had been informed about his arrival or what they should do with him after he landed. The wing commander who took charge of him seemed faintly amused that he should be so surprised.

'It's par for the course, captain. Nobody's ever expected. You get urgent orders to report to some place you've never heard of and when you get there they've never heard of you.' He laughed. 'You say you're in OSS. What the hell is that?'

'The Office of Strategic Services.'

'Never heard of it. Is it American?'

'Yes. It's part of the army.'

'Well, I've sent a signal down to London to see what they want me to do with you. Meantime, have a meal in the Mess and get some sleep. It could be a couple of days before we discover who owns you.'

It was the first time that Malloy had been outside the United States and the first time in his life where he had felt ill at ease with men who were of his own age. They weren't unfriendly, they passed down the mustard, salt and some kind of tomato sauce in a bottle. But they were pilots, navigators and air-gunners and he was an outsider with nothing to contribute to their talk. He could barely understand half of it. They had a special coded jargon that was their own. They kept talking about 'wizard prangs' and roaring with laughter at a pilot with his arm in a sling. He could hardly believe it when he found out the next day that a 'wizard prang' was crashing an aircraft. And they were amused at it. When he asked where he could find a phone to call home he was told that there were no overseas telephone calls allowed apart from official ones.

As the days went by without word from London he sometimes wondered if it wasn't all some elaborate scheme to test out his morale, but gradually he was absorbed into the squadron and became aware that their exclusive attitude was born of knowing that the odds were against them surviving the next sortie over Germany. In the second week there were two non-returning air-crews after a raid on Hamburg.

At the end of the second week he was called to the Squadron Office and the CO of the unit told him that he was to travel to Manchester where he would do his parachute course.

At the RAF parachute school on the outskirts of Manchester it was as if some official word of approval had gone out. He was the object of curiosity. The Yank. And Malloy found himself responding.

In the echoing hangars, in the creaking baskets of captive balloons and in the bellies of aircraft he was America's representative. Joked about, teased and genuinely liked, he was at home at last. In the Mess at night he talked to young men who came from the poverty-stricken backstreets of industrial cities and others from middle-class homes. There were young men from the upper classes who he disliked instantly, only to find them as brave and as unsure as the rest of the men on the course. He learned a lot about how to not be an American in just over three

91

weeks. When he was ordered to report to OSS HQ in London it felt like he was leaving home.

Malloy was aware that his uniform was what got him a taxi at Euston Station. Not because he was a soldier. Not even because he was a captain. But because he was an American and he'd got dollars.

At the house in Grosvenor Square he'd been introduced to a Lieutenant-Colonel Kelly who in turn had taken him the short walk to Baker Street where he had been introduced to Major Wallace. Major Wallace was a Scot, and he was SOE. He would be Wallace's protégé while he was undergoing his SOE training.

The major had taken him to dinner at the Dorchester and as they walked through the darkened London streets he heard his first air-raid warning.

The major said, 'We'll be OK in the hotel. Safer in there than out here anyway.'

A dance-band played as they ate dinner and several people came to their table to chat for a few moments with Wallace. Most of them pretty girls in khaki uniforms.

'You married, Malloy?'

'Yes, sir.'

'It's Mike, and you're Bill, aren't you?'

'Yes.'

'When you write to your wife there's a nice little item from today's news to tell her. Today the British government announced that for the duration of the war there is to be no embroidery on women's underwear.' He roared with laughter. 'That'll shake the Germans.'

'What's the purpose of that regulation?'

'God knows.' He smiled. 'In wartime it gives all the old aunties in the Ministries a wonderful chance to make people's lives more miserable than they already are.'

'Most people over here seem pretty cheerful to me.'

'In a way they are. Everybody's got a job. Everybody's earning money and that includes women too. People who've been on the dole for years have suddenly become valuable. No wonder they like it.'

'What did you do before the war, Mike?'

'I was a lawyer, criminal law-courts.'

'I was a lawyer too.'

'I know. Is that what you're going to do when you get back?'

'I'm not sure. Depends what things are like. The war's going to change a lot of things.'

'Like what?'

'Everything. This war is going to change countries as well as people. It's going to be a mess. And I guess it'll take at least as many years to clear up the mess as it takes to win the war.'

'You don't have any doubts that we'll win it?'

Malloy looked shocked. 'Of course not. Do you?'

Wallace shrugged. 'We were fighting the Germans and the Italians on our own for over a year. We'd have been fools not to wonder if we'd survive. Now that your people are in it with us it changed overnight.' He paused. 'But it's still got to be won.'

At the next day's briefing Wallace got straight down to business. 'I want to make clear that you're completely independent. You're only with me for special training that will make your job in France easier. You're still one of Kelly's men. Not under us for discipline. We aren't trying to take over any of OSS's operation. All we want to do is to make sure that our experience of operating in German-occupied France is passed on to you. When you've finished the course you can operate how you choose, you can ignore what we've told you – or use it – it's up to you. D'you understand?'

'Yes. But I don't understand why you're telling me this.'

Wallace shrugged. 'Your people here in London have their own ways of doing things. That's the way you go. And there are people in Washington who think we are trying to impose our methods on OSS so that we can take them over or at least control their activities if they don't mesh with ours. Your people here wouldn't let us do that even if we wanted to. They know the score – the politicians in Washington don't. OK?'

Malloy smiled. 'Sounds like home.'

Wallace shrugged. 'You'll be going to a place in Hampshire called Beaulieu. A large estate with a mansion. That's where SOE people are trained. You'll be trained on how to use a radio, how to encode and decode, how to carry out surveillance, how to drop a tail, map reading, recognition of German troop insignia and weapons and lastly – how to behave if you're caught by the Germans.'

'Sounds like I'll be busy. How long does it take?'

'You'll be there about six months.' He stood up. 'By the way, there's mail for you at Grosvenor Square. I've arranged for a car to collect you from OSS and take you down to Beaulieu.'

At Beaulieu Malloy was billeted in a house on the big estate that was allocated to house SOE people who were going to operate in France. None of them used their real names. Malloy's field name was to be Maurois with the same first name – Guillaume. He had been shown his documentation but it would not be handed over until he was in transit.

Spending most of his time with people who insisted on speaking only French improved Malloy's French and gave him a more realistic idea of what things would be like when he was in Occupied France. The instruction was intensive and the training hours long. But what he learned by being with French people was almost as valuable. The surrender to the Germans was a bitter memory and the politics of Vichy were constantly debated. He learned too that for most of them the only thing that mattered was not winning the war but the liberation of France. Malloy was uneasy that he would be working so closely with people whose views were so narrow and isolated, but the British he met on the course had objectives more like his own.

The defeat of the Nazis and the liberation of Europe as a whole.

Finally he was fitted out with clothes that had been bought from refugees from France, two American fillings in his teeth were removed and substituted with appropriate fillings by a French dentist. An instructor went carefully over his documents. An identity card, a travel permit, a medical certificate that he suffered from asthma so that he would not be taken to work in Germany.

Back in London two OSS officers had gone over his briefing again and had given him the details of the network he would be attached to. It was a network commanded by a British SOE officer named Parish. The same age as himself. They would provide funds, food and shelter and radio communications with OSS London. They would help him but would not be responsible for his work. They would only intervene if it seemed that something he was intending could affect the security of the network. He would be leaving in three days' time from an airfield in the East Midlands and he was not being dropped but taken by Westland Lysander to a reception group near Chartres. They also went over with him large-scale maps of the area covered by the network. The network leader already knew what Malloy would be there for.

Both Colonel Kelly and Major Wallace had travelled with him in the British Army Humber staff car but the conversation had been desultory and routine as if they were all too embarrassed about what they were doing to mention it aloud. Malloy thought that it must be like this in the mourners' limos following a hearse to a cemetery. For security reasons you were not allowed to say goodbyes at Beaulieu and there had been no sense of occasion in the house in Grosvenor Square. Nobody had even wished him good luck.

The car turned right down a country lane and a mile further on it turned onto a concrete strip and stopped at a red and white pole across the path. A man in RAF uniform came out of a wooden shack, a Sten gun cradled in the crook of his right arm. The driver wound down his window and passed a card to the guard who studied it carefully then opened the rear door and looked at the passengers. Then he walked round to Malloy's door, opened it, looking at the card again before he looked at Malloy. He nodded his head to the driver and pointed towards a red light in the distance.

There was dance music coming from the wooden building where they stopped and the driver led them on foot past other wooden buildings to a brick building where a guard stood with a rifle. Major Wallace led the way, pushing open the door and moving the black-out curtain to one side and Malloy blinked in the sudden light inside the building. An RAF officer came to meet them, hand outstretched. 'You're early, Wallace. Would you all like a meal?'

Wallace looked at Malloy who shook his head and said, 'I'd like a coffee if you've got one.'

Twenty minutes later Malloy was naked in the shower and when he stepped out to dry himself a man in civilian clothes looked him over. Back and front. 'No operation scars, are there?'

'No.'

'Let's see your hands.'

Malloy held out his hands and the man checked them carefully, then said, 'Scrub your nails thoroughly and then get dressed.' He pointed to Malloy's French clothes on a wooden table.

There was a small canvas bag on the table and when he looked inside there was an old-fashioned cut-throat razor, shaving soap and a shaving brush. There was a change of underwear, two pairs of socks, a bottle of vitamin tablets and a multi-bladed penknife. As he closed the bag Major Wallace came in with a leather pouch.

'This is for the network, Bill. Mail and instructions. You only hand them over to Captain Parish himself.' He paused. 'They're ready if you are, old chap.'

'I'm ready. Where's the colonel?'

'Waiting for you at the plane.'

As they walked out into the darkness Malloy's eyes gradually adjusted and he saw that in fact the area was bathed in the light of a full moon. What the RAF men called a 'Bombers' Moon'.

The squat Westland Lysander looked like a giant dragon-fly with its wings, with their strange dihedral, seeming to be hovering as a cloud passed across the face of the moon.

Malloy was introduced to the RAF pilot and Colonel Kelly shook his hand, wished him luck and patted his shoulder. Major Wallace smiled as he shook Malloy's hand. 'Best of British luck, my boy. Take care.'

Then he scrambled up the short metal ladder into the passenger cockpit, the hood coming over and the engine rasping into a deafening crescendo. A slight wiggle from the tail, a short run and they took off into the dark blue sky.

A hundred miles south of the top security airfield at Tempsford the RAF's newest bombers, Lancasters, were taking off to bomb the U-boat yards in Danzig.

13

Andrei Aarons wasn't happy with his new rôle. He was a thinker, an arguer, a persuader – not a spy. But if that was what Moscow needed him to do he would do it to the best of his ability.

He was surprised at the contacts that they had told him about and wondered how long they had been spying for the Soviets. It didn't help that his new bosses had told him that he was to trust none of them. Not only not trust them but to take any opportunity he might have for testing and checking their loyalty.

The first man he had to contact was a man named Scholes. Sol Scholes. He'd been given an address on 27th Street between Eleventh and Twelfth Avenues. They said he'd been an engraver in Petrograd and had fled to America in the early thirties.

The building was an old warehouse that had been roughly converted into cheap, rented units occupied by small engineering companies where two or three artisans turned out small items for major companies. The blanks for safety-razor blades, small pressings, cardboard boxes and ammunition boxes. They were doing well now that America was in the war. Sol Scholes' place was a two-storey building with a sign that said 'Scholes Tailoring'.

When he rang the bell at the outer door a young woman opened it and when he asked for Mr Scholes she pointed to a flight of worn wooden steps leading up to the second floor. There was an old lady sitting on a chair at the top of the stairs and when he asked for Scholes she said nothing but waved briefly to a door on the right. Aarons knocked on the door and then without waiting for an answer he opened it.

There was an elderly man sitting at an oak table. He was looking at something through a magnifying glass on a swivel stand. For a moment he looked up at Aarons and then pointed at a wooden chair by the table. Without looking up he said, 'And what can I do for you, my friend?'

Aarons said quietly, in Russian, 'Arise ye workers from your slumbers.'

The man looked up slowly, 'Who was the Islavins' friend?' he said in Russian.

Aarons smiled. 'Lev Tolstoy.'

The man smiled back. 'It must have been you who worked out the passwords.'

'Why do you say that?'

'Because those idiots in Moscow wouldn't know Tolstoy from Shakespeare.'

Aarons nodded. 'You've got something for me.'

'Yes.' He looked at Aarons. 'You got the cash?'

'What cash?'

'Look, buddy, let's not play games. They told me what you needed. And it's gonna cost you four hundred bucks.'

'You mean you charge them for your help?'

'You bet your ass I do. This is my business. Why d'you think I do this?'

'For the sake of the Party.'

'You must be out of your mind, comrade. I don't give a shit for the Party. Never have and never will. You want those documents you pay for them like anybody else.' He leaned forward, looking at Aarons. 'You sure you're who I think you are?'

'Who do you think I am?'

The old man shook his head. 'No way, my friend. You're shaping up like FBI to me.'

Aarons reached inside his jacket and took out an envelope. Slowly and carefully he counted out four hundred dollars in ten dollar notes. He slid the rest of the bills back in the envelope.

The old man stood up unsteadily, tried a couple of times to slide the money into his trouser pocket and when he failed he pushed it into a drawer in the table. Then he walked over to where a framed photograph of Abraham Lincoln hung on the wall. Carefully, he took it down and put it on the floor. Aarons saw the grey-green door of a small safe with the large dial of a combination lock. The old man stood in front of the safe so that Aarons couldn't watch him twisting and turning the dial. When the safe door swung open the old man reached inside, brought out a package, closed the safe, spun the lock and put back the photograph before he walked back to the table.

He sat down carefully and opened the packet, taking out several items, looking through them one by one before he looked across at Aarons.

'You think four hundred bucks is a lot of money, don't you?'

'It is,' Aarons said rather sharply.

The old man nodded. 'That's what you damn Reds ain't ever worked out. Some poor bastard's got to make a profit before you can hand out the apple-pie to all and sundry. What you lot do is to make sure the fella makes the pie don't get to eat any of it.'

'So why do you come to us for business?'

The old man cackled. 'I don't, comrade, I don't. It's you lot come to me.' He paused, and now his face was serious. 'Let me tell you what I've done for your dollars, my friend.' He picked up one of the papers and waved it at Aarons. 'This is your birth certificate. Genuine – not copied or forged, but the real thing. By the way your new name's Slansky. Igor Slansky. But – do you realise what I had to do to get it? First I had to hunt around the cemeteries to find someone born in the same year as you were and it has to be someone who died soon after birth. That takes time, mister. Then I apply for a duplicate birth certificate in that person's name. With this I got your supporting documents – driver's licence, social security card and so on. I got you a passport. All they want is a birth certificate which I got certified at the Health Department for a couple of bucks. Anywhere else you'd pay five hundred bucks for just a phony passport.' Scholes looked at Aarons, shaking his head as he said, 'You don't give a damn about all this, do you?'

Aarons was silent for a moment and then he said, 'Don't you care about Russia?'

Scholes smiled. 'No. But if you asked me if I care about the Russian people then I'd say yes. I was there, my friend, when it was all happening. We had eight weeks of communism, the dream come true. Then the power-hungry men strangled it and called it Bolshevism. If it suited them they called it Socialism. Anything to keep control. And after that we had the Moscow Mafia. You do as you're told or you go to a labour camp if you're lucky. If not they kill you. Like many others I dreamed dreams . . .' overcome with emotion he had to take a deep breath, '. . . and your friends stamped our dreams into the ground.' He wagged a finger at Aarons. 'You're like a man in a film cartoon who walks off the edge of the cliff and goes on walking on thin air – and then he looks down – and he falls. One day you'll look down, my son. Just a question of time.'

Again Aarons was silent for a few moments and then he said quietly, 'If I need documents for somebody else can you provide them?'

Scholes shrugged. 'I need the relevant details. Date of birth and so on.' He paused and smiled. 'And four hundred dollars.'

Aarons stood up and walked slowly to the door where he turned and said, 'Thank you for your help, comrade.'

In the room in the Flatiron Building Aarons sat at the small desk looking at the documents. He ought to get similar documents for Ivan if he was going to use him full-time but that would create problems when Ivan married his girl. Maybe it would be better to use Anna and get documents for her. There was so much he had to do in the next few weeks. So many people to contact, and then plan how to use them. Maybe Ivan could just go out and find the dead-letter drops and one of the others could do the pick-ups.

His next call was at an address near Madison Square Garden in an alley off 31st Street. It was a narrow-fronted shop with a sign that said, 'Martin Electrics'. The dusty windows showed rows of valves, condensers, knobs and switches that made the place look more like a junk shop than an electrics store. He pushed open the door and a man came out from a back-room wearing a grubby singlet and brown chinos. He was in his forties with a pale face and a pair of wire-frame spectacles pushed up onto his forehead.

'Are you the guy asking on the phone about rectifiers?'

Aarons shook his head and gave him the password. For a moment the man looked as if he didn't recognise the question but Aarons saw the recognition dawning on the man's face and then he gave the response. Then the man held out his hand, 'Cowley. Roger Cowley. You'd better come in the back.'

The room he was taken into was as untidy as the shop-window but on a shelf above the work-bench was a row of measuring meters and a board with screwdrivers, pliers and boxes of screws neatly set out in rows.

Cowley cleared a pile of tattered instruction books from a chair and waved for Aarons to sit down.

'You know anything about radio, friend?'

'No. I had some basic training but it was only on how to use a short-wave receiver.'

'I show you something. Come with me.'

Aarons followed him up a wooden stairway to an upstairs landing where Cowley turned left, unlocked a door and waved Aarons inside. The room was small but unlike the workshop below it was spotlessly clean. There was a long working surface along one wall and an array of radio sets with metal cases. Cowley pointed to one of them. 'That's the one I'll be using for you, mister. The US Navy's top set. A real beauty.' He pointed at various other sets. 'The FBI use that one for communications with Washington. It's not bad. That small one is US Air Force air to ground. The green one is used by special squads of the NYPD for emergencies and that Eddystone set's used by most embassies all over the world.'

'How did you get them?'

Cowley smiled. 'Being in short-wave radio's like being in a club. You can get anything if you'll pay the right price. I do repairs for the Navy and for the local FBI guys. The services have collared all the best radio mechanics. I can do overnight what'd take them a week or ten days.' He pointed up at the ceiling. 'I got four different antennas up on the roof. Gets me anywhere in the world.' He smiled. 'And I don't even have to hide the set I'll be using for you.' He waved his hand at the line of radios. 'Just one among many.'

Aarons took a folded sheet of paper from his inside pocket and handed it to Cowley. 'They said you'd need this.'

Cowley opened the sheet and read it carefully before he looked up at Aarons. 'This is OK. Both those frequencies will work but they'll have to come down a bit in the winter months. But we can talk about that. I'll want you to keep your stuff down to no more than two hundred characters, outside two fifty.' He looked at Aarons. 'You'll have encoded them before you hand them over, yes?'

'Yes. And what you get back will be encoded.'

'And two hundred bucks a month for two timed schedules a week and one emergency any time. That OK?'

'Yes.' Aarons paused. 'These other radios. Do they mean you can listen in to the Navy and the FBI and the others?'

'Sure. So long as it's voice and not coded Morse.'

'Could you do that for me and give me reports? I could pay you extra. An hourly rate perhaps.'

'OK. How about five bucks an hour but I get paid even if there's no traffic. We can do it on a random basis for a month and then if you want to specify the source you can do so.'

Aarons nodded. 'I'll pay you four hundred now on account. When can you start?'

'Any time you want.'

'I'll come back tomorrow with a message to let them know we're available and warn them to start monitoring.'

'OK. Evening if you can.'

In the next ten days Aarons had contacted a diamond merchant on West 47th Street, a Czech photographer, a professor of physics at the University, an official of the longshoremen's union, a woman who lectured on Psychology at Brooklyn College, a waiter at the Waldorf-Astoria and a free-lance journalist who covered defence and the war in Europe.

They seemed a strange group of people that he had inherited from whoever his predecessor had been. And they in turn had their own networks of informants and cut-outs. He had been given no background information on any of them and he had no idea of what their motivation might be.

The only obvious one was the diamond merchant, Moshi Wald, a Jew from Kiev, half-Russian, half-Polish who still had a love for Russia that grew on his homesickness. That and an easy profit from his commission on selling the diamonds that were part of Aarons' funds. And that was his only service to the cause. That and his silence. He asked no questions and gave honest evaluations of the stones, ready to pay cash on presentation even before he had sold them. Aarons brought him the latest Party pamphlets and a few pre-war novels on each visit.

When it came to people like Lev Cohen, Professor

Cohen, the information he passed on was highly valued by Moscow but it had taken Aarons several meetings before he understood why Cohen cooperated. They met usually at an Italian café near Washington Square, usually in the evening after Cohen's day's work was over. It was at one of those meetings that Aarons realised that Cohen was not, despite his information, one of those who wished Moscow well.

He was in his early forties, a dapper man with a Douglas Fairbanks moustache and his black hair creamed back slickly so that it showed the lines of a comb.

'D'you read this material I give you?' Cohen raised his eyebrows quizzically.

'I photograph it.'

'Do you understand it?'

Caution made Aarons avoid answering. Instead he said, 'Why do you ask?'

Cohen smiled, a brief, cold smile. 'I guess that's answer enough. If you understood it you'd realise that the last stuff I gave you was vital material.' He paused. 'Have they commented on it yet?'

'No. But they've received it. I know that.'

'They'll ask you to find out how I've got it.' He paused and sipped his beer as if he needed its support. 'And I won't tell you, my friend. And they'll want more and you can tell them that I'll want real money from now on and proof that they're meeting their obligations at the other end.'

'How do you want them to provide proof?'

'They told you of the deal?'

Aarons hesitated because they had not told him of any deal and then he said, 'You tell me. Let's make sure that there's no misunderstanding.'

'The deal is that Manya is not harassed and is safe. Safe from everything. Not only safe from you people but safe from the Germans.' He leaned forward as he went on. 'Photographs, declarations, letters from her. I tell you now that if anything happens to her then I not only cease

105

to cooperate but I'll go to the FBI and tell them what I've been doing. No matter if I go to jail or anything else.'

'What did you mean when you said, "safe from my people"?'

'Safe from the secret police or the army, whoever you work for.'

'Tell me about Manya.'

'So they didn't tell you?'

'No.'

'At least you're honest, my friend.' He sighed. 'In 1936 I went to Berlin to work in the experimental physics department at the university. Moscow gave me permission to go. In fact they encouraged me. I was thirty then and Manya was nineteen. We wanted to marry but they said we had to wait. In 1939 I was dismissed from my job at the laboratory. They said quite openly that it was because I was a Jew.

'Moscow told me to apply to come here to the USA. Because of my qualifications and expertise there was no problem. I was offered a teaching post at UCLA and a year later the offer came from New York University. The deal with Moscow was that Manya would be allowed to come over in a year. Before the year was up the Germans invaded and that was it. Then I heard that Manya had been arrested and sent to a labour camp. I raised hell about this and after two months I got a message saying it was all a mistake and she was now back in Moscow and safe. Since then all I've had is two letters from her, but they were obviously dictated. Like I said, I don't trust Moscow.'

'Would you trust me to find out what's happening?'

'I don't trust anybody any longer. But I'd like to know what they tell you.'

'I'll see what I can do.'

14

The Lysander flew low across the Channel and came in over the French coast well south of the landing place. Malloy had been shown large-scale maps of the area where they would land. It was to the north-east of Chartres, a small village called Gallardon.

The plane banked, the pilot looking for the markers, but it had taken two sweeps across the fields before they spotted the flares and the pilot turned the plane into the wind and they came over the tree-tops to land in the field. The drill was that the passenger had two minutes only to get out and any waiting passenger had to be aboard in the same time. Malloy slid down the side of the fuselage missing the short ladder and the pilot threw out the two canvas bags. There was no return passenger and the pilot kept the engine running, waving as he set the plane rolling forward over the bumpy tussocks of the field.

For a moment Malloy was alone, watching the Lysander as it lifted up over the woods into the midnight sky. Then a hand was on his shoulder, roughly turning him around and he saw the face of the man whose photographs they had shown him. For a moment he was silent and then he said softly, '*J'ai deux amours*.' The man smiled and said, '*Mon pays et Paris*,' and he said it like Josephine Baker sang it, making two syllables out of '*pays*'.

The man picked up one of the bags and signalled to Malloy to pick up the other bag and follow him. As his eyes adjusted to the moonlight Malloy saw that there were now three men ahead of him, turning from time to time to check that he was still there. At the edge of the woods they stopped and one of them put his finger to his lips and then whispered, 'We stay here tonight because of the curfew. OK?' Malloy nodded and followed the man to a small clearing in the woods. There was brown, dry bracken piled up in heaps and the first man said, 'You'll be comfortable on the *fougère* for tonight.' As Malloy rearranged one of the heaps of bracken the three men came over and the first man held out his hand. 'Boudin. Welcome.' He turned to the next man. 'Just Jean-Paul, yes?' The man held out his hand and nodded without speaking and then the third man said, 'Theo, welcome. We got coffee for us and bread and cheese.' He pointed to an open hamper and Malloy walked over with the others. He was careful to eat very little and to take only a few sips of the bitter coffee. Then Boudin said, 'You sleep now for tomorrow. We shall keep watch.'

Malloy slept only fitfully. He was a city boy and the rustling of birds and small animals in the woods kept him awake, It was already light when Boudin shook him awake with a cup of coffee. 'We'll be moving on in ten minutes. We'll be travelling on a farm vehicle.' He paused. 'Are you a Catholic?'

'Yes. Not a very good one but . . .'

'That's no problem but you'll be staying with the priest. He's got a converted village hall next to the church where he looks after old people. You'll be with them, as his assistant.'

'When can I meet the railway people?'

'You'll have to wait until we contact Parish to confirm that you've arrived.'

'How long will that take?'

'About a week. Maybe a bit more. Just have to see how it goes.'

Ten minutes later Boudin led Malloy down a narrow track in the woods to where an ancient truck was parked in a narrow lane, its engine running. Boudin pointed to a space between the bales of straw and Malloy climbed aboard. Boudin sat in front with the driver.

It took nearly an hour to get to the church on the outskirts of the village. The priest was waiting for them and after a few words with Boudin the priest took Malloy into the church, walking up the aisle and then over to an open door to a corridor which led to the priest's quarters.

The priest was a small man with a round smooth face, red cheeks and bald at the front. He wore a pair of granny glasses with thick lenses. He pointed to an armchair. 'Do sit down, my boy.'

When Malloy was sitting the priest said, 'My name's Père Levêque. Henri Levêque. You are welcome to stay here but I want to warn you to be very discreet – very careful. All we Frenchmen want the Germans to go but not all Frenchmen feel that the Resistance is helpful. They think that perhaps it brings trouble for innocent people and gives the Germans an excuse for revenge and brutality.'

Maybe it was tiredness or tension that made Malloy say waspishly, 'And how do those Frenchmen think the Germans will go without the Resistance?'

The priest smiled. 'My friend, I don't defend them. I am just warning you for your own sake.' He paused. 'And for the sake of those who are helping you.'

Malloy smiled and shrugged. 'I apologise, Father. It was a foolish comment.'

'I think the British captain will be coming to meet you in the next few days. Have you met him already?'

'No. What's he like?'

'About the same age as you. Quiet but very tough. The French respect him and his network is very successful. They don't cause trouble except for a good reason.'

'Tell me about the people in the place where I'll be staying.'

'It's just next door. Used to be the village hall but we've turned it into a refuge for old people who have no relations to care for them.' He smiled. 'Some of them are rather disturbed. Mentally disturbed. Some of them are just senile and some are just old and lonely. We shall say that you are the janitor, the caretaker. There are two rooms put aside for you.'

'Thank you for your help. I hope I can help you in some way.'

'Maybe. Maybe. Just send the Germans back to Germany and that will be more than enough.'

Malloy had not been allowed to bring maps with him but there were pre-war maps in the priest's small library and Malloy studied them again, refreshing his memory of the main lines of the French railway system, SNCF. He had been given a Walther PPK pistol and fifty rounds and he cleaned and oiled it thoroughly, wrapped it in an oily rag and buried it in the garden the first night at the church.

He was reading a week-old newspaper when the man walked into his room on the fourth night. There was no need for passwords, they had both seen photographs of each other.

The man smiled and held out his hand. 'Glad to see you.' He glanced around the room. 'You seem to have settled in OK. Was it a good flight?'

Malloy smiled. 'Yes. But it seems a long time ago. I can barely remember it.'

'You want to talk about your mission?'

'Sure. I'll talk all night if you will.'

'London didn't tell me much for security reasons, but I understand your main concern is the railways.'

'That's correct.'

'Tell me a bit more so that I can put you in touch with the right people.'

'Right. My orders are to build up a network that can provide us with the fullest possible picture of what's moving on the rail system so far as the Germans are concerned. Troop movements, movements of strategic equipment and materials. Repair facilities, use of rail in communications with Italy, Germany and Switzerland.

Some interest in traffic to and from Spain. Then a sabotage and target map. Bridges, marshalling yards, strategic switching points, telegraph system, repair shops, locomotive sheds, fuel stores – anything that could hinder German troop movements.'

'My God, that's some task. What kind of people are you looking to recruit?'

'Just people who work on the railways. We need specialists in control and admin, people who can give us overall inside information. But most of what we need can come from low-grade employees – secretaries, typists, signalmen, drivers, station staff and clerks. They don't need to do anything. Just keep me informed.'

'I'm afraid what I'd planned to support you just won't work. I imagined that most of the time you'd be based here or at least in the area covered by my network. But you're going to be all over the place. You're going to need your own radio operator to travel around with you. That's going to be a problem. From what London told me it seemed that my radio chap here would be enough. But I need him here. I really need two radio operators even now.' He smiled. 'By the way, I don't know if they told you but my name's Parish. I'm a Scot, and from your name I reckon you must be American-Irish.' He smiled. 'Or is it Irish-American?'

Malloy smiled. 'My old man explodes when people call him that.' Malloy shrugged. 'We're just Americans.'

'Sorry. But tell me about your lot – or whatever they call themselves – what are they – some kind of private army?'

'No way. Our remit is much the same as SOE's. But we cover intelligence gathering – not just sabotage.'

Parish smiled and said nothing.

'Does any other network have a radio operator to spare?'

'If they have they won't let on. Radio operators are like gold-dust.'

'Shall I contact London and see if they've got anyone?'

'Waste of time, pal. If they'd had one they'd have sent him with you. They know the problems.'

'And I'm OSS not SOE.'

'Makes no difference. I think you're being over-suspicious. Let me think about it overnight. We'll talk again tomorrow.' He smiled. 'How do you get on with the reverend?'

'He's fine. No problems there.'

Parish stood up. 'I've got to see some of my people. I'll be back tomorrow. Don't worry. We'll solve it some way.'

It was mid-afternoon when Parish came back but he wasted no time.

'I've been on to London. They haven't got an operator to spare. Neither have your people. But what I have squeezed out of them is a radio.' He grinned. 'I think I made them feel guilty, they're giving us a Mark III suitcase transceiver. Dropping it next full moon in five days' time. Including spares and operating instructions.' He smiled. 'They show you how to use one?'

'No. I wasn't allowed to go to Thame. Just Beaulieu, and a brief look at all the SOE sets.'

'This one's the best so far. Weighs less than fifteen pounds. And Yank 'lock-in' valves.' He laughed as he saw the disappointment on Malloy's face. 'And I think I've got you a man who can operate the radio for you.'

'Tell me about him.'

'He's French, but speaks enough English to get by. He has contacts all over France. Excellent Resistance history. Right in it from the start of the Occupation. Very clued-up chap. Name's Pascal, everybody calls him Jo-jo, God knows why. Good Morse, good technical knowledge of radios but hasn't worked on an SOE network. I'm not sure but I think he's probably a Commie. A lot of them are.'

'You mean you allow communists to join the Resistance?'

112

Parish laughed. 'It's their Resistance, not ours. And it's their country. We're only here to help.'

'Do OSS know that we're using Commies?'

'I've no idea. Who cares anyway?'

'When can I talk to him?'

'Tomorrow. But remember – we don't talk politics with anybody. It's not our business. Talk politics and you'll be in dead trouble – so will I.'

Parish brought the man to Malloy the next morning, introducing them briefly and then leaving them.

Malloy said, 'Do sit down. Would you like some coffee?'

Pascal smiled and nodded. 'He told you already my English is not good.'

Malloy smiled back, 'We can speak both languages and get by. I'll be back in a moment.'

In the small kitchen as he waited for the water to boil he thought of the man in the other room. He wasn't at all Malloy's idea of a communist and Malloy realised that he had no real idea of what he expected a communist to look like. He was slim and fair-haired and he smiled easily and spoke quite softly. A bit older than he'd expected but he looked fit and wiry enough.

As he put the coffee cups on the table he said, 'Did they tell you what I'm here to do?'

'Just an outline. Checking on how the *boche* use the railway and getting together a network of informants. You've got a radio coming and you don't know how to work it, yes?'

'Yes. Can you work it?'

'If it's got instructions I can work any radio.'

'And you can read and send Morse?'

'Yes.'

'Where did you learn to do that?'

'That's my business, comrade.'

'I'm sorry.' He paused. 'Is it OK to leave what you've been doing?'

113

'Yes. What you are doing is more important.'

'Why do you say that?'

'It will take more than the Resistance to beat the Fascists. It will need an invasion. You only need the kind of information that you want if you're going to invade. Others can do what I was doing.'

'And you don't mind working with an American instead of an Englishman?'

'The captain wouldn't like that. He's very proud of being a Scot.' He shrugged. 'Doesn't matter to me who you are if you're working against the Fascists.'

Malloy went with Parish and four of his men to the dropping zone on the edge of the woods at Epernon. The flares had been placed but not lit and they sat in silence looking up at the clear sky, straining their ears for the drone of the Hudson aircraft. Malloy had turned to look quickly at Parish when he heard a bark in the woods behind them. But Parish smiled and said softly, 'It's only a fox.'

It was one of the Frenchmen who first heard the plane, pointing up at the sky, his arm slowly following the sound of the distant plane. Three men scrambled forward and lit the flares. It was five minutes before the plane came in over the woods. It made a second circuit and then Malloy saw the parachutes drifting down silently as the plane headed back to base. There were three parachutes for Parish's network and one with Malloy's radio in its two special airtight containers.

As usual the parachutes had been buried in the woods for recovering later and their loads concealed under leafy branches piled on top of them. They waited until first-light when everything was loaded into an ancient baker's delivery van.

Three days later Pascal was satisfied. If Malloy wanted to try to contact London he was ready to try. It was two hours before the next scheduled contact and Malloy worked out a short coded message with a request for a confirmation that it had been received.

Pascal had rigged up a simple wire antenna that went up to the attic and he sat looking at the set. He turned to Malloy.

'It's a beautiful set. Super-het, two wave bands. Better than Parish's radio. Much, much lighter. And a nice, easy Morse key.'

Malloy smiled at the enthusiasm and gave Pascal the paper with the five-letter groups of his coded message.

An hour later Pascal was frowning with concentration as he tapped out the message, then turned the switch to reception and adjusted the headphones as he waited. Fifteen minutes later Pascal was writing out the groups of letters on a sheet of paper.

Malloy decoded the message. It merely acknowledged reception and gave a frequency for emergency use that was monitoring all Resistance frequencies round-the-clock.

They were looking at a map of France and planning where to go when Pascal said, 'Can I have a look at your papers?'

'Why?'

'I want to know if we'll have any problems.'

Malloy walked over to his bed, lifted the mattress and took out a bundle of papers held together by a rubber band. He handed them to Pascal who looked through them carefully, one by one. When he'd finished he looked at Malloy.

'They're very good. How did they get the medical certificate?'

'I've no idea.'

Pascal smiled. 'They're better than mine. Why did you choose that cover name?'

'I didn't choose it. I think it was used because it suited the documentation. Why did you ask?'

Pascal smiled. 'I had a girl-friend before the war in Paris – her name was Maurois. A nice name.'

'When can we start?'

'I want to make a deal with you first.'

'What kind of deal?'

'We'll be going to a lot of cities and towns. I've got places in most of them that are safe. And people I know. I think I know my way around this country better than you do. Can I decide where we stay and that sort of thing?'

'I don't see why not.'

'What about money? We'll need plenty of money.'

'That's OK. I've got access to money.'

'Let's plan the visits tonight for the next two weeks and start off tomorrow morning. We can take the bus to Chartres and go straight to Paris.' He paused. 'Have you had your papers checked at all since you've been here?'

'No. I've not been out.'

'Let me go over it with you so you're not scared and you know how to behave.'

'Good idea.'

Two hours later he was glad to have Pascal with him. He knew all the questions that the police or the Germans would ask him. And the answers he should give.

They were checked by the police at Chartres Station and by a Gestapo officer when they got off the train in Paris and a second German as they left the station. They had separated and the German had gone over his papers slowly and carefully.

'Name?'

'Maurois. Guillaume.'

'Where are you going?'

'I'll be here in Paris for two or three days.'

'What are you doing in Paris for three days?'

'To buy books.'

'What kind of books?'

'Law books. I'm interested in being a lawyer.'

The German seemed in no hurry to let him go. He looked at the papers again but then finally handed them back, nodded and moved away towards the ticket office.

Pascal was waiting for him outside the station as Malloy

took a deep breath before putting the papers back in his jacket pocket.

'What happened?' Pascal asked, and he listened as Malloy told him. Pascal shook his head. 'You got to stand up to the bastards. You were too polite and that makes them think you're scared, so they want to find out why.' He shrugged. 'You'll learn. We've got to walk for about fifteen minutes.' He laughed. 'We'll be bedding down over a butcher's slaughter house. My friend here will have found a few people to talk to you about SNCF.'

By the end of the week Malloy was pleased with what had been done. He had four vital contacts. The secretary of the scheduling director at the Gare du Nord, who had handed him copies of the German controller's instructions to all senior railway officials. Plus a policy document outlining the priorities to be given to the movement of German freight and personnel. A signalman who operated the signals network for all main lines out of two Paris stations. A station clerk who could supply daily reports on the movement of food transporters. And finally a retired SNCF senior official who had been brought back by the Germans to act as adviser to the German High Command in Paris on the use of the national rail resources in both Occupied and Unoccupied France. He would also be able to supply permits for travel in restricted areas. He had given Malloy copies of the schedules for rail traffic servicing the German U-boat bases on the Biscay coast. Pascal obviously knew his way about Paris and Malloy realised that it would have taken him months to establish even one of the contacts he'd made. Malloy was impatient to get back to the village and suddenly Gallardon seemed like home.

Back at the village Malloy spent two days listing the contacts he had made giving them just code names. Then he made two long lists. One a list of the documents and information he had obtained, and the second a list of the

117

kind of information that he could obtain from these sources. It took him another two days to encode his reports and then Pascal broke them down into four transmission schedules. Finally he asked for a Lysander flight to pick up the documents.

His report was acknowledged without comment and on the following transmission he was told to refer to Parish regarding the Lysander flight.

Parish told him that there was no Lysander flight planned but after contacting London Parish had been given details of a Lysander flight to another network and offered to send one of his own men on the cross-country journey. Malloy gladly accepted.

15

As Cohen stirred his coffee he said, 'And still no news of Manya, but they still take it for granted that I'll cooperate.'

'There is a war on, Professor. I've raised the matter twice.'

'Say I tell you that I've got some important news but I don't pass it on until I get a response from them about Manya?'

Aarons shook his head slowly. 'I wouldn't pass on a threat, Lev. It would make things worse.'

'How?'

'They wouldn't trust you after that.'

Cohen smiled, coldly, 'They don't trust me anyway. They don't trust anybody. Not you, not even themselves.'

'What's the news?'

'The Americans are up to something.'

'Like what?'

'I don't know. But something's going on. Two physicists and a mathematician have been spirited away in the last ten days. They just went overnight. Nobody will say where they've gone but one of them sent a post-card to his girl-friend who's a lab assistant in my department. The post-mark was Santa Fe in New Mexico. And he gave no address where she could contact him. She asked the faculty head where he was and he'd said he couldn't tell her for security reasons. He implied that all three of them had gone to the same place.'

'What do you think they're doing?'

'One of them had worked for Fermi in Washington in 1939, and both of them had been working on experiments on the products arising from bombarding barium with neutrons. And the mathematician had been working on the theory of chain reaction in certain rare metals.'

'I don't understand.'

Cohen smiled. 'Your people in Moscow will understand all right.'

'They instructed me to pay you a thousand dollars.'

Aarons saw the anger in Cohen's eyes as he said, 'I don't need their money. All I care about is the girl.'

'I'll keep trying, Lev.'

Cohen shook his head. 'Why did I ever trust them? I must have been mad.'

'Calm down, Lev. I'll do my best. I promise you. But like I just said there *is* a war on. Even if they say yes there's the problem of getting her here. I can't think how we could do it, can you?'

'If they'd kept their promise she'd have been here before the war started.'

'I'll meet you here Saturday, same time.' Aarons stood up. 'Don't leave with me, hang on for ten minutes or so.'

Aarons spent the night encoding the basic details of the document photographs that Cohen had given him and then had posted the film to the address in Toronto for sending to Moscow by diplomatic bag. He also recommended that some positive gesture was made regarding the girl.

Cowley transmitted Aarons' coded messages on the 4 a.m. schedule and then Aarons went home.

At 11 a.m. there was a telephone call from Cowley, carefully worded, telling him that he should pick up the electric iron as soon as possible.

In his office at the Flatiron Building he decoded the message from Moscow. He was to ask Cohen if he knew about something to do with 'the poplars'. If Cohen cooperated maybe something could be done about the girl.

Aarons had no means of contacting Cohen without going through the procedure. The chalked cross on the door of the derelict building near the Brooklyn library. He had Cohen's home phone number but it was never to be used. But it was an emergency and a Sunday and Cohen would probably be at home. He'd have to take the risk.

Cohen himself answered the phone and Aarons just said that he wanted to talk about Manya. He didn't give his name but arranged a meeting in an hour's time.

Cohen was waiting for him outside the coffee shop where they usually met and Aarons suggested that they went to a local bar for a drink.

They sat at a table at the back of the bar and when the waiter had brought their beers Aarons said, 'I've got a question to ask you. I don't know what it means. But they indicate that if you can assist them they will do something positive about Manya.'

'What's the question?'

'Like I said, it makes no sense to me so I'll ask it exactly as I received it.'

'Was it in English or Russian?'

'Russian, I've translated it into English myself. Word for word.'

'OK. Go ahead.'

Aarons spoke slowly, in almost a whisper. 'Do you know about the poplars and can you give them a useful contact?'

Cohen frowned. 'I don't get it. It's just . . .' he shrugged, '. . . it's just meaningless. What poplars? What contact?'

'Think hard, Lev. They obviously think you'll understand.'

'I don't, my friend. I really don't.' He looked at Aarons, 'Have you got any idea what they mean?'

'It must be to do with your work, Lev. There's nothing else.'

121

'What have they been most interested in out of what I've told you? What have they followed up?'

Aarons thought for a moment, his eyes closed, then shrugged as he looked at Cohen. 'Two things I guess. The thing you photographed – a paper on something like – calculations on slow neutrons by a guy at Colombia University.'

'And the other thing?'

'You told me about some physicists who'd kind of disappeared but one sent a card to his girl-friend post-marked somewhere in New Mexico.'

'It was Santa Fe.'

'Does any of that help?'

'I can guess what they're after but this stuff about the poplars doesn't make any sense. You're sure it was the poplars?'

'Quite sure.'

Cohen leaned back in his chair looking at the ceiling, 'The poplars – the poplars.' He shook his head. 'I wouldn't know a poplar if I saw one.'

'Maybe we're taking it too literally. Maybe it's some sort of code.'

'What's "poplar" in Russian?'

'*Topolb.*'

'Could almost be an anagram.' He shook his head. 'Beats me. I don't get it.'

'This project these physicists are working on, does it have a code-name?'

'Yeah but it's nothing to do with poplars or any other tree.'

'Is it top secret?'

'Yeah. If the military found out about the card to that girl they'd have them both in St Quentin.'

'Is it that important?'

'It could be. Nobody outside the project knows. They probably don't even know inside.'

'You know all these physicists personally?'

122

'Sure. There's others I know too from other universities.'

'It's obviously one of these people they want to have as a contact.'

'So why don't we ignore the poplars bit and I'll give you a possible contact.'

Aarons shook his head. 'No. That thing about the poplars is some kind of bench-mark, a clue of some kind. Or maybe a test of what you know.'

'They know what I know, for Christ's sake. I've already passed the basic material to you.'

'Yes but maybe it's the contact that matters.' He said softly, 'Tell me the name of the set-up.'

Cohen looked at his beer and then at Aarons. 'It's called the Manhattan Project.'

'Any reason why it should be based at Santa Fe?'

'Security I guess. It's surrounded by desert.'

'What's Santa Fe mean in English?'

'Fe means faith so I suppose it's holy faith – something like that.' He looked up quickly at Aarons. 'What's "the poplars" in Spanish?'

'I've no idea.'

'You got anyone who speaks Spanish?'

Aarons smiled. 'The bartender's an Hispanic, I'll ask him.' He stood up, walked over to the bar, paid for the beers and ordered two more. When he'd paid for those he said, 'Do you speak Spanish?'

The man shrugged. 'Of course. Is my language.'

'How do you say "the poplars" in Spanish?'

The man frowned. 'What is poplars? I don't know it.'

'They're trees. Tall trees.'

The man shrugged. 'I ask my daughter maybe she know.'

He wiped a cloth over the counter and went into the office behind the bar. He was gone several minutes and when he came back he said, 'She not know. She look in dictionary. Here she write it out for you.'

On the piece of paper it said – 'Poplars in Spanish is

123

"Los Alamos". Also place in New Mexico near Santa Fe.'

Aarons folded the paper, passed the man a dollar and smiled. 'Thanks for your help, señor.'

The man laughed and stuck the dollar in his shirt pocket. As he sat down at the table Aarons pushed across the paper to Cohen. 'It was both. Checking on what you knew. Did you know that was where it was?'

Cohen nodded. 'It's one of the places I heard mentioned. But I'd no idea where it was. There were several others.'

'Can you help with the contact?'

'Yes. But not until they do something about Manya.'

'Tell me about the contact.'

'He's a scientist. Young. Not an American. I've heard that he's a communist sympathiser. A bit of a loner.'

'Where is he?'

'He's at the site at Los Alamos.'

'What's his name?'

Cohen smiled and shook his head. 'Manya first. Then the name.'

'They're in a hurry, Lev. Why not trust them just this once?'

Cohen laughed softly. 'Not in a million years, my friend.'

'Would you trust me?'

'Oddly enough – I would. But this doesn't lie in your hands. They don't have to do what you ask.' He paused. 'As a matter of interest have you thought of how you'd get her over here?'

Aarons nodded. 'Yes, as a matter of fact I have.'

'Tell me.'

'Plane to Stockholm. Swedish airlines to Toronto and after that there's no problem.'

'How long?'

'Allow two weeks.'

'I mean when does she leave?'

'I'll have to come back to you. If she phoned you from

124

Stockholm that she was OK, would you accept that and give me the contact name?'

Cohen nodded. 'Yeah. I almost believe you mean it.'

'I'll have to phone you at the university or home at short notice. I'll say my name's Hart, OK?'

'Yeah. Any time.'

It had taken longer than Aarons had estimated. It was two weeks before she landed at an air-strip at Malmö. She made the phone-call to Cohen who passed him the envelope as they walked in Bryant Park.

Aarons coded the name and it went to Moscow via a radio in a farmhouse by the lake-side near Kingston, Ontario. It was just the name. Klaus Fuchs.

16

Ivan reached up and slid the bolt across at the top of the door, put the catch on the lock and bent down to push home the bottom bolt. Anna was counting the takings for the day. He turned to watch her. There was no denying that she was very beautiful. Long black hair, big, dark, heavy-lidded eyes and that wide, full mouth that gave a calmness to her face that made her still seem like a young girl. But she was thirty-three years old and she had no life until she had met the man she called Sam. She had met him when he came in for a book on Chopin. That was four years ago and she'd seen him twice a week after that. Sam wanted to marry her and they would have made a good pair. But she wouldn't marry him because of Andrei. Andrei knew nothing about Sam. It never seemed to enter his mind that Anna might want a life apart from the bookshop. Anna said that Andrei needed her and that what Andrei did was more important than anything else. Andrei and Chantal had agreed right from the start not to have children because of Andrei's work. So Anna still went on with her secret love affair. Only he and Anna and Chantal knew about Sam.

They all liked Sam. He was thirty, gentle and easy-going. He played piano in night-clubs and had had offers of good money to go to Chicago and Los Angeles but he loved Anna too much to leave New York.

He saw her close the exercise book where she kept the accounts and look over at him.

'What are you dreaming about, my boy?'

'I was thinking about you and Sam.'

'And what were you thinking?'

'That it was a shame that you two aren't married.'

'Why a shame?'

'Because you're a pair. Nice people. You belong together.'

'You don't have to be married to be together. Being married is just a formality.'

'You love him, don't you?'

'Of course I do.'

'And he loves you. It's crazy. Why don't you let me talk to Andrei about it for you.'

She shook her head. 'He has enough things to occupy his mind. Maybe one day.'

'I can't see what difference it would make to Andrei or his work if you were married.'

For a few moments she stood looking at him without speaking, and then she said softly, 'Have you looked at Andrei recently? He's thirty-five next birthday but he looks like a man of fifty. Think about his life. He loves Chantal but he sees very little of her. The work he does is for a cause. Not for himself. He daren't have a friend. He can't even confide in Chantal for her sake. No hobbies, no holidays, no kids, no time for anything but his task.' She paused. 'We're all he's got, Ivan. And I'm not going to do anything that could disturb him. Never.'

'Does Sam know about what Andrei does?'

'No. Of course not.'

'Are you sure that the cause is worth the sacrifice?'

'Anything I do or don't do is for Andrei – not a cause.'

'Does Sam mind not being married to you?'

'Sam understands.' She smiled. 'That's why I love him.' She paused. 'And how are things with you and Rachel Henschel these days? She's not been here for weeks.'

'Drives me crazy. I waited all that time for her to be of age so we could be married. And now she's old enough – what happens, for God's sake? Says she needs to know more about life before she settles down.'

127

'Better now than after you're married.'

'All it means is she goes around with other guys. And she don't wear my ring any more.'

'And you?'

'What's that mean?'

'I've heard that you've got quite a few pretty girl-friends.'

He smiled and shrugged. 'That's just to make her jealous.'

Anna laughed. 'I'd still put my silver dollar on you being married to Rachel.'

He shook his head slowly, smiling. 'I hope you're right, honey.'

Parish heard the news on the BBC's French Service and he realised at once that it would affect all the networks in France including Malloy's operation.

Malloy was reading a book to a group of five or six of the old men when Parish signalled to him. Malloy read to the end of the chapter and then joined Parish in the corridor that led to his own rooms.

As they walked together Parish said, 'What were you reading to the old boys?'

Malloy held up the book. It was Alphonse Daudet's *Lettres de mon moulin*. He smiled. 'I've read it to them three or four times but they never seem to get tired of it. It's gentle and about the countryside. I think it reminds them of when they were young.'

By then they were in Malloy's place.

'I just heard the news on the BBC's French Service. It's going to make problems. Or it could do. I thought I'd better warn you.'

'What is it?'

'The Americans landed over a hundred thousand troops in North Africa yesterday.'

'Where?'

'In Morocco and Algeria, that means they were probably fighting some of the Vichy French. Seems like two French ships were sunk in the harbour at Oran. I guess they must have resisted. When the French scuttled their navy ships at Toulon last month when the Germans tried to take over the fleet, that was OK. They accepted that.

But they won't like this. Eisenhower apparently did a broadcast saying that the French were not the enemy but a lot of Frenchmen are not going to see it that way.'

'Why have they landed there? I thought the Brits were about to run Rommel out of North Africa.'

'Politics I guess.'

'I don't get it.'

'Your people are spending millions of dollars a day on the war, the White House probably thought it might be a good idea to show the voters that they were getting something for their money.'

Malloy looked at Parish for several long moments and then said, 'We're on the same side, Parish. Fighting the same war.'

'But we've been fighting it longer. And we didn't wait until we were attacked.'

Malloy stood up. 'You didn't exactly rush to help the Austrians or the Czechs when Hitler marched in, did you?'

Parish laughed. '*Touché*. I guess cowardice and diplomacy are the same thing under different names.'

Malloy looked at Pascal as he sat shivering in the barn.

'D'you realise what it is next Friday?'

Pascal shook his head. 'What is it, some crazy Yank holiday?'

'It's Christmas Day, my friend. We'll take a few days off.'

Pascal looked unimpressed. 'Better we spend our time planning. You said you'd got an idea you wanted to talk about.'

Malloy smiled. 'OK. We'd better get on our way.'

They had spent four days on the farm just outside Brest in a vain attempt to get into the town but Brest was a German Navy base and had been made a Defence Zone with security that was too risky to try to penetrate. Even skilled workers with all the correct documentation had to pass through a maze of check-points and random searches. But they had talked with one of Pascal's communist contacts who had arranged for them to meet a signalman who was working for the Germans handling the traffic of all German troop trains.

It took them three days to get back to the village and there had been a drop while they were away and a bundle of mail for Malloy. It was only the second lot of mail that he had received in five months.

There were seven letters from Kathy and he sorted them into date order before he read them. They were full of chat about the apartment and their friends, and anecdotes about several visits to his father. She'd seen a film that she was sure he would like called *Casablanca*. There was a song in it called 'As Time Goes By' that was very 'them'. She had decided to have a flat-mate, a girl named Milly who worked in the same office as she did. Milly's husband was Navy and 'somewhere in the Pacific'. Malloy's father had taken a part-time job at a local plant making domestic radio sets.

Despite the newsiness of the letters it all seemed a long way away. Part of another world. A world he didn't belong to any more. A world he faintly resented. It was crazy to resent the fact that people still went to the cinema back there and that so few seemed to be in the services. She had mentioned one of his schoolfriends she had met when visiting his father. The schoolfriend now had a Pontiac, an apartment in Manhattan and two restaurants. Malloy was no gourmet and on the whole was not all that interested in food but he resented the fact that there was no rationing back home. He had a vague feeling that for a lot of people the war was the best thing that had ever happened.

He read all the letters three times and then burnt them. She had written out the words of a song they both liked.

I'll walk alone because to tell you the truth, I'll be lonely
I don't mind being lonely when my heart tells me you
Are lonely too.

He felt guilty as he read the words. There was no doubt that he missed Kathy but she was no longer part of his life. Even America was no longer part of his life. He lived under the laws of an occupying power in a country that was not his. For the first few weeks it had seemed a strange, disjointed existence. Almost no more than an extension of his life under training at Beaulieu. But now, months later, the two rooms in the building next to the church were home. His relationship with Pascal and Parish were what mattered. Even the war itself was strangely remote. The war was in Russia and the Far East, not in Europe. His life was with people who merely hoped that things would change. Only a handful were ready to take action and risks to make those changes happen. The Resistance was looked on by many French people as no more than a provocation to the Germans that could cost innocent lives and even more draconian regulations.

Bill Malloy was still very uneasy about the fact that so many of the people who offered their services and who gave shelter and advice to him and Pascal were quite openly communists. But despite his unease he had a sneaking admiration for these men and their courage, and what he found even more surprising was that when they talked politics they sounded remarkably like his father.

18

Two days after the Christmas holidays Aarons had taken his wife on a sight-seeing trip to Manhattan. They did the usual visitor's things. Up to the top of the Empire State Building, Central Park, the concourse at Grand Central Station, the Chrysler Building and the Rockefeller Center. He had taken her for lunch at Stouffers and to several of the big stores in the afternoon, then to the movies to see *For Whom the Bell Tolls*. They had a steak dinner at Joe Madden's on West 56th and then to Times Square to see the lights until the Motogram spelt out its nightly message – '*The New York Times wishes you good night*'.

After Prospect Park they were the only passengers in their carriage on the subway back to Brighton Beach. He sat with his arm around her, her head on his shoulder, each thinking their own thoughts. Andrei aware that the time he spent with Chantal was far too little because of his work and Chantal was surprised that her husband knew New York so well. As they walked from Brighton Beach station back to the shop she said, 'Do you like America, Andrei?'

'Why do you ask?'

'You seem so at home in New York. You know where everything is. You seem to belong there, not down here.'

'That's because I spend so much time there. It doesn't necessarily mean that I like it.'

'Do you?'

For a few moments he was silent, then he said, 'I've grown to admire the people. They're optimists. Full of enthusiasm, like children. But it's a cruel system for the losers. It abuses people. Their philosophy is that you can have anything you want. Money, power – anything. So long as you're ready to pay for it. They've made money into a god. I find them just a little bit frightening.'

She laughed. 'They didn't look very frightening today. Not to me anyway. They seemed quite jolly.'

'You make my point. They were jolly. They were enjoying themselves. But there is a war on, and they're making money out of the war, the ones who don't have to go. And in Russia this very day I suppose ten thousand people were killed. Those people in New York didn't care. They didn't even think about them.'

She laughed as she tucked her arm in his as they crossed the Avenue. 'You're just a typical tragic Russian, always dwelling on the cruel fates and making them worse. I'd better take you down Coney tomorrow to the fair.'

'It'll be closed for winter.'

She laughed aloud. 'There's my boy. Always looking on the bright side.'

As 1943 moved on there was good news for Aarons. Von Paulus had surrendered his army south-west of Stalingrad and Winston Churchill had presented the Sword of Stalingrad to Stalin at the Allies' conference in Teheran. And as if to match all this his network was providing a wide variety of information useful to Moscow.

The gossip of generals and admirals at the Waldorf came within hours from his waiter and visiting politicians were equally indiscreet. Almost daily details of shipments of war supplies and men heading for Africa and Britain came in from his faithful longshoreman.

But oddly enough it was Myron Harper, his journalist contact, who provided most of his hard facts about the military.

Aarons had first met Harper in Los Angeles. Already writing political and military pieces for several newspapers. Already a card-carrying member of the Party and a committed supporter. But Aarons had told him to resign his membership, using the Nazi–Stalin pact as his reason. He had never flaunted or even admitted his communist leaning and he was far too useful to Aarons to risk him being labelled as a 'Red'. In 1939 Harper had moved to New York, writing mainly about the war in Europe and European politics. Aarons had fed him information from Moscow that made his forecasts of events in Europe prescient enough to be studied by influential people in both the military and the White House. Much of what he passed on to Aarons was gossip, but it was the gossip of the military top brass, the Senate and Congress. Part of his success was due to the fact that he had refused several offers from Washington papers. That made him a safer confidant than a local newsman could ever be. He was not involved in sharpening other people's axes and neither sympathetic nor adversarial about either of the two political parties. Although his information came from gossip his writing was about events and trends.

Myron Harper had rooms at the Plaza and that was where they generally met. He was a fan of Scott Fitzgerald and he claimed that some characters in *The Great Gatsby* had used the Plaza. Myron Harper was the only one of Aarons' contacts with whom he felt able to be almost entirely frank.

As they settled down in Harper's living room the writer said, 'The word is that the Red Army took half a million prisoners outside Stalingrad. Is that what you heard?'

'Just over three hundred thousand.' He smiled and shrugged. 'Nobody's going to argue if you call it half a million.'

'Have you had any news about North Africa?'

Aarons shook his head. 'It's not an area that interests me. Maybe others cover it.'

'Well maybe you should give it some attention. Or Moscow should. There's a lot going on there at the moment.'

'Tell me.'

'Eisenhower has taken Patton away from his field

command and I understand he's now responsible for planning the invasion of Sicily. They would only be interested in Sicily to use it as a spring-board for the invasion of Italy. You've got a lot of Party members in Italy. Moscow should warn them so that they can have a plan of how to take control as the Americans and the British push out the Germans.'

'I'll pass it on.'

'You'd better start thinking too about what happens here in America when it's all over.'

'Why?'

'There are going to be a lot of problems. When the relief and the euphoria are over the servicemen are going to see that everyone here has been making a pile of dollars while they've been slogging it out in Europe or the Far East.'

'That's not going to be the main problem.'

'Oh? What is?'

'We, the Soviet Union – will have beaten the Germans on our own. There'll be a new power structure after the war. And Russia will be a major power. The Americans won't like that. The Red Army are heroes now but that'll change overnight. We'll be the enemy then.'

Harper smiled. 'You're such a goddam Russian, Andrei. You always see dark clouds ahead. The Red Army's kicking the shit out of the Wehrmacht in Russia. The Americans and the British are doing the same in North Africa. Italy's about to be invaded. But for my friend Andrei it's all a waste of time. What makes you such a pessimist?'

'It's just that somebody has to look ahead and try to imagine what's going to happen and how to deal with it.'

'And you're that someone?'

'Yes.'

'Will you go back to Moscow when the war's over?'

'I shall do whatever I'm required to do.'

'And your family? Do they have no choice in this?'

'We'll see when the time comes.' He turned to look at

Harper. 'And you? What will you do when it's all over?'

Harper laughed. 'I'll go to Moscow and see what they're up to. I'll expect you to tell them to give me the red carpet treatment. An interview with Uncle Joe. A guided tour round the Kremlin and a beautiful Intourist girl to keep me company. Or maybe one of those young lovelies from the Bolshoi.'

Aarons smiled. 'I'll make sure you get everything you want, my friend.'

'Tell me. Does it seem odd to you to be spying for them when you know so little about them?'

'What I do I do for the Party not individuals. And I'm not a spy.'

'What are you then?'

'I'm a bookseller and a citizen.' He smiled. 'And sometimes like you I talk to people.'

'How about a game of chess?'

A young boy delivered the note to Aarons. It was from Dr Zetkin. Klara Zetkin. She sometimes bought second-hand books from the shop. She was half-German and half-Russian and her surgery was in a small house in one of the side roads near the bus-stop.

He had to wait about half an hour before it was his turn. She was a handsome woman in her early forties and had lived in America for at least twenty years.

'I wanted to talk to you, Mr Aarons, about your wife, Chantal.'

She saw the alarm on his face and she went on. 'She's not well. Not well at all. I thought that I should talk to you first before I talk to her.' She folded her arms and leaned on her small desk. 'I'm afraid that I think she has an infectious disease called tuberculosis. She's going to need a lot of care.'

'How did she get it?' Aarons said quietly.

'At the moment I don't know. It's an infection but it can come from eating or drinking infected food. I'll have to check the rest of the family, you included. Just to make sure that it's an isolated case.'

'What is the treatment for this?'

'I've got to have some X-rays done to locate the actual infection area but I'm almost sure that the trouble is in one of her lungs.' She looked at him. 'Forgive me for asking, Mr Aarons, but do you have money? I'm talking about several thousand dollars.'

'I could try and borrow it. What is it for?'

'For two things. She will need to be in a sanatorium for quite a long time. Could be three months, even longer. That is quite expensive but there is a drug. A new drug, not yet on the market and all the indications are that it is very effective. It's called streptomycin. I should like your wife to be treated with that drug. As soon as I have located the zone of infection. That too would be very expensive.'

'I'll find whatever money is needed.'

'We could be talking of as much as ten thousand dollars because of the long time of rest in the isolation hospital. There's a hospital in Manhattan that has considerable experience of handling and treating tuberculosis but that would be even more expensive.'

'Could I pay by the week?'

'The drug would have to be paid in a lump sum but I could try and negotiate a weekly payment for the sanatorium.' She stood up. 'Leave it to me to sort out the best thing to do.'

Aarons stood up unsteadily. 'How bad is she?'

She knew when she had to lie or half-lie and she said, 'I'm optimistic let us say. We've caught it early.'

'How did you find out about this?'

'She was feeling very tired. She came to me for a tonic. I decided to check her over.' She walked him to the door. 'If you care to wait until my surgery is finished I could perhaps let you know a little more.'

'I need to make some phone calls. I'll come back in half an hour.'

*   *   *

Aarons sat in the coffee shop and coded the message to Moscow asking if he could use money from the funds. Ignoring his usual careful security he phoned it through to Cowley and told him to use the emergency schedule, and repeat it on the afternoon schedule.

There were dollars enough in his KGB fund and he was sure that when they knew about Chantal's illness they would agree. He would only be borrowing the money. He had made that clear.

Aarons phoned Cowley twice in the next hour. The message had been transmitted and acknowledged but there had been no reply.

He walked back to Dr Zetkin's surgery. The surgery was closed and he rang the bell and waited in the street. After waiting for ten minutes he walked back to the book-shop. The doctor was there, supervising two ambulance men who were loading a stretcher into the vehicle. As he hurried forward the doctor stopped him.

'I'm afraid you'll have to keep away, Mr Aarons. It's highly infectious. I'm having her taken to our local hospital, they have an isolation ward.'

'But I haven't even spoken to her about all this.'

'I'm afraid she's in no state to talk. She's got a high temperature from the fever. She'll be in good hands.'

'What about the hospital in Manhattan?'

'Right now she needs urgent medical care. It's a critical period. You can let me know about the hospital and the drug in the next few days. You'd need to allow about two thousand dollars for the drug.'

'I'll bring you half tonight. Is that all right?'

'Yes. Of course.' She saw the tears in his eyes and put her hand on his arm. 'There is a fund which the City of New York set up to help immigrants with health problems. I've spoken to their president, a friend of mine. If your wife stays in the local hospital they will pay all the nursing and accommodation fees. Don't worry, we shall do our best.'

*　　*　　*

It was three weeks before Andrei was allowed to see his wife through the observation windows at the hospital. She was asleep and she looked thin and pale. But she always had a pale complexion. When his visit time was up a nurse took him to see Dr Zetkin in the waiting room.

'She's making reasonable progress, Mr Aarons. I'm very hopeful. It takes time to assess the drug dosage but we seem to have it right. There's no spread of the infection to other parts of the body and that's a good sign.'

'I'm very grateful, doctor. How long will it take?'

'If things go on I guess it would be another two months and then at least a month's convalescence.' She paused and looked at him. 'I think you'll have to accept that it will take a long time before she's properly fit again.'

He handed her an envelope. 'That's the rest of the money for the drugs. Can you tell me what I shall owe for the hospital treatment?'

'The fund I told you about are paying all the hospital charges and that will continue until your wife is discharged.'

'Could you tell me who I can write to to thank them for their help?'

She reached for a prescription pad and wrote out a name and address. As she handed the slip to him she said, 'They'll appreciate a letter.' She paused. 'Just one more thing. As you know I've checked you all for the infection and you're all clear but there are lots of factors that contribute to this disease. One of them is stress.' She paused. 'I got the impression that despite appearances there's some kind of tension in your family. Do you know what I mean?'

'We keep to ourselves if that's what you mean.'

'Mr Aarons. That's not what I mean and you know it's not. Let me be frank with you. I see your wife seriously ill in this place. Your sister Anna is thirty-three. Far too good-looking not to be married. Your brother is thirty or so. Also not married. But when I ask them questions they respond as if I were the police accusing them of some crime.'

'I think you're mistaken, doctor. We just live very normal lives.'

She shook her head. 'You're responding the same way yourself. It's time you did a little self-analysis, Mr Aarons. You've been in Brighton Beach for, what is it now, over four years. I heard about you way, way back.' She smiled. 'A dedicated man. And dedicated men, in my experience, are all too often oblivious to what's going on around them. I'd like to suggest that you think about what I've said.' She shrugged. 'You don't have to take my advice but it might be worthwhile thinking about it.'

'You don't understand. I love my wife.'

'I don't doubt that.' She smiled. 'I hear that you've borrowed money from half a dozen local people to pay for the drugs. Good for you.' She paused. 'I once heard you give a talk at the library about Communism. Some people heckled you and I was impressed by your arguments against them. You're good at arguing, Mr Aarons, but that doesn't mean you're right.'

Aarons half-smiled. 'You're not bad at arguing yourself, doctor.'

'Think about what I've said.'

Aarons nodded. 'I will.'

For the first six weeks Aarons lived through a nightmare of indecision, doubt and guilt. Messages still came through from Moscow wanting information on a wide range of subjects. But no response to his request about the money for Chantal. And the daily reports from the sanatorium that gave him no peace because they varied from slow recovery to lapses of remissions that made them no more than daily torments. The fever in her body matching the fever in his mind. He ignored Moscow's demands but kept vague contacts with his network.

They were allowed to see her, one at a time, through the glass partitioning, as she lay there, eyes closed. Sometimes pale-faced, sometimes with the flush of fever on her cheeks. They were aware that it was no more than a ritual, that served no real purpose. It distressed them afresh and Chantal's mind was somewhere far away.

In the third week of the second month he was called to the hospital where Doctor Zetkin was waiting for him. He was told that she was dead. The bacilli had eventually won the fight despite the drug and had spread through other parts of her body. It was recommended that she should be cremated rather than interred. He could feel his heart beating inside his head as he stood there. The doctor took him to the small pharmacy in the hospital and he drank a sedative she gave him, without even being aware of what he was doing.

Finally he looked up at the doctor's face and said, 'Would it have made any difference if she'd gone to the hospital in Manhattan?'

For a moment she hesitated, then she said, 'There's no way of knowing but experts in a particular disease are obviously more successful in treating it than non-experts.'

'You think she might have lived?'

'Yes, I do.' And he saw the anger in her eyes before she turned and walked away.

19

They had spent the two days of Christmas finalising the material for London. London had copies of all the Michelin 1/200,000 maps and Malloy's work had covered maps 51–75 which meant that they covered the Belgian border, all of Occupied France and about a quarter of Unoccupied France down to Perigueux and Bordeaux. All the map references were based on the Michelin maps.

The routine radio messages back to London gave whatever details they obtained about German troop movements, identifying the units concerned where possible and their starting and destination points. But way back London had asked for him to identify suitable targets for bombing or sabotage and Malloy was satisfied that he and Pascal and their network of informants had done a good job. Michelin sheet numbers and map references pinpointed bridges, viaducts, marshalling yards, repair sheds, locomotive sheds, strategic junctions and signalling and telephone junction boxes, and the main strategic railway junctions. There were well over 500 targets identified. But the paperwork was too extensive to be sent by radio and it was the third week in January before a Lysander pick-up for Parish's network could be used to pass the material back to London.

There was no response from London for ten days and then Parish told him that London were sending a Lysander with a new radio operator for Parish's network and that he was to go back with the plane.

'Why do they want me to go back?'

Parish shrugged. 'No idea, my friend. Why should they tell me? I'm not part of OSS, I'm just your nursemaid while you're in France.'

'Is that how you see it?'

Parish laughed and punched him lightly on his arm. 'Don't take things so seriously. I was only kidding.'

'When does the Lysander come?'

'A week tomorrow. It's full moon plus one. I've got a few packets for London if you'll take them with you.'

Despite the full moon it wasn't a good night for a pick-up. There was a high wind that sent the clouds racing across the sky so that the light on the field was constantly changing. And it made it difficult to hear anything other than the wind in the trees as they stood at the edge of the woods.

They had been checked twice on the journey down to Orleans. Once by German soldiers from a local anti-aircraft battery and once by an officious sergeant in the Milice. But both times their stories had held together and they had been sent on their way. The rest of Parish's men had gone separately without being checked.

There were six of them. Parish, himself and four of Parish's men. He had no responsibility for the pick-up but he was aware that there was some tension in the others. Their faces turned upwards, pale in the fleeting light of the moon. The Lysander was overdue by ten minutes but Parish said that it was probably because of the strong wind. Parish was using a new piece of equipment for the first time. An S-phone which meant that he could talk directly to the pilot once he was overhead. One of the problems was that they had decided not to use flares as markers because of the wind and they couldn't use their torches for long periods because batteries were so scarce.

Then he saw Parish hold up his hand for silence and turn towards the north-west. He could see him talking but couldn't hear the words. Parish ordered the torches on and then Malloy could hear the plane's engine and seconds later he saw it in the brief light of the moon as it came in low over the woods on the far side of the field. Five minutes later he was airborne with the plane heading almost due west to avoid the Luftwaffe base at Tours. They landed at Tangmere, an RAF fighter airfield in Sussex, because they were low on fuel. Major Wallace was there to meet him.

'How're you feeling, Bill, tired?'

'I'm OK.'

'We could stay at a hotel in Chichester for the night or I've got a staff car to take us up to London. We've booked you in at the Dorchester. Which do you prefer?'

'Let's get up to London, shall we?'

In the car he asked Wallace how long he would be in London.

'I don't know. SOE are only responsible for your transport, it all depends on what your OSS people want.'

'Do you know why I've been recalled?'

'No idea, my friend.' He smiled. 'If we're not told we don't ask.' He paused. 'Anyway, how are you getting on with Jim Parish, is he providing what you want?'

'He's fine. Cool, calm and collected and very efficient.'

'I'm glad to hear it.'

Malloy had an early breakfast in his room. Powdered egg from the States and two pieces of toast. The room waiter told him that there would be a fresh egg every second day during his stay at the hotel.

There was no call for him and he went for a walk up to Hyde Park Corner and along Oxford Street. He was shocked by the damage that the Luftwaffe had inflicted on the city but the people he spoke to, the newsvendor and a policeman, seemed to be taking it all as a payment towards victory. They certainly weren't cowed and frightened as the French newspapers had said.

When he got back to the hotel the clerk gave him his room key and told him that his visitors were waiting for him in his room. He guessed that one of them would be

Kelly but he had no idea who the other person would be.

Kelly was sitting on the edge of the unmade bed and standing by the window was Lieutenant Colonel Williams who he had last seen in Washington.

Williams smiled, 'Glad to see you again, Bill. I've brought you some mail – it's on the table there.' He looked at Malloy, 'And how're you making out over the water?'

Malloy shrugged. 'I guess you'd better ask Colonel Kelly.'

Kelly just pointed to the armchair, waving for Malloy to sit down. Kelly was a Bostonian and not given to unnecessary pronouncements.

'The reason why I wanted to see you is that we'd like to move your operation up a gear. What you've done so far is much more than we expected. You've got a great network of informants but there's no good getting information unless you can pass it back to us in time to act on it. I've arranged for two senior officers from General Eisenhower's staff to join with us in trying to devise some way to process your intelligence in a matter of hours. They're very impressed with what you've been sending back.' He paused and looked at his watch. 'Let's meet at our office in Grosvenor Square at 4 p.m. OK?'

'That's OK by me.'

Kelly handed Malloy a brown envelope. 'There's pounds and dollars for your incidental expenses. Let me know if you need more.'

Malloy went slowly through his mail. Four letters from Kathy which he put to one side and the rest was like messages from another planet. A book-club subscription reminder, two offers of life-insurance, a mailing shot for an S and L, an alumnus letter from the university and a statement of his account from the bank. He tore them up and threw them into the waste-paper basket beside the bed, and wondered why Kathy had forwarded them when she could have dealt with them all herself.

He stood at the window looking down at the traffic on Park Lane and then across to the bare trees in Hyde Park.

Despite the wind and the rain he could see two riders in the park. A man and a girl riding their horses down the sandy track of Rotten Row, dodging the branches as they swung in the wind. Then a squall covered the window with raindrops and he closed his eyes. For the first time in all the months he'd been away he wondered what the hell he was doing in a hotel room in London. He didn't belong here, nor in France. And what was worse he didn't belong in New York any longer. Each country had eaten up the one before. He was like some garden plant that people kept digging up to check that the roots were OK. And now there weren't any roots left. He didn't belong anywhere. But the others, Parish, Kelly and Williams, seemed to take it all in their stride. To them, what they were doing absorbed their lives, but what did he care about what trains in a foreign country were carrying German troops and supplies. The information he supplied was just one small piece in a giant jigsaw puzzle, and if it wasn't there it wouldn't be missed.

Kelly introduced the two officers from Eisenhower's Staff, Rogers and Westphal, both wearing the single star of a brigadier-general. Wallace from SOE was there too and was introduced as an observer.

Williams looked around the table and then said, 'Gentlemen, you've all seen the flow of material that has come from Captain Malloy. I understand you've already made good use of some of it. But I want us to consider how we can speed up the whole process. I'd like one of the planners to put Bill Malloy and the rest of us in the picture. Maybe you, Greg, could lay it out.'

Brigadier-General Rogers looked at Malloy, 'I endorse what Colonel Williams has said about your material. But I must tell you that when the time for the invasion of Europe arrives the information you can give us about the movement of enemy troops and materials could save us thousands of lives . . . maybe tens of thousands of lives, provided we get it in time to react appropriately. This means jacking up the risks to you and your people and I want to hear your views on that.'

'I'd need to know what you have in mind before I could judge the risks involved.'

Rogers nodded towards his colleague Westphal who lit a cigarette before he started talking.

'You've got one radio operator and by courtesy of British SOE you can call on one more operator but only in real emergency. Our information is that the nearest German direction-finding unit is in Orleans, and it's only there on detachment from Paris for one week a month. There's a map on the wall behind me and you'll see that I've put pins in where you have informants and I've used cotton to link them back to your base.' He shrugged. 'It's crazy. Not your fault. If you hadn't done so well acquiring people it would have got you by. But right now we're wasting valuable time and valuable sources.' He put down his cigarette in a glass ashtray. 'How does most of your information come back to you?'

'By telephone. Sometimes by couriers where they have travel permits. But mainly telephone. One contact to another and eventually back to me.'

'You only use your radio back and forth to London?'

Malloy nodded. 'Yes.'

'How long did it take you to recruit the key people you've got now?'

'Eight, nine months. I'm still looking for more.'

'And they've all kept their jobs so that they can pass you information?'

'No. They kept their jobs because they need jobs. If they felt that passing me information endangered their lives or their jobs they'd stop contacting me.'

'They'd surely be willing to join the Resistance full time? Some of them.'

For long moments Malloy was silent. Then he said, 'I'm afraid you don't understand the situation in France. Most people see the Resistance as a provocation to the Germans which only causes trouble for the civil population.'

'So what motivates the people who you have recruited?'

'Politics.'

'Explain.'

'Most of them are obeying the orders of political parties so that they can claim power when France is liberated.'

'Which parties are these?'

'Mainly the communists but there are a few socialists among them.'

'You mean you're using Commies as your informants?'

'I'm not interested in their politics. All I want is their cooperation.'

Westphal leaned back in his chair, looking first at Rogers and then at Williams.

'Were you guys aware of this?'

'No.' It was Rogers who answered him.

'What about you, colonel?' said Westphal. 'Did you know?'

'I didn't *know*. But I'm not surprised. I go along with Malloy. Their politics are their business. If they'll help us win the war – good luck to 'em.'

Mike Wallace said quietly. 'If I could perhaps intervene. Our policy in SOE is to accept communists so long as they are not controlled by anyone except us. Some of our best resisters are communists.'

Williams said, 'I suggest we ignore the politics – at least for now – and carry on talking about the brigadier's plan.'

Westphal looked at Rogers who shrugged noncommittally and Westphal said, 'OK. This is what I planned. How long would it take you to recruit six full-time couriers who could be trusted?'

'I've no idea. Some months. Two, maybe three.'

'Too long. I need your stuff coming back to me by March.'

'Why March?'

Westphal ignored the question. 'Money no object. Whatever it takes.'

'What about additional radio operators?'

'Two. Trained and French speaking. French-Canadians.'

'When are they available?'

'Right now.' Westphal paused. 'We'd like to suggest that you place one of them somewhere near Chartres and one very near to Paris.'

'It would be risky for both of them. The Gestapo and the SD and the Abwehr are very active in Paris.'

'We thought you should move to Paris to control them.'

'Why all the sudden expansion and the hurry?'

'You work it out for yourself. Keep it going for two months and that's enough.'

Malloy looked at Wallace but his face was impassive.

'OK. When can I see these two?'

'Tomorrow morning here. OK?'

Malloy nodded.

As Wallace walked back with Malloy to the Dorchester he said, 'Don't take too much notice of Rogers' and Westphal's views on communists. You've got to remember that they're soldiers not intelligence officers. They're career officers and I guess they see things in black and white.'

Malloy didn't hide his anger. 'In that case maybe they should stay out of other people's business.'

'Are you happy with what they're suggesting?'

'Of course I am not.'

'Tell me why?'

'It's being done in too much of a rush. It's not properly thought out. It could be a complete shambles.'

'In a way it's a tribute to the work you've done.'

'How come?'

'When the invasion comes, information on German troop movements and supplies will be vital. Your operation really could save thousands of lives.'

'So why didn't they come up with this months ago?'

Wallace sighed, 'Until you had shown what could be done it wasn't part of the game.'

'So why is getting this in place by March so important? Why the mad rush?'

'Think about what you've just said and you'll come up with the answer. Anyway, tomorrow we'll go over what you feel you need. They meant what they said – money's no problem. Think about it.'

The two French-Canadians were a pleasant surprise. They were brothers and had lived in France until they were teenagers. Tough, and competent radio operators, they gave him his first ray of hope that the plan might work. It was agreed that they would wait for two weeks so that Malloy could find them safe-houses, one near Paris and one near Chartres before they came over.

He had a final working meeting with Kelly. Williams was already on his way back to Washington, and one of Kelly's sergeants gave him a long briefing on the German order of battle in France.

Two days later he parachuted from a Hudson and was picked up by Parish and four of his men. The plane circled again and dropped four cylinders of plastique, grenades, and ammunition for their Sten guns.

It was the night of the 21st of January 1944 and Parish told him that the BBC French service had said that the Royal Air Force had dropped over 2,000 tons of bombs on Berlin the previous night. The next day thousands of British and American troops stormed ashore at Anzio, thirty miles south of Rome.

The next morning he had a meeting with Parish and Pascal, telling them what London had asked for.

When he was through Pascal sat silent without comment waiting for Parish to speak.

'Why did you go along with it?'

'You think I shouldn't have agreed?'

'It's bloody crazy, man. You'll be spread so thin on the ground you'll never have it under control.'

'They only want it to work for a few months.'

'Why?' Pascal asked quietly. 'Why only a few months?'

Parish looked at him. 'Use your head, comrade. Once the invasion has been going for a couple of months we shan't be interested in the French railways. The Germans will be well east of Paris. Either that or we shall have all gone down the drain together.'

'You mean . . .' Pascal hesitated.

'Yes, I mean . . .' He paused. 'Let's talk about how we make this crazy thing work.' He looked at Pascal. 'Can you find a safe-house near to Paris and one near Chartres?'

Pascal closed his eyes, thinking, then opened them as he said, 'I could fix one in Melun for Paris but the only place I could do in Chartres is in the city itself.'

'How safe would they be?'

'Committed people who hate the Germans. One lost a husband and a son to the Germans. The other one I have known for years. I use it myself.'

Malloy said, 'How long will it take for you to arrange this?'

'Three, four days.'

Malloy said, 'Do you want me to come with you?'

'Are you going to do what they want and base yourself in Paris?'

'Yes, but I won't move to Paris until the two radio operators are in place.' Malloy turned to look at Parish. 'Could you lend me two Frenchmen for a couple of weeks just to save time.'

'What for?'

'I'll need to set up a chain of telephone contacts from the informants back to me so that Pascal and I can feed it to the radio men. We'll have to make Pascal's radio into a mobile unit as a back-up.' He turned to Pascal. 'Find me at least three places I can use in Paris and one in Chartres that you can use yourself. I'll go over with you some basic verbal codes that our people can use on the phone. If we could get someone who works on a telephone exchange in Paris or Melun it could help us a lot. Or a telephone operator at a works that operates day and night.

Some sort of factory. Even one that's working for the Germans.'

Pascal nodded. 'When can I say that the invasion will start?'

'You can't say. We shan't know until we get the coded messages on the BBC French Service.'

'It would help in getting volunteers if they knew that the invasion was not far off.'

'We can't tell them anything. We don't know anything ourselves. We can make some guesses but even those we keep to ourselves.'

'We're asking a lot from these people. If any of them were caught they would be shot without trial or mercy.'

'So would we, Pascal. And it is their country that they want liberated. It will cost a lot of American lives no matter how well it goes.'

Parish intervened. 'For Christ's sake let's not fight about who of us are the heroes. You and I are soldiers, we've been trained, and we're volunteers. Pascal here and the others are civilians. We need their help. Please God they just give us what they can. French soldiers held off the Wehrmacht at Dunkirk so that 350,000 men could escape to England and fight again.' His face was flushed with anger as he looked at Malloy. 'Just remember that. You people left us to fight alone until the Japs attacked you at Pearl Harbor.' For a moment he closed his eyes and when he opened them he said, 'I'm sorry but you've got me doing it too. Let's get your show on the road.'

It was a week before Pascal came back. He had arranged for three safe-houses to be made available. One in Chartres, one in Paris and one just outside Paris in Melun. But the real news was that Pascal had found five people who would not only provide telephones but would be willing to take messages. All of them regularly received calls day and night. Incredibly, one was an operator on the main telephone exchange in Melun. Another was a policeman in a Paris suburb. They were all already members

153

of Resistance networks who had agreed that they would cooperate with Pascal. There were also two additional couriers, one a postman and the other a taxi driver, both of whom had passes that allowed them to circulate freely. An attic room was available for Pascal and Malloy in a three-storey house at the top of the hill in Montmartre. An ideal location for Pascal's transmitter.

The French-Canadian brothers, the Jarrys, Pierre and Paul, had parachuted down safely four days later.

20

There had been little time for the brothers Jarry to settle in but they had been well-briefed in London about their tasks and Malloy and Pascal had spent two long days going over the procedures that had been worked out for the new operation. The brothers seemed to take it all in their stride and Malloy felt a surge of confidence in his team.

Pierre Jarry was installed in a loft which was part of a stables on the outskirts of Chartres and Paul Jarry was based at a private house in Melun just outside Paris.

Pascal had already set up the teams of couriers and message-takers and a link-man who would pass the information immediately to one of the Jarrys.

Malloy and Pascal moved on two days later to Paris where Pascal had arranged for them to rent the attic rooms of a café in St Germain in the rue de Beaune near Quai Voltaire. It was patronised by both Germans and local French people and the constant flow of people provided good cover for Pascal's frequent comings and goings.

Within a couple of hours of their arrival the system was working and Malloy was hard-pressed in encoding the radio traffic to London. There was more chance of detection-vans operating in Paris and that meant finding alternative sites for Pascal's radio and after two weeks of intense pressure Pascal found a courier who would take encoded material down to Paul Jarry in Melun for onward transmission.

By the end of March Malloy had asked London to specify areas of priority otherwise they would be overwhelmed and the operation would grind to a standstill and what might be vital information would have to take its turn in the queue with the chance of its value being negated or diluted.

London agreed immediately and the next day a list of a dozen priorities came over. Half of them concerned Wehrmacht troop-movements east to west towards the Channel ports and their hinterland. Even nil reports were to be included. London mentioned that transmissions in daytime hours could be considered as there was so much radio traffic in the Paris area at that time that it could make detection more difficult for the Germans.

The only problems in March were the power-cuts for the civilian population. They came without warning. Only the Jarrys' radios were operative for several days. And as May came in the pressure from London was increased. The priority classifications were void. London wanted everything, even movements of troops in the south of France.

Malloy barely ventured outside on the streets and Pascal had told him that he wouldn't be fit to carry on if he didn't relax and get some fresh air.

They had walked down the next afternoon to the *quai*. It was the 1st of June 1944. Blue skies and a warm sun sprinkling the Seine with sparkling diamonds as they sat on a bench near to an old man with a fishing rod.

He tensed as he saw a group of German soldiers walking towards them and Pascal said, 'Don't worry. They're on leave. They put them up in an old warehouse in the rue du Bac. Those guys are just kids from a machine-gun battalion.'

'How do you know that?'

Pascal laughed. 'You gave me talks on recognition. That leather pouch on his belt is supposed to hold tools and an anti-aircraft sight for his MG43.'

'And you still remember all that stuff?'

'Yes. Never know when it might come in handy.' He

paused. 'There's a lot of messages in the last week on the BBC French Service. Could mean something's boiling up.'

'How do you get time to listen to the radio?'

'I don't. People tell me.'

'What else do they tell you?'

'Rommel's been posted here as commander of the Channel defences.'

'Anything else?'

'Yeah, the Allies took Rome yesterday but the Germans wouldn't let the newspapers print it today. There's a lot of changes going on at the Kommandantur. Civilians going back to Germany and soldiers taking over.'

'What kind of people tell you these things? Are they reliable?'

Pascal laughed. 'Of course not. Most of them, it's just gossip but it's generally right. Especially if they're Party members. They know how to sort the wheat from the chaff.'

'You still believe in all that?'

'All what?'

'Workers of the world unite, down with capitalism and on with the class war.'

'You think that's all it is?'

'What is it then?'

'It's the basis for trying to create a world where everybody gets a fair deal. Where everybody gives what they've got. Those with talents give their talents and others give their labour. Where every man has a job by right, and medical care and a roof over his head.'

'And if he doesn't toe the line he gets sent to Siberia.'

Pascal smiled. 'Let's win the war first, comrade, and then we can argue.'

'If they were all like you, my friend, then I'd join myself.'

Pascal laughed. 'Thanks. I'm flattered. We'd better go, we've got a heavy schedule tonight. Paul's coming up himself early evening to take back some of my load.'

*   *   *

157

On the 4th of June London was asking for even more specific information. They would monitor his frequencies round the clock so that no time was lost. Their requests were about German units moving away from the Channel ports eastwards, and getting this type of information quickly put great pressure on the couriers and telephone contacts. Malloy wondered why London were so interested in troops moving away from the coast, it was usually incoming troops that interested them.

The following day it seemed as if London had gone berserk. They asked for hourly transmissions with no priority restrictions. Anything he got, they wanted it. All their previous rules on radio security seemed to have been abandoned.

The next day, Tuesday the 6th of June he had gone down to the café to cadge a spoonful of sugar for his breakfast coffee and the place was in turmoil. The radio was on full blast, quite openly tuned to the BBC French Service. Eisenhower's voice announcing that the invasion had started. Then the French translation. It was repeated again and again interspersed from time to time with reports that troops had already landed on French soil.

The several groups of early-morning customers stood listening in silence and there were no signs of excitement. That would come later if the invasion was successful but at that moment they were aware that the landings meant the destruction of villages and towns and the deaths of many French men and women.

It was Pascal who brought home other realities to Malloy when he said, smiling, 'I guess at least a hundred thousand people joined the Resistance today.'

When he saw the surprise on Malloy's face Pascal grinned. 'All those bastards who've been collaborating with the Germans will be desperate for some insurance for when the *krauts* have left. A Resistance ID card will be worth a lot of francs.'

'What do you think will happen to collaborators?'

'Women will have their heads shaved if they're lucky

and men will get shot.' He shrugged. 'Let's get back upstairs. I've already missed a schedule but I guess London will understand.'

As Allied troops fought their way across the plains towards Paris it was becoming more difficult for Malloy's couriers to move about. The French Milice working for the Germans were everywhere. They worked outside the law and murders were a daily occurrence. Street checks and arrests on suspicion made life in the city precarious and even Pascal no longer ventured out unless it was really necessary.

By the third week in June there was little information coming through but the pressures from London had eased too. It was in that week that Pascal heard that Parish's network had been wiped out and that Parish himself had been killed.

It was on the Wednesday of that week that the mix-up with London started. London were acknowledging messages quoting reference numbers that had not been sent. When Malloy queried the references London seemed confused. At the mid-day schedule on the Thursday there was no acknowledgement. Pascal tried to make contact every hour but London didn't respond. Pascal told him that he had tried all their frequencies including the emergency ones and there was not only no response but there was no carrier wave. London had closed down on them.

After two more days with no response from London Malloy was at his wits' end. He had been left high and dry. He closed down on his network and told his people that they had a technical fault on the radio. The fault was being rectified.

The tension in the streets was mounting as news and rumours of the Allied advances spread. There seemed only one thing left that he could do and that was to try and contact London through one of the Jarrys.

Mid-day on the third day Malloy slipped out of the café

159

and along the *quai*. He had to walk nearly two miles before he found a telephone that was working and not in sight of German patrols.

He called the Melun number first but after a long wait and several attempts there was no reply. It was exactly the same with the Chartres number. He walked around for an hour and then went through it all again but there was no response from either number. He walked back along the river road, tired and confused and the light was beginning to fade as the café came in sight.

He walked under the arch to the alleyway that led to the small yard and the fire-escape stairs to the top floor. There was a light in their window and Malloy was glad to be back despite his problems.

At the top of the stairs he saw the chink of light under the door and wondered if by some miracle Pascal had contacted London while he was away. He opened the door and went inside. It wasn't until he turned to close the door behind him that he saw the man sitting at the table. He was wearing the SS uniform of a *Standartenführer*, a colonel, his hand was resting on the table, a Luger in his hand, his cap on the table beside the gun.

The man pointed with his other hand at the bed against the wall. 'Sit down,' he said in not very good French.

As he moved to the bed and sat down Malloy could see the aerial wire trailing down from the ceiling in the far corner of the room. The radio wasn't there. And he saw no sign of Pascal.

'Who are you working for?'

'I'm studying to be a lawyer.' He pointed at the books on the shelf, but the SS man didn't look away from his face.

'We started monitoring your radio traffic ten days ago.' He smiled. 'We sent a few messages of our own. They accepted them for a couple of days. But they closed down. I expect you noticed. What are your orders now?'

Malloy didn't reply and the German stood up and called out something in German. Two men came out of the kitchen. One an SS sergeant and the other a Milice officer. Malloy realised that if the Milice were there it might mean that they still thought he was a Frenchman.

The SS sergeant walked over and stood behind him, taking his wrists and clamping them tight with handcuffs. They took him down the inside stairs and through the café. The place fell silent as they threaded their way through the tables.

There was a black Mercedes and a white Peugeot with Milice markings parked in the street and he was shoved onto the back-seat of the Merc with the SS colonel, the sergeant in the driver's seat.

They went down to the *quai* and across the bridge and he closed his eyes trying to collect his thoughts. It seemed a long time before the car stopped. He was half asleep from sheer exhaustion when he was dragged out of the car, vaguely aware of being in the forecourt of a big house with lights in all the windows and inside the big open door.

Then he was in a panelled room that had been made into an office. There was a big mahogany desk with several phones and the SS colonel was sitting on the edge of the desk looking at him.

'Do you want to talk, my friend or do you want to do it the hard way?' He shrugged. 'It's up to you.'

When Malloy didn't speak the colonel said, 'Any citizen found working for the enemy is executed summarily. We don't play games, we don't have the time.'

'I'm a captain in the United States Army, my name is Malloy, my number is 10350556 and that is all that I am required to say under the Geneva Convention.'

The colonel smiled. 'You are not a prisoner of war, Captain Malloy. You are a terrorist involved in espionage and you have no rights under the Geneva Convention or any other convention. Tell me what you were sent here to do.'

Almost without thinking Malloy shook his head and the SS colonel reached for the phone, but left his hand just above the instrument. 'If you don't talk, Malloy, you'll be handed over to people who'll make you talk. We want to know what you and your network were doing and we're in a hurry.' He paused. 'If you want to play the hero – go ahead. On your head be it.'

The blue eyes looked at Malloy for long moments and then he closed his hand over the phone, lifting it to his mouth and speaking in German.

A couple of minutes after he hung up two men came into the room. Both wearing the uniforms and insignia of Gestapo sergeants.

The journey in the prison van took about fifteen minutes.

For four days they worked on him until his eyes were closed, his fingers broken, his body burning with pain, the stink of suppurating wounds around him as he lay on the concrete block in the cell.

Two days later a guard unlocked the barred door of the cell and a uniformed woman pushed a trolley inside. She stood looking at him for long moments and then turned to the trolley. Slowly and gently she wiped his bruised flesh, binding his fingers and putting a powder on his open wounds. When she was finished she stood back and looked him over.

'I'm arranging for you to have some soup and bread. Make sure you eat it up. You need to put on some weight.'

'Where am I?'

'You don't know?'

He shook his head and cried out with the pain.

'You're in Fresnes prison.'

'How long have I been here?'

'A week.'

'What's happening? The war?'

'I'm not allowed to talk about that.'

As the walls and floor of the cell seemed to dissolve he lay back on the cement block and sank into a coma.

A week went by and the woman visited him every day, checking his condition. On the third day she said very quietly as she bent over him, 'Are you the American captain?'

'Yes.'

'What's your name?'

'Malloy.'

'I've got a message for you from another prisoner, the Russian.'

'I don't know any Russian.'

'Says he uses the name Pascal.'

'What was the message?'

'To tell you that he didn't talk. They don't know anything from him.'

'Did they beat him up too?'

'Yes. I'm afraid they did.'

'Can you give him a message from me?'

'I can't. He isn't here any more. He was being sent to one of the German concentration camps. He left three days ago.'

'What date is it?'

'It's the third week in July.'

'And the invasion?'

'People are saying that they'll be in Paris in six weeks.'

'Are they sending me to a camp?'

'I don't know.'

'How did you know that Pascal was a Russian?'

'He's a well-known man in the Resistance. He lived here in Paris long before the war.'

'How long before I can get on my feet?'

'At least another two weeks provided you do as you're told.' She paused. 'You've got a high temperature. You must rest all you can.'

Two days later a guard had contacted the prison doctor and after a brief examination Malloy had been transferred to the prison hospital bay. He was diagnosed as having pneumonia. A further examination defined it as bacterial pneumonia and the only treatment he got was a hot-water bottle twice a day to ease the pain in his chest.

Day after day he lay there, panting, coughing blood, his temperature rising and falling erratically, delirious at night. It was three weeks before the fever subsided and Malloy's mind got back into the world again. The pain on the left side of his chest was still there and sitting up in bed took all his strength. There were two other prisoners in the hospital bay and a guard with a pistol stood just outside the barred gate. An orderly came twice a day with food. A thin soup, a piece of acorn bread and sometimes offal, kidneys or liver swimming in a greasy gravy.

Then one day the guard unlocked the door, leaving it open, beckoning to him, but he was too weak to move. The guard walked over to him and helped him to his feet. With his arm round Malloy he led him slowly forward to the gate and then to a window in the thick stone wall. The guard pointed down to the streets.

There was a cavalcade of cars and khaki-clad troops but Malloy couldn't see them, his head rolled forward and the guard dragged him back to his bed.

It was the 25th of August and Paris had been liberated. That night a Free French patrol had entered the prison, bringing food and medical supplies and two doctors and two nurses.

When the prison records had been examined by a French intelligence officer a call had been put through to SHAEF headquarters who in turn had contacted London. A few days later Malloy was in St Thomas's Hospital, London. An OSS officer came to see him. It seemed that Lieutenant Colonel Kelly was back in Washington. They were doing their best to get him a flight back to the States to save him the long sea journey.

He asked about why they had broken off radio contact but the man didn't know. He gave the impression that it was all in the past and there were other more important things occupying OSS minds at the moment.

Two days later Malloy was flown back to an airfield in New Jersey, the only passenger in a bomber taking engines back for servicing, and half a dozen coffins.

21

Kathy Malloy stood beside Lieutenant Colonel Kelly as the huge B-27 rolled to a standstill. The ground-crew wheeled over the ladder and Kelly took her arm and led her to the foot of the steps. The door in the fuselage opened slowly and a man appeared at the top of the steps, shading his eyes from the evening sun. As the man walked slowly and awkwardly down the steps she wondered how long it would be before Bill came out from the darkness of the door.

She was vaguely aware of the first man walking slowly towards her and Kelly saying quietly, 'You greet him first.' And she couldn't believe it, that pale, haggard face and the trembling body was her husband. For a moment she wanted to turn her anger on Kelly but she held out her arms and put them around the bony shoulders. 'It's lovely to see you, Bill. It's been so long.' She put her head on his shoulder and wept.

Kelly stood to one side, uncertain what to do. They had told him that Malloy had had proper medical treatment and was fit enough to return to the States. He hadn't expected to be faced with a wreck of a man who couldn't speak and could barely stand up. But Kelly was OSS and knew by instinct what was happening. This was a homecoming that was fast turning into a wake unless he took it in hand.

Kelly wasn't given to throwing his rank about or blustering but when he'd phoned Washington from the building on the airstrip he'd told them to use any pressure that was needed to get him a suite at the Waldorf by the time he got there in about forty-five minutes. He was also insistent that they got hold of an army doctor for when they arrived.

His army driver had taken every short cut he knew but it had seemed a long silent journey before they drew up outside the hotel. There was a message at the desk that the doctor was in the bar.

Kelly sat waiting with Kathy in the sitting room of the suite while the doctor examined Malloy. He took nearly an hour and when he came out with his black bag he sat down facing them.

'I've given him as thorough a check-up as I can outside a hospital.' He smiled at Kathy. 'Let me say first of all that he's not as bad as he looks. Physically, he just needs rest, good food and a pleasant environment. You won't recognise him in a few weeks' time. He's young and tough and everything's healing up quite well.' He turned to look at Kelly.

'The main problems are psychological. He's been beaten up, humiliated and that's bound to have an effect. I suggest that he is discharged from whatever your unit is and that he's given a month or six weeks' paid leave.' Turning to Kathy he said, 'Have you got a home to take him to, Mrs Malloy?'

'Just a small apartment.'

'Do you work?'

'Yes.'

'Could you give up your work and take him down to some resort? Florida or California. Where there's sun and no more evidence of war?'

She looked at Kelly who said, 'No problem, the service will see to all that.'

The doctor stood up. 'OK. Now don't worry, Mrs Malloy, he's going to be all right.' He picked up his bag. 'I'll look in every day until you leave.' He nodded at Kelly who stood up and walked with him to the door.

In the corridor Kelly said, 'Did you mean all that? It wasn't just bullshit for his wife, was it?'

The doctor half-smiled. 'I'm a doctor, colonel, I may be in uniform but so far as your officer in there is concerned he's a patient. He's had a bad time but he'll get over it. His wife's going to need some help however.' He smiled. 'I guess you'll see to that.'

It was September when they boarded the plane at La Guardia for Los Angeles and that night they had driven up to Carmel where a politician friend of Kelly had put his villa at their disposal.

The Mexican gardener had waited for them and his wife had left salad and cold meats for them in the refrigerator. He showed them over the house and told them that he and his wife would be there every day to look after them.

The villa had its own garden and swimming pool and in the lights on the patio they saw the bougainvillea that smothered the roof and the bunches of hanging grapes on a vine covering the wooden patio ceiling.

When they had eaten Kathy took him out to a couple of striped canvas chairs under a honeysuckle.

As they settled down she said, 'Are you glad we came?'

He shrugged. 'I guess so, honey.' He smiled. 'You always know what to do with me, don't you?'

'We've got four months to unwind here and it was very good of Kelly to fix it for us.' She paused. 'He thinks a lot of you. You know that.'

'I guess so.'

'What's that mean?'

He reached out for her hand. 'Just that, kid. Let's forget him and the rest of them.'

'OK. Let's talk about when it's all over. What shall we do and where shall we live?'

He leaned back in his chair. 'I'd like to go back to New York. How about you?'

She smiled. 'Like it says in the Bible. Whither thou goest . . .'

'I'll go back into law and make some money. And if we can afford it we'll get ourselves a weekend place in the country or by the sea.'

'And what do you want me to do?'

He looked at her quickly. 'Whatever you want. But something that really interests you.'

'I'd be happy to stay at home.'

'You're too bright just to do that.' He smiled. 'We'll think of something.'

'What about a family?'

'You mean children?'

'Yes.'

'Is that what you want?'

'I'd like to talk about it and see what you feel.'

'It would scare me, Kathy, after what I saw when I was away. I wouldn't really want the responsibility. I used the resources I've got to keep myself sane. I don't think I could cope with any extra responsibility.'

She smiled, but it took an effort. 'Let's wait and see. We've got plenty of time to see what happens.' She stood up. 'It's time we were in bed, it's been a long day.'

After two months of the sun and air and peacefulness of the small town Malloy was physically fit again and beginning to make moves towards getting a job. And again it was Kelly who put a word in the right ear. His old friend, Hancox, who had originally spotted Malloy for OSS was consulted. It was Hancox's view that the end of the war, which was now in sight, would mean a tremendous amount of legal work concerning the government, its departments, and industry and commerce. His chambers were prepared to offer Malloy a junior partnership to prepare for this influx of work, and a senior partnership if everything worked out as Hancox expected.

Malloy had flown up to New York for two meetings with Hancox. The financial arrangements were generous and the work itself suited him but Hancox had had to convince him that he was not being offered the job just because he was a war veteran. Hancox had told him that the terms offered him were only in line with the big increases in everybody's earnings in the war years. When it came to finding accommodation in New York he realised that Hancox wasn't kidding.

Kathy had gone with him on the second trip to New York and had spent two days looking for a new home for them. They discovered that there was a chronic shortage of apartments – there had been no building since 1943 and wartime rent controls encouraged tenants to hang on to what they had.

They eventually settled for an apartment in a converted brownstone on the East Side between 48th and 49th streets. A large living room, a double bedroom, a small study and a well-fitted kitchen and bathroom. And only fifteen minutes' walk from Hancox, Yarrow and Partners' new offices.

It was March 1945. He had been at the law firm for two months and seemed to have settled in without any problems. He had taken her out for dinner at a small French restaurant they used frequently.

Pierre, the owner, had become a friend and Kathy was sometimes just a little irritated that they talked in French so much. At the same time she was secretly quite impressed by the fact that her husband could speak French so fluently.

There was a red rose in the vase on the table to mark the fact that it was her birthday and she was wearing the pearls that he'd given her. Pierre came and sat with them at the table and as always chatted away in French and she realised that she resented that she was always left out of the conversation. And subconsciously she knew that part of her resentment came from the fact that when he had those nightmares he was always talking and shouting in French. There had been only a couple of recurrences of the bad dreams since they had come back to New York but Pierre and his chat was a reminder that there was a

169

part of her husband's life that she was excluded from. She resolved as she sat there that she'd do something about it. It was bad manners on Pierre's part to say the least.

They went on to the Barclay for a night-cap on the way home and then walked back to the apartment. As she hung her coat in the hallway she decided that she would tackle him about the Pierre business right away.

As she walked back into the living room she saw him standing by the window looking out towards the river. He hadn't realised that she was there and as she observed him she was startled by the sadness of his face. His mind was obviously far away, his eyes closed, the deep lines at the sides of his mouth exaggerated by the lights from outside. She had seen pictures of faces like that in magazines like *Life*. Pictures of refugees. Jews lining up for the gas-chambers. People with no hope in their faces. Expecting nothing, fearing the worst.

There was no way she was going to harass him about talking French.

22

On New Year's Day, 1946 a Red Army artillery unit in Berlin were hosts to a detachment of American infantrymen, some of whom had slogged their way up the spine of Italy with General Mark Clark. After toasts had been drunk to 'Uncle' Joe, Harry Truman, Rokossowsky and Eisenhower, one of the Americans, a sergeant, raised his glass to 'getting the hell out of Europe and going home'. One of the Russians noticed that every US soldier not only drank to the toast but was angry that he was not back home already. 'Why the hell is there space on the boats for GI brides but not for us?' The Russian happened to be the artillery unit's commissar and after some checking of other American units he sent a long report on American servicemen's morale direct to his boss in Moscow.

Serov was employed at that time as an interpreter for a US Counter-Intelligence unit and had sent a similar report to Moscow about low morale in the American forces in France.

There had been similar reports from Tokyo, Hawaii, London and Vienna, and Moscow knew it was on to a winner. For three weeks of virtually non-stop planning meetings a combined operation was put together by the Comintern and the KGB. As the list of subversives, agitators and malcontents in the US armed forces built up it was Lensky who pointed out that their reports from the embassy in Washington and their man in New York indicated that it was not only the American forces who suffered from low morale but there was wide-spread civilian discontent about conditions, pay and prices. The two strands could be welded together and exploited. The United States was in a mess, uncertain of where it was going, divided and restless. An ideal target waiting to be struck. The cauldron of internal strife was already boiling. All it needed was a little spice and some stirring. With a small-town haberdasher in the White House Moscow could show the world where the real power lay in the post-war world.

When strikes had paralysed General Motors, the oil, lumber, textile and electrical industries, and newspapers had started talking about the workers' 'revolt' and labour's 'rebellion', President Truman had reached the low point of his Presidency. When the GM strike had been settled and then for 750,000 steelworkers to bank their furnaces and walk out to be followed by 400,000 soft coal miners it seemed like the end of the line. When the railroads' two key brotherhoods announced that they would withdraw their men in thirty days President Truman had had enough. He called the leaders of the railroad unions to the White House and offered them generous arbitration awards. When they refused the offer he looked at them and said, 'If you think I'm going to sit here and let you tie up the whole country you're crazy as hell.'

When they still wouldn't budge he stood up. 'All right. I'm going to give you the gun. You've got forty-eight hours – until this time on Friday – to reach a settlement. If you don't, I'm gonna take over the railroads in the name of the government.'

'That won't get the men back to work, Mr President.'

'Then you'll all be drafted, regardless of age or situation, into the army. Mark my words, my friends, I mean every word of it.'

Two hours later when the President informed his cabinet of what he intended to do his attorney general shrugged and said simply, 'Unconstitutional.' The

President said curtly, 'We'll draft 'em first and think about the law afterwards.'

When he told his press secretary to clear the networks for a fire-side chat he handed him a draft of his speech for copying and said, 'Get it typed up. I'm gonna take the hide right off those sons of bitches.'

The President's opening words of his fire-side chat were less demotic but even more biting. 'The crisis of Pearl Harbor was the result of action by a foreign enemy. The crisis tonight is caused by a group of men within our own country who place their private interests above the welfare of the nation.' He went on to announce that he was calling Congress in session on Sunday afternoon at four o'clock. If the engineers and trainmen were not on the job by then, he would turn them over to General Hershey.

Sunday afternoon came with no surrender from the union bosses who were closeted in a room in the Statler Hotel with a hard-faced government negotiator.

The President entered the House chamber through the Speaker's office and the piece of paper in his hand as he mounted the podium was asking for authority as the commander in chief, 'to draft into the Armed Forces of the United States all workers who are on strike against their own government'.

The President was five minutes into his speech when the phone went in Sam Rayburn's office and a few moments later a scrap of paper was shoved in front of the President. He glanced at it, looked up and smiled around the chamber. 'Gentlemen, the strike has been settled.'

The ovation was the prelude to passing the legislation he asked for on the spot. The angry president of the railwaymen announced that every penny of the union's 47 million dollar funds would be spent defeating Truman in the election in 1948. And John L. Lewis said, 'You can't mine coal with bayonets.' But Truman was in the mood to bring to an end the mine leader's arrogance and irresponsibility.

Sixty-two per cent of the country's electricity and 55 per

cent of its industrial power was based on coal and there was no point in getting the railwaymen back to work if the miners' strike meant that there was no coal for the locomotives. The miners' strike was, quite openly, a challenge to the government by one man. The confrontation was inevitable.

But President Truman had a natural instinct for knowing what the average American was thinking. Mainly because his thoughts were much the same. And instinct told him that John L. Lewis had lost this battle way back in 1943, when, as he put it, 'Lewis had called two strikes in wartime just to satisfy his ego'. Lewis had called out 400,000 men from the mines with no thought for the GIs fighting in Europe and the Pacific. And Truman remembered too that scathing editorial in the Middle East edition of *Stars and Stripes* that ended with 'Speaking for the American soldier – John L. Lewis – damn your coal-black soul'.

The strike was in its sixth week already and the President was more subtle in his moves this time. With the Secretary of the Interior now the coal industry's boss, the President side-tracked Lewis, and the miners were offered most of their demands and an agreed contract was signed. Then the overwhelming ego of Lewis betrayed him. Raising a trivial issue over vacation pay he repudiated the contract and declared that every clause would have to be renegotiated.

The government lawyers told the President that the only recourse available was a court injunction against the union and that was not possible because of the Norris-La Guardia and Wagner Acts. The President ordered them to go ahead all the same because those Acts, he decreed, only covered private employers, not the government.

In the weeks before the court hearing the unions closed down again on Lewis's edict of 'No contract, no work'. Trains ran out of coal and electric power was down to a few hours a day in many States.

In court Judge T. Alan Goldsborough cited Lewis for

contempt of court and two days later ruled that 'The defendants, John L. Lewis and the Union of Mine Workers of America, have beyond a reasonable doubt committed and continue to commit a civil and criminal contempt of this Court'. The fine would be 3,510,000 dollars. Lewis's lawyers had to restrain him from haranguing the judge. It was the largest fine in labour history and Lewis was immediately hit by the government with every available legal weapon from writs to restraining orders.

A few days later he called a press conference at the UMW headquarters and announced that all miners were to return to work immediately on the conditions previously agreed in the contract.

In Manila, 20,000 servicemen booed Lieutenant General W.D. Styles and the indiscipline spread to every theatre where US troops were stationed. In Yokohama Secretary Patterson was howled down as he tried to explain the problems of demobilisation shipping.

In Paris the Red Cross Clubs had boards exhorting servicemen to 'Back up your Manila buddies', and a mob marched down the Champs Elysées waving flags and chanting 'We wanna go home'. And in Frankfurt a mindless, howling mob of four thousand GIs rampaged through the streets and were only turned back by the bayonets of the MPs.

The very newspapers who had played their part in supporting the GIs' demands to be sent home now demanded that they should be brought under control and referred openly to 'a breakdown of army discipline'. General Eisenhower told Congressional leaders that there was now a real danger that the United States 'would run out of army'. He added that he was sure that the outbreaks had been deliberately organised by subversives working to a deliberate plan to undermine the morale of the army. What disturbed his listeners most was that it might become necessary to let US influence in Europe go by default to 'some other country'. In the post-war euphoria it was not done to speak of any nation as a potential enemy but his audience knew who he meant. There had been ten million men in the Red Army in Europe, and they were still there. All of them. And they were not indulging in wanna-go-home riots.

Despite these battles and concerns it was a letter that President Truman had received from a man he respected that worried him most. It had been handed to him by the British Ambassador almost a year ago. And for some reason which he couldn't have explained he had not shown it to any of his cabinet. The letter had been so far-sighted and what it forecast had already come true. And he had a dreadful feeling that what it merely hinted at was about to happen. He hadn't heeded the warning. Imbued with Roosevelt's determination to try and work with the Russians and his suspicions of British intentions in the post-war world, he had ignored the facts. They now had to be faced and he sat at his desk in the White House and read the letter again. It was from Winston Churchill and was dated May 12, 1945.

Prime Minister to President Truman.

I am profoundly concerned about the European situation. I learn that half the American Air Force in Europe has already begun to move to the Pacific theatre. The newspapers are full of the great movements of the American armies out of Europe. Our armies also are, under previous arrangements, likely to undergo a marked reduction. The Canadian Army will certainly leave. The French are weak and difficult to deal with. Anyone can see that in a very short space of time our armed power on the Continent will have vanished, except for moderate forces to hold down Germany.

2 ... I have always worked for friendship with Russia, but like you, I feel deep anxiety because of

*their misinterpretation of the Yalta decisions, their atti-
tude towards Poland, their overwhelming influence in
the Balkans . . . the difficulties they make about
Vienna, the combination of Russian power and the
territories under their control or occupied coupled with
the Communist technique in so many other countries,
and above all their power to maintain very large armies
in the field for a long time . . .*

*3. An iron curtain is drawn down upon their front.
We do not know what is going on behind . . .*

*4. Meanwhile the attention of our peoples will be
occupied in inflicting severities upon Germany, which
is ruined and prostrate, and it would be open to the
Russians in a very short time to advance if they chose
to the waters of the North Sea and the Atlantic . . .*

23

Anna watched Aarons as he listened to the news on the radio. She wondered so often about what went on inside his head. Chantal's death had left him even more aloof and silent than he was before. He never spoke about her after the cremation but her clothes and things were left just where they had always been. She had tried so hard to make him take an interest in other things than his work but it was pointless. But he often sighed deeply when he thought he was not observed. She wondered what he would say when she told him her plans. At first she had thought that Chantal's death meant that he would need her even more. But gradually she had realised that individual people meant nothing to Andrei. He cared about the world, not people. She took a deep breath. 'Andrei.'

He looked at her. 'What is it, Anna?'

'I want to talk to you.'

He switched off the radio and smiled. 'Go on.'

It was the first time she had seen him smile for months and for a moment she wondered if it was the right time to speak.

'I'm going to be married next month, Andrei.'

He shook his head like a dog coming out of water and the shock on his face disturbed her.

He swallowed and then said, 'Tell me about it. Who is the man and how long have you known him?'

'His name is Sam. Sam Fisher. We've been seeing each other for almost six years.'

'What does he do?'

'He's a pianist. A jazz pianist. He plays in clubs and hotels in Manhattan.'

'I had no idea. Why didn't you tell me before?'

'Chantal felt that it might get in the way of your work so I decided to wait.'

'Why would it have been a problem?'

'He's not a Party member. He's not interested in politics. You might have worried that I would talk about your work.'

'And why now?'

'I think we've waited long enough and I don't think that you need me any more.'

'Tell me about him. What sort of man is he? He must love you very much to have waited so long.'

'He's very gentle. He is dedicated to his music.' She smiled. 'A bit like you.'

'Does it mean you'll leave here?'

'Yes, we've got rooms near Prospect Park. But I'll go on working in the shop if you want me to.'

He nodded. 'When can I meet him?'

She shrugged. 'Any time.'

'There's no need for you to be involved in my work but we need the income from the bookshop and I'd be grateful if you carried on working here.'

'Of course I will.' She paused. 'Can I ask you something? Something personal.'

'Try me.'

'You must miss Chantal a lot.'

'I do, Anna. It haunts me.'

'I don't understand.'

'I feel I didn't do enough to help her.'

'What else could you have done?'

'The doctor told me of a hospital in Manhattan that specialised in treating patients with consumption. I didn't have enough money to pay for it and I asked my people in Moscow if I could borrow the money from my funds.'

'And what did they say?'

'Nothing. They didn't reply one way or another.'

'Are you sure they got your message?'

'Quite sure.'

'So what could you have done?'

'I could have just borrowed the money or used the money. Without their permission.'

'So why didn't you?'

He shrugged. 'Some people I have to deal with will only do the work for money. They squeeze us dry. I despise them for abusing the Party.'

'Go on.'

'I thought she was all right in the local hospital. I didn't realise how bad she was.'

She saw the tears on his cheeks and moved over to sit beside him, taking his hand in both of hers. 'You couldn't have known. How could you? I'm sure that they did all that could be done.'

'I wasn't even there when she died.'

'Andrei, she was unconscious for three days before she died. You couldn't have comforted her.'

'It was unforgivable.'

'Nothing's unforgivable. Grieve you must but your life has to go on. You have so much to do.'

'I know. I'll get on with it.'

'Just remember one thing, Andrei. There are no experts in loving and no scholars of living. We all just do our best.' She kissed him gently on his cheek.

But as she went to the kitchen to make his hot chocolate she wondered how he could still serve those monsters in Moscow, who so abused the people they pretended to protect.

A week after Anna's announcement Aarons got the orders to go to Vienna.

He travelled by bus to Toronto then by plane to Paris, where he had to wait for two days for a Soviet transport plane that was taking relief supplies of medical stores to Vienna. A car was waiting for him at Schwechat and as the driver tossed Aarons' bag onto the back seat he said to Aarons, 'It's a long time ago, comrade.' Then, seeing Aarons' blank look he held out his hand. 'Spassky, Gene Spassky. Saw you off at the station when you were on your way back to Paris. And I've been handling a lot of your traffic from New York. Welcome to Vienna.'

'I'm sorry. I didn't recognise you.'

'Jump in, we don't want to hang around. There's always people watching who comes in on Soviet planes.'

'Nice car – what is it?'

Spassky grinned. 'Nearly new BMW, we took it over from the deputy head of the Vienna Gestapo.'

As they turned onto the main road Spassky said, 'It's about eleven miles to the city centre. Have you been to Vienna before?'

'No.'

'We took it over in 1945 and now it's divided into five zones for the four Occupying Powers. One zone, the central First District is the International Bezirk. Outside the city boundary we control everything. The British are in the old embassy area and in Heitzing, the Yanks are in the best mansions and we're in two hotels on the Ringstrasse. That's where you'll be staying. A bit crowded but not bad.' He laughed. 'Trust the spies to get a good billet.'

'Do you know why they want me here?'

'Lensky's coming from Moscow to talk with you and I think he'll want you to go back to Moscow with him for a week or so. They want to talk to you about the Americans. They reckon you know them better than any of the diplomats.' He laughed. 'You should do. You actually live with the bastards, not in some bloody embassy.'

'What's Lensky doing now?'

'You'd better ask him, comrade. I know that he and some of the others rate you as our number one agent in the States. You'll get the red carpet treatment, don't worry.'

'And what do you do these days?'

'Much the same as way back. A kind of trouble-shooter. Plugging the holes in Churchill's Iron Curtain.'

181

Aarons was given a spacious room at the Imperial Hotel which looked over the Ringstrasse to the Soviet's other HQ in Vienna in the Grand Hotel. There were flowers and a bowl of fruit on the sideboard and an envelope with a red wax seal with his name on. When he opened it there was a thick wad of 50 schilling notes and a message saying that Lensky would be seeing him the next day.

Spassky had introduced him to the senior officers of the Vienna Residency and he had been invited to eat with them in the evening. He had been taken to a conference room where agents were being lectured about the American and British agents in the city. A projector throwing photographs onto a screen. Men's faces with their names and the lecturer giving details of the kind of work that they did. Some in uniform and some in civilian clothes.

He listened with interest to the details of one man. The picture on the screen was of a young man in his early twenties. A pleasant open face, hair blowing in the wind and sergeant's stripes on his battle-dress sleeve.

'The name is Williams. Trevor Williams. Twenty-four years old. Rank – sergeant. Unit – 291 Field Security Section. Speaks Russian and German. Used on surveillance in civilian clothes. Interests – music and photography. Bought Leica IIIb camera on black-market for cigarettes. Has girl-friend Ursula Fleischer, lives in rooms on the Ring paid for by Williams. Further details available File 0/291/8.'

There followed pictures of agents' cars and their registration plates and some background information on the top men of the British and American intelligence organisations. After a short break there was an instruction film showing how to use a three-man 'box' for surveillance of a trained agent.

The evening meal was in the same conference room. About thirty officers. Good food, local wine and a pianist playing the romantic melodies that Vienna had always inspired. Half a dozen senior men took him into a small annexe and asked him to talk about the United States. Not his work but his assessment of the Americans' intentions. He was surprised from their questions how little they knew about conditions in America. Glances exchanged as he talked of the food and goods available in the stores and sharp questions as to why if things were as good as he described were there strikes and discontent. They were tough, dedicated men but strangely ignorant and naive about the rest of the world. It didn't seem to enter their minds that their own agents and the Comintern might have contributed to the unrest. And it wasn't his job to inform them. To each his own sphere of operations. There was even disbelief and distrust on some of their faces. But Aarons was used to that. In the days in America when he had been working for the Comintern he had seen the same look on the faces of Party members who didn't accept his explanation of Moscow's actions. But more often than not he had been proved right as time went by. Patience had always been his virtue.

Spassky had taken him to Lensky's suite of rooms. There were several men talking with Lensky but Lensky broke away from the group and walked over, hand outstretched, a hug, a kiss on each cheek and then a nod of dismissal to the waiting men.

When they were alone Lensky said, 'I'm glad you were able to come, Andrei. I wanted to talk to you before I take you to Moscow.' He smiled. 'There are a lot of people who want to talk to you. You're a very important man these days.'

Aarons half-smiled. 'I really don't think so.'

'My dear chap, you're unique. There's nobody else who has achieved the total approval of the top men in the Comintern and then gone on to even more approval for his work for the intelligence service.'

'I just do what I was trained to do.' He shrugged. 'I carry out my orders as best I can.'

'You're a modest man, Andrei. Almost too modest.'

He paused. 'I sometimes wonder if you wouldn't be more useful in Moscow.'

Andrei shrugged. 'Whatever you wish, Comrade Lensky.'

'We'll see. We'll see.' Lensky reached into his jacket pocket and brought out a folded sheet of paper, handing it to Aarons who unfolded it and read it. It was a letter on official internal notepaper, a statement confirming officially that he was now an intelligence officer with the rank of full colonel, and signed by the deputy-director in charge of administration.

Aarons looked up at Lensky. 'Thanks. But I don't need sweeteners.'

'It's not a sweetener, my friend. It's just formal and official recognition of work done. I just wish your father was still alive to enjoy it. He would have been so proud of you. Now let me tell you about some of the people you'll be meeting in Moscow. We shall be flying there tomorrow afternoon.'

They had landed at a military airfield south-east of Moscow. A large black car had taken them into the city and Aarons had been given rooms in the same block as Lensky's home. They ate together in a small restaurant in the building in Dzerdzhinski Square. When the meal was over he had walked with Lensky to Red Square and Lensky had pointed out Lenin's Mausoleum, St Basil's, the Historical Museum and the walls of the Kremlin.

As they sat on a bench by the Tomb of the Unknown Soldier Lensky said, 'Are you warm enough? It's cold for only September.'

'I'm fine.'

'Good. I wanted to talk to you before we start our meetings tomorrow. You know more about what's going on in New York and Washington than in Moscow. I thought you ought to know some of the background on what's going on here.' He paused and looked around then back at Aarons. 'There's a great struggle for power. Stalin encourages the rivalries. At the moment there are several different areas of strife. In the Politburo between Malenkov and Beria. Differences on agricultural policy. We fall far short of our needs for grain. The generals want their share of power and that affects our foreign policy. What worries me most is our almost complete ignorance of the rest of the world. Especially Europe and the United States. We have basements full of reports and summaries of reports and they are all quite useless. Why? Because the people who write them write what they think the Politburo wants to hear.' He spread his arms. 'So we not only have unreliable information but we add to the prejudices of top men in the Kremlin who've never even been out of the Soviet Union. We can't form foreign policy without having the facts. The truth.'

'How do I come into all this?'

'Andrei, when you were doing the job for the Comintern, you sent back reports that gave us an accurate picture of what Party members in America were saying and thinking. They were the only accurate reports we got.

'Since you've been working for us you've used your knowledge of America and Americans to send us information that has been invaluable. In many cases you obviously didn't know yourself the importance of what you were passing to us. But you gave us the pieces to fit in the jigsaw. Other people gave us gossip and in many cases it was just lies to justify their existence.'

'You still haven't told me how I come into all this.'

'In the time that you're here – no, before I say that let me say that your work has been read by many, many people. Important people. Influential people. Some of them set great store by your opinions. Others question them. So in the time that you're here you'll be talking with a lot of different people. I want you to be aware of these internecine rivalries that are going on. Not to be afraid to say what you mean but to say it bearing in mind that all your listeners have axes to grind that might be blunted by what you say. You understand what I'm getting at?'

Aarons smiled. 'I guess so. Tell me about Stalin.'

Lensky shook his head. 'Let me know what you hear before you go back. By the way, there are two names I'll mention to you among the others you'll meet. Petrenko and Noskov. They're significant. So watch your step.'

As Aarons lay in bed that night he was aware that despite what Lensky had said he was obviously expected to justify some of his reports and actions over the years in America. Lensky was obviously a man of great power in the Kremlin. He was no less friendly than he had always been but Aarons was aware that there had been none of the usual enquiries about his family. And no mention of Chantal's death. He also found it not so easy to speak Russian again. He found that he missed the easy fluency of New York slang.

The next morning the two of them had strolled through the Aleksandrovskii Gardens to the Kutafia Tower where both guards had checked Lensky's identity card and read carefully an official letter giving clearance for Aarons. They were checked again as they crossed over the bridge to the Trotskalia Tower. From there they had been escorted around a courtyard where young guards in uniform were goose-stepping, rehearsing for their watch at Lenin's tomb.

Aarons noticed that everywhere was spotlessly clean, paved with new stones, the buildings freshly painted and restored to look like new. The people seemed to be visitors. To the obvious disapproval of their escort Lensky stopped to show him one of the falconers with a goshawk attached by jesses to his leather gauntlet. The Kremlin area had always been pestered by too many crows and because the sound of gunfire in the Kremlin would be an embarrassment the falcons were used to keep down the crows.

Inside the Council of Ministers building they walked down long corridors on crimson carpeting, past offices with names on their doors. There was no name on the door that the guard opened. Inside was a room with comfortable leather armchairs, at least a dozen of them and a row of telephones on a trolley near the window. Tall, wooden double-doors gave onto a large room with a long table. There was a group of men, some in uniform, some talking, hands in pockets, some drinking coffee. They stopped talking and turned when Lensky led him into the room. After brief greetings they took their places at the table and a man in the grey clothes that junior intelligence officers tended to wear, placed triangular cards giving the name of each man around the table. One by one Lensky introduced them but without any identification of their jobs. One man half-smiled but the rest of them just nodded, their faces impassive. Only Petrenko of the two names Lensky had mentioned was among the people around the table.

When the introductions were over Lensky said, 'You've all read the summary that my staff have made giving details of the work done for the Comintern and for us by Andrei Grigorovich Aarons – and perhaps I should mention that he was recently promoted to colonel. He's on detachment in the United States. He is attached to Directorate S of the First Chief Directorate.

'Let me emphasise that this is an informal meeting. No notes to be made of questions or answers. This is only a short visit to Moscow by Colonel Aarons but there will be opportunities for individual interviews with him if it seems useful to me. So – please go ahead. Rykov, perhaps you'll start and we'll go round the table clockwise from you.'

There were eight men around the table and Rykov was sitting opposite Aarons.

'The discontent in the American army, comrade, what can we do to help it along?'

'It's too late to do anything now. Most of them are already back home. It's no longer an issue.'

'What part did our people play in the protests?'

'My own network was not involved at all, but there were a lot of our people in the army, ex-CIO men and union officials used to organising protests. But most of it was spontaneous.'

'Why did the officers let them get away with it?'

Aarons smiled. 'The officers wanted to go home too. You have to remember that Americans have a natural dislike for any kind of discipline. Their constitution is based on individual rights. There's very little about a man's obligations to the state or the government. You have to see them as what they are. Rather like children in many ways. Irresponsible, rather selfish and living in a society which tells them that it's every man for himself.'

A man at the far end of the table said, 'Oranskii. When we arranged for your documentation in New York we included a driver's licence in your cover name. You refused to accept it. Why?'

Aarons shrugged. 'Because I can't drive a car. If I came under suspicion and it was discovered that I had a licence to drive but wasn't able to drive they would ask why I needed a licence and how I'd obtained it.'

'There are plenty of reasons you could give them.'

'Comrade Oranskii, I'm a bookseller not a lawyer.'

'That's just a cover, you don't have to behave and think like a bookseller.'

'That's where you're wrong. It's not a cover. I *am* a bookseller. I buy and sell books. I live off the proceeds of my bookshop not off State funds that are needed for other things. If ever I stop thinking and believing that I'm a bookseller I shall cease to be a useful asset in New York.'

Two or three of them spoke at once and Aarons nodded towards a man with a moustache who said, 'I'm Ustinov.' He paused. 'When you were working for the Comintern way back you gave explanations of Soviet actions that some American Party members disagreed with. Who, in

188

Moscow, supplied your information and arguments?'

Aarons smiled. 'I gave the explanations that I considered a correct interpretation of Moscow's actions and motives. There was very little communication back to here in those days. And there was seldom any need for consultation. It was best that I was not pre-informed. I got the news like any other Party member – from newspapers and the radio.'

'Did you ever disagree with Moscow's actions even if you didn't say so?'

'No. The actions that some people disagreed with always had a rational explanation to my mind. I gave them that explanation.'

'And they always agreed?'

Aarons laughed. 'Not always. There are always people who see themselves as strong supporters – but who want to criticise. They think it's leadership, but others see it as self-importance. The odd ones don't matter. It's useful sometimes to let them be the devil's advocate.'

A man who gave his name as Gitlov said, 'If you were needed to do other work have you anyone in your network who could take over?'

Aarons shook his head. 'No. For two reasons. First of all my kind of network should be run by a Russian national, a Soviet. And secondly nobody else in the network knows any of the others. It would be too time consuming and elaborate to use a traditional system of cut-outs. If any one person was caught by the FBI the only other person he or she could expose would be me.' He smiled. 'And like I said it would be hard to prove that I was anything other than a bookseller – because I am just that.'

'What do you see as the most likely cause of you being uncovered?'

'I think my weakest link is communication both ways. Most of what I get comes here by radio. That means more schedules to cut down transmission times or someone to come up with a speedier kind of Morse. Some day the FBI will have more radio-detection facilities than they have at present.'

As time went by it became more like chatting than questions and answers, and with a break for lunch the talk had gone on for nearly four hours before Lensky closed the session.

Back in Lensky's apartment Lensky was obviously pleased with Aarons' performance. Gone was the rather passive man who Lensky usually saw and here was a man confident in his decisions who had obviously impressed most of the men at the meeting. And none of them were men who were easily impressed. The KGB promotion had been a gesture, a recognition of Aarons' loyalty and work. But at the meeting Aarons had looked and sounded like a colonel, an expert talking about his speciality.

There had been several meetings the next day with individuals and the word seemed to have gone around about the man in New York. A loyal Soviet but who could think like Americans thought. There had been ten minute interviews with Malenkov, Beria, Khrushchev and Marshal Zhukov and he had been taken to a reception in the Kremlin for the French Ambassador where he had not only seen Stalin but had been taken over to have his hand shaken by the great man himself.

On the last day of his visit Lensky told him that he was to be given unlimited funds and was to extend his network to cover more contacts with politicians and advanced technology. They wanted information on technical advances that would save them the billions of roubles that would be involved in research. So far as the politicians were concerned they wanted him as a reference point on American intentions. The feeling of Congress and the attitude of the public to current events. Lensky made clear that the Washington embassy's views would be the official source but from time to time Moscow would want his thinking and analysis.

He was flying back via Helsinki and Toronto and as they

waited at the airfield Lensky said, 'You've done well for us, Andrei, but what pleases me most is that you've impressed people while you've been here. They'll take a lot of notice of what you think in future. You're not part of the internal fighting. I've made sure that you've met all the rivals so that whoever comes out on top in the end they'll see you as a valuable aid to their thinking. You're on nobody's side, you're neutral. And you're in New York not Moscow, thank God.' He smiled. 'I was going to say take care of yourself but I think you're one of those people who just go on their own sweet way and somebody above looks after them.'

24

As they ate their evening meal together Aarons realised that to the other three he was an outsider. Someone outside their easy-going circle. Ivan obviously knew Sam Fisher well. He must have known about Anna and Sam for years. They were like old friends the three of them, relieved now that the introductions were over and that there was no longer any need for any subterfuge.

He had never seen Anna looking like that before. Not just beautiful but smiling, relaxed and confident. And he realised that it was her relationship with Sam Fisher that gave her that confidence.

He liked Sam Fisher, he was a smiling man and gentle and showed no sign of resentment that Andrei had been the unwitting cause of them not being married long ago.

After the meal Anna had said that she was going out for an hour with Ivan to choose a birthday present for Rachel Henschel.

As they settled down with their coffee Aarons said, 'I'm sorry that I seem to have got in the way of you and Anna being married. I didn't know, I assure you.'

'Not to worry, Andrei. We've been very happy together.' He smiled. 'But I'm glad we've met at last.'

'Anna told me that you play piano in clubs and hotels in New York. How long have you been doing this?'

Fisher laughed. 'Since I was sixteen. I was lucky. It's the only thing I ever wanted to do.'

'What kind of music do you play?'

'Depends on the place. Sometimes it's Gershwin, or

Berlin or Kern. Sometimes it's jazz. Blues and rags. That sort of stuff. Stride piano for the clubs with pink lampshades and Scott Joplin if the lights are bright.'

'What's stride piano?'

'Well, technically single bass notes on the first and third beats and chords on the second and fourth. Like Fats Waller plays.' Fisher smiled as he saw Andrei's blank look. 'You've never heard of Fats Waller?'

'I'm afraid not.'

Fisher laughed amiably. 'We'd better take you in hand. Have you ever been to a night-club?'

'No. Never.' Aarons shook his head and looked amazed at the question.

'I'm playing in a club tomorrow night. It's quite pleasant. No hookers. No gangsters. How about you bring Anna, it's a club she likes.'

'Where is it?'

'It's on West 52nd between Fifth and Sixth Avenues.'

'Are you sure I won't be an embarrassment to you?'

Fisher looked surprised. 'Why should I be embarrassed?'

Aarons shrugged. 'I don't drink. I don't know about jazz. And I don't know how to behave in a night-club.'

'Anna will look after you. I'm doing a special George Gershwin evening. Both his parents were Russians from Petrograd. Some musicians say they can hear a Russian sound in his music. See what you think.'

The trip to the club had been a surprising success. Andrei had loved the music and was impressed by Sam's playing. Sam was obviously a star performer so far as the club members were concerned and so many people had come over to chat to Anna. There had been only a moment's hesitation when the waiter asked Andrei what he would like to drink.

'Could I have a glass of cold milk?'

'The drinks are on the house, Mr Aarons.'

'That's very nice. Well, maybe a hot chocolate if that's possible.'

'Certainly sir,' the waiter said and back in the kitchen he'd sent one of the boys to an Italian coffee shop down the block.

There was a Gershwin tune that Andrei particularly liked, Sam had played it three times for him. It was a tune called 'Liza'.

Andrei stayed for two hours and then left to catch the last subway train back to Brighton Beach. Anna stayed on with Sam Fisher.

It was 4 a.m. when Sam Fisher drove Anna back home. The roads were virtually empty and they had stopped to look at the building in Prospect Park where they were to rent their apartment. Sam wasn't rich but he earned good money and the new place was being redecorated inside. There was enough space for Sam to have a piano and music room.

As he stood with his arm around her waist he said, 'There's enough room for Andrei to live with us if you wanted.'

She looked up at his face. 'What made you say that?'

'He's going to be very lonely when you've gone.'

'But that's how he's always been. He's always been a loner. Even when Chantal was alive.'

'I think you're wrong, honey. That's just a pose.'

'Why should he pose?'

'I don't know but it is just a pose. I'm sure of that.'

'How can you be so sure?'

'The Gershwin piece he liked so much – "Liza." Gershwin's ballads all have words. They say what they're about. And when a piece has words it belongs to the singer not the composer. "The Man I Love" and "Somebody Loves Me", for instance belong to half a dozen vocalists.' He smiled. 'Only jazz buffs remember who wrote "Tiger Rag" but how many people could tell you who wrote "Please"? They would probably say Bing Crosby wrote it.'

'I still don't understand.'

'Everybody thought that George Gershwin was a loner. That's what he seemed to be. That was what he wanted to be. But he wasn't a loner. The melody of "Liza" is the real Gershwin. Lush and loving, warm and longing. He came to hear me play some years ago and I spoke to him about "Liza". I said what I just told you. He got up from the table and walked away.'

'What made you think of all this?'

He smiled and shrugged. 'It's part of music and playing music. You don't just think about the notes on the paper but the white spaces in between as well.'

'And Andrei is the spaces in between.'

'You've got it, honey.'

'And what am I?'

He laughed. 'A beautiful chord in B flat minor – *sostenuto*.'

'You're an idiot and I love you so much.'

'It's freezing, we'd better go.'

As Anna lay in bed she thought about what Sam had said about her brother. She felt guilty that she wasn't able to tell Sam about Andrei's work. He never talked with her or Ivan about it but she knew that the things he asked them to do were all part of it. A chalked cross on a wall, a package in the cistern of a toilet in the cinema in Brooklyn. Dialling a telephone number and when it was answered saying that one word and then hanging up. A card tossed into a trash basket at the Union Square subway exit. Standing by a certain painting in the Museum of Modern Art so that a man could slip a catalogue into her shopping basket. The picture was always Picasso's *Guernica*.

Cohen and his Manya had moved to a studio on East 10th Street near Washington Square. Manya was working on the cosmetics counter at Macy's.

They were married in the third week of February and

Aarons had attended the wedding but had not gone to the reception. Thanks to Aarons the bride's nationality on the marriage certificate was Canadian.

In the same week Anna and Sam were married. Aarons had looked so solemn that several people had assumed that he was the father of the bride. They had a family party that night at the club where Sam had taken Andrei. There was a seven-piece jazz band that night but Sam had played one tune for his bride. It was 'Love Walked In' and Rachel Henschel had sung the words at the microphone and had been applauded by all the patrons.

Anna and Sam went back to their apartment at Prospect Park and Ivan disappeared with his girl.

The rooms above the shop seemed very empty as Andrei made himself a jug of hot chocolate. Despite the late hour he had opened the parcel of books that he had bought earlier that day at Weiser's near Union Square.

25

Serov knew that the airports would be watched by men from the embassy and he took a train from Paris to Brussels and then a local train to Bruges.

He spent three days in Bruges, walking around the beautiful old town, trying to decide what exactly he should do. He had no contacts in Britain and the only contact he had in America was Malloy. He had no idea how to contact Malloy and he would have great difficulty in getting a visa for the USA. All he could do was make contact with the US embassy in Britain and see if they would help him contact Malloy.

He made his way to London without any problems and booked in at a small hotel in Sussex Gardens and asked where the US embassy was located. They showed him on a street map and he walked along Bayswater Road to Marble Arch, then down Park Lane, turning off to the left to get to Grosvenor Square.

At the foot of the wide steps to the embassy he hesitated for a moment, then took a deep breath and walked on up to the door. There was a US Marine on duty in the foyer and when Serov looked around for some indication of the right place to go the marine said, 'Can I help you, sir?'

'You have CIA officer in the building, yes?'

But the embassy Marines were trained not to answer that kind of question. The Marine said patiently, 'Who do you want to see?'

'Any CIA man. Any intelligence officer.'

'Can you tell me what it's about?'

'I'm a Soviet intelligence officer. I want to come over, to have political asylum.'

For a moment the Marine sergeant looked intently at Serov's face, and then he said, 'Come with me, sir. I'll get someone to talk to you.'

The sergeant stood close to Serov as they walked down a wide corridor with the sergeant talking into a portable telephone so quickly that Serov couldn't understand what he was saying.

As they got to the far end of the corridor a door opened and another Marine sergeant came out, and the first Marine handed him over.

'This is the gentleman who wants to speak to somebody.'

The other sergeant smiled. 'Come in my office and make yourself comfortable, Mr . . . I didn't get your name, sir.'

'I did not give my name.'

'OK, sir. Do sit down, make yourself comfortable. I've asked for somebody to come and see you.' He smiled. 'I guess you'll understand that I need to just check you over.'

Serov shrugged and raised his arms, standing there passively as the sergeant patted him over. But he was clean.

It was nearly twenty minutes before a tall grey-haired man walked into the office. He looked at Serov for a few moments and then nodded to the sergeant who left the office and the civilian took the sergeant's seat at the desk. His face was impassive as he leaned forward, his elbows on the desk.

'How can I help you?'

'Are you CIA officer?'

'Just tell me how I can help you.'

'I am major in the Soviet intelligence service. I want to talk to Mr Bill Malloy.'

'Who is Mr Malloy?'

'He was captain in OSS during the war. We were in Resistance together.'

'Where?'

'In France.'

'What were you doing there?'

'Working for Captain Malloy.'

'But you're Russian, aren't you?'

'Yes. But I lived in France many years before the war.'

'How long have you been in intelligence?'

'Since just before the war in Europe.'

'What rank were you?'

'Now I am major.'

'Your name?'

'In French Resistance it was Pascal. In real it is Serov. Igor Alexandrovich Serov.'

'What were you doing for them after the war?'

'I spot for them. Agents of influence. I know many important French people.'

'Why do you want to meet this man Malloy?'

'I want to come over – to have political asylum.'

'And why Malloy?'

'He is only man of yours that I know and trust.'

'Are they looking for you – your people?'

'Not yet. In three, four days maybe.'

'That means you were an illegal. Not based on the embassy.'

'Is correct.'

'You'd better sleep here tonight. Do you have any bags?'

'No, nothing.'

Friedman went back to his office and made notes of his talk with Serov and then put a call through to Langley, to Harris. He was put through almost immediately.

'Harris.'

'Hank, we've got a walk-in. Says he's a Soviet. Been operating in France as an illegal.'

'What do you think? Is he a plant?'

'Who knows. But I think we'd better take him through the course.'

'Why's he come to us not the French?'

199

'He wants to talk to an American named Bill Malloy. Says Malloy was in OSS in France during the war and he worked with him. Says he's the only man he trusts.'

'I'll check the records and call you back. What's your guy's name?'

'Cover name was Pascal. Claims his real name is Serov. Rank of major. Igor Alexandrovich.'

'OK.' Harris paused. 'You've got him there?'

'Yes.'

Harris was waiting for them at the airport and took them straight to a car without going through the immigration check. Serov had slept on the long flight but by the time they got to the safe-house he seemed overawed by the traffic and bustle of Washington on a Saturday night.

Harris showed Serov the suite of rooms he would occupy on the top floor of the pleasant old house. He seemed impressed, and they ate, the three of them together, in a large room that covered the whole of the ground floor. They were sitting around a low coffee table after the meal when Serov said, 'What did Malloy say when you told him?'

'We haven't contacted Mr Malloy as yet, Serov. He's no longer in the intelligence business.' He smiled. 'But there's no reason why you shouldn't meet him when you and I have had a talk.'

Serov shook his head. 'First I talk with Malloy. Then if he says OK I talk with you.' He shrugged. 'And anyone else. But first Malloy.'

Harris glanced at Friedman who leaned forward and filled Serov's cup from the coffee jug. 'Tell us about your work in France, Mr Serov. Just a general outline.'

'And if I don't talk with you people you don't let me stay in USA?'

'Mr Serov, you're an experienced intelligence officer, you must know that no intelligence organisation would accept a man from the opposition without trying to make sure that his reasons for coming over are genuine.' He stood up, smiling. 'Tomorrow you and I will go shopping. Get you some clothes and things. There are shaving things in your bathroom. Have a good night's sleep. I think we both need one.'

'Am I safe here?'

'Absolutely. Don't worry about that. I shall be here too. I'll show you back to your rooms.'

When Friedman came back Harris was waiting for him with fresh coffee.

'Were you able to trace this guy Malloy?'

'Yes. He's a lawyer. He's a partner in a Manhattan law firm.' He looked at Friedman. 'I don't see why we should involve him. Not at this stage anyway.'

'Why not?'

'It's not his business. If Serov wants to defect then he's got to talk to us.' Seeing Friedman's frown he said, 'Maybe when we've got him straightened out we'll see if Malloy wants to talk to him.'

'Are you doubtful about Serov?'

'I'm always doubtful about walk-ins until we've put them through the wringer.'

Friedman smiled. 'I must get some sleep.'

26

A month of talking and questioning went by before they were satisfied that it was unlikely that Serov was a plant. Experience made them cautious. Too often in the past a defector had been hailed as a great prize in the continuous intelligence game, only to be doubted or even exposed as time went by. There was no litmus paper that turned purple as proof of genuineness. Moscow's plants were not sent like lambs to the slaughter. They had sometimes been singled out and trained over years for their role, and all the interrogations and polygraph tests wouldn't dent, let alone break, their covers.

But Serov had none of the arrogance of some Soviet defectors, and he asked for no great rewards. Just the chance to live with CIA protection in the United States without harassment and free from the bureaucracy that he had come to despise and hate.

The information that he gave them about both past and current Soviet operations in France was useful but not dramatic. His knowledge of the rivalries and machinations in Moscow politics were, in fact, invaluable, but at that level of the CIA it was just seen as gossip. They valued most his detailed knowledge of how the Soviets had penetrated French politics and the French security services. There were lessons to be learnt there. His knowledge of the inner workings of the Moscow political scene seemed an irrelevance. The names were unfamiliar and there were too many to be absorbed. All the details were noted but at that time in the Cold War what mattered to the CIA was the Soviet's intelligence operations in the United States.

Three months after Serov had walked into the embassy in London he was offered new documentation and a modest post in the CIA's analytical section evaluating French documents. He had asked a couple of times about meeting Malloy but there had been no response from his handlers. When Serov discovered that one of the other men in the section had been in OSS in France he asked him about Malloy. The man had worked in the south of France whereas Serov and Malloy had been in Occupied France. But the man had vaguely heard of Malloy and thought that he was now a lawyer in New York. When the man found that Serov was originally Russian he said his wife was Polish-American and told him that there was a place in Brooklyn where everybody was originally Russian or Polish. You could hardly hear anyone speaking English. They had Russian newspapers and magazines, Russian delicatessens, cafés and shops. The man had laughed and said that New Yorkers called it 'Odessa by the Sea' although its real name was Brighton Beach and you went through it on the subway on your way to Coney Island.

Serov had hesitated for two weeks, curious to see this Russian community but worried that he might be recognised. It seemed unlikely because he had spent most of his time in France. His visits to Moscow had been made in typical secrecy and his time there had been spent with people who were too important and privileged to end up in a Brooklyn ghetto. It seemed crazy, but he was homesick for Moscow. Maybe not Moscow itself but for silver-birch trees and *piroshky*. Even in France he had sometimes felt this homesickness. But in those days he could just go to Moscow and a day with those bastards would be cure enough.

It was a Saturday when he took the bus to New York and made the long subway journey to Brighton Beach. It was just like he'd been told. He stood at the cross-roads and looked across at the dilapidated clapboard building that advertised Bar-mitzvah instruction on a crudely painted board. Facing him across the street was a car-repair shop and next to it a paint and wallpaper store. He looked up at the street signs and followed the sign that said Brighton Beach Avenue.

Both sidewalks of the avenue were crowded with people. Shopping, window-gazing, talking in groups. He heard snatches of conversation in Yiddish and Russian. At the entrance steps to the subway he crossed the avenue and stopped to look in a junk-shop. There was a row of old-fashioned charcoal irons, a tray of dusty medals, odd pieces of decorated china, a concertina, and a violin without strings and an album of faded postcards with views of Petrograd. Serov moved on slowly, past a book-shop where he glanced briefly at the secondhand books arranged in rows. They were mostly Russian politics but in the centre of the front row was a book in English. Isaiah Berlin's *Karl Marx*. As he passed on to the jewellers shop he stopped, standing still, thinking. It was the French translation of that book that the Soviet intelligence service used in France as a means of recognition. You asked to see the book. They told you it wasn't for sale. You gave the password and then they gave you the meeting place, the time of the meeting and the day. For several moments he hesitated then he went back and looked again at the book. Then he looked beyond the book inside the shop. There was a dark-haired woman at a desk, typing slowly with two fingers on an old-fashioned typewriter.

As the woman pulled the sheet of paper from the type-writer she glanced briefly towards the window and Serov before she rolled another sheet of paper into the machine. Serov saw that she was extraordinarily beautiful. The calm face and the dark heavy-lidded eyes reminded him of someone. He couldn't think who. Maybe it was some film actress he had seen. She didn't look like an agent but he was tempted to see what happened.

The brass bell over the shop door clanged as he pushed the door open and the woman looked at him, smiling, 'Can I help you?'

She spoke in English but Serov said in Russian. 'I'd like to buy the biography of Karl Marx in the window.'

The smile on the woman's face faded and for a moment she looked embarrassed. Then she said quietly, 'I'm not sure how much it is. I'll have to ask the manager. I won't be a moment.'

He watched her walk to the stairway half-way down a narrow corridor. He looked around at the walls of the shop and the shelves of books as he waited, most of them were second-hand. But all of them obviously cared for. Then she came down the stairs followed by a tall man. And as the man came out from the shadow of the corridor he stood quite still, staring at Serov. They recognised each other immediately but there was disbelief on both their faces.

It was Serov who spoke first. 'I can't believe it, Andrei.'

Andrei smiled. 'Me too, comrade, me too.'

They hugged and kissed, laughing, but there were tears on their cheeks and the woman stood watching them, smiling. Anna didn't remember Serov from the days in Paris.

As Andrei poured a cup of tea for his visitor he wondered if Serov had been sent over by Moscow to check on him. And he wondered why Serov had grown a beard. It didn't suit him. But he had no intention of asking him. It was Serov himself who said, 'Are you still Comintern now, Andrei, or intelligence?'

'Why do you ask? You must know already.'

Serov shook his head. 'I don't know, Andrei. But I need an answer.'

'Why?'

'That means you haven't heard about me.'

'About what?'

'I defected, Andrei. Walked out and asked the Americans for political asylum.'

'I don't believe it. Why should you do that?'

Serov shrugged. 'I'd had enough. The rivalries, the corruption and the terrible cost to the people.' He sighed.

'Maybe over here you didn't know what was going on. How often do you go back to Moscow?'

Andrei smiled. 'Not as often as they want me to.'

'They're like wild animals, Andrei. Living like Tsars while the people starve. There are millions in the slave labour camps. Stalin killed every officer from marshal down to colonels. When the war started the Red Army had no senior officers.'

'Why should he do that?'

'He saw plots everywhere. He was paranoid. Everyone was an enemy, a rival. You've no idea what it was like. All those dreams we had were just that – dreams.' He paused. 'Tell me about you.'

Andrei shook his head, slowly. 'That wouldn't be wise after what you've just told me, would it?'

'You don't trust me, do you?'

'It's not a question of trust. It seems that we're now on different sides of the fence.' He paused. 'Do you work for the CIA now?'

'I just evaluate documents in the French section.' He smiled and shrugged. 'It's not much more than a clerk's job. I could leave if I wanted to. They weren't all that excited at my arrival.'

'When were you last in Moscow?'

'About a month before I walked out. Roughly six months ago.'

'What was your job in Paris?'

'Spotting people of influence who could keep us informed on French policy and internal politics. And people of influence who could help put over the Party policy.'

'Were you successful?'

'Yes. I think so. I got commendations from Moscow. I was treated as one of the *nomenklatura*.'

'Did you marry?'

'No. That would have got in the way of my work.'

'There must have been something that made you change your mind. What was it?'

Serov looked towards the window and then back at Andrei. 'When I realised that I no longer believed what I was telling other people. When I realised that good, honest people – Party members – believed what I said only because it was me who was saying it.' He shrugged. 'I knew too much, Andrei. I knew what was really going on and I wasn't prepared to deceive those people any longer. Nor deceive myself either.'

'Do you live in New York?'

'No. In Washington.'

'Do you want to sleep here for tonight?'

Serov looked surprised. 'Are you sure you don't mind?'

Andrei stood up. 'Of course I don't mind.' He smiled. 'You may be stupid but you're still Serov and that's all that matters.'

Serov looked at him and said quietly, 'That's the nicest thing anyone has said to me for a long, long time.'

'So. Do you want to stay?'

'Yes, please.'

'Why are we speaking Russian?'

Serov laughed. 'Because it's easier than American.'

Despite what Serov had told him he said nothing to the family and when they all ate together that evening they spent their time talking about when they were all in Paris. Andrei said very little, listening to the rest of them chattering about those days that had seemed so innocent and full of hope.

The next day he had taken Serov to the beach and as they sat looking at the sea Serov said, 'Don't let any of them know that you've met me, or you'll end up in one of the Gulag labour camps.'

'You really think that I matter so little to them?'

Serov shook his head in disbelief. 'You haven't learned a thing, Andrei, have you? They wouldn't hesitate for a second. None of us matter. We're just puppets on a string.' He looked at Andrei as he spoke. 'The revolution ended when Stalin took over. When you and I were telling everybody about the wonders of communism there was no such thing. What Moscow gave us was Bolshevism. Dictatorship by a handful of men with a hundred thousand hangers-on waiting for their turn at the pig trough. They have luxury houses, radios, furniture, everything they want. But the people live in poverty, afraid of the local Party men who rule their lives.' He shook his head. 'Is that what you work for, my friend?'

'But you were one of the privileged yourself. Why the sudden change?'

Serov turned to look at Andrei. 'It wasn't sudden.' He paused as if searching for the right words and then said, 'Haven't you ever – just once maybe – thought that it was dictatorship not a government in Moscow?'

Andrei didn't reply and Serov went on. 'You don't have to answer me, Andrei. I know the answer. You're the same as me. You come from a family background that was always Marxist. You took it all for granted. You never worked it out for yourself. And you end up as a Jew without a religion and a Russian without a country. You've made your life in the Party and you've given up the rest of the world as the price you pay. How many friends have you got, Andrei? None. Party people like you pretend that you don't need friends. Not even Party friends. The truth is you couldn't trust any one of them for a second. You never worked it all out for yourself. You took it from your father and then the Party training. You were great at arguing the Party line but just think back. All you were doing was making a case for something that Moscow had done that even Party members found unacceptable. You were a stooge, Andrei, a *schlemiel*.'

Andrei smiled. 'If we've gone over to Yiddish there's an old saying – a fool can ask more questions in an hour than ten wise men can answer in a year.'

Serov laughed. 'There's another one too – fools search always for yesterday.' Then, his face serious again, Serov said, 'You should know better than me what you're here for. You're in intelligence because the Comintern doesn't work any more in America. Americans can see through all the Party lines. Soviet propaganda doesn't work here so people like you are only here to spy. The Party members here are the neurotics not the down-trodden. Even back in the Soviet Union nobody believes that Moscow are "the saviours of peace" and "the true democracy". It was a dream, Andrei, and it didn't work. They didn't even intend it to work, it's time to wake up.'

Andrei stood up slowly, brushing the sand from his clothes. 'We'd better go home. It's getting cold.'

'I'll get the subway to the bus depot and get back to Washington.' He looked at Andrei's face. 'Have you had enough of me?'

'What's that mean?'

'Can I come and see you all again?'

'Of course you can.'

'Are you going to tell Moscow that you've seen me?'

Andrei glanced briefly at Serov. 'You'd better leave that to me.'

Serov said, 'Can I ask you a personal question, Andrei?'

'I should think so.'

'When we were both in Paris I can remember you marrying a girl. A French girl. What happened to her?'

'She died.'

'I'm sorry, Andrei. Very sorry.'

'Phone me before you come next time.'

'I will. I will.'

As Aarons undressed that night to go to bed he arranged his clothes carefully on the chair beside the bed. He couldn't put out of his mind what Serov had told him. But it wasn't the first time that he had heard those stories. Some of it was probably true but exaggerated. It was like when a couple fall out of love and can only see the bad in someone they had once deeply loved. But he had no intention of mentioning Serov's visit in his reports to Moscow.

Serov had two rooms just north of Dupont Circle. It

was an old house and his rooms had high ceilings and big windows. There were two photographic prints on the main wall. One by Ansel Adams and one by Robert Doisneau that reminded him of Paris. There was a second-hand black and white TV on a small table alongside a record-player. Two armchairs and a coffee table were set in the bay window and a small dining table with four simple wooden chairs were in one corner of the room. The building he worked in was within walking distance of his rooms and he ate at a small French restaurant a block away from his home. Most of his colleagues saw him as living a strange restricted life as a recluse. But for Serov it was a small haven of peace without the torment of his conscience, no longer committed to supporting a regime he had grown to resent and even hate.

The accidental meeting with Andrei Aarons had only confirmed that he was right to have walked out. He was sad for his old colleague. The loyalty, the enthusiasm and the talent that had been so coldly abused from youth to middle-age.

27

In the first six months after his return from Moscow Aarons extended his network slowly and carefully but despite Moscow's comments and instructions he found it impossible to abandon his in-built interest in politics. He spent a lot more time with Myron Harper and most Wednesday and Sunday evenings they played bridge with two of Harper's friends. Although the other two had no inkling that Aarons was anything other than an unusually knowledgeable bookseller they assumed that like themselves he was on the left in politics.

The third player was another political journalist who wrote for a weekly magazine and was based in Washington although his home was in Brooklyn. The fourth player was a woman who worked for the New York headquarters of the Democrats. In her middle thirties, she was both intelligent and attractive and in private was quite openly sympathetic towards the Communists.

It was at one of the Sunday evening games that they sat around talking as usual of what was going on in New York and Washington. Nick Coletti had brought two bottles of wine and had poured them each a drink and there had been the usual cracks about Aarons' preference for hot chocolate or cold milk. When they were finally settled down the woman, Jo Lafferty, said, 'Has anyone read the piece by Walter Lippmann in the Tribune?'

Coletti laughed. 'You mean the reference to Mr X?'

'Yeah that's the one. Who is Mr X?'

'He's George Kennan, was at our embassy in Moscow

for a stretch.' Coletti looked at the others. 'Kennan did a report for Truman saying that the Soviet Union contained the seeds of its own decay and would eventually disintegrate. He went on to say that the Soviet Union must be resisted and confronted at every point where they are encroaching on the interests of a peaceful and stable world.'

Myron Harper said, 'And Truman believes him, hence the so-called Truman Doctrine. The Reds must be opposed on all fronts.'

Aarons said nothing as Jo Lafferty added, 'And Lippmann was saying that we couldn't do it even if we wanted to. We haven't got the forces to do it.'

Harper laughed. 'Nevertheless that's going to be our policy while the little guy from Missouri's in the White House.'

Aarons said quietly, 'How do the people in the White House justify such a policy?'

Harper shrugged. 'Because Moscow has been under the delusion that they won the war alone. And quite openly they're telling the world that they are the masters now. They look like drunks looking for a fight. And our little man was the wrong guy to try it on. Somebody should have warned 'em.'

Aarons said, 'Do you think he'll get a second term?'

Jo Lafferty said, 'Inside the Party they don't think he'll make it. They think Dewey will get a landslide.'

'What are Dewey's views on the Soviet Union?'

Coletti laughed. 'Nobody knows. Our Tom isn't talking policy until he's safely in the White House.' He stood up stretching his arms. 'You want a lift, Joanna?'

'That's very *galant* of you, Nicholas. Thank you.'

Aarons stayed on after the two had left and Harper brewed them a pot of tea. As they sat opposite each other Harper said, 'There's going to be a big campaign against the Party, Andrei. I've heard talk of a committee being set up to search out communists in government jobs. There's even talk that they're going to attack the Hollywood studios. Especially writers and directors.' He paused. 'You'd better warn your people. It's going to be rough.'

Aarons had sent a report to Moscow but there had been no comment from them.

By January 1948 Aarons was faced with a difficult decision. His network had grown, and living in Brighton Beach meant too much time and energy was spent in travelling. But he needed the bookshop as his cover. Common sense said that he should sell the bookshop and open another somewhere in Manhattan. He could sell the shop at enough profit to rent a central shop but Aarons resented having to make the move to facilitate his work for Moscow. For him, running a network was just a matter of careful administration and caution. He was aware of its potential dangers but indifferent to the possibility of being caught. He was quite sure that nobody would penetrate his security or his cover. Moscow seemed to be pleased with the information he passed back to them, but his mind was always focused on the successful development of Marxism. All those years working for the Comintern had taught him how to read the thoughts behind the actions of the men in the Kremlin. And his years in the United States had made it possible for him to think like an American. And now, as they faced each other, pawing the ground, he could have been of real help to Moscow. Their ambassador in Washington had no idea of what ordinary Americans thought. He never met any, he lived a secluded life of comparative luxury. He couldn't even speak the language.

Why couldn't those men sitting around the table listening to him see that he could help them far more his way than working out dead-drops in outside toilets, derelict buildings, holes in trees in Central Park and under benches in Bryant Park? And all for what? A copy of the minutes of some Congressional committee, a training manual for US Navy radio operators, the blue-prints of a gyroscopic sight for the guns on new tanks, a copy of the White House's internal telephone directory and the radio frequencies used by the FBI in Washington. Maybe he should talk to Lensky.

Two well-established Armenian refugees had bought the shop and Aarons had sold them most of his stock. It would not be suitable for a shop in Manhattan.

He had taken a two-year lease on a shop on West 41st Street between Fifth and Sixth Avenues, a shop with two floors of living accommodation above it. Both the shop and the living quarters were almost derelict but he had made so much profit on selling the Brighton Beach shop and the stock that he could well afford the cost of repairs and decoration.

The new shop was within walking distance of the New York Public Library and he was going to specialise in classics and scholarly books. Ivan had agreed to move with him and once they were established he intended hiring an assistant to help Ivan. They stayed at a nearby hotel for three weeks until their new place was ready but in the meantime Aarons bought books for his new stock and left details of the shop at the library, where one of the librarians had told him that Trotsky had been a frequent reader when he was in New York. They saw Anna and Sam several times where Sam was playing. It would be an exaggeration to say that Aarons was happy in those few weeks but both Anna and Ivan noticed that he was more relaxed than they had ever seen him before. At least since Chantal's death.

28

Serov was amazed at the grumbles of some of his American colleagues complaining about life in Washington DC. He enjoyed his life and became more and more a typical American immigrant, sometimes a little homesick for his roots but on the whole enjoying the optimism and energy of Americans.

His life became even more enjoyable when he found a girl-friend. But it would be more accurate to say that she found him, for Serov kept himself to himself, intent on offending nobody in his new environment. She was a waitress at a local café and she had rather liked the diffident man who came in every day for a coffee and a beef sandwich. She had got into conversation with him one day when she saw him reading a film magazine. They talked about *From Here to Eternity* which neither of them had seen. She'd eventually worked him round to asking her to go to see the film with him.

When she had got to know him better she was amused by his pessimism, and as they sat with a beer each one evening after a trip to the movies she said, 'You know you'll never be an American if you don't get more positive.' She laughed. 'Even Bing Crosby sings about "accentuate the positive".'

'You don't like how I am?'

She smiled. 'I like you a lot, honey, but you always look on the bad side of things.'

'Like what?'

She shrugged. 'I can't explain. I spoke to my dad about

you.' She smiled. 'He says it's because you're a Russian. He says all Russians are gloomy and all Americans are optimists. If things are bad they'll get better. You understand?'

He smiled. 'I'll try to be like that.' He paused. 'Do you really like me a lot?'

She burst out laughing. 'There you go again. Yes, I like you a lot.'

'Enough to marry me?'

'We've only known one another a few months. Let's just see how it works out.' She put her hand across the table on his. 'You must come and meet my family. You'll like them.'

'What does your father do?'

'He's a mailman and Moma works in a laundry.'

'It must be nice having a family.'

'How about next Sunday – come for lunch?'

'Are you sure?'

She laughed. 'I'll send you an engraved invitation.'

Serov had made the long journey down to Brighton Beach and had been shocked when he found that Aarons no longer ran the bookshop, but the new owners gave him Aarons' address in Manhattan.

At the new shop Aarons was out and Serov sat talking with Ivan waiting for Aarons to come back.

'Are you married, Ivan?'

'No.'

'Girl-friend?'

'Kind of.'

'What's that mean?'

'She can't make her mind up. Playing the field. Seeing if anything better turns up.'

'And you?'

'I've given her two months. If she ain't made her mind up by then I'll call it a day.'

'What's she looking for?'

'Who knows. A guy with a red convertible and plenty

216

of spending money.' He paused. 'How about you. You got a girl?'

'Yeah. How's Andrei?'

Ivan shrugged, smiling. 'Who knows. You never can tell with him.'

'Did he tell you about me?'

Ivan nodded. 'Yeah.'

'Was he angry with me?'

'I've never seen Andrei angry. Never. It's not his way.'

'Why have you moved up here?'

'You'll have to ask Andrei.'

'Do you remember me from Paris?'

'Just vaguely. It's a long time ago.' He looked towards the door. 'Here's Andrei now.'

They had eaten at a small Italian restaurant just off Times Square and afterwards Andrei had taken Serov back to the apartment. As Serov looked around he said, 'Why did you move up here?'

'We needed more space.'

'Isn't it more dangerous up here?'

Andrei smiled. 'Selling books isn't dangerous, Igor.'

Serov shrugged. 'They'll get you one of these days. The Americans have got a mania about Reds. Why don't you just stick to the books. Can you live on the books?'

'That's what I do live on, my friend.'

'Did you tell them you'd seen me?'

For a moment Aarons hesitated, then he shook his head. 'No. I didn't tell them.'

'Why not?'

Aarons shook his head. 'What did you do when the Germans took France?'

'I worked in the French Resistance.'

'With the English?'

'The network I worked for was run by an American. He was OSS.'

'What's that?'

'The Office of Strategic Services. It's the CIA now.'

217

'What were you doing after the war?'

'I stayed in France. I was working for Moscow. Spotting and recruiting agents of influence.'

'How did you get over here?'

'I got to London and went to the US embassy.' He smiled. 'I was a walk-in. I had a long de-briefing. I don't think they were very impressed.'

'And now?'

'Like I told you, I work in the CIA's French section evaluating documents.'

'Have you got what you wanted?'

'I just wanted to get away from those bastards in Moscow.'

'Who was your controller in Moscow?'

'A guy named Kalmyks. First Directorate.'

'What was wrong with him?'

'Nothing. But like everybody else he just did what his bosses told him to do.'

Aarons smiled. 'That's what most people do.'

Serov looked at him. 'Would you send a man to a Gulag camp just because you wanted to screw his wife? Would you want to be part of a set-up that sent millions of people to work-camps where they starved them to death. People who'd done no more than grow a few potatoes for their families to eat or because the local commissar wanted to get promotion?' He paused. 'When I say millions I don't mean just a lot of people I mean millions. Literally millions.'

'What's a Gulag camp?'

'You don't know?' Serov smiled. 'You're kidding.'

'I'm not.'

'The Gulag is an organisation that controls forced labour. They have prison-camps all over the Soviet Union. You want ten thousand men to build a road and some bastard just takes a town in Khazakhstan and ships the whole population off to where you want them. Enemies of the people.'

'But the constitution doesn't allow that. It's against the law.'

For long moments Serov looked at Aarons' face and then he said quietly, 'Don't you read the newspapers, Andrei, or listen to the radio? It's all been written about.'

'I assumed that it was anti-Soviet propaganda.'

'I told you, Andrei, the last time I saw you. The people in the Kremlin are gangsters. The whole country is a prison. All that stuff of Marx and Lenin went out of the window long ago. They just wave those names around like banners to cover what they're doing. It's crude power politics. Every man for himself. When were you last in Moscow, for God's sake?'

Andrei shook his head.

'D'you know something, Andrei?'

'What?'

'You know more about what's going on in America than you do about Russia. There you just know about what goes on in the Kremlin. And you don't even know much about that. You aren't a Russian. You never have been. You weren't brought up there. You don't know what it was like then or what it's like now. You live in limbo and you stick to some dream your father told you. He didn't know how it would all turn out. But you do. You can't be that stupid.' He stood up. 'I'm sorry, Andrei. I didn't mean to be so – so unkind, so critical. I got carried away.' He shrugged and smiled. 'And I really came to tell you I'm getting married.'

'Congratulations. Who is she?'

'Her parents were Italian. But she was born here. She works as a waitress. Angela. Angela Corelli.'

'I'm glad. You deserve a break.'

For a moment Serov was silent and then he said quietly, 'What makes you think that?'

Aarons shrugged. 'You've worked hard all your life for what you thought was a good cause. You risked your life in the Resistance to defeat the Germans. Not many men

219

have done so much, with so little reward. Maybe your lady is the reward.'

Serov shook his head slowly, 'You're a strange man, Andrei. And a good man. I think about you a lot. I hope that one day I can do something to help you.'

Aarons put his arm around Serov's shoulders. 'Let's agree not to talk about politics.'

Serov smiled. 'OK. That's a deal.'

As Aarons made himself a glass of hot chocolate that night he thought about Serov when they were both young men in Paris, talking and arguing but so sure that the dream was going to come true. And then Chantal. Were they all really so naive as to think that you could change the whole world just by argument and discussion? Maybe it wasn't innocence but arrogance. They had seemed such good days in Paris. Days of sunshine and promise.

But the reality was always different. Even with religions it was like that. You started as just a believer and then you discovered that behind the scenes men were fighting for power, manoeuvring to be bishops, or archbishops. Powerful men deciding who would be Pope to make sure that they got preferment and power for themselves.

Christianity and Communism were so much alike. Both of them would work and either of them would make for a better world. If only it wasn't for people. It was people who wouldn't let it work. They didn't want equality, they wanted to be individuals and independent of any higher authority.

The Americans had recognised this when they worked out their constitution.

They had been wise men those Americans all those years ago. He remembered reading through all the articles and amendments in his first days in Brighton Beach, waiting for the family to come over. And he'd learned the words of the preamble by heart and he still remembered them – '. . . *we, the people of the United States, in order to form a more perfect Union, establish Justice, insure dom-*

220

estic Tranquillity . . . promote the general welfare and secure the blessings of Liberty to ourselves and to our posterity . . .' Even with his poor grasp of the language at that time it had seemed romantic, even poetic. And all the words they cared about had capital letters, like Liberty and Justice. Even tranquillity had a capital letter. It still moved him. It didn't really work, but to him what mattered was that those men way back had tried to sort out what men and women really wanted. Like him they could be accused of dreaming dreams. He felt a great affinity to those men.

29

Aarons was surprised when he got to Myron Harper's apartment that Sunday evening and found that they were alone. When he asked why the others were late Harper had poured him a coffee before he responded.

'They've dropped out, Andrei. We'll have to find another couple to make up our four.'

'Why have they dropped out? Are they offended or something?'

'They no longer sympathise with your views or mine.'

'Why didn't they say so? Why so sudden? We could just have not talked about politics.'

'That was more the attraction for them than the bridge games.'

'So?'

Harper shrugged. 'They think . . . they've changed their minds. They feel that they've been deceived.'

'By me you mean?'

'Not you particularly but the whole apparatus of the Party.'

'But I still ask why so suddenly?'

Harper smiled. 'It's St Paul on the road to Damascus. A sign from God.'

'What was the sign for them?'

'When Moscow closed down our access to Berlin and we had to organise nine hundred Dakota flights a day to feed the people of West Berlin.'

'Why that?'

'Tell me,' Harper said, 'what do you think of it yourself?'

'I don't know. I guess they've got a good reason. What do those two think it is?'

'They think that it's proof positive that Moscow is bent on confrontation and aggression. Ready to risk another war. Which is what could have happened if the Americans had insisted on their rights under the Allied Commission.' He sipped his coffee and then said, 'The Americans were strong enough in themselves and their beliefs to back down.' He paused, looking at Aarons. 'And now the whole world knows that the men in the Kremlin are just bully boys, looking for a fight.'

'That's ridiculous, Myron. Is that what you think yourself?'

'Let's say that it's made me think about some fundamental things. Beyond the Berlin airlift, even beyond the Party.'

'What things?'

'How many people in the Kremlin decided to confront us about access to Berlin? Just roughly. Three, a dozen, a hundred maybe.'

'Probably Stalin, Molotov and three or four others and maybe two from the army.'

'So let's call it a round dozen.' Harper shifted in his chair and leaned forward. 'Do you think it's right that just twelve men should be able to decide to risk another war?'

'So how many people should be involved?'

'You're not getting my point, Andrei. What I'm saying is that I can't understand how it comes about that a handful of men should be able to decide the fate of millions of people. Not just in war but in peace too. And not just in the Soviet Union, but everywhere. Who the hell are these men who can take over whole nations and decide how people shall live.'

Aarons shrugged. 'In Moscow's case they are the elected leaders.'

'Oh, come off it, Andrei. There are no free elections in

223

the Soviet Union. You vote for the Party or not at all and in some back room a handful of men decide who gets the power and how it's shared out.'

'Just like the Democrats and the Republicans do in the so-called smoke-filled rooms.'

'You've made my point, Andrei. Here there are at least two parties and the power lies with Congress, openly and publicly.'

'So here you bribe politicians and judges.' He paused. 'So what made you change your mind so suddenly?'

'It wasn't sudden. I didn't like the coup in Hungary. Nor the take-over in Prague. When the Soviets walked out of the Allied Control Commission in Berlin I really started thinking. And when we had to start the Berlin airlift I knew that it was time to think again.'

'So now you're anti-communist and we don't meet anymore.'

Harper smiled. 'No. On both counts. And I'm not talking about Communism, I'm talking about Moscow. I'm not pro-Soviet anymore but I'd be glad to meet you the same as we always have but I'd like it to be a two-way deal in future. I give you the Washington gossip and you give me the Moscow gossip.'

'I'm not in Moscow. I couldn't do that even if I wanted to.'

'But you have instincts and views, Andrei. You get my honest opinion and I get yours.'

'That would be a poor deal for you. Like I said, I'm not in Moscow. I would have nothing to give you.'

'I'll take the risk, Andrei. I've known you a long time. We're not so far apart in our thinking.'

'I'm afraid we are, Myron. Very far apart.'

Harper smiled. 'See you next Sunday, usual time. We'll play chess instead of bridge.'

'Are you being controlled by the FBI, Myron?'

Harper laughed. 'No way. I've always kept my personal views on politics to myself.' He paused. 'And you. Are you working for the Russians?'

224

'I'm a bookseller, Myron.' He stood up. 'I'd better get on my way.'

'Think about what I've said. We could still be useful to one another.'

30

Even with the benefit of hindsight nobody could say what went wrong with 1948. Truman was handsomely back for a second term, the war was over, America was getting back to normal and Europe was trying to decide where it wanted to be in the post-war world. But it was as if the two great powers, the United States and the Soviet Union, were hell-bent on irritating each other until something got settled. Nobody quite knew what the something was. Like two savage dogs they snarled at each other across the world as if they were intent on tearing each other to pieces.

The glib explanation was that they were each looking for world domination. Pessimists on both sides reckoned that their antagonists were shaping up for World War III. From time to time they drove each other to a fury of action and abuse that defied reasonable explanation.

The battle-ground was mainly the hearts and minds and territory of Europe. Each pressed its cause in its own inimitable way. The Russians by domination and the Americans with a generous helping hand. And both came to find their clients both ungrateful and unrewarding.

The Soviets couldn't understand why their satellites' inhabitants wanted to flee to the West when the Soviet Union had single-handedly won the war and freed them from the Nazis. And the Americans were baffled as to why a country that had given a hundred billion dollars in foreign aid should have to install shatterproof window glass in its European embassies and offices because they were so frequently the targets of hostile demonstrators. Each gave what they valued most and found it incredible that they should be abused for so doing. Soviet power despised along with the US dollar.

What made it worse was that both powers knew that they couldn't just wash their hands of their ungrateful allies. Even for the Unites States thousands of miles from Europe the administration knew that attractive as it might seem isolationism was impossible. And as if it provided some kind of relief they snarled and lunged at each other like pit-bull terriers and simple words like Communism and capitalism became epithets in the propaganda dialogue.

And on a more homely level American travellers complained about inflation when a room for the night could cost $12. In the Soviet Union the $12 would rent you a room for three months but there would be five other people sharing the room.

So in 1948 Moscow set about aggravating the Americans by trying to cut off Berlin from the Allies, and Congress, feeling only vaguely guilty, turned a blind eye when McCarthy and his henchmen started their attacks on the Reds. A bad time was going to be had by one and all. A few quiet voices muttered – 'Those whom the Gods would destroy . . .' but they never finished the sentence and anyway nobody listened. Euripides wasn't likely to unseat Norman Mailer on the list of bestsellers for 1948.

31

A lot of Aarons' traffic with Moscow was now coded material by post via Toronto. As he sat decoding the latest messages he realised that he would have to expand his network. Myron Harper's apparent change of heart didn't affect his operation because he had never been part of the network, his only use was political information and Aarons was no longer responsible for providing that sort of background material. But Moscow seemed to be continuously expanding the range of their tasks.

The latest request was for information on US Navy submarine communication systems and for details of a new gun-sight but it took weeks and sometimes months depending on when the ultimate source was on leave from the navy. He had a man who specialised in reading and evaluating patents applications and technical magazines who could start the trail off for the gun-sight. The kind of money involved in this sort of work seemed incredible but when he had queried it with Moscow they had told him to pay whatever it cost.

When he had absorbed the basic information he burnt the two pages of instructions in the bathroom bowl, pouring in water until it was no more than black flecks in the water. Then he pulled the plug and poured down a cupful of the liquid that plumbers use to loosen up blocked pipes. He left the tap running for fifteen minutes before he turned it off.

It was almost midnight as he made himself an omelette

and opened a tin of peaches and a tin of Nestlé's condensed milk.

Ten minutes later Ivan came in, hanging up his coat and then joining Aarons at the small kitchen table.

'You hear the news tonight, Andrei?'

'No, I haven't had the radio on.'

'Truman says the whole country has got to be defended against the Reds.'

Aarons shrugged. 'They're always saying things like that. Forget it.'

'Sounds to me he meant business.'

Aarons looked at Ivan. 'Tell me, brother, if you had the choice of living here in America or in the Soviet Union which would you choose?'

'Are you planning to go back then?'

Aarons shook his head. 'Let me put it another way. If somebody in Germany were given the choice which do you think he'd choose?'

'Depends on the guy, Andrei.'

'Why?'

'Well if a guy's a winner he'll choose the States, if he's a loser he'll choose Russia.'

'How do you make that out?'

'Well if you're a go-getter you'll come here because the rewards are good, but it's a bad place for losers. Russia's great for losers. You'll have a job. You'll probably hate it but it's a job. You'll have a roof over your head.' He grinned. 'But you'll share it with five or six others. You'll get medical treatment if you're ill provided you know some Party guy who'll get you in. You won't have to make any decisions; like in the army, you'll do as you're told. Winners don't want to be told by anybody.'

'And how did you work all that out?'

Ivan shrugged. 'Everybody knows it, you don't need to work it out.'

'Are you a go-getter then?'

'You bet.' He smiled. 'By the way, can you pay me

more? I could get more than you pay me sweeping the streets.'

Andrei nodded. 'Yes. You should have asked me before.'

Two weeks later Aarons got a coded message from Lensky to meet him in Vienna. He had booked to Rome and then taken a flight to Vienna.

A man he didn't know had approached him at the airport and after they had gone through a password routine he had been driven to a large house in its own grounds outside the city boundaries.

There was only Lensky at the house apart from the servants and plain-clothes guards who were all Soviets not locals. Lensky looked tired and Aarons realised that Lensky was now an old man. He ate slowly and without his old relish and at the end of the meal he led Aarons into the large living room, pointing at the leather chairs around a low table.

'I need your help, Andrei.'

'Just tell me what you want.'

Lensky smiled faintly, without conviction. 'I appreciate your loyalty but there are things you need to know before you make any decisions.' He paused and looked at Aarons. 'The wrong people are making the decisions in Moscow right now and they haven't the wisdom to see where it's heading us. Those of us who want to take another route no longer have any influence. Our time will come but . . .' He shrugged, '. . . it may be years before it does. And we may not survive that long.'

'So tell me what I can do to help you?'

Lensky shook his head. 'Not so fast, Andrei. When I tell you what it's about you may feel the other people have got it right. I don't want blind loyalty, I want your advice.'

'About what?'

Lensky shrugged slowly, 'World War III. The end of the world. God knows.' He shook his head. 'I just need to talk to someone who hasn't got an axe to grind. Someone who's sane and not involved in Kremlin politics.' Lensky stood up and looked towards the window, standing there silently for several minutes before he turned to Aarons. 'You know – I don't even know where to begin.' He shrugged. 'It's time you stopped calling me Comrade Lensky. It's Jakob.' He shook his head. 'You don't know how lucky you are. Away from it all. Still loyal to the Party. Still . . . innocent. I don't want to spoil it for you. You're safe over there. They can't infect you with their sickness.' He shook his head. 'What a world we live in.' He drew a deep breath. 'No, that's wrong, the world's all right, it's the people who ruin it.'

'Sit down and tell me what's worrying you.'

'Aren't you tired after your journey? Maybe we should leave it until tomorrow?'

Aarons smiled. 'Let's talk now.'

Lensky sat down facing Aarons and he took off his glasses and put them on the low table, rubbing his eyes before he leaned back in the armchair.

'There are God knows how many factions and schisms inside the Kremlin but the two that really matter are the Stalinists who want to take over the whole world and those who want to give the people a better life. And right at the moment the Stalinists have got the upper hand. The army's behind them and so are the state security services. It's not easy, you know, to convince people that doing nothing may be better than making the whole world communist.'

'They'd say that spreading Communism was one of the fundamentals of Marxist-Leninism.'

'Sure. But by conviction, by persuasion, not by threats and the overthrow of governments. And the objectives have to be right.' He shook his head. 'These people aren't going to give their conquered countries a better life. It's power they want.' He waved his arm impatiently. 'And why not give our own people a decent life before we take over other people's lives? God knows our people need

231

it. They've just become statistics and pawns in a terrible game.'

'Jakob. Tell me something good about the Soviet Union.' The question seemed to stop Lensky in his tracks. He leaned back in the chair, his eyes closed. It seemed a long time before he opened his eyes and leaned forward again.

'Just the people, Andrei. Just those patient, loving people. Nothing but them.' He sighed. 'And the music, the literature from the old days, the Bolshoi . . .' he smiled, '. . . and Moscow Dynamo.'

'So what's bad?'

'Corruption of every kind. The abuse of authority. The abuse of the law, and power in the hands of despots who can send hundreds of thousands of people to forced labour camps. Or just one man because he gets in somebody's way. Privilege and bribery on a scale you wouldn't believe. Nepotism at every level.' He shrugged. 'A dream turned into a nightmare.'

It shocked Aarons to hear Lensky making the same criticisms of the Party that its political enemies always made.

'So why does nobody expose it? Why don't you use your influence and protest?'

'My dear boy if anyone heard me say what I've said to you tonight I would be floating in the Moskva river tomorrow. If I was lucky. If not, I would be lying on the cement floor of a cell in the Lubyanka with my fingers broken, maybe my legs and arms too, if I had any teeth left they would be hanging loose. Maybe six months later you'd read a small piece in *Pravda* or *Izvestia* saying that the Jew Lensky had been tried as an enemy of the Revolution, found guilty and executed by due process of law as laid down in the Constitution.'

'But the Constitution specifically prohibits all that.'

'Neither the Constitution nor the law matters to these people. They do what they want. They *are* the law.'

232

'Are conditions for the people as bad as the overseas propaganda says they are?'

'They don't know the half of it. These men have turned humans into garbage, and there's an almost visible mist of misery over every town and village. Even the fields and the forests haven't escaped. Except for the privileged few, the *apparatchiks* and the *nomenklatura*, we have created a nation of prisoners. In what other country in the world is it an offence to want to live somewhere else or pay a visit abroad? Or an offence to listen to a foreign broadcast or read a foreign magazine or book? They are afraid that the people will discover how the rest of the world live. They've made even the mind a frontier.'

'And what can I do to help you?'

'I want to know from you about what is happening in the United States.'

'Why?'

'You can't imagine the ignorance of the men in the Kremlin about Europe and the United States. Information comes from our embassies and our agents abroad, but if it gives a true picture, which it seldom does, it is ignored and the sources are looked on as suspect or worse. I want to be able to use my past record of loyalty and work for the Party to influence what they do. And to do that I need to know what the people in Washington are thinking and planning.'

'To what end, Jakob?'

'To try and avoid another war.'

'Is it that possible?'

'We are spending 35 per cent of our national product on arms. Guns, tanks, planes, warships, men. And we shall have our atom bomb too before long.'

For a few moments Aarons didn't respond, and then he said quietly, 'Do you really think that you can make a difference?'

'I don't know, Andrei. But I must try. I think there is a chance. Some of them are not far from being psychopaths but there are others who could be diverted if they

233

thought they were going to lose because of their aggression.'

'Lose what?'

'Their privileges, their dachas, their Western goods, their luxury apartments, their status.'

'But I don't cover that sort of work any longer. You know that. You were there when they told me that my role was running an espionage network.'

'And they still want that. But I ask you to delegate as much of that work as you can and give me the information I need.'

'Why do they want me in Moscow?'

'Just a routine meeting. They're satisfied with what you're doing. I guess they'll want to extend your brief. If any of them start fishing around on Kremlin politics . . . you don't know what they're talking about. It's nothing to do with you. Your mind is on your network in New York. Understood?'

'Yes.'

'Will you help me?'

'Can I ask you something?'

'Of course.'

'*Was* it all just a dream, and doomed to failure?'

'No. If I thought that I wouldn't go back to Moscow. I'd just disappear. Mexico or Brazil. I want the dream to at least have a chance to succeed. If we can show that it works in the Soviet Union the rest of the world might be ready to try it themselves. Not by occupation or force of arms or threats. But because it's good.'

'OK, Jakob. I'll help you any way I can.'

Lensky smiled. 'Tonight I'll sleep in peace and I haven't done that for a long while.'

'You've given me a lot to think about. How can we keep in touch without going through channels?'

'I've got a friend in New York. You can talk to her as if you were talking to me. She'll pass on anything, verbal or otherwise. I'll give you her address when I see you off on the plane from Moscow. You'll be flying via Stockholm.'

The meetings in Moscow had been routine. They had added two more targets to his brief. One of them was a report on the FBI. Its structure and pay scales. And the other was a survey of the latest drugs available without prescription. He had previously sent them basic details of the FBI's New York offices but it was obvious from their probing about what qualifications a man had to have to be recruited by the FBI, and the pay that various grades of FBI officers would earn, that they were hoping to recruit somebody from the FBI themselves. He had hinted that they would be wasting their time. If they ordered him to try it he'd ignore the order.

He had meetings with other Kremlin people, officials concerned with foreign policy and trade. He had spent three days in Moscow and there had been time for him to stroll around the centre of the city. He had been aware of the long queues and when he had chatted with people who were lined up he was surprised to learn that they sometimes didn't even know what they were queuing for.

Lensky rode with him to the airport and handed him a book of poems and said quietly, 'The name, telephone number and address are in this book. Burn it when you've memorised it.'

'Does she know the current passwords?'

'Yes.' He paused. 'And she's totally loyal. Disenchanted but loyal.'

32

The bus from the airport dropped Aarons at Grand Central and he walked down 41st Street as it started to rain. At the shop he searched in his pockets for the keys and a man with an umbrella stood beside him, looking in the shop window and Aarons heard the man say, 'Don't look at me, Andrei, and don't talk to me. It's Myron. Myron Harper. I just wanted to tell you I've been subpoenaed to appear before McCarthy's congressional committee. They're already checking on all my friends and contacts. I just wanted to warn you. I won't be giving them any names I promise you. But others might. You've got to be very careful.'

He walked away before Aarons could respond.

As Aarons made his way upstairs to his apartment he was shocked at Harper's news. And grateful that he'd taken so much trouble to warn him. He found out later that Harper had watched the shop for four days.

There was a pile of mail on the table in the living room, most of it business mail. There was an envelope that had not gone through the mail with his name handwritten on the cover. When he opened it he found a note from Serov to say that he had tried to contact him and was coming to see him in a couple of days' time at the weekend.

As he stirred his glass of hot chocolate he remembered seeing newspaper photographs of the Senator who was in charge of the committee. There was the Senator and a lawyer, his assistant. A man named Cohen, or was it Cohn? It was he who provided the Senator with his material for questioning witnesses. He would have to find out more about them. But there was nobody in his network who was a member of the Party and only two had been members way back. Harper and the longshoreman. But he'd had their Party records destroyed long ago.

The next day Aarons walked down to the address Lensky had given him in Greenwich Village. The name of the woman was Tania Orlovsky and the house was in what was more or less a lane not far from Washington Square. It was a row of houses that had once been the servants' quarters of the big houses on the next street. Number 31 was a three-storey house in reasonable repair. At street level what had once been a stable had been converted into what looked like a garage. A flight of four stone steps led to a door painted a bright blue with brass fittings and on the wall beside the door was a plate with name labels. Apartment 3 gave the name Orlovsky.

Aarons pressed the bell and a few moments later there was a buzz and the blue door clicked open. The stairs were narrow but carpeted and the handrail was new and varnished. On the top floor there was a short corridor with a window at the far end that cast a square of sunshine on a print of an Impressionist painting, framed and hanging on the plain white wall. The door to the apartment was plain wood varnished with an elaborate Arabic 3 in polished brass at eye level. Aarons rang the bell and heard the chime inside the apartment.

When the door opened a young girl stood there, her hair wet and tangled, tying the cotton belt of a bath-robe. Aarons guessed that she must be in her early twenties and she was very beautiful.

'Is Mrs Orlovsky available at the moment?'

The girl smiled. 'There is no Mrs Orlovsky.'

Aarons frowned. 'Are you quite sure?'

'Maybe you want Tania Orlovsky.'

'That's right.'

'I'm Tania Orlovsky.' She smiled. 'You'd better come in.'

It was a much larger apartment than he had imagined, the living room was spacious, walls and ceiling white and only minimum furniture that looked as if it was Swedish, plain wood and soft leather cushions.

'Would you like a coffee?'

'Thanks.'

She came back a few moments later with a Thermos and a tray with cups, sugar and a small jug of milk.

'Help yourself.'

'Didn't our friend in Moscow give you a password?'

'Yes, he did. I forgot all about it.' She smiled. 'But I knew straightaway who you were.'

'How?'

She shrugged. 'He'd told me about you. And anyway you've got that typical Russian look about you.'

Despite himself Aarons smiled. 'What's a typical Russian look?'

'Tragedy and worse to come.'

'Sounds terrible.'

'Not really, Americans go for it, especially if you're Jewish as well. Sticks out from all that American optimism. Makes you a character, to be listened to. Who wants a cheerful philosopher?'

'How long have you known our friend?'

'Ever since I was born.' She laughed as he was obviously trying to work it out. 'Didn't he tell you? He's my grandfather.'

'I didn't even know he was married.'

'They weren't married. He was afraid that because he was a Jew she could be harassed by the Bolsheviks. He moved her to Vienna and then here in the States. He loved her very much and she loved him too.'

'Is she still here?'

'Kind of. She died about two years ago.' She smiled. 'It always seemed strange to me that two people could love one another so deeply and have to live so far apart. But

I guess that was part of the loving. Caring for the other one more than you care for yourself.'

'I've not heard anyone use that word Bolshevik for years. Why not Communists?'

'Oh . . .' she said, looking surprised '. . . because they are Bolsheviks – they're not Communists and never were.' She shrugged. 'It was the Bolsheviks who spoilt it all.'

'How?'

'Communism would work but nobody's ever tried it. Like Christianity would work but nobody's ever tried that either.'

'Are you a student?'

'No way. I'm a photographer.' She gave a deprecating shrug. 'I'm quite well-known.'

'What kind of photography?'

'Portraits of important people for magazines, and street photographs for myself. One pays for the other. That's my studio on the ground floor. I bought a long lease on the whole house a couple of years ago when leases were cheap. The rent for the second floor pays for everything.'

'How long does it take for you to be in touch with our friend?'

'If it's very brief, and verbal – an hour. If it's documents then two days, sometimes three.'

'And how can I contact you?'

'Here, you've got my telephone number. I'll give you my studio number downstairs and my answering-service number – they'll get in touch with me wherever I am. I'll give you a priority word so they know it's urgent. Any ideas for the word?'

'What about Neva – the river?'

She shook her head dismissively. 'Too Russian – why make the connection? I know what we'll use – possum – like Americans use it for lying-low – playing possum – pretending to be dead.' She laughed. 'It's rather cuddly too. A bit like you.'

Aarons stood up. 'I must say thank you for your cooperation. It will help a lot. I'll be in touch.'

'You're welcome.'

He smiled. 'You sound very American.'

'I am, possum. I *am* American.' And she laughed at his obvious confusion.

Serov had arrived mid-morning on the Saturday and had insisted on taking Aarons out to lunch at an Italian restaurant just off Times Square. When they got to the coffees Serov said, 'You seem very down, Andrei, what's bugging you?'

Aarons half-smiled. 'Bugging me? Hasn't taken you long to talk like an American.' He sighed. 'I guess I'm tired of being told that the people in Moscow are just a bunch of crooks, or worse.'

'You must be used to that. You read the newspapers, you hear the radio so you know what they're doing. You may not like it but that's what it is.'

'I always thought it was propaganda against the Soviets. Part of the war. Capitalism versus Communism.'

'But you're beginning to realise that most of it's true, yes?'

'Yes.'

'What made you see the light? What made you change your mind?'

'Let's go and sit in the park and talk.'

Serov paid the bill and they walked down to Bryant Park. They found a bench in the sun and Serov said, 'So tell me, what made you change your mind? What's new?'

'Nothing I guess. Just that people I respect, people I trust seem to be losing the fight in the Kremlin.'

'Have you just come back from a visit?'

'Yeah.'

'Did you talk to Lensky?'

'Maybe.'

'I tell you what – if Lensky's worried about what's going on then there's real trouble.'

'Tell me about Lensky.'

'I don't know all that much. He's a Jew. Comes from a

240

really rich family with vast estates outside Moscow and in the Ukraine. They gave them to the workers long before the revolution in '17. He served as an officer in the Tsar's army but came out and became a lawyer. He was always part of the group. Lenin, Trotsky, Marx, Karensky at one time. But he was always in the background. Never looking for power. Trying to keep the peace. And on the whole he succeeded. He didn't gossip, was always totally discreet. He knew how to analyse problems and work out the best solution.

'When I was in Paris I realised he was in intelligence, but as a political adviser. He did work for the Comintern as well.' Serov turned his head to look at Aarons. 'I'd say he's getting a very rough ride at the moment.'

'Why do you think that?'

'Those bastards in the Kremlin are ready to risk a war. They aren't sure how far they can go without the Americans picking up the gauntlet. They want to rule the world, Europe, Asia, South America, everywhere. And the only people who can stop 'em are the Americans. They've got no idea of how the free world thinks, especially the Americans. They get fed real crap by the embassy.

'And the Yanks are only just beginning to understand that Moscow doesn't have the same inhibitions as Washington. I've heard Washington people saying that Moscow wouldn't start a war in Europe because the Red Army would lose a hundred thousand men in the first few days.' Serov waved his arms. 'Even if that was true it wouldn't stop them for a second. What's a hundred thousand dead if it gets you even more power? There'd be no riots in Red Square or round the Finland Station. But lose a tenth of that many American lives for the sake of Europe and you'd have Congress in uproar and the whole country going crazy.

'So in Washington they try to work out how to stop the aggressions without starting a war and they too don't have enough information about what the people in the Kremlin

241

are thinking. They're both playing Blind Man's Buff. It's crazy.'

'That's what's worrying Lensky. He wants me to keep him in the picture about what they're thinking in Washington and the White House.'

'That's great but who's going to do that for the White House?'

'Maybe they've got their own man in the Kremlin.'

'I can tell you for sure they haven't. He'd have to be a genuine Soviet, have been around the top brass for a long, long time and ready to risk his life. Why the hell should he? If he knows what's going on he's part of it and getting all he wants already.'

'What about a man like Lensky?'

'He'd never do it. He's got a broader outlook than the rest of them but he's still part of it. And he's still waiting for the dream to come true despite what he knows.'

'Is there anyone else you can think of who could do it?'

'Yes.'

'Who?'

'You, my friend. You understand them both. You've got Lensky in Moscow, there'll be a Lensky in the White House somewhere.'

'And who do I cheat on?'

'Nobody. You give honest advice to Lensky and honest advice to somebody here.'

'Lensky wouldn't agree.'

'So you don't tell Lensky about this end of the story. You give him straight honest advice. Not biased either way. You do the same here.'

'And not tell them either?'

Serov shrugged. 'You'd have to work that out. They're not idiots and they'd be getting more information than they're getting now. Despite your advice either side could still go ahead and do it the wrong way but they'd at least know the odds before they placed their bets.'

Aarons smiled at Serov. 'You're as crazy as the rest of them. I'll take you to a night-club tonight for a change.'

'You. A night-club. You're kidding.'

'I'm not. My sister's husband plays piano in a night-club. He's great. You'll love it.'

'As long as he plays "Manhattan" I'll be happy.'

33

'There's a gentleman asking to see you, sir.'

He shook his head. 'I can't, Jo. Tell him to make an appointment.'

'He says it's personal. To do with the war.'

'The war? What's his name?'

'It's Serov, but he said that when you knew him his name was Pascal.'

'Good God. You mean he's here?'

'Yes.'

'Show him in.' He paused. 'Phone Macey and make some excuse. I'll see him later.'

Malloy was standing by the window as his secretary opened the door and said, 'Mr Serov to see you, sir.'

Malloy walked forward, smiling, his hand held out. 'I can't believe it but it's great to see you.' He pointed at the chair in front of his desk. 'Sit down. What are you doing in New York?'

'It's good to see you too. I work in Washington. It's a long story.'

'So tell me. And how did you find me?'

'I looked up your name in the New York telephone directory. But there were pages of Malloys and O'Malleys. I'd never seen your name written down. A girl at the library found me a directory of attorneys and helped me track you down.'

'How long are you here for?'

'I live here. Not in New York but in Washington. I've been here some time.'

'What happened to you? I drove everybody crazy trying to trace where you'd gone from Fresnes.'

'They shipped me off to a concentration camp. It was liberated by the British. I was in hospital for some months and then I went back to Paris.'

'What were you doing?'

Serov took a deep breath. 'I was working for the Russians. After some time I defected and now I'm doing an office job in the French section of the CIA.'

'My God. Tell me about it. Is there anything I can do to help?'

Serov told him his story but made no mention of Aarons. When he had finished Malloy said, 'And all they use you for is evaluating French section documents?'

'I was glad to do anything they gave me, Bill. Just pleased that they let me stay.' He paused. 'You didn't fancy joining CIA when they started it up.'

Malloy laughed. 'Nobody asked me. No, that's not fair. I wanted to earn some real money. Anyway I'm a lawyer not a spook.'

'But you still keep contact with the old OSS people.'

'I spend a lot of time in Washington so I bump into them from time to time. Some of them stayed on when it became the CIA but most got out as soon as they could.'

'I've got something important that I want to talk to somebody about. Who should I talk to? It's got to be whatever goes beyond top-secret.'

'Is this something to do with the Soviet Union?'

'Yes.'

'Are you still involved with them?'

'No way. I hate their guts. And if they knew where I was they'd probably kill me. They don't like defectors.'

'Can you tell me about it. Just a rough idea of what it's about.'

'That's part of the reason I came to see you. You're the only American I can trust.' He paused. 'I *can* trust you, can't I?'

'It depends a bit on what it is, Jo-jo. I need some rough

245

idea of what it's all about before I can make any promise.'

For several moments Serov was silent, and then he said, 'The Russian who runs Moscow's most important espionage network in New York is disillusioned about the men in the Kremlin. I think if it was done in the right way he'd be willing to help us.'

'You mean he's ready to defect?'

'No. It's more complicated than that.' He paused as if he were trying to sort out the words. 'This is a man who mixes with the top men in the Kremlin. He knows what they're thinking.'

'I don't understand, Jo-jo. Would he be on our side or theirs?'

'Both or neither if I guess right about his attitude. All he's interested in is preventing another war.'

'Unless there's more to it than you've told me I can't see anyone going for it. It could be a plant. A disinformation operation.'

'If you knew the man you'd know it couldn't be that. I've known him since we were young men in Paris before the war and that's a long time, Bill.'

'And what if they discovered what he was up to?'

'They'd kill him. They trust him and he's never given them bad advice. He wouldn't agree with the description, but he's an intellectual although he doesn't see himself in that way.'

'You're keeping some things back from me, aren't you?'

'Yes.'

'Why?'

'Because I feel partly a traitor to him for telling you what I have told you already. I'm certainly not going to reveal enough for him to be identified without knowing what the reaction would be this side. In Washington.'

'I don't have any idea what their reaction would be. I'm long out of this sort of business. It sounds kind of crazy to me, Jo-jo. I'm sure you mean well but it doesn't make any sense.'

'I haven't explained it very well, Bill, it needs talking

246

about with someone right at the top. All I hoped for was that you'd be able to introduce me to someone who was high-up enough in the White House to appreciate what this could mean.'

'Have you even hinted of this to anyone else?'

'No. And if you can't help I shall forget it.'

'How long can you give me to think about it?'

Serov shook his head. 'I guess there's no time limit but I just feel that if something's going to be done, now is the time. Before it's too late.'

'You think it's that bad?'

'I think there are going to be confrontations where knowing what the other side are thinking could save us making mistakes.'

'If I were to describe this to somebody what should I say that sums it up? Something that makes them take notice.'

Serov was silent for a few moments, looking towards the window, and then he turned to look at Malloy. 'Ask him if the President would like to know where the Soviet Union's next aggressive move against the United States will take place?'

'You think your man knows this?'

'If he doesn't he could easily find out.'

Malloy looked at his watch and then at Serov.

'Can you stay in New York an extra day?'

'If it will help, yes. I'll have to phone the office.'

'OK. Let's do this. Give me until six o'clock and we'll meet in the bar at the Waldorf, OK?'

'Whatever you say.'

'Whatever happens come and stay at my place tonight.'

'Thank you.' He stood up and Malloy walked with him to the door. 'I'm so glad we've met up again, Jo-jo. We've got a lot of missing pieces to fill in for each other. And let me say it – I'm flattered that you trust me.'

'I do, Bill. I've often thought about you.' He smiled. 'We didn't do a bad job together all those years ago.'

*　　*　　*

Hancox sat listening impassively as if he were listening to the details of some complex fraud case, while Malloy outlined his talk with Serov. When Malloy finished Hancox said quietly, 'And why are you telling me this, Bill?'

'I thought with your connections you might be able to advise me on who to talk to about it. Somebody high enough to appreciate the potential of all this.'

'The man Serov. Do you trust him?'

Malloy smiled. 'I guess by now I don't trust anybody entirely. I trust his loyalty. He was tortured and sent to a concentration camp because he wouldn't talk about our operation. He did wonderful work for me. I'd have been lost without him.'

'So what is it that you *don't* trust about him?'

'I suppose I don't trust any communist.'

'Nothing specific?'

'No.' Malloy smiled. 'Just prejudice.'

Hancox pursed his lips. 'A popular prejudice, my boy, these days.'

'But if we want inside information it's not going to come from anyone who isn't a Commie.'

'But you can be sure that nobody at the top is just going to give the nod to something like this without a lot of checking.'

'Serov isn't going to tell us who the man is unless he's satisfied that it will be handled the right way. The man concerned doesn't even know that Serov is doing this. He hasn't said that he wants such an operation.'

'The FBI could probably come up with the name of two or three possibles.'

'I don't think so. The man's been operating here in New York since before the war. And if anyone made the wrong move he'd just light out in a matter of hours.'

'It sounds like your friend Serov has convinced you.'

'He has. Convinced me that at least we should pursue it further.'

'It means that you want me to talk with someone important about an anonymous man who's a senior Soviet agent

248

operating in New York, who is well connected in the Kremlin, who might, and we don't know for sure, who *might* be willing to advise us on the thinking of the Kremlin vis-à-vis the United States. And the pay-off would be that we apprise him on current White House thinking vis-à-vis the Russians.' He shrugged. 'Not a very credible story, Bill, is it?'

'The story's credible enough if you bear in mind that the only reason this guy would do it is because it could keep peace between the two major powers who seem to be squaring up to one another. If somebody would listen we'd have to work it out step by step.'

'Let's face the facts, my boy. The only reason why you find it credible is because it comes from your friend Serov. The main reason why I would pursue it is because I trust your judgement. And from that point on it all depends on somebody trusting my judgement. The people I have connections with don't go much for trust.'

'Then we'll have to forget it. I'd have to ask you not to mention that the possible collaborator is based in New York.'

'Why not?'

'Somebody might turn down the idea but feel that looking for the man was a better deal.'

'The more I think about it the crazier it seems.' Hancox stood up slowly. 'Is there any time limitation?'

'Serov will be staying at my place tonight. I think the sooner he gets an answer the better.'

'Why?'

'He's acted on impulse and I'd guess that by now he's beginning to regret it.'

'I'll see what I can do, but I don't hold out much hope. I'll get in touch with you one way or another tonight.' He shook his head slowly. 'Don't expect much.'

When Malloy met Serov at the Waldorf he realised in a few minutes that his diagnosis of Serov's reaction was correct. He was full of doubts now about the scenario he had described, and guilty that he could have compromised his friend by his impulsive action. Malloy took him back to his home straightaway in the hope that talking with Kathy about other things would take Serov's mind off the problem.

He had phoned Kathy earlier to warn her that he was bringing home a visitor and he had explained briefly who Serov was.

To his surprise Kathy took to Serov immediately. Amused by his politeness, the kissing of hands and the bunch of flowers from the kiosk at the Waldorf. There was a telephone call as they ate their meal but it was from one of Kathy's friends.

There were two further phone calls during the evening but neither was from Hancox. It was almost midnight when Malloy finally got the call from Hancox.

'I hope I've not kept you up, Bill.'

'That's OK.'

'When you posed this little problem I wasn't sure where to go, but in the end I decided that all the traditional routes were just that – traditional. Anyone who'd even consider this would have to be very aware of its potential value without wanting to work out how it could affect their own interests. So I went as high as I could. Very near the top. And I was very surprised. Instant recognition of the possibilities and immediate willingness to explore it further.'

'That's great news. Can I ask who it is?'

'You can ask but I can't tell you.' He paused. 'Your friend, when does he have to go back to Washington?'

'He's supposed to be back there now.'

'OK. Ask him to go to the Tabard tomorrow at around 7 p.m. and ask for me. I'll have a room there. And we'll see how it goes from there.'

'I'll do that. Thanks for the effort.'

'I think it's going to work out. Maybe not exactly as we talked but on the right lines.'

'And no problems about our friend's friend's security?'

'No. No problem. Sleep well.'

And Hancox hung up. Malloy sat in his small study for several minutes before going back to join Serov and Kathy.

As Serov walked from his rooms to the Tabard Inn he wondered why he hadn't let well alone. He was content with his quiet life and now overnight he was involved with people of importance and influence. Why the hell didn't he mind his own business instead of creating problems for both himself and Bill Malloy? And now an even more important man, the senior partner of the firm of lawyers where Malloy worked. But now he'd started he'd have to carry on for Malloy's sake.

It was three days before Malloy saw Hancox again and the senior partner had been amiable but without making any mention of the meeting with Serov or its outcome. On subsequent office meetings with Hancox the senior partner had made it subtly but patently clear that he didn't want to discuss the Serov business.

Malloy had put the episode out of his mind, not without some mild resentment at not being taken into Hancox's confidence. And then two months later Hancox had walked into Malloy's office late one afternoon, sitting himself down in the client's chair and slowly and elaborately clipping a cigar and lighting it before looking at Malloy.

With a half-smile he said, 'You've put up a good show of being patient, Bill. I'm sorry I couldn't let you in on what was going on. I didn't know much myself.' He paused. 'It seems to be working out. Slowly, but good foundations have been laid.'

'Am I allowed to ask what's happened?'

'Are you doing anything special tonight?'

'No. Kathy's away for a couple of days.'

'I'll get Sue to book us a table at the Metropolitan and we can eat, it's usually quiet on a Wednesday. And then we can talk.'

The Metropolitan Club at Fifth Avenue and 60th had been founded by J.P. Morgan, allegedly for friends who had been blackballed elsewhere. But that was a long time ago and now it was extremely choosy itself.

The food was plain but good and neither of them had been disposed to linger at the table. They had found two comfortable, leather armchairs in the corner of the lounge and when the club servant had brought them coffee Hancox drew his chair nearer to Malloy.

'The man I finally decided to talk to is right at the top . . .'

'Where at the top, the FBI or Langley?'

'Neither. He's at the White House. In due course I'll be able to tell you who he is. And if everything goes together you'll meet him.'

'Why the White House, not one of the agencies?'

'Because if this thing is done it'll have to be done away from any intelligence outfit. Serov's friend, let's call him "X", is in a dangerous position, or would be if anyone from the CIA or the FBI knew his identity. From talking to Serov it's clear that "X" would only go along with this on his own terms.'

'And what would they be?'

Hancox smiled. 'It's only a guess. He doesn't know anything about this effort, but we're sure that "X" would only cooperate if he felt that it was not only on a very high level but as a means of keeping the peace between us and the Soviets.

'The guy in the White House and I have talked at length with Serov about "X" and I'm convinced that Serov has read him well. The reason why it's taken so long is that we've been doing a kind of dry-run on this.'

'What's that mean?'

'We asked Serov to ask him about McCarthy's Red hunt, and ask him what advice he would give to the Kremlin about it. Should they intervene or protest or put pressure on the Jews in the Soviet Union as a reprisal.'

252

'What was his advice?'

'To do nothing. To accept that there was a strong feeling against communists in America but that McCarthy was going too far. He was becoming above Congress and an embarrassment and Congress would put a stop to him sooner or later. Meantime the rest of the world will read about it and see newsreels about McCarthy and that will make them dislike Americans.' Hancox smiled. 'And very shrewdly he pointed out that it was harassment of creative people, writers, film people, artists and even musicians. Whilst those were the kind of people who were most respected and privileged in the Soviet Union. And now McCarthy is on screen every day hounding government servants. And the White House share his assessment. McCarthy's like Hitler. He'll go too far and Congress is being abused and will turn on him.' Hancox paused. 'The last part of the dry run was for Serov to ask "X" where he thought the Soviets will make their next aggressive move against the US.'

'What did he say?'

'It was a surprising answer. Unexpected anyway. He said it would be in East Asia.'

'Does he mean China?'

'I don't know. That was his answer and we're waiting to see what happens.'

'We could wait a long time.'

'Maybe. But Serov said that "X" spoke as if it were imminent.'

'When did "X" say this?'

'Just over two weeks ago.' He leaned forward towards Malloy. 'The whole exercise has made my man in the White House appreciate the value of knowing what the other side is thinking or planning. There's no doubt in Serov's mind that "X" feels that the Kremlin are looking for trouble. And "X" doesn't like it. He's very worried.'

'There's no chance that your White House contact would tip off one of the agencies to put surveillance on Serov to try and identify "X"?'

'No chance at all. He's got great hopes that if this is done carefully and well it could be an invaluable aid for the President.'

'Does the President know?'

'I can't discuss that. I don't know for sure anyway.'

Two weeks later on Sunday the 25th of June 1950 the North Koreans invaded South Korea.

34

There was a note stuck on the apartment door. It just said – 'In studio T.O.' It was written in a rounded innocent script and the only affectation was that there was a small circle over the 'i' instead of a dot.

For a moment Aarons hesitated and then he walked back down the stairs to the narrow cobbled alleyway. There were two big garage doors painted in bright red, white and blue vertical stripes and there was a smaller door let into the right-hand garage door. He tentatively turned the brass door-knob and the small door swung open into what seemed like total darkness. And then as Aarons' eyes became accustomed to the darkness he could see that he was behind a black curtain and there were bright lights visible through the thin material. He gently pushed the curtain aside and blinked in the bright lights of the studio.

He saw Tania bent over a camera on a tripod, the long lens pointed toward a girl in only a bra and panties smiling to the camera. He heard the thump of the camera and then Tania stood up straight and turned to look at him. He felt pleased that she recognised him so quickly and then she turned to the model.

'OK, honey. Same time tomorrow.'

Tania walked towards him, still smiling. 'It's been weeks since I saw you. Let's go upstairs and have a coffee. You haven't seen the studio before, have you?'

She took his hand and led him to the camera, 'This is a Hasselblad, a Swedish camera, much easier to use than those old Graphics and Graflexes.' She waved her hands at the lights on stands and overhead. 'These are electronic flashes, the same colour temperature as daylight.' She paused and turned to point towards the doors. 'I do mainly fashion and portraits but I get quite a few car shots because I've kept the big doors. It's fine having one of those lovely loft conversions but you can't get a car up there.'

He looked at a large photograph on the wall, 'That's Paris, when were you in Paris?'

She laughed. 'You flatter me, that's by a guy named Cartier-Bresson. He's very special. And so's that guy.' She pointed at a photograph of a desert scene with a solitary yucca. 'That's by Edward Weston but he uses huge 10 x 8 cameras to get that long range of tones.' She smiled. 'But he's an artist and I'm just a craftsman. Let me switch off the lights.'

As they walked up the stairs to the apartment she linked her arm in his. 'You look tired, are you eating properly?'

Aarons laughed. 'I'm OK. Am I taking up too much of your time? I've got an envelope for our friend but I can just hand it over. You mustn't stop work just for me.'

'I've finished work for today. This morning's shoot was only for a reference sheet for the model. She's just starting with an agency.'

'Do you do landscapes like the one on the studio wall?'

'No. They're beautiful but I'm more into people.'

'What kind of people?'

'Professionally it's models; pretty girls and handsome men. But for myself I'm doing a book about New Yorkers. All kinds, winners and losers. Rich men, poor men, beggarmen and thieves.' She laughed. 'We've got all those. Black and white. Sutton Place and Harlem. But I'm talking too much, let's go in the kitchen and I'll do the coffee and you can sit and watch.'

As she prepared the coffee he wondered what kind of men friends she had. She was so beautiful. The mane of black hair, the big dark eyes, the neat nose and the soft wide mouth. Even making the coffee the movements of her hands were graceful. And almost as if she knew what he was thinking she turned her head to look at him.

'Have you got a girl-friend, Andrei?'

'No, I'm afraid not.'

'Is that because you miss your wife?'

'How did you know about that?'

'Grandpa Lensky told me. And those shits in Moscow didn't let you borrow some money.' She looked at him, frowning. 'How could you go on working for them after that?'

'I guess I don't really work for them.'

She frowned. 'I don't understand.'

He shrugged. 'It sounds dreadfully self-important when I say it out loud but for me I work for all people who don't get a fair chance in life.'

'And you think Communism could put that right?'

'It's the only way I know that aims to do that.'

She turned to stand looking at him, shaking her head. 'How old are you, Andrei?'

'Forty-one next month.'

'I'm twenty-four but you make me feel like Methuselah.'

He laughed. 'Why?'

'Because you're so unworldly. I don't know whether you are an innocent or just naive. You know so much about what's going on in Moscow and here in the States and you still believe that crap.' She shook her head. 'I don't get it. Anyway . . .' she said dismissively '. . . with cream or with milk?'

'Milk would be fine.'

Aarons reached for the black brief-case beside him on the white leather couch. The brown envelope he took out bulged with its contents and he looked at the girl. 'Do you want me to split this up into two envelopes?'

'No. That's OK.'

She held out her hand for it and took it into the next room which he assumed was a bedroom. She came back a few minutes later.

257

'How long before they get it?'

'They'll get it by Saturday.' She smiled. 'What do you do at weekends, Andrei?'

'They're just the same as any other day to me. I just get on with my work.'

'Have you heard of Sag Harbor?'

'Isn't it a rich people's place on Long Island?'

She smiled. 'You're a snob, Andrei, aren't you?'

'How do you make that out?' He looked genuinely surprised.

'You judge people by their money, not by what they are.'

'How else would you describe Sag Harbor?'

'I'd point out that it was designated by George Washington as the first Port of Entry for the first immigrants. Then I'd say that it was old and historic and beautiful. And for those with a social conscience I'd tell them that John Steinbeck lived there for many years.

Aarons laughed softly, 'You dug a trap for me.'

'You need civilising, my friend. You're a bit of a country bumpkin.' She grinned. 'Anyway – back to Sag Harbor. I'm driving there on Friday night – a client has lent me his house for the weekend. How about you come with me?'

'I'm no good at parties. I never know what to talk about.'

'Who said anything about parties? It's just you and me and my cameras.' She smiled. 'And you'll have to carry my photo bag of lenses and stuff.'

'Are you sure I won't be a bore?'

She shook her head as if in despair and then stood up. 'Be here about five on Friday evening. OK?'

'OK.'

It was in the early hours of the morning when she eased the car into the wide driveway of the house. Before she switched off the car lights he saw the house. It was a magnificent place, white clapboards recently painted, with

258

blue shutters at the windows. Spanish-type arches along a patio and then the extended length of the house that was covered with Virginia creeper. Aarons guessed that it must be the house of a very rich man.

Tania seemed familiar with the interior layout of the house, giving him the choice of two comfortable bedrooms before taking him to a beautifully fitted kitchen with its own dining area. She made Aarons a glass of hot chocolate and a small pot of tea for herself.

'Are you tired, Andrei?'

He smiled. 'Not as tired as you must be after that long drive.'

'I'll have to fix for you to have driving lessons, it's crazy in this day and age not to be able to drive a car.'

'Who's the owner of the house? He must be very rich.'

'Just a friend. He seldom comes here. He lives in Manhattan.' She stretched her arms. 'It's time for bed or we shall be too tired to swim tomorrow.' As Aarons stood up and walked towards the bedroom he'd chosen she said, 'Sleep well. If there's anything you want call me.'

'Thank you.'

She shook her head slowly as he turned and walked away. It was hard to believe that this was the man that Grandpa Lensky had talked about. A man who had risked his freedom and possibly his life all those years working for the Party. And now was a colonel in intelligence and their star agent in New York. He was like a child. Too grateful for a kind word and yet suspicious of a friendly gesture. How could he be so intelligent and still be contented with the grim, grinding routine of his life? And how could those bastards in Moscow have tamed him and trained him to devote his life to their furtive affairs? But Lensky had said that he had the best analytical mind that he'd ever come across. This gauche, unsophisticated drudge of a man. He needed taking in hand.

She had persuaded him that it would be a good idea to stay on over Sunday night and drive back mid-day on

Monday. And after their evening snack she was looking through the gramophone records alongside an expensive radiogram.

'What kind of music do you like, Andrei – no don't tell me – it'll be Tchaik and Rach won't it?'

Aarons laughed. 'You're dead right.'

She looked at him. 'You know – that's the first time I've ever seen you laugh. The Sag Harbor air must be doing you good.' She paused. 'Back to the music. You ever heard of a guy named Korngold?'

'No.'

'Most people haven't. He writes music for films so with a name like that he's wide open to cracks like – oh yes, Korngold – more corn than gold – but he wrote a beautiful fiddle concerto. See what you think of it.'

She sat down watching his face as he listened to the music. For her Korngold was like a piece of musical litmus paper. If you were dismissive or indifferent to it then you were an outsider, but if you were moved by it then you were worth bothering with. She saw the tears on Aarons' cheeks and was happy about him. He was curable, or at least he could be patted into shape and made human. He would probably always be a Stoic, it was too late to change that, but maybe she could make him into a vulnerable Stoic. Vulnerability for Tania Orlovsky was what humanity was all about. What disturbed her was not so much Aarons as herself. She knew that she didn't really need to put him through her little Korngold test. All that old Russian blood in her veins was leading her astray. She knew that she was half in love with Andrei Aarons and she didn't know why.

As she watched him listening to the music she wondered what he would do if she just upped and told him she loved him. She smiled to herself as she imagined the horror on his face. He'd probably head back to Moscow.

But she learned her first lesson about surprises when, as she was driving them back to the city, he offered to take her to a night-club that evening. She would have bet her silver dollar that Aarons had never been in a night-club in his life. He had wondered why she laughed aloud when he explained about Sam and his sister.

Sam had taken Andrei off in the interlude to meet the other musicians in the band and Tania sat alone with Anna.

'How long have you known Andrei?'

Tania shrugged and smiled. 'A few weeks.'

'He said you'd taken him to Sag Harbor for the week-end. That must be the first holiday he's had in his life. How did you persuade him to go?'

Tania laughed. 'I just told him.'

'I've never seen him looking so alive, it must have done him good, the fresh air.' She paused. 'Or maybe it was you. How did you meet him?'

'We had a mutual acquaintance. A relative of mine.'

'Your name's Russian, do you speak Russian?'

'I can but I don't. I read Russian books sometimes – novels and poetry. Classics not modern stuff.'

'Can I ask you something personal?'

'Of course.' She smiled. 'But maybe I won't answer. So ask away.'

'Why do you bother with Andrei? He must seem rather dry to you.'

Tania shook her head slowly. 'Not dry, reserved maybe but not dry. It happens to people who devote their whole lives to some cause or other.'

'You still haven't said why you bother with him.'

'I admire him, his devotion to a cause, his mind and his loyalty.' She shrugged. 'I guess I just like him the same way you do.'

'How do you know what way I like him?'

'He told me how you had waited so long before you married – waited for his sake.'

'Are you part of his work?'

'Not the way you mean. I guess I love the dream but I know too much to believe in it. Do you believe in it?'

261

'No. I've never believed in it but I believe in Andrei and I go along with it.'

'Does he involve you in his work?'

'He used to but that stopped when I got married.'

'Because Sam didn't know about Andrei's work?'

'Yes. He still doesn't know.'

'What about your brother? Is he involved?'

'You'd better ask Andrei.'

Tania looked away and then back at Anna. 'They're coming back. Don't worry about Andrei. He'll be all right.' She smiled. 'Is it OK to bring him here again?'

'Of course. Sam's very fond of him.'

She stood looking around the living room. It was the first time that he had invited her back to his apartment. It was a large room with a high ceiling and it had obviously been recently painted. All of it white. And those were its only virtues. To describe it as masculine would be an abuse of words. It was a room entirely without character. Not a picture, not an ornament, not even a book, and God knows where he had found the furniture. It looked as if it was from some film-set for a film about Russian peasants. The best that you could say for the furniture was that it was built to last. It was not badly made, the heavy mahogany and the horse-hair stuffing were genuine but both ugly and incongruous in this setting.

When he came back with tea for them both she said, 'Who was that man you spoke to in the shop?'

'I knew him long ago when I lived in Paris.'

'But you were both speaking Russian.'

He smiled. 'He is Russian. Or he was, he's American now.'

'Is he on your side?'

He shrugged. 'He was once but not any more.' He smiled. 'About like you. On nobody's side.'

'What does he do now?'

Aarons shook his head. 'Don't ask.'

'Right,' she said, yawning. 'Can I bring you a few things to brighten up this room?'

He looked as if he was surprised that the room needed brightening up, and then he said, 'That would be very kind of you.'

She laughed, shaking her head. 'You idiot. You don't have to thank me. I'm a friend.'

35

Abe Karney was ex-US Marines, ex-Harvard Law School and ex-two wives. A large man with a large face and a belly that was beginning to look like a beer drinker's gut. A stranger could have taken him for a retired wrestler or an ex-pro football player and Karney did nothing to dispel that image. But, in fact, he was one of the shrewdest minds in the White House. And what was more important he was one of the very few men whom the President trusted.

Karney had no axes to grind, he was financially successful and backed by old family money. He had no yearning for power or status and had no official title in the White House administration. When the media referred to him as merely 'one of Truman's cronies' he made no attempt to deny it or justify his relationship with the President. In commerce and industry they were beginning to call men with his talents 'trouble-shooters'. He received no stipend from any government source but the running costs of his three-man staff were paid for from a small fund made available to the President for 'Research and Evaluation'. His staff consisted of a secretary, a young woman researcher and an ex-journalist.

With no authority of any kind beyond the knowledge that he was the President's eyes and ears he put out political fires between the top echelons of departments with a mixture of amiability and commonsense that made warring parties remember his interventions as both impartial and just. Those who resented the outsider found that their careers were not as secure as they had imagined. The interventions were not frequent because sometimes an invitation to a game of golf or to a White House dinner was hint enough without the problem subject ever being mentioned. A smile from Abe Karney could seem like a warning if your conscience was troubling you.

As the car edged its way into the short drive in front of the house Karney closed the outer doors and walked to where the driver was getting out of the car. He held out his hand to his visitor. 'Glad you could make it, Jake. Bella's out at some charity thing but she's left us some cold-cuts and stuff. Let's go inside.'

His visitor looked at the house. 'This is beautiful, Abe.'

'My old man bought it direct from Robert Simon when he was trying to turn Renton into a garden suburb. Before he went broke and had to sell out to Gulf Oil.'

'How is Bella?'

'Go up the steps. Bella? Has her good days and her bad days. They're trying new drugs on her. She'll be OK. Just takes time.'

Jake Hancox and Abe Karney had been friends when they were boys in a small town near Lake Champlain in Vermont.

As they helped themselves to food from the dishes on the sideboard Hancox said, 'That last book your Bella wrote – *Always Tomorrow* – I tried to work out which of those guys was you.'

Karney laughed. 'None of them was me. She never writes that sort of novel – by the way d'you know what they call those damn things when the characters are based on real people – they call 'em *romans à clef*. But she always puts at least one real son of a bitch in the story and everybody swears it's me.'

When they were seated and stabbing into the food with their forks Karney said, 'You come up with any ideas on this thing, Jake?'

'I get ideas on the hour every hour and each one's crazier than the previous one. What about you?'

'Well, the problem is that we don't even know what the

265

problem is. We don't know if this guy will go along with the idea. We don't know what would convince him that it's for everybody's good. His people as well as us. And there's a dozen little peripheral problems. We're walking around in the dark.'

'What do you see as the peripheral problems?'

'Most important is who's going to handle him. Can't be the FBI. They'd have a fit if they knew that we're even talking about such a thing. The CIA is too new. And it isn't secure enough. If something leaked out then our guy would end up in the morgue. Either here or in Moscow. And let's say we get it going, who's going to be privy to the information? As far as I can see it's got to be direct to the President. So only three people know what's going on. Truman, your guy and whoever handles him.'

'What does the President think?'

'No problem. Wants all the dope on Moscow he can get.'

'And willing to cut out the FBI and the CIA?'

'Yeah. No problem.' Karney smiled ruefully. 'I guess that's what he likes most about it.'

'What do you think about it from an intelligence point of view?'

'Well, its great advantage is that the President himself can specify what he wants to know about. It may not always be possible to oblige, but the rest of the material he gets from all sources is about what the agencies have happened to find out and that ain't necessarily what the little man wants to know about.'

'Say we make the approach and the guy turns us down flat. What then?'

Karney shrugged his big shoulders. 'I don't see that it matters. OK, he tells Moscow. So what?'

'And how do we know that he's not foxing us and playing it both ways?'

'That's part of the deal, isn't it? Two way traffic. He can give his views on what Washington are thinking but it'll just be his views and he's got no access. But what we get from him is straight out of the Kremlin where he's respected and seen as part of the inner circle or very near.'

'The big snag that has worried me is how can we guarantee that he won't be spotted at some time by the FBI and picked up?'

'We can't give any guarantee he won't get collared, that's up to him and they haven't spotted him in over ten years. But if he does get caught then OK we step in and stop the action.'

'With what explanation? We can't tell 'em that the President's running his own little private espionage operation.'

'I wouldn't worry about that stage. There's always some bullshit story we can give them. That or threats. Jobs, heads rolling etcetera. Sufficient unto the day, my friend. Have you spoken to Malloy about taking control of the operation if it gets off the ground?'

'No. Do you think it's time to do that? Not premature?'

'You got doubts about him?'

'No. I think he's got everything we need. Intelligence background, patriotic, a lawyer's analytical mind, energetic, virtually non-party political. What more could we ask for?'

'A knowledge of the Soviets? More awareness of international politics?'

'Better without that. He wouldn't be there to evaluate. He'd just be a contact, a hand-holder, a listener.' Hancox smiled. 'A high-grade nanny and delivery man.'

'Try him out, Jake. See how he responds.'

'What are you dealing with at the moment, Bill?'

'I've just finished the report for Defence on procurement contracts.' He grimaced. 'They're not going to like it but at least they'll be well prepared when the Congressional Commission starts.' He paused. 'And I've started on my investigation of the Lowden Trust.'

'How long will that take?'

'Quite a time. It's a possible Breach of Trust matter and the assets are widely dispersed.'

'Could Julian Manton take it over, d'you think?'

'I'm sure he could.' He paused. 'Has something else come up?'

'Yes, but not a legal matter. It's our old friend Mr X again. The friend of your old wartime colleague. The people in Washington would like to take it further. And they want you to take over the whole operation.'

'How long would it take?'

'I've no idea, Bill. First of all you'd have to get alongside Mr X, but I guess your friend could see to that. Then you've got to analyse how best to approach the possible deal.' He shrugged. 'And if you made it work it would be an on-going thing.'

'But I'm a lawyer, Jake, not a spook.'

'If you made this work you would have direct access to the President. You'd have one other very high-up contact in the White House. I would be out of it. Your friend would be out of it. Only you, the President, and the man I mentioned would know what was going on. You can imagine that if it worked you'd be far more valuable than if you were to stay as a lawyer.'

'Would I still have the firm as my base?'

'The firm would certainly be a cover if you wanted it that way. And I can say now that you'd be a senior partner no matter what the outcome. When you were not involved with the other thing you would function here to suit your availability.'

'Do *you* want me to do this, Jake?'

Hancox was silent for a few moments and then said, 'As senior partner in this firm -- no. As a patriotic American then the answer's yes. The fact that the man right at the top wants it has to be enough for the likes of me.'

'I guess that goes for me too.'

'Good, good. Let me bring you up-to-date.'

36

'Why the red light everywhere?'

'It's what you have in a darkroom, Andrei. Photographic papers aren't sensitive to red light. Come over here.'

When he stood beside her she said, 'Watch this.'

She slid a large sheet of paper into an enamelled tray half-full of liquid and as he watched he saw the image form. It looked like the base of a column and some words which he could not make out. She held it up for a few seconds to drain off the surplus liquid then slid it into another dish. 'That was the developer and this is the stop-bath and then it goes in the fixer. We can put the lights on then while it's washing in the sink.'

He looked around the darkroom. There were two enlargers, timers, developing tanks and a cork board with hooks for scissors and small implements he couldn't identify.

When she switched on the main lights he had to half-close his eyes to get used to the brightness. She took his hand and led him over to a work-bench on the far wall and turned to him. 'These are for your room.'

She pulled aside a sheet of brown paper and he saw two large photographs, mounted and framed. The first one was of a line of limousines outside the main entrance to the Waldorf with chauffeurs and flunkies opening the doors for people in dress clothes obviously going to some important dinner. The second photograph was of a line of tired, ill-dressed people queuing at a soup kitchen. She let him look for a moment then said, 'The third one is the one in the sink. Come and look at it. It'll be the centre picture between the other two.'

As they stood at the metal sink she said, 'It's the foot of the Statue of Liberty.' He'd not seen the words before.

> Give me your tired, your poor,
> Your huddled masses yearning to be free,
> The wretched refuse of your teeming shore.
> Send these, the homeless, tempest tossed to me.
> I lift my lamp beside the golden door.

For long moments Aarons stood there looking at the photograph and then he turned his face to look at her. 'Who wrote those words?'

She smiled. 'Her name was Emma Lazarus, a New York Jewess. Died in 1887. She was a very good poet but nowadays people imagine she was some old dear like Ella Wheeler Wilcox writing good thoughts for the day. Some even say that those words are hypocritical. That what really happens to poor people in this country belies those words.'

He nodded. 'I can understand that but that isn't what matters.'

'Oh. What is it that matters?'

'What matters is that she had those thoughts and enough people felt the same way to put them on the Statue of Liberty.' He turned his head to look at her. 'Americans mean those words even if they don't live up to them.'

'They're very you, Andrei.'

'In what way?'

'A great feeling for humanity and an inability to face the basic facts of life.'

'What basic facts of life?'

She laughed softly. 'Another poet said it better than I can. A Scot who married an American. Robert Louis Stevenson.'

270

'Go on.'

'He said – "Saints are the sinners who keep on going." They were contemporaries, Emma Lazarus and him.' She paused. 'But you're absolutely right. What matters is that that was how people wanted it to be.' She shrugged and smiled. 'We'll get it right in the end – you'll see.'

'Thanks for the photographs and all the trouble you . . .'

She stamped her foot, 'Don't say that. Don't be like that.'

'Like what?'

'Don't be so . . . so grateful. I enjoyed doing the photographs for you.'

'What can I do to please you?'

For long moments she looked at him, smiling. An affectionate smile as she shook her head slowly. 'You know, Andrei, what makes the difference between most people and an artist is that most people look without seeing.' She paused. 'And I guess that some people listen without hearing.' She took his arm. 'Let's go upstairs and eat.' She laughed as she squeezed his arm. 'Just an omelette and then some strawberries and cream.'

They had finished their meal and were playing chess when the bell rang and when he opened the street door Aarons had hesitated for a moment when he saw that it was Serov. Then he invited him in and upstairs he had introduced him to Tania Orlovsky. With the introductions over she went to the kitchen to make them coffee and when she came back with a tray Aarons said, 'My friend here wants me to meet his fiancée. They both live in Washington. I thought we might all go to Sam's club on Saturday evening to celebrate.'

'A good idea, Andrei.' She looked at Serov. 'Do you like jazz, Mr Serov?'

Serov smiled. 'Is "Tiger Rag" jazz?'

She laughed. 'Kind of. We'll get him to play it for you and your girl. What does she do?'

'She works in a small restaurant as a waitress.'

'Is that where you met her?'

'Yes. I used to eat there every evening.' He laughed. 'I still do.'

'D'you speak Russian, Mr Serov?'

'Yes. I was born Russian.'

'How do you like Washington?'

'Better than Moscow but not as good as Paris.'

'You know Paris well?'

'Yes. I lived there for many years.' He shrugged. 'That's where I first met Andrei.' He smiled. 'We were just very young men in those days. Not very wise in the ways of the world.'

She laughed, glancing at Andrei. 'I don't think he's changed much.'

Serov stood up. 'Shall we come here first on Saturday, Andrei?'

'Yes. Come about seven and then we'll all go to the club.'

After Serov had gone they finished the game of chess and as Aarons put the pieces back in the box she said, 'Does he know about you, Andrei?'

He nodded. 'Yes. He was part of it, way back. But he defected. He worked for an OSS network during the war. He's been very lonely over here. I'm glad he's found a girl-friend.'

'What does he do in Washington?'

'Works for the CIA.'

'You're kidding.'

'No. He just works on documents for the French desk.'

'And you trust him not to tell them about you?'

'Yes.'

'And Moscow – do they know that you're in contact with him?'

'No. I haven't told them.'

'Why not?'

He shrugged. 'We were friends, comrades.' He smiled.

'We shared that dream. He no longer believes it – but he's still a friend. I understand.'

'What do you understand?'

'When people try to make it a better world for us to live in they will make mistakes. Serov was too close to Moscow. He saw the mistakes and in the end, for him, the mistakes were more real than the dream.'

'And why aren't you affected the same way?' she said quietly.

'Because I wasn't so close to the mistakes and because the dream for me was for the whole world not just for the Soviet Union. It's like those words on the Statue of Liberty in my photograph. I can't forget them. I love them. And the words of the Constitution. They dreamed of the same world. The Americans have made terrible mistakes too.'

'But there's a difference, Andrei. A big difference.'

He smiled. 'Tell me.'

'The Americans admit their mistakes. People can say fully what they think. There's no knock on the door in the middle of the night. And no Gulag camps.'

'What about Senator McCarthy and his committee who have trials by the newspapers and television. And the negroes in the south who are harassed by the police just because they are black. Is that justice any more than Moscow's justice?'

'Do you really believe that there's nothing to choose between them? Millions of people come here for a new life, a better life. Are they all fools? And how many people leave their homes for a new life in the Soviet Union?'

For a few moments Aarons was silent and then he said, 'No. They're not the same. America is a better place to live. But there weren't twenty million Americans killed in the war and the country wasn't devastated by an invading army. I do what I do because I want the Soviet people to have good lives too.'

273

'So why doesn't Moscow collaborate with the Americans, and make it so. Why are we the enemy?'

'Because there are people on both sides who have a vested interest in making it so.' He paused. 'It's a lack of knowledge and understanding. What does the average American know about Russian people? Nothing good is said about them, ever. And the average Russian has been told for decades that America wants to destroy the Soviet Union. I want the people in Moscow to know more.'

'And when they know more will they change their thinking?'

'I don't know, Tania. I want them to at least have the chance to think again.'

She shook her head, but she was smiling as she stood up. 'I must go.'

'We'll take a taxi.'

'You don't have to bother.'

He laughed. 'Shall I stamp my foot and say – don't be so grateful?'

She smiled. 'You're learning, my boy, you're learning.'

On the Saturday night Aarons had ordered champagne to toast Serov and his bride-to-be, and Tania had been amused to see him sipping the champagne as if it were hemlock.

They had been to the club a number of times and she had taught him a couple of simple dance steps so that they could shuffle together round the small dance-floor when the jazz was converted into 'Smoke Gets in Your Eyes' or Gershwin's 'Fascinating Rhythm' done as a fox-trot.

Sam was playing a solo while the other four went for a beer and he was in the last few minutes of 'Rhapsody in Blue' when Serov said, 'I don't believe it.' He was looking at a couple standing by the hat-check girl's small counter. Aarons and Tania followed Serov's eyes. He turned to Aarons. 'That's the guy who was my boss in Occupied France, and that's his wife Kathy. I didn't know he was interested in jazz.' Aarons looked at the couple and then

274

back at Serov's face. 'Do you want to ask them over for a drink?'

'Are you sure you don't mind?'

'Of course I don't.'

'Angie's never met him. That would be great.'

He stood up, pushing back his chair, waving at the couple as they stood at the top of the steps that led down to the tables. Serov walked over to them and they stood there talking for a few minutes and the man looked over at them as Serov pointed to their table. The man smiled and nodded then followed Serov who introduced them, Tania, Angela, Anna and Aarons. Two extra chairs were found and another bottle of champagne. Aarons noticed that Bill Malloy barely touched his champagne.

There was much chatter about Serov's and Malloy's time together in France but no mention of Serov's defection or what had happened to them when they had been taken by the Germans.

Sam came over and after the introductions had taken the girls and Serov to meet the rest of Sam's quintet in the bar.

Malloy said, 'Are you a jazz buff, Andrei?'

Aarons smiled. 'I'm afraid not. I come because of my brother-in-law.'

'Igor tells me you're a specialist bookseller. What kind of books do you sell?'

'I used to have a shop in Brighton Beach and then it was mainly books in Russian and Polish. Novels, politics, history. And some in Hebrew. But now I'm in Manhattan it's mainly rare books, old books. And they cover all sorts of subjects. Religion, sermons, science, politics.' He smiled. 'They make a lot more money than the others.'

'I gather you and Igor more or less grew up together in Paris.'

Andrei smiled. 'Tania says we still haven't grown up. I suppose Paris was a good place to be young in.'

'My memories of Paris aren't so pleasant. I was in prison there after the Germans rounded up my network.'

'Have you been back?'

Malloy shook his head. 'No.' He smiled, embarrassedly. 'I guess if I'm truthful I didn't much like the French. I didn't like them before I went and I liked them even less when it was over.'

'Why was that?'

'They seemed to expect everyone else to liberate them but complained that their country was damaged in the process.'

'And Serov?'

'He wasn't French, he was Russian. He taught me a lot.'

'About what?'

Malloy smiled. 'Communism for a start. Like most Americans I hated the idea of Communism but when I listened to Serov and his friends talking politics they sounded just like my father.'

'Was he a communist?'

Malloy laughed. 'Maybe he was, but he certainly didn't know it. He was just a working man who cared about other working men.'

'What do you do, Mr Malloy?'

'It's Bill.' He shrugged. 'I'm a partner in a law-firm here in Manhattan.'

'What kind of law do you do?'

'Mainly trust funds and evaluating government contracts with major industries.'

'Do big companies try to cheat the government?'

Malloy smiled, wryly. 'Let's say they sometimes try to build in what we refer to as non-appropriate allowances.'

Then the others came back to the table. They stayed chatting for another hour then Malloy and Kathy left and shortly afterwards Tania and Aarons left.

They walked down Fifth Avenue to 41st Street and Aarons' place. She linked her arm in his as they walked.

'What did you think of Serov's friend?'

'Seemed a nice enough guy. What was his wife like?'

276

'Not so solemn as he was. But obviously thinks he's something special.'

'And what did you think of Serov's girl?'

She laughed. 'Angela? She's just what he needs. Pretty, lively, warm and typically American.'

'What's typically American?'

'Optimistic, cheerful. Pleased with life. Haven't you noticed that Igor is getting to be quite human these last few times we've seen him?'

As they waited for the lights at 45th Street he turned her towards him and put his hands on her shoulders as he looked at her face.

'Why do you bother with me?'

For several moments she looked back at him and then she said quietly, 'Because, Andrei Grigorovich Aarons, I don't *bother* with you – I love you.'

He was silent for a few moments, then he said, 'I can't believe it.' He shrugged. 'I wish it was true.'

'It's true, my love. I liked you the first time we met but it's much more than just liking now.'

She saw tears in his eyes then he rested his head on her shoulder. Her hand gently stroked his neck. When he lifted his head he was smiling, and she kissed him gently on the mouth. It was beginning to rain and he looked up at the sky and said, 'I'll always be happy in future when it rains.'

'Why?'

'Because this is my lucky day and it's raining. And I ain't ever going to get wet in the rain ever again.'

She smiled. 'Let's go. It's time we were in bed.'

He glanced at her face as they crossed the street and as she looked back at him she winked. 'Yes, I did say *we*.'

37

In the White House that Christmas President Truman wrote in his diary – '. . . I have worked for peace for five years and six months and it looks like World War III is near.'

The war in Korea had become a disaster. With conflicting views on Chinese intentions from MacArthur and the intelligence agencies it seemed that the nightmare would never end. There was to be no Christmas for the President.

In New York the Aarons family had gathered for a meal and at the end Andrei told them that he and Tania were to be married in the New Year. He was surprised and relieved that they all seemed so pleased. Serov and Angela had married two weeks earlier and had joined them for the Christmas holidays.

The day after Christmas the Communists recrossed the 38th parallel and the President had received a hand-written note from General MacArthur who demanded that Congress should now recognise that a state of war existed with the Chinese as well as the North Koreans, and followed this up with the recommendation that the United States should drop thirty to fifty atomic bombs on air bases and other strategic points in Manchuria, then land half a million Chinese Nationalist troops from Formosa with two divisions of US Marines at either end of the border between Korea and China. Finally, after the defeat of the Chinese they should 'lay down a belt of active cobalt all along the Yalu River'.

On New Year's Eve 1951 the whole family plus Malloy and Kathy were celebrating at Sam's club. Celebrating not only the New Year, but Andrei's forthcoming marriage and the fact that Sam was now the owner of half the equity in the club. Even Ivan was there with his Rachel. Serov and Angie joined them just before midnight. And as they all joined hands to sing 'Auld Lang Syne' half a million Chinese and Koreans poured through the American defences on their unstoppable sweep to take Seoul.

The next months were field days for the isolationists like Joseph Kennedy and Hoover but to the American public even the official policy of local containment rather than unlimited warfare seemed nothing short of treason. In the White House the President saw it as proof that all over the world the Communists were intent on bringing America to its knees. And it was a time when to the man in the street Joe McCarthy seemed the only hero he'd got left. Every shabby lie he uttered seemed to work, and his hatreds had become uncontrollable. It was Congressman Nixon who stopped the drunken McCarthy from physically beating up Drew Pearson in the men's room of a Washington club. It wasn't a good time for politicians or journalists.

It wasn't too good for soldiers either. Unlike Eisenhower, MacArthur was not widely admired by fighting men, and in Washington the Joint Chiefs of Staff had realised as far back as January that the General had lost confidence in himself and was fast losing the confidence of his field officers and troops. By early March the President decided that it was time for a cease-fire and negotiations.

When MacArthur got his instructions from the President to this effect the General told the press that he would negotiate on his terms and offer Peking total annihilation. He then appealed to the House with scathing comments on the White House and the President. In the early hours of 8 April the President announced that the General had been relieved of all his commands.

Rarely had a President of the United States been so reviled. The public, frustrated by the war that no one could win, were up in arms. The flag was burned or flown at half-mast, effigies of Truman were burned in public places, clergymen reviled him from their pulpits and one Los Angeles newspaper suggested that the President was befuddled by drugs.

The returning MacArthur was invited to address the House and after his speech Representative Dewey Short of Missouri said – 'We heard God speak here today.'

As the fighting in Korea ground on and settled to a bloody stalemate the public virtually ignored the far away war and turned its mind to what seemed to be an economic boom. The war's only legacy seemed to be an even more zealous loathing of communists and fellow travellers. Mickey Spillane and his Mike Hammer novels epitomised the vigilante instinct for violence that seemed to be latent in every American. It sensed that the civilised West were helpless against the brute force of their enemies and maybe their hope lay with the violent men in their midst who weren't afraid to take the law into their own hands. Even the more cautious who didn't approve of McCarthy's methods felt that maybe he'd got the right idea.

It was in June 1951 that the Atomic Energy Commission agreed to the financing of America's first H-bomb plant. It looked as if the two world powers were testing each other out to see which one of them was most ready for World War III.

38

Aarons was surprised when he saw the 'For Rent' sign pasted in the window of Cowley's shop but assumed that he was moving to larger premises.

Cowley came out from the back-room, a soldering-iron in his hand.

'Is business that good?' Aarons said, pointing at the sign.

'I'm closing down, chief. Moving out of New York.'

'Why?'

Cowley shrugged. 'I'm tired of working for myself.'

'What about my work?'

'Have to call it a day. But you've got other radio people, haven't you?'

'What makes you think that?'

'I've heard at least two different operators on my scanner.' He smiled. 'I recognised the five figure groups and the tops and tails you use.'

'What are you going to do?'

'Moving down south. The government are setting up a radio surveillance place. State of the art computers and radios like you've never seen – me neither.'

'To do what?'

'Can't really talk about it but you'd better warn your people, they'll be monitoring everything that's on the air. Not just in the States. All over the world.'

'And what will you be doing?'

'Maintenance, general dogsbody. Good money, pension, medical insurance – the lot.'

'How long before you close down here?'

'About four weeks. I'll give you fair warning.'

'Is this new place FBI or CIA?'

'Don't think it's either.' He shrugged. 'I could be wrong.'

Aarons nodded and held out his hand. 'Hope it's all you want it to be.'

'You got anything for me?'

Aarons hesitated for a moment and then took an envelope from his jacket pocket. 'There's the cash and a short message. It's not urgent.'

Back at his apartment Aarons had encoded his report to Moscow and given it to Ivan to take down to the dentist in Brighton Beach who was a radio ham and had been his first operator. He still needed him for routine traffic to Toronto where it was passed on to Moscow. The news about Cowley and the new government radio surveillance set-up was bad news. He wondered vaguely if there was more to Cowley's defection than he had said. But maybe it was the money and the pension. He had seen Cowley several times in the last three weeks and he hadn't given a hint of his new plans and he must have been negotiating with them during that time. Had he been careless or had Cowley been working to somebody's instructions?

Two days later he got orders from Moscow Centre to meet a contact at the house on Long Island.

He took a train from Penn Station and a bus to Garden City and walked the rest of the way. The area always reminded him of Paris. The long tree-lined boulevards and the grand houses. It was dark and the house itself was surrounded by tall trees. The wrought-iron gate swung open easily and he walked up the gravel pathway with lawns on each side to the glassed-in porch of the old house. There were lights on all over and the sound of a radio from an open window. As he reached for the bell the door opened.

It was Harris himself who opened the door. He was a tall, lanky man with heavy glasses that gave him an academic look. And he had once been an academic, at a university in Texas. But his appetite for teenage students had made him unemployable in teaching circles and he now earned a meagre living doing desk-research for commercial companies, including banks and sharebrokers. He earned rather more doing the same sort of work for Aarons.

Harris waved him towards the open door of the living room. 'Hi,' he said, 'the guy's waiting for you. I'll leave you to it. Give me a shout when you've finished.'

Aarons had been to the house several times before, and knew that Harris used the room for his work. The walls were lined with bookshelves and there was a large plain table piled with newspapers and magazines. And in a chair on the far side of the room was a man he recognised from one of the Kremlin meetings. At least he recognised his face but couldn't remember his name.

The man stood up and held out his hand, smiling as he said, 'It's Yakov, Igor Yakov. We met in Moscow.'

Then Aarons noticed the uniform and Yakov laughed softly, 'Don't worry. It's cabin crew uniform on Aeroflot. Moscow wanted me over here quickly.' He shrugged. 'This was what your people worked out. I go back on duty tomorrow morning.'

'What's the hurry?'

'Your report on your radio operator. The one who's going to a new installation.'

'Let's sit at the table.'

When they were seated Aarons said, 'What's the problem?'

'Moscow has had other reports on this new organisation. They think it's going to be the most important US intelligence agency – more important than the CIA and the FBI. The reports indicate that it will be responsible for monitoring radio and telephone operations all over the world. There's no doubt that it's very high-technology.'

He paused. 'They want you to concentrate on this outfit. Money no object.'

'I don't even know where it's located. And I've no technical background.'

'No. But you've got your radio man.'

'He isn't going to risk giving me top-secret information. He's too keen on his job and a government pension.'

'Experience says that it's always only a question of finding the price.'

'I don't have funds that would stretch that far. I'd have to drop the rest of my operations.'

Yakov stood up, walked over to where he had been sitting, reached down beside the chair and picked up a worn black leather case. Walking back to the table, laying down the case and opening it, he drew out three large green envelopes and handed the top one to Aarons. The envelope was not sealed and he opened it, drawing out the contents carefully.

The first item was a letter between sheets of tissue paper and a description. It was a letter from Voltaire to Algarotti and the description gave its date as 1751. The second item was Stalin's copy of Trotsky's pamphlet on the rôle of trades unions. Signed by Stalin on the cover and annotated by him in pencil. A note said that this was the first time that a pamphlet belonging to Stalin had ever been on sale.

There was a letter signed by Leon Trotsky and written in English to an American Trotskyist named Dwight Macdonald. Then notes autographed by Stalin to Voroshilov were followed by a bundle of ten letters signed by Molotov to his sister. Finally there was an autographed postcard signed by Lenin to the Bolshevik Dr Schklowsky in Berlin.

Aarons laid them all carefully aside and looked at Yakov.

'What are these for?'

'To fund the operation.'

'How can I authenticate them?'

'In this envelope . . .' he handed the second envelope to Aarons '. . . all the receipts are from established and

284

independent dealers in rare books and documents.'

'But they're so Russian it will draw attention to me.'

'None of the authentication sources are in Russia. Two are in Paris, one in Vienna and another in Berne. The bills of sale are receipted and are all genuine.' He handed Aarons the third envelope. 'Don't bother to read it now but it's a list of books that I shall give you. Rare books, first editions, signed by the authors. An expert in Moscow values the material at about one hundred thousand US dollars. It could be more.'

Aarons nodded. 'I think it could be far more than that from what I've seen already.'

Yakov shrugged. 'So that's your basic fund for the operation. Buy your friend Cohen the radio man. But you'll need others as well. There's more back-up funds if you need them. But we must have results.'

'Tell me about the other reports that you've had.'

'There were only three. No more than you had had except that one source said that the site of the organisation was to be at Fort Meade in Maryland. Could be wrong of course.'

'What do they want to know?'

'Everything. Equipment, people, daily operations, scope, who's in charge, what agency funds the operation. Nothing's too small.'

'It'll take me time to work out a system.'

Yakov shrugged. 'It'll take the Americans time to set it up too.'

'If Cohen won't cooperate it will mean starting from scratch. It's in a part of America that I don't know at all. My operation is New York based. I can't leave it to run itself.'

'Why not send Harris down there. Just on reconnaissance. If he does well let him stay.'

'He's an American. I'd only trust a Soviet.'

Yakov smiled. 'The men in Moscow would approve your caution, Andrei. But they'd take real risks to be able to penetrate this monitoring set-up.' He stood up. 'But they'll trust your judgement whatever you do.' He smiled. 'And believe me there are not many men I could say that about, in or out of Moscow.' He waved to a side table. 'The books are on there. I'll have to go, my friend.' He smiled. 'They keep a tight hold on Aeroflot cabin-crew.'

Back at his place Aarons looked through the rest of the material that had been given to him. It was incredible. Six volumes of La Fontaine inscribed by the author, three volumes of the first edition of Karl Marx's *Das Kapital*, all the volumes of the first edition of Tolstoi's *War and Peace* each inscribed by the author, another copy signed by Stalin of Trotsky's pamphlet *The rôle and tasks of Trade Unions,* and even an original lithographed plate of one of Verlaine's poems illustrated by Bonnard. It was a treasure trove that was almost invaluable. Not only wealthy collectors but universities and museums would almost certainly be eager buyers. He wished that he had time to enjoy the dispersal of such wonderful material.

The only consolation that he had was that after Yakov had left he had talked for two hours with Harris and had made arrangements for him to go down to Maryland for a week to see what he could find out. He had the technical know-how and the perfect background for such an attempt.

Anna had insisted that they went in separate cars to City Hall. She said it was bad luck for the bride-to-be and the groom to go together. It was a Thursday and there were only two other couples to be married by the City Clerk.

As they sat waiting Anna looked at her brother. She had made him buy a new suit and had bought a white carnation for his button-hole. She wondered if he was thinking of Chantal and that wedding in Paris all those years ago. He had been so eager to be married then but his enthusiasm for people and causes had drained away over the years. She had talked with Tania about him. It was obvious that she loved Andrei but she was very different from Chantal. Independent and not submissive. She understood how a girl like Tania could admire a man like Andrei, but she wondered what made her love him. When she'd asked, Tania had smiled and said she didn't know. In a way it seemed almost a maternal love. And maybe that was what he needed.

She looked at the others. Serov and Angie had become a typical American couple and Malloy sat between Sam and Kathy. And Ivan sitting there with his latest girlfriend. Her vague worries lifted as she realised that none of the couples seemed obviously suitable for one another. Not even her and Sam. Maybe that was what made marriages work. Then the clerk was beckoning them inside his office.

They lunched at the Waldorf and in the afternoon they went to the cinema to see Gary Cooper in *High Noon*. They spent the evening at Sam's club and he played 'Love Walked In' for Tania and Andrei, 'Manhattan' for Serov and Angie, 'Twelfth Street Rag' for Ivan and his girlfriend, and 'She's My Lovely' for the Malloys. And to everyone's surprise Andrei had bought a very beautiful diamond ring for his new wife. A good time was had by all, and only Anna's mind went back to the days in Brighton Beach when only survival mattered, and a walk to Coney was a special treat.

39

Hancox had listened to Malloy's conversation with Serov without joining in but when they seemed to have finished he took over.

'Bill, you seem to be disagreeing with Mr Serov about Aarons. Where does the difference lie?'

Malloy shook his head. 'It's not really a difference, just a different reading of Aarons' character.' He pointed to Serov. 'Igor sees him as an idealist, a man who is loyal to a lost cause, and maybe easy to influence.' He paused. 'I've met Aarons a number of times now and I can see why Igor thinks the way he does. Aarons is an idealist but he's intelligent enough to realise that the Soviet experiment is nothing more than a dictatorship. And underneath that rather soft personality there's a very tough guy. He wouldn't have survived so well if he wasn't tough.'

'So what are you saying?'

Malloy shrugged. 'All I'm saying is – don't see Aarons as a pushover. He isn't. Sure he cares about the masses, the human condition, but he's a very successful spy, operating here undetected for years. He'll realise straight away that my meeting with him in the night-club was a set-up. He won't like that. He won't like Serov or me for doing it. We've got to do something to counter that.'

'What do you suggest?'

'I think there's only one way we can do it. Give him some piece of information that's top secret that Moscow really wants.'

'Such as?'

Malloy shook his head and looked at Serov. 'I don't know, maybe Igor could test the water.' He paused. 'What do you think, Igor?'

Serov shrugged. 'Let me fish around and see what I can come up with.'

Hancox said quietly, 'OK. You do that Mr Serov, but a word of warning. If he takes the bait and we give him what he wants then it's part of a deal. We don't put the deal forward afterwards. He says what he wants and it's a test of our good faith. If we deliver then he goes with our suggestion.'

Serov spoke up. 'But we are not suggesting an exchange of espionage material – just he tells us of current Kremlin thinking and we put him in the picture on Washington thinking.'

'Yeah. That's what it is,' Hancox said. 'Both camps get a window on the other side. What they do about it is up to them.'

Malloy looked at Serov. 'When are you going to approach him?'

'As soon as I can. Tomorrow if it's possible.'

As Malloy and Serov went down together in the elevator Malloy put his arm around Serov's shoulders. 'Are you still feeling guilty, Igor?'

'Not really. I've got your word that Andrei will not be betrayed to the CIA or the FBI. The rest is a genuine attempt to do good for both sides.'

It was two days before Serov was able to contact Aarons and as Aarons poured him a cup of coffee Serov was torn with doubts and fears of the consequences if Aarons turned on him as a betrayer. His hand trembled as he took the cup.

'You OK, Igor?'

'Yeah. I think maybe I'm starting the 'flu.'

'You said on the phone that there was something urgent.'

'Do you count me as a friend, Andrei?'

Aarons looked surprised. 'Of course.'

'Do you trust me?'

Aarons was silent for a moment. 'Igor, you know my work. I can't afford to trust anyone entirely.'

'I understand, but do you see me as a man who would deliberately do you harm?'

'No. Of course not.'

'Do you remember some time back saying that you were tired of finding excuses for some of the things that Moscow does?'

'Yes.'

'You felt that you gave them an honest picture as to what is going on in the States. At least with Lensky you could be frank.'

'You're beginning to worry me, Igor.'

'Just listen to me, Andrei, I swear I only want to help.'

'Help who, the CIA?'

'This has nothing to do with my work.' He sighed. 'You know how closely I worked with Bill Malloy in France. I trust him like I trust you. I want you to talk to him.'

'What about?'

'He thinks that the Soviets and the Americans are heading for a war because neither side is getting a true picture of the other side's real intentions.'

'Go on.'

'Do you agree with what I've just said?'

'It's possible.'

'Malloy thinks that you could provide a balance. You know what the people in the Kremlin are really thinking and if you were given access to the top of the US government you could understand what *they* are thinking.'

'Or what they tell me they're thinking.'

'I'm talking about one-to-one contact between you and the President.'

'You're out of your mind, my friend.' Aarons laughed sharply. 'Can you imagine me even getting inside the White House?' He shook his head. 'You mean well, Igor, but you're dreaming wild dreams.'

290

'But if it *wasn't* a dream?'

'Go home, Igor, have a whiskey and lemon and a good long sleep.'

'Andrei . . .' Serov said quietly, '. . . it's not a dream. It's already been arranged.'

'Is this some sort of trap?'

'I swear to you, Andrei. It is exactly what I have said. Malloy's boss has arranged it because he trusts Malloy's judgement. The President has agreed.'

'Do they know what I do here in the States?'

'Yes. But only four people know apart from me. They have no intention of using that as leverage. If you refuse, things will go on just as they are now. Nobody in the FBI or CIA will be any the wiser.'

'How long have you been working on this?'

'I guess about two months. From the day when I felt you were tired of seeing both sides making stupid mistakes.'

'Who suggested you should talk to me about all this?'

'Nobody. Malloy spoke as if he was as unhappy about what was happening between the Soviets and America as you were. You both used almost the same words, it was like listening to an echo. I thought about it many times and then I spoke to him about you. No name or anything. Gave him your background and suggested this idea of mine. He spoke to a man he trusted, his boss, a top attorney. At first he said what you said – that we were out of our minds. Then he thought about it and he quizzed me for hours about you. And did you know about the idea? It took about two months and then I made it so you could meet Malloy. He liked you and it was back up the line. Right to President Truman.' He shrugged, 'And here I am.'

'And I'm supposed to become a double-agent. Spying on the Kremlin for Washington and on the White House for Moscow.'

'No. Nothing like that, Andrei. Nothing contrived at all. Just give your views on what Moscow are thinking. Just what you yourself feel they're thinking.'

'And for Moscow?'

'You can ask the President about US policy and attitudes. Even discuss them with him. Just their general attitude to world conditions, especially the Soviets. Whether you pass it on to the Kremlin is up to you. Nobody will check on you.'

'I can't believe this, Igor. It's just not credible. Politicians don't do such things.' He frowned. 'What would happen if I went to a newspaper with this?'

'They wouldn't believe you. You don't believe it despite the fact that you know me and you know Malloy. If you don't believe it why should a journalist?'

'And all this has actually been discussed with the President?'

'Yes. And he's agreed.'

'How do they expect me to have access to the Kremlin if I have to fold up my network?'

'You don't have to, Andrei. It's accepted that that would be part of the deal. They're not offering immunity if you get caught by the FBI but what you do for Moscow is a separate issue.' He looked at Aarons, 'I think if this works they would give you protection anyway. They don't want to say so right now in case you were tempted to go over the top on your intelligence work because you relied on them providing immunity.'

'I'll need time to think about it, Igor. It's a bit of a bombshell.'

'I know. But there was no other way I could think of to tell you about it. I can arrange for you to talk to Malloy or Hancox or both if that would help.'

'Just let me get it straight. I just tell the President what people in the Kremlin are thinking and in turn he'll put me in the picture about his thinking.'

'And he'll ask you to comment on both lots of information. Maybe even ask your recommendations of how to keep things under control.'

'And the only reason for doing this is to prevent unnecessary tension and aggression.'

'Yeah.' Serov shrugged. 'And of course nobody knows whether either side will heed what you tell them. Other people on both sides will have conflicting views.'

'How long can I think about it?'

Serov shrugged. 'They've got to wait as long as you choose to make them wait.'

'It would be a terrible responsibility, my friend. I could misread situations.'

'It will be other people who decide what their attitudes will be. But both sides will be better informed because of you.'

'Let me think about it.'

'And we keep it strictly between ourselves.'

'At this stage, yes. But I should want Tania to know. Not the details but the essence of what I'd be trying to do.'

'It's better if she's not involved, Andrei.'

'She's involved already, my friend. She's my wife.'

When Serov had left Aarons stood at the windows that looked over 41st Street. He stood looking down at the people on the far side of the street, hurrying about their business, indifferent and ignorant of what was going on in the world outside the United States. Heading for home or the movies or even a last chance to see *Oklahoma*. And some would want nothing more than an evening listening to the radio, the *March of Time*, *Charlie Chan*, *Dick Tracy* or one of the soap operas that were supposed to show what family life was really like. And in those crowds there were people from every country in Europe. These were the huddled masses from those lines on the Statue of Liberty. And no matter what the critics might say they were undoubtedly living better here than ever before. But despite all those immigrants America still seemed totally ignorant about Europe and the rest of the world. America didn't need the rest of the world, so why should they care. Old allies had turned on them. The French under de Gaulle had been encouraged to despise everything

American, the Russians were now America's open enemies. And the English still laboured under the delusion that they'd won the war alone and were looking for handouts. And who was he that people thought he could help to put right the ignorance and misunderstanding that might lead to another war? That was what ambassadors were for. But he knew that the reports of the Soviet ambassador in Washington would be ignored by the Kremlin and if the ambassador didn't say what Moscow wanted then he'd be replaced.

He thought about Malloy who was obviously just as much a victim as he was. From a working-class background but no way a sympathiser with Communism. Not an international idealist either. He obviously detested the French. Saw them as effete and hypocritical. And Moscow thought much the same. But only an American could have dreamed up a scenario like Serov had described. It was crazy but maybe it could work. If either Moscow or Washington actually wanted war then they'd go ahead when they thought the time was ripe. But maybe if they understood each other better it could change the atmosphere of constant suspicion. Who knows? He could remember something that Serov had said many years ago, or was it the Spanish girl who had said it? Whoever it was, had said that he was a Jew without a religion and a Russian without a country. He smiled to himself. Maybe those were as good a set of qualifications for this crazy set-up that you could get.

He told Tania about Serov's proposition while they were eating. When he'd finished he looked at her and said, 'What d'you think?'

She shrugged and smiled. 'Sounds crazy to me so it's probably worth trying. More important is what you think.'

'I just wonder if they think I'm more important than I really am.'

'Grandad Lensky told me way back that they set great store by you and what you do.'

'But they took me off politics and kept me on intelligence work.'

'Honey, the good Lord himself couldn't keep you off politics. You've been into politics since you were a kid. Anyway they don't expect you to know every detail of what's going on in the Kremlin.' She laughed. 'Even people in the Kremlin don't know it either.'

'Maybe it comes down to a question of loyalty.'

'That's rubbish and you know it. Tell me . . .' she paused '. . . do you think Moscow would drop atomic bombs on America?'

He smiled. 'No.'

'Why not?'

'There'd be no point. There'd be nothing left. There'd be no prize.'

'And do you think we'll drop atom bombs on the Soviet Union?'

'No.'

'Why not?'

He shrugged and smiled. 'I'd reckon that was an un-American activity. They don't want a war. They want to go on enjoying themselves.'

'You know damned well that America wouldn't do a thing unless Moscow attacked them first.'

Aarons shook his head slowly. 'It's not as simple as that. There are powerful people on both sides who would be all for starting a war. Not a world war. Just taking over some country for strategic reasons or because they have some valuable resources. They can both fight proxy wars. But those can develop into major confrontations.'

'What sort of people would want that in the Kremlin?'

'The military. The hard-liners.'

'And here? Who wants to make wars in Washington.'

'The people who make huge profits from armaments.' He shrugged. 'And the Red-haters.'

'All the more reason why you should try to pour oil on troubled waters.'

'Putting politics aside – what would you like me to do?'

'You really want me to say?'

'Yes.'

For long moments she was silent, then she said, 'There's no point in me saying what I'd like, is there?'

'You're my wife, that's enough.'

'OK,' she said quietly, 'with my income from the studio and what you make on the books, we could live quite happily.' She paused. 'That's what I'd like.'

He reached across the table and put his hand on hers. 'Try to understand, my love. It's like breathing – I couldn't stop even if I wanted to.'

She smiled. 'I don't expect you to change your life, honey. Just a touch on the brakes here and there. Don't worry.'

'And this thing of Serov's?'

'Do it. Try it.'

Aarons phoned Serov and asked him to arrange a meeting with Malloy. He wanted to meet him alone. Serov had called back almost immediately. Would Aarons meet Malloy at his house. Mr Malloy's wife, Kathy, was in Florida and they would be alone.

When they had settled down in Malloy's small but comfortable study Aarons wasted no time.

'We both know what we're here to talk about, don't we, Bill?'

'Yes.'

'I'd like to ask you whose idea this is? Who first thought of it?'

'It was Serov's idea. He put it to me some months ago.'

'What did you think of his idea?'

Malloy shrugged. 'Frankly, I thought it was crazy.'

'So why did you take it further?'

'I thought about it for several days. I couldn't get it out of my mind.' Malloy shifted uneasily in his chair. 'As you know, I'm a lawyer. I spend my time on checking facts and seeing if what has been done meets the laws of the land. That tends to make you a rather conservative thinker. Imagination isn't necessarily an advantage for corporate law. I wondered if I was the right man to make a decision on Serov's idea.

'Don't get me wrong. I worked with Serov in Occupied France and even though I never agreed with his politics in those days, I trusted him.' He paused. 'I still do. But although he's come over to our side I still felt some doubts about his political judgement. My boss, Mr Hancox, is a man I totally respect. So I decided to talk to him about it.' He smiled. 'At that time Serov had kept you anonymous. Never gave your name or anything to judge you on. But he told me what you were doing. That scared me.

'Anyway Hancox had the same reaction as me. At first he thought it was crazy. Then he had second thoughts. He talked to an old friend of his who is a close friend of Truman. Hancox was surprised that that man saw possibilities in it. I arranged with Serov to meet you socially and I couldn't really believe what I'd been told about your work. You were too sane, too intelligent . . .' He laughed softly, '. . . and too American.'

Aarons didn't react. 'Then what?'

'It was put to President Truman. He didn't hesitate. He thought it was workable. That it might help. It seems he thinks that things are going to deteriorate even further between Moscow and Washington.'

'But he's got the CIA, why doesn't he use them to find out what he wants?'

'I think for two reasons. The practical reason is that he can only get from the CIA what they're capable of getting. And as far as the Soviet Union is concerned, that ain't much. Secondly he sees all US official sources as biased. Fitting the facts to their theories. He'd like somebody he could talk to who has no axe to grind. Who knows both sides and understands both sides.'

'How does he know that I'm impartial?' He shrugged. 'Why should I be?'

'He's just got to accept Serov's evaluation and mine, at

297

this stage. I guess you'll both make your minds up about the arrangement when you've tried it for a bit.'

'Serov says that they would accept that I should still operate my network.'

'Yes, that's agreed.'

'Why?'

'They realise that without that you would have no access to the Kremlin.'

'But I would get no immunity from the FBI?'

'I raised that point and they said that that was the weak link in the chain. There's nothing illegal in what we've talked about but to give you immunity for other things would be a serious offence. The FBI and the CIA would be angry that they weren't made parties to the arrangement. Even if pressure was put on them they could be dirty enough to leak it to the press. Do you want immunity?'

'No. I'd trade it for an assurance that whatever happens to the arrangement, even if it doesn't work, that they would never tip off any agency about my network or me.'

'Take that as agreed.'

'You're sure?'

'Quite sure.'

'Who knows about this?'

'You, me, Truman, Serov, Hancox and Truman's friend Abe Karney.'

'Who will know the on-going details?'

'Just you, me and the President. The others are already out of the picture. But when you talk with the President it will just be the two of you. Nobody else will know what you've both talked about. I shan't ask you what you talked about, neither will anyone else. I'll just be a messenger for both you and him when either of you wants a meeting.'

40

For months the press had been full of scandals that con-
jured up new words like 'call-girls' and 'party girls', who
were used by business to get contracts and favours. But
when President Truman announced that he would not run
again for the Presidency it seemed to trigger an onslaught
by the Republicans on the corruption of the government
itself. It had been no secret that the President appointed
old friends to government office at many levels. And now
the word to describe them was 'cronies' which implied
that their misdeeds were accepted by the President as fair
rewards for old friends.

Day after day the press revealed graft and corruption
at all levels of the administration. Sometimes sub-
committees were set up to investigate. The most pres-
tigious of these was the Fulbright committee which the
President had said was 'asinine'. But day after day in the
Senate Caucus Room the President's cronies were
exposed as lining their pockets at the public's expense. It
showed that even officials of the Bureau of Internal Rev-
enue were indictable for conspiracy to defraud the
government.

The Republican campaign was so ruthless that even
such men as Dean Acheson, and General Marshall who
was entirely non-political, were targets for the attacks.
The General was a public hero, beyond criticism and that
was considered a threat by the Republicans. When
McCarthy charged Marshall with 'a conspiracy so
immense and an infamy so black as to dwarf any previous

such venture in the history of man', there were even Republicans who thought that maybe the campaign had gone too far. But the campaign of calumnies continued. The public no longer responded to the gutsy little man from Missouri. His courage and honesty were obvious but his judgement seemed to be flawed.

The door of the house was ajar and Malloy led Aarons up the stone steps and when they were inside Malloy closed the door behind them. A few moments later Malloy introduced Aarons to Abe Karney. He gave no name, just introduced him as 'my friend'. Karney asked no questions but led them upstairs to a small room that had been converted into a study, its walls lined with shelves of books.

On a side table was a thermos of coffee with a jug of cream, a bowl of sugar and cups and saucers. There were several bottles of mineral water and beside a tray of plates with an assortment of sweet biscuits was a telephone. He was told that it would be at least an hour before his visitor arrived. There was a pile of the day's newspapers on a trolley and Karney had told him to make himself at home. His visitor was unlikely to detain him for more than half an hour but he was not to leave the house himself until Karney gave him instructions.

There was a table with four chairs, two leather armchairs and a couch that looked as if it were sometimes used for taking a nap. When he was alone Aarons took a book from a shelf and sat reading it at the table. It was John Gunther's *Inside USA*. He had sold several second-hand copies at the shop and had read it when it was first published in 1947. After ten minutes randomly turning the pages and reading brief items he put the book aside. He had asked Malloy how the meeting would be structured and Malloy had said that it was not intended to be structured. In fact it wasn't even a meeting. It was just two men chatting.

Aarons wondered what Truman would want to know. And he wondered what questions he should put to the

President. The more he thought about it the more unrealistic it all seemed. What on earth was he doing here? An illegal refugee Jew from Moscow about to have a clandestine meeting with the most powerful man in the United States. He had read about Truman's background but it was of little help. He had no idea of how a man from such a humble, everyday background got to be the President of the United States. In the Soviet Union he would have to have some sort of power-base. A trades union, the military, an ethnic group or long service as a party organiser. Truman had been a shop-keeper, a haberdasher, and not even a successful one. He'd gone into local politics but wasn't a charismatic personality. And local politics in Missouri were notoriously corrupt. How did such a patently honest man survive, let alone succeed, with such a background?

Then he heard car doors banging and voices in the street below the window. He walked to the window and looked down through the net curtain. There were two limousines and two police motor-cycles. He saw Malloy's friend walk down the steps and stand at the gate. The two cars were side by side on the quadrangle beside the house. Two men got out of the first car and looked around slowly and carefully and then one of them leaned down and opened the rear door of the car without taking his eyes away from the area. He saw a short man with a tweed fisherman's hat and a heavy overcoat get out of the back seat of the car. He walked towards the gate where Malloy's friend was waiting. The light from a street lamp reflected briefly on his glasses. It was Truman. He turned to give a brief signal to the men by the cars who stood there silently with two of them pacing slowly around the whole area of the quadrangle. Another two standing leaning with their arms on the roof of the second car. Then Truman and Malloy's friend disappeared into the house.

It was another fifteen minutes before there was a knock on the door and the door opened and he was there alone.

The President of the USA, looking just like he did in the press pictures.

Truman looked at Aarons for several moments and then said, 'Let's sit at the table.' He pulled out a chair and sat down, and Aarons did the same.

'They told me to call you "A", is that OK with you?'

'That's fine, sir.'

'Let's cut out the bullshit. We're just two men chatting, aren't we? You probably know, my name's Harry. Can I start?'

'Sure.'

'We don't pull punches or we're wasting our time and our opportunity to do some good. So. Why are the people in Moscow so aggressive towards us?'

For a few moments Aarons hesitated, then he said, 'I can only give you some possible reasons. They feel that they won the war alone. Twenty million Soviets killed, our cities destroyed. America was never occupied by the Germans. Now the Soviet Union and the States are the super-powers. We're not used to being top dogs and there are jealousies about being number two. And the United States wants the whole world to stamp out Communism.' Aarons shrugged. 'There are other reasons, the armed forces have shown that they can beat the Germans and I guess peace can seem pretty tame to a general with vast military resources and only ten rows of medals.'

'When you talk about us being anti-communist do you have in mind McCarthy and his committee?'

'He's a very obvious part of it but he doesn't really matter.'

'Why not?'

'Moscow's view is that outside America McCarthy and his tactics are so fascist that he does America more harm than he does us.'

'Is that why your people haven't done anything about him?'

'What could we do? He's a Senator. A war hero and . . .'

'What the hell do you mean – a war hero?'

'He was tail-gunner in a bomber.'

'He sat in the tail-gunner's seat as a passenger on a military plane a couple of times in the Pacific. He spent his service behind a desk.'

'But he was wounded in combat.'

'Was he, shit, he injured his leg when he fell downstairs, drunk, on a troopship. He started this committee because he was scared that the good folk of Wisconsin were sick of him. He's what we call a boodler. A boozer and a gambler who paid for his vices by taking bribes from corporations that had business with Washington. He needed some issue to help him survive. Could have been anything but some son of a bitch put him on to communists.'

'So why don't you stop him?'

'He's on the way out. He's worn out his welcome.' He shrugged. 'And it's a free country.'

'He's ruined a lot of people's lives. Creative people, writers, film people, scientists, scholars and government officials.'

'Sure. Democracy too costs lives.'

'Can I ask you something?'

'Fire away.'

'What would make the United States start a war against the Soviet Union?'

'We wouldn't start one. But if the Soviets made a move against us then we'd respond.'

'What kind of move?'

Truman was silent for long moments. 'If they made a move against one of the NATO countries. Or if they found some country to accept atomic weapons within striking distance of our backyard.'

Aarons smiled. 'It sounds as if the so-called superpowers are just scared of one another rather than looking for conquests.'

'You could be right.' He paused. 'Tell me. What made you a communist? What was the attraction?'

Aarons shrugged. 'My father never stopped talking

about the revolution that was coming to set us all free. I was just a boy and I heard it every day. I guess it's like being born a Roman Catholic. You just accept the rules even if you don't agree with all of them.'

'Was your father a politician?'

Aarons laughed. 'No, he was a glove-maker in a small factory.'

'What kind of gloves?'

'Gloves for rich women.'

'Is he still alive?'

'No. He died when I was a kid. We were Jewish and we had to emigrate to Paris.'

'Did he go back after the Revolution?'

'No.'

'Why not?'

'Because we were Jews.'

'So much for the brotherhood of man.'

'Jews have the same problem here.'

'But they don't flee the country.'

'Why is Communism feared over here so much?'

Truman stood up slowly and shrugged off his jacket, hanging it over the back of one of the other chairs before moving over to the couch and lying back against the cushions, one leg stretched out on the couch, the other trailing alongside the couch. The alert eyes focused on Aaron's face.

'It's not feared so much as hated and despised. And it's not a question of Communism itself. It's loathing of any system that only survives by a huge apparatus of suppression of its own people.'

'But if that's what the people want.'

'That's bullshit, Mr A, and you know it. They don't have any choice.' He wagged a finger at Aarons. 'People have always got excuses for doing wrong. A fella was telling me the other day that bribery and corruption are a good thing. You get quick responses that way. You pay the guy who matters and you get the contract, but if you go through proper channels it could take you six months and you could still lose out. Speeds up the economy he says. I told him it can speed up the trip to a Federal penitentiary as well.'

'Who's going to be the next President?'

'Who do your guys think it will be?'

'Adlai Stevenson.'

Truman shook his head slowly. 'No. A Democrat won't make it this next time round. It'll be Eisenhower. The people want a change. Don't matter if it's for good or bad. The liberals have had their day. Ike makes out that he's non-political. And if that means that he don't give a shit either way he's right. He's a trimmer, is Ike. He was in Wisconsin a few weeks back and he endorsed McCarthy for re-election. In the press hand-out of his speech he'd defended Marshall from McCarthy's libels but on the day he cut it out. He's more ambitious for power than he makes out. Maybe that's not a bad combination. Could be a good President as far as your people are concerned. He was a very successful soldier so he knows what wars are all about. He's got nothing to prove so he'll be all for peace. But what you've got to worry about are the people he appoints to key posts. The Republicans in power now are the extremists and they'll want their pay-off for getting him into the White House. If he appoints men like John Foster Dulles you've got trouble. Hates Communism, would like to liberate Eastern Europe. A meddler is Dulles.' He paused. 'Tell me, do they take any notice of what you say in Moscow?'

Aarons smiled. 'People who I trust tell me that they do.'

'You say people who you trust. What people don't you trust?'

Aarons shifted uneasily on his chair, at a loss as to what he could say, and Truman, feeling that he might be probing too deeply said, 'Not names necessarily. Just your impression.'

Aarons sighed. 'If we're to do any good, you and me, I guess we have to be truthful. There is only one man in the Kremlin who I know well enough to trust. The others are just faces and names, they make the machinery work but only Stalin decides what should be done. Nobody knows what goes on in his mind. Those who are close to him, fear him. He's ruthless but very shrewd. He's a peasant.'

'Have you ever met him?'

'Once, briefly, and with other people.'

'What happened?'

'We shook hands, an aide mentioned my name to him and he stared at my face for a moment and then said he was grateful for the work that I was doing.'

'Here in America?'

'Yes.'

'You don't look like a spy, but God knows enough people have told me I don't look like a President. So what?' He paused. 'How much notice do they take of the information supplied by the intelligence people? Do they mistrust them too?'

'It's not a question of trust. It's a question of where power lies at the time. If I was based in Moscow I wouldn't be able to give my opinions as freely as I do now. The man I trust, I tell him as openly as I'm talking to you now, but he's an exception. He influences other people.'

'Would he protect you if it were necessary?'

'He would try.'

'And?'

'Who knows?'

'D'you reckon we're doing any good – you and me talking like this?'

Aarons nodded. 'Yes, I do. I was never sure about whether America wouldn't make a so-called pre-emptive strike against the Soviet Union. Now I'm sure you won't.'

'You think the others will believe you?'

'I wasn't thinking of them. I was thinking of me. I felt guilty about talking with you about Soviet attitudes. It seemed a bit like treason. I feel justified now. We both want the same thing for our countries. Maybe we can convince others as time goes by.'

Truman swung his leg down from the couch and sat there looking at Aarons.

'Don't expect too much, my friend.'

'You think we're wasting our time?'

Truman pushed his glasses back up his nose. 'No. We were neither of us sure how it was going to turn out, this talk. It's easy to say that we were hoping to make a contribution to peace, it's a helluva lot different actually doing it.' He paused, looked away towards the window for a moment and then looked back at Aarons. 'I meet a few Soviet officials, diplomats and so on. And we talk a few polite words through an interpreter. And I read summaries of CIA reports on the Communist Bloc but I've never had the chance to talk to an ordinary Russian about what he thinks about his country – and mine, of course. You're not an ordinary Russian of course. You're intelligent and well-informed but I get the impression that you're telling me like it is. Not better or worse than it actually is.' He shrugged irritably. 'The official reports I get are about numbers not people, and half of them are grinding some axe. More money for the Pentagon or funds for some crack-pot outfit who are supposed to be the saviours of some place in Africa or South America who'll save the place from Communism.' He rocked slowly as he sat on the couch. 'The least we've done is get to know each other.' He paused. 'You still happy to keep in touch?'

'I'll do anything I can to help you and my own people.'

Truman held out his hand. It was a quite leathery grip. Then he picked up his jacket, slinging it over his shoulder as he opened the door and let himself out. Aarons heard him shout, 'Abe, where are you?' and then he was alone. A few minutes later he heard the voices, the car engines and then the rasp of the two Harley Davidsons. Ten minutes later Malloy came in with Abe Karney, both of them so obviously avoiding questions that they made it as embarrassing as if he'd had a furtive assignment with a girl.

Aarons was back in New York just after 2 a.m. Tania had waited up for him but she had fallen asleep in her armchair, a book on the floor beside her. He bent down, picked up the book, straightening a crumpled page before he looked at the title. It was *The Catcher in the Rye*. He made them both a glass of hot chocolate and after he had woken her they sat talking for almost an hour before they went to bed. He gave her no details of his talk with Truman but he told her that it seemed to be worth continuing if he was asked.

Aarons sat checking the figures in the small notebook. He had made 75,500 dollars so far from the material that Moscow had provided and he estimated that at least as much again would come from what was left. Two university libraries had paid high prices and the curators had recommended private buyers for half a dozen other items. He now had a dozen bank accounts and a couple of deposit boxes, one in Manhattan and one in Albany.

When he rang Cowley's number it was answered immediately.

'Yeah.'

'Is that Jim Cowley?'

'It is.'

'I'd like to see you about a repair, how about tomorrow?'

There was silence for a moment then, 'OK. I'll be here.'

The message meant that he would be at Cowley's place in an hour.

The windows of the shop had been boarded up and the door was locked. He rang the bell and a few minutes later it was unlocked and Cowley waved him inside, locking the door as Aarons stood by the counter in the shop. He followed Cowley into the workshop which was empty except for several stacks of magazines and service manuals.

Cowley leaned against the work-bench.

'Thought I'd seen the last of you, skipper. I'm off at the week-end. What can I do for you?'

'Can we talk about money?'

Cowley laughed and folded his arms across his chest as he leaned back against the wall. 'I'll always talk money, my friend, you know that.'

'Can I ask what you'll be getting at your new job?'

Cowley grinned. 'You won't believe me if I tell you.'

Aarons shrugged. 'Try me.'

Cowley spread out his hand, pointing to one finger after another as he spoke. 'A guaranteed minimum of a hundred bucks a week. A hundred. Twenty-five a month rent assistance, unemployment and health insurance paid by them. Three weeks paid holidays and plenty of over-time at double rate in the first couple of years.' He smiled. 'What d'you think of that, eh?'

'I'll pay you the same.'

For a moment Cowley hesitated, then he said, 'I've signed a contract and I've got a house down there on special terms. I couldn't give up all that.'

'I'm not asking you to. I want you to take the job but I want you to go on working for me as well.'

'I'm not allowed to own a transmitter or a transceiver, not even as a hobby. They've cancelled my amateur licence. I don't even have a call-sign anymore.'

'That doesn't matter. I want you for other things. Just information.' He paused. 'Are you interested?'

For a few moments Cowley was silent, then, 'And that's all I have to do?'

'Yes.'

'And you'd pay like you just said?'

'Yes. And a bonus right now of a thousand dollars.'

Cowley stood there thinking, nodding his head as if agreeing to his unspoken thoughts. 'I'd go to jail if they found out.'

'How could they find out? There would be nothing in writing. It would be just you talking to me or somebody

I send down to you. Say a couple of hours a week at a time and place to suit you.'

'Give me an idea of what you'd want to know.'

'What's the place like. How many people. What kind of people. Equipment. Objectives. Names of top people.'

'How do I get the money?'

'Separate bank account. Anywhere you want. I could arrange it for you over the border in either Toronto or Mexico City.'

'Starting when?'

'I've got the bonus in cash right here. The payments start as of now.'

Cowley took a deep breath. 'OK. It's a deal.'

After six of the weekly meetings with Cowley at small hotels on the outskirts of Baltimore Aarons had contacted Moscow and suggested a meeting somewhere with Soviet experts on communications and electronics. A reply came back immediately. The meeting was to be in Moscow as soon as possible. He should travel via London and Stockholm.

41

Lensky met him in at Moscow airport. He had travelled on a Canadian passport but there had been no problems until Moscow where he had been made to wait until his passport had been checked by the border police in the office behind the control area. Lensky had come back with the passport himself.

'They're such fools. Your visa is out-of-date in six days' time and you said you weren't sure how long you'd be here. But the code on your visa is a special code and intended to make sure that no attention is drawn to you as you come through immigration.' He shrugged. 'So much for bureaucracy.' He smiled. 'It's good to see you again. You'll be staying at my place. I've got a car outside.'

They had eaten at Lensky's place and afterwards they listened to the mid-evening news from Radio Moscow. When Lensky switched off the radio he said, 'I'd better fill you in on the local situation. The new head of our organisation is Semyon Denisovich Ignatyev. A Party *apparatchik* from the Central Committee.'

'What happened to Abakumov?'

'Ah, our dear Viktor . . .' Lensky smiled, '. . . he really asked for trouble. Two private brothels, people say they were the prettiest whores in Moscow, and importation of foreign luxuries on an unbelievable scale. It was embarrassing – Abakumov was popular with our colleagues here in Moscow. Stalin sent Khrushchev to the officers' club to explain his arrest. So we had a mixture of Viktor's moral turpitude and illegal importation and corruption. Then for a few months we were stuck with Sergei Ogoltsov. But he was only acting head.'

'And Ignatyev?'

'His first priority was handed down to him by Stalin personally – the exposure of the Zionist plot against the State. And of course that means we're back to the purges of the Jews. Every officer who was a Jew was removed in the first few weeks. There'll be show trials, here in Moscow, in Georgia and in Prague. Prague first as a practice run to see how it goes. They've been preparing that for over a year and for the first time in a show-trial defendants are going to be identified as Jews. The legal people have been arguing for weeks as to whether the prosecutor says "Of Jewish origin" or "Jewish nationality" or simply "Jew". They didn't use those tactics even on Trotsky or Zinovyev.'

'Is that why I was called back?'

Lensky shook his head. 'No, or I'd have warned you not to come. They've got a list, a very short list I might say, of what they call acceptable Jews. The official title is "hidden Jews".'

'Are you on the list?'

'Yes. So are you.'

'And what happens to the Jews?'

'Some are sent to labour camps,' he shrugged and said quietly, 'and some are killed.'

'You mean murdered not killed.'

'Whatever word you use it's the same result.'

'And I'm supposed to help these people or I too end in a Gulag camp?'

Lensky shrugged. 'In the States you've got McCarthy.'

'McCarthy is not the government. What he does is not government policy. His time's coming to an end very soon.'

'What makes you think that?

Aarons shrugged. 'He's begun attacking the army. They will finish him.'

'Are you getting disillusioned?'

Aarons shook his head slowly. 'I don't know why, because I don't remember much from when I lived here as a boy, but I'll always love Russia and Russians. It's just an instinct, I must have inherited it from my father.'

'If they wanted you to come back to Moscow – would you come?'

'No. Tania wouldn't leave the States.'

'Is a woman more important than your country, your people, Andrei?'

'I don't answer questions like that anymore. I don't even ask myself those questions.' He looked at Lensky. 'So why am I here?'

'This new signals place in Maryland. It's a top priority as you know, even before your reports came through. They want to talk to you about it. You said you wanted a meeting with some experts. Now they've seen your reports they can't wait to talk to you. Right now you're well in favour.' Lensky smiled. 'You always have been of course. No fireworks, no complaints, no arguing – just hard work and doing what you're asked to do.'

'Sounds like a reference for a not very bright servant.'

Lensky didn't answer. 'How's Tania?'

'She's fine.'

'Does she know you're here?'

'Yes.'

'Did you notify Moscow that you were married again?'

'No. My wife is none of their business.'

'They may not agree. What makes you think that?'

'Because when I begged for the loan of money to nurse Chantal they didn't even reply. That's enough for me.'

'I shouldn't share those thoughts with other people here.'

'I'm tired, I'd better go to bed. What time's the meeting tomorrow?'

'Ten, there's a car coming for you. I won't be there at the meeting.' Lensky paused. 'Who's going to be the next President in the States?'

'Who do you think?'

'Stevenson.'

'It'll be Eisenhower.'

Lensky looked surprised. 'What makes you think that?'

Aarons gave Lensky his reasons and wondered what Lensky would say if he told him that his careful analysis had come direct from the President of the United States.

They talked a little longer and in a more friendly vein and then Aarons went to bed, setting the small travelling alarm-clock in a red leather case that Tania had given him.

The meeting had been in a room on the tenth floor of the Comecon building and there were only three people apart from Aarons. They introduced themselves as Beletsky, Denikin and Glazkova. The first two were scientists and Glazkova, a young woman, didn't identify her rôle and Aarons assumed that she was probably a commissar, sent as an observer from the Party Committee, which was more or less independent of the intelligence chain of command.

Beletsky seemed an amiable man, used to running meetings and getting cooperation from people who were disinclined to talk freely until they had tested the temperature of the water.

Beletsky smiled at Aarons. 'The material you sent us was fine but we thought that perhaps you had made more notes that we could talk about.'

'It's part of the deal that I've made with my informant that I don't ask him for documents and that all his reports to me are verbal. I have to make up my notes from memory.'

Denikin asked. 'According to your file, comrade, you're not experienced in this area – electronics and signals stuff.'

'No. No experience at all.'

'It would help us a lot if you could get your contact to provide documents or his own written reports.'

'If I asked he wouldn't agree and if I pressed he'd break off the contact. We have to do the best we can on the

314

present basis. Maybe you can brief me with specific questions.'

'Is your contact a Party member?'

'No. I think his father was, but he died some years ago.'

Denikin said, 'If we supplied you with a small tape-recorder that you could conceal would that help you?'

'Comrade, I've been doing this work for many years and I've built up quite a large network of informants. They trust me because I make sure that if they were interrogated the FBI would have no documentary proof of their committing any offence. When I get documents they are very useful for us but they are not top secret.' He smiled. 'They trust me because I don't play games. I take every precaution to protect them. And to protect myself of course. So no hidden tape-recorders.'

Beletsky took over again. 'You're quite sure that your contact said that this place was called the National Security Agency?'

'Yes.'

'And it's not controlled by the FBI or the CIA.'

'It's entirely independent but it has connections with the CIA.'

'And it is intended to intercept, monitor and record all radio and telephonic communications, not just in the USA but all over the world.'

'That's what the staff are told.' He paused. 'They are also told that it is the most important of all the US intelligence organisations and will grow and expand very quickly.'

'He also mentioned code-breaking.'

'There is a big section being built up that covers codes, cryptology, high mathematics. Continuous recruiting from industry, commerce and the universities.'

'And the Soviet Union is top target?'

'Not only us but all Communist countries especially those in eastern Europe.'

Beletsky nodded. 'We'll give you a list of questions that we'd like you to put to your contact. Two things are urgent as far as we are concerned. We'd like to know what equipment is installed, particularly computers, and who are the suppliers. Second we'd like a chain-of-command diagram with titles of different sections and names of middle status people. Especially people with problems, and names and backgrounds of people who get dismissed.'

'I'll see what I can do. Of course it's early days, maybe five or six hundred people but they're talking about two or three thousand staff.'

'Are we funding you enough?'

'So far I'm OK.'

'Does this hold up your usual network tasks?'

'Not yet.'

'Could your contact recruit other people?'

'I wouldn't trust him to do that. The only reason I used him is because I've known him for a long time. He does what I pay him to do. He's greedy for dollars. It's a business. If he sold me out to the authorities he'd lose more than half his income. They wouldn't compensate him for that.'

Beletsky nodded. 'You know best but we're desperate for all we can get on this place. No money restrictions.' He turned to Denikin. 'Your turn.'

Denikin smiled. 'We'd like you to spend the rest of today and the whole of tomorrow with us so that we can give you some basic knowledge of what this kind of installation does and how it does it. Just the basics so that you can follow better what he tells you and push for more if it seems worthwhile.'

Aarons nodded. 'I'm at your disposal.'

That evening Lensky took Aarons to a reception at the headquarters of the Moscow Party given by the Moscow Party Secretary. They had walked there and Lensky seemed on edge. He talked about the battles for power being waged inside the Party and Stalin's growing paranoia. Stalin frequently talked aloud to himself and

316

Khrushchev had heard him say, 'I'm finished. I trust no one. Not even myself.'

'The doctors say that he hasn't more than six months to live. God knows what will happen then. There are dossiers on everyone – generals, politicians – the lot.'

'Who will take over?'

'It will be either Khrushchev or Malenkov. But Beria will cause a lot of trouble until things are settled. You'll be introduced to K tonight. I told him about your theory on Eisenhower being the next President. He says you're wrong but he's too shrewd not to listen to what you've got to say.'

It was almost midnight when Lensky took his arm and led him over to where Khrushchev was standing with two other men. Aarons was introduced and Khrushchev looked at him with those shrewd peasant's eyes.

'So you think we're wrong in looking forward to Stevenson in the White House?'

'Yes, comrade, it will be Eisenhower.'

Khrushchev waved his glass around in his podgy hand as if he were appealing for support from the other two men. But they said nothing.

'Tell me why you're so sure.'

Aarons went through the scenario again and Khrushchev listened as he drank his vodka. Then he said, 'So we can expect a bigger budget for the army, eh?'

'I think he knows them all too well to let them increase their spending. And he won't be looking for adventures.'

'Is that what your American friends think?'

'Those who are interested in politics share your views and ordinary people won't be interested in any candidate until the primaries start.'

'It's ordinary people who get them into the White House.'

'Of course. And when Ike's name comes up that will be enough. He's a war hero. He's not corrupt and he's much admired.'

'But he's not a political figure.'

317

'That will help him. They don't much like politicians.'

'What about all the Republican top men, will they stand for a general taking their prize?'

'They'll be glad to have such a clean candidate.'

'So where will the trouble come from for us?'

'I think Foster Dulles might be his Secretary of State. He's a convinced anti-communist. He could be trouble.'

An officer in security service uniform brought Khrushchev a note. He read it and handed it back, saying, 'I'll see him in the alcove. Give him a drink.' He looked at the other two and said, 'That bastard Beria, I wonder what pot he's stirring.' He turned to Aarons and shook his head. 'They tell me you do a good job for us over there. Keep at it.' He paused. 'By the way do you meet our Ambassador there?'

'No, comrade. I had orders not to.'

Khrushchev laughed, 'You're very wise. He thinks McCarthy will be the next President.'

The time spent with the two scientists had been interesting and they were obviously much concerned that he should be as well armed for dealing with Cowley as possible.

The night before he left they ate as usual at Lensky's place. They were always much concerned that there was no chance of him being seen by anyone from the US Embassy.

After they had eaten Lensky poured himself a drink and his housekeeper brought Aarons a mug of hot chocolate. Aarons smiled. 'You've got a long memory, Jakob.'

'I shouldn't be alive if I hadn't.'

'Are you worried about something?'

Lensky shrugged and smiled. 'We Russians are always worried about something. You used to be the same but something seems to have changed you.'

Aarons smiled. 'Not something – somebody.'

'Tania?'

'Yes.'

'What does Ivan do these days?'

318

'He works for me as a courier.'

'And Anna?'

'She is married. She just cares for her husband.'

'What does he do?'

'He plays jazz piano in a night-club which he owns.'

'Which one would be the one to betray you?'

'None of them.'

'And who amongst your network would sell you down the river?'

Aarons shrugged. 'Who knows. Each one knows very little. They don't even know that there is a network.'

'Do you like America?'

'I like some things. The optimism, the instinct of being friendly, the opportunities and the freedom.'

'Freedom to persecute blacks and Hispanics? Freedom to shoot a man just because you don't like him? What freedom?'

'The freedom to talk like you and I talk but not with lowered voices. And not assuming that maybe your room is bugged. And knowing that nobody can send me to a prison camp for something I said or because some Party hack wants to sleep with my wife.'

'And all their politicians are corrupt. Just find the right price.'

'They are corrupt here too. You don't trade roubles because there's nothing to buy with them. You trade favours and privileges, somebody's life. And you trade freedom despite our Constitution.'

Lensky smiled. 'When did you read our Constitution?'

'When I was in Paris.'

'Do you still speak Russian when you can?'

'Of course not. I'm an American bookseller. I spoke Russian when I was at Brighton Beach but not in New York.'

'But there are immigrant Americans from Russia who still speak the language at home.'

'But they don't do what I do.' He shook his head. 'I've survived because I take no unnecessary risks.'

319

'You're very sensible. Take no notice of my questions. They may not be what they seem.'

'You're being very mysterious, Jakob. Why?'

'Because when all the cards have been played I want to know who I can trust.'

'Is it really that bad?'

'They are going to adopt a policy of aggression against the United States. Not actual war but harassment all round the globe.' He sighed. 'And I've no idea how far they'll go.'

'The Americans won't let them go too far, Jakob.'

'Don't be so sure. Our people think the Americans will back down.'

'I think that they're wrong.'

'There aren't many people who think confrontation is a mistake. And they aren't going to say what they think, believe me.'

'So what is the point of me reporting how things really are in the States, to you?'

'I'm not sure, Andrei. I'm an old man, and I'm tired from struggling. Sometimes I wonder if I'm wrong.' He sighed and looked at Aarons. 'And sometimes I wonder if I'm mad.' He paused. 'Talking to you is a kind of therapy – a life-line to sanity.' He settled back in his chair. 'I've always read a lot but these days I read only *les philosophes*, Descartes, Montaigne, Wittgenstein, Russell.' He waved his hand languidly and let it fall, shaking his head as he looked at Aarons. 'I envy you, Andrei. At least you live among optimists.'

Aarons smiled. 'You shame me, Jakob.'

'Why? In what way?'

'More and more I get sick of people. It would be so easy for the world to live in peace . . .' he smiled, '. . . if only there were no people.'

Lensky smiled. 'What does your Tania say to all this?'

'She's sixteen years younger than I am but despite that she seems older and wiser than I am.'

'In what way?'

320

'She says that I'm wishing my life away. She thinks I should do something with energy and enthusiasm. The books – anything.' He smiled. 'I think in a way she feels that men behave like spoilt children. Rather cruel children. School bullies.'

'She obviously loves you.'

'I'm very lucky. She makes my life a real life, not just an existence like it used to be.'

'Good, good.' Lensky leaned forward to touch Aarons' arm, the talk about Tania already dismissed. 'You know, Andrei, I sometimes think that there's nothing to choose between them. They're both the same – we're wasting our lives, the likes of you and me – we should let them get on with it. The hell with them.'

Aarons smiled. 'You don't mean it, do you?'

Lensky shuffled embarrassedly. 'No. I wish I did.' He paused. 'This bloody country is like a drug – and I'm an addict.'

'For what?'

'For all those real Russian things. Tchaikovsky, Rachmaninov, Tolstoy, Chekhov, Dostoyevski – poor Mandelstam even. We can't let them be pushed aside for pamphlets about economics and the dialectic of materialism.'

'So why did you join the Party way back?'

'I thought it would improve the lives of peasants and workers. Give everybody a chance to enjoy being alive.'

'And has it done that?'

'You know it hasn't. We've just changed from Tsars to commissars. Ignorant louts after power and privileges. So-called realists.'

'Why don't you leave?'

'And go where?'

'America.'

Lensky smiled wryly. 'And you think they care about music and poetry and literature?'

'They care about individual rights.'

'Ask a negro about individual rights or a Puerto Rican. See what they say.'

'I said they *care* about those rights. They haven't made it work yet but you don't end up in a labour-camp if you air your views.'

'Why do you carry on, Andrei? You could earn a good living over there.'

'Somebody's got to try, Jakob. I'll keep going until somebody proves that I'm wasting my time.'

'And how will you know?'

Aarons shrugged. 'It's a negative proof. If they don't start another war that's all I want. For people to listen instead of just shouting in ignorance.'

'Well,' said Lensky standing up slowly and unsteadily. 'Remember poor Osip Mandelstam. They said he was one of the *raznochintsi*, the classless intellectuals who were like St Petersburg – facing both east and west. He died on his way to a labour camp in '38.'

Aarons laughed quietly, 'Nobody's ever going to see me as an intellectual.'

'By the way,' Lensky said, 'K is already saying that he thinks Eisenhower will be the next President. He may be a peasant but he's a very shrewd one. Let's go to bed.'

It was snowing when Aarons landed in New York and he took a taxi back to 42nd Street and got out at Bryant Park, walking the rest of the way. He still kept to his old habits of precautions against being followed.

Sam and Anna were there and he and Tania arranged to meet them at Sam's club that evening.

After they left Tania said, 'Bill phoned and asked for you to call him back.'

'Did he say it was urgent?'

'He didn't say so but he sounded concerned that you were away and wouldn't be able to contact him for some days.'

'Did he ask where I was?'

'No.'

'Shall I ask them to join us at the club tonight?'

'Do you want to?'

'It would be convenient.'

'Shall I ring him for you and you could have a nap?'

'OK. Say 9 o'clock at Sam's.'

'Don't forget it's elections tomorrow.'

Aarons smiled. 'I hadn't forgotten, honey.'

At the club Malloy and Aarons had wandered over to the bar. Malloy had a whiskey and the barman smiled as he pushed the usual glass of milk across for Aarons. Moving away from the bar they stood in a small alcove where extra chairs were stored.

Malloy raised his drink. 'What is it you and Tania say – *Na zdrovye* – cheers.'

Aarons smiled. 'Cheers.'

'I've had word from the man. Spoke to me personally. I had to meet him after he visited some school. He's spoken to Eisenhower in very general terms but Eisenhower wasn't interested. But the man wants to keep in contact with you on the same basis. Mutual discussion and mutual briefing. He thinks he can still influence policy makers both in the White House and on the Hill.' Malloy smiled. 'He was concerned that you might be offended by Ike's lack of interest. What do you think?'

'Well, I'm certainly not offended. I think it showed exceptional courage for our man to go with this crazy set-up in the beginning. If he wants to keep in touch I'll be happy to cooperate. It will be easier when he's no longer the man. And just as useful in many ways.' He paused. 'He didn't give Eisenhower any clues as to my identity?'

'No, and he doesn't know enough to give anyone a lead by mistake.' He smiled. 'I gather he was impressed by your attitude.'

'What attitude?'

Malloy shrugged. 'Your even-handedness about both sides.' He waved towards their table. 'We'd better get back and give the girls a whirl.'

42

General Eisenhower became President Eisenhower on the 20th of January 1953 and Stalin died on the 5th of March.

On May 4 over two thousand Germans from the Russian sector of Berlin marched over to the West, and in the Communist Zone of Germany two million people were refused ration cards because of the shortage of food. The Communists refused Western offers of relief supplies to ease the famine.

In June Soviet troops fired on protesting workers in East Berlin, killing twenty-two of them. Two days later the Rosenbergs were executed for spying in the USA. The following day Aarons received instructions to go to Moscow immediately.

Lensky, as always, met him off the Stockholm plane and took him back to his apartment. He could see from Lensky's face that he was under some sort of pressure. As Lensky closed the door of his apartment he held up a piece of paper for Aarons to read. It told him not to talk about anything other than the weather and family affairs.

Half an hour later they were sitting on a bench under the trees in Vorontsovo Park. There were small children playing games under the watchful eyes of *babushkas* and groups of old men walking slowly down the wide pathways, eyes alert but backs and shoulders bent by a lifetime's hard labour.

'What did the message say that brought you here?'

'Just "come immediately", and the password.'

'What password?'

'*Soyus*.'

'Why so long getting here?'

'Some sort of service engineers' strike at Toronto airport. Why do you ask?'

'You had a lucky escape, my friend. That recall message went to all overseas residents from Beria. Did you ever meet Beria?'

'No. Why should I?'

Lensky smiled. 'That question shows how lucky you are – Beria's your boss. Or to be more precise, he was your boss – until yesterday.'

'What happened?'

'I'd better go back a bit. After Stalin's death Beria saw himself as the kingmaker, deciding who would be Stalin's successor. You've got to remember that he had secret files on every member of the Presidium. Embarrassing, incriminating and scandalous material. And the members of the Presidium knew he'd got them. He'd used them before.

'He began throwing his weight about right after Stalin's funeral. He didn't seem to realise that he had built up a great barrier of hatred. When there was the workers' uprising in East Berlin he went there personally to take charge. Instead of cooling things down he sent in armour and troops. Taking advantage of him being away it was decided to call a meeting of the Presidium and deal with Beria in his absence. Somehow he learned of the meeting and phoned the Secretariat who told him it was just a routine meeting. But he flew straight back to Moscow.

'The group against Beria was Khrushchev, Bulganin, Marshal Zhukov and Malenkov. At the start of the meeting Beria asked what was on the agenda. Malenkov was supposed to denounce him, but when the chips were down he didn't have the guts. Khrushchev and Bulganin denounced Beria and somebody, I think it was Malenkov, pressed a secret button under the table and seconds later in came Marshal Zhukov at the head of a group of armed

326

army officers and took Beria away.' Lensky sighed. 'That was yesterday.'

'Are they going to try him?'

'They'll talk about a trial in camera. But there'll be no trial.'

'So what will they do?'

'They've done it, Andrei. They shot him last night.'

For a moment Aarons was silent, then he looked at Lensky and said quietly, 'What kind of people are they, Jakob? This is gangsterism. The Mafia.'

'Beria was no angel, Andrei. He had a house in Vspolny Pereulok and he used to drive around the Moscow streets late at night looking for teenage girls. He'd drag them into his car, take them back to his house and rape them again and again. There were over four hundred names of victims on a list in his house when it was searched. He was a degenerate of the worst kind.'

'But that wasn't why he was shot. He was shot because he was getting in the way of people greedy for power.'

'So what do we do about it?'

'You tell me.'

'God knows. I just wanted to warn you about what's going on so that you can be prepared for when you're talking with them.'

'If the meeting was called by Beria do they still want to talk with me?'

'Yes, they will.' He paused. 'You should act as if you don't know what has happened. You're just here to discuss your operations in New York.'

'Do you think your apartment has been bugged?'

'I'm sure it has.'

'What's your position in all this?'

'I think they tolerate me because I've never had any ambition to be a member of the Presidium or taken sides in any of the in-fighting at the top of the Party. I'm a kind of uncle they can talk to who tells them the truth but doesn't criticise them. In a peculiar kind of way they trust me, especially about the West and its ways. Their ignorance of the world is appalling and I'm a sort of reference point. What will the Americans do if we do this or that, or why do the Americans not see things our way.' Lensky smiled. 'Like the Romans had oracles, they've got me. Like the women in magazines that girls write to about whether they should sleep with their boy-friends. And whatever you say they'll still probably do what they intended to do anyway. But when they find they're pregnant then they'll take notice. Like children, they're primitives – can't cope with being thwarted.'

'No enemies, Jakob?'

'Not really. I'm more like a crystal ball than a person and a crystal ball never harmed anyone. Like the women who read their astrological forecasts – if they like them – OK. If they don't – forget them.'

'Are you still a spy?'

'Who told you I was a spy?'

'A girl who was on my training course way back. I met her again years later. She seemed surprised that I didn't already know.'

'I never was.' He smiled. 'But if somebody thinks I am – well, it does no harm.'

'So what are you?'

'Officially – what I get paid for – is as a consultant on Soviet history. In fact I guess I'm what Americans would call a dogsbody. A very discreet listener and an even more discreet commentator for any member of the Presidium who wants a shoulder to cry on or an audience for pent-up anger.'

'Are you safe from all the in-fighting?'

'I'm not sure, but I think so.' He stood up slowly. 'We'd better get back to my place. They want to see you this afternoon. It's Friday so they won't take long – they all want to rush off to their *dachas* with their latest girl-friend.'

Aarons laughed. 'I can't imagine Khrushchev with a girl-friend.'

'Don't be too sure, my friend. Don't be too sure.'

The afternoon meeting had gone quite smoothly. There had been no mention of internal problems. A brief talk about Eisenhower and Dulles and then he was passed over to the technicians whose sole interest was about the functions of the installation at Fort Meade. This time it was just Beletsky and Denikin, Glazkova was in hospital with a broken leg. They both seemed pleased with the information that he was providing.

Denikin got down to business. He looked at some notes and then at Aarons. 'First of all the main-frame computer. Your contact calls it a CRAY-1 and he says it's made by . . .' he glanced again at his notes, '. . . an outfit at Chippewa Falls in Minnesota. We'd like to know more about that plant. What's the name of the manufacturer and is there any significance in its name. Is CRAY-1 some sort of code-name or an acronym?

'And secondly we want to know its capacity. Your contact calls it a number-cruncher but we need to know more than that. Can he get you a specification or some reference? For instance how does it compare with an IBM 360? And why didn't they use IBM as suppliers? OK?' He looked at Beletsky, smiling. 'Your turn.'

Beletsky shoved a typed sheet across the table. 'Try and memorise the questions, comrade. I want to know how the place is organised. Names of departments and special groups. Especially people concerned with evaluation. If they're going to do surveillance on the scale your contact indicates they've got two more problems when they've got it. How do you print it out and how the hell do you evaluate it? You'd need thousands of people working round the clock. They must have some electronic system. What is it?'

Aarons asked, 'Can I keep the notes overnight? I'll leave them with Comrade Lensky when I go to the airport tomorrow.'

Beletsky nodded. 'Just burn the sheet and flush it down the pan.'

Denikin said, 'One last point. Can you find out what security checks are done on people they recruit? Especially lower-grade people.' He sighed. 'How are your funds?'

'They're OK.'

'Let us know if you need more. This is top priority for us.'

Lensky woke Aarons the next morning. There had been a telephone message. His flight back to Stockholm had been put back for a day. Khrushchev wanted to see him late that afternoon.

As they had coffee together Aarons said, 'What does he want with me?'

Lensky shrugged. 'I've no idea. I understand somebody mentioned that you were in Moscow and he said he wanted to see you before you went back. He wasn't free until this afternoon. I was told that it would be just you and him.' He paused. 'He's almost certain to be made First Secretary sometime in the next few months.'

'What's he like?'

'Well, you've met him. He's not a dissembler. He's much what he looks like. Did a good job in the war. Energetic and shrewd. Some people say he's a reformer and could make a real difference to the Party.'

Aarons had been shown into a small room at the back of the domed building of the Council of Ministers. The guide who escorted him told him that this was where Lenin had lived and studied, and that sometimes his fourth floor study with its original furniture and books was opened for members of the public.

The room was furnished like any New York club. Leather armchairs and settees, panelled walls, high ceilings with chandelier lighting, one wall lined with books, a long table with seating for a dozen people and a drinks trolley with crystal glasses.

It was only a few minutes before Nikita Khrushchev

330

bustled into the room followed by two men who he turned and waved away, turning to check their exit until the heavy door closed to behind them.

He waved to one of the armchairs. 'Sit down, sit down.' He turned to the drinks trolley. 'What do you want to drink?'

'Perhaps an orange juice.'

Khrushchev frowned in disbelief, 'You got some illness, comrade?'

'No.'

'You mean you drink orange juice voluntarily?'

'I prefer milk but it isn't always available.'

Khrushchev turned away, shaking his head. 'There's some juice somewhere here. Help yourself.'

When they both had their drinks and were seated Khrushchev said, 'Tell me about Eisenhower and his people.'

Aarons thought for a few moments. 'Well, Eisenhower seems to think that business people and lawyers are the best government officers. Dulles was a lawyer, his deputy was the head of Quaker Oats. The Secretary of Defence used to be the head of General Motors.' He shrugged. 'It was a cabinet to please Wall Street.'

'Yeah, but what are they like? Who's going to make trouble for us?'

'Not Eisenhower. He genuinely wants peace. But most of all he wants a quiet life. The public love him.'

'What about McCarthy?'

'He won't last long.'

'How is it they haven't caught up with you all this time?'

For long moments Aarons was silent, and then he said, 'I don't really know.' He paused and smiled. 'I think they would have a hard job pinning anything on me.'

'Why, do you pay off some cop?'

'No, that would be crazy. I keep no written records of anything. What I get comes back here within the hour if it's transmittable and if it's not it goes within the hour up to my contact in Toronto.'

Khrushchev nodded as if he understood. 'You don't *look* like a spy. You don't even look like a colonel.'

Aarons smiled. 'I don't feel like it, comrade Minister. I feel like a bookseller.'

Khrushchev didn't look particularly impressed or amused.

'This man McCarthy, why does he always attack intellectuals – writers, film people, actors, scientists and so on?'

'They influence people's thinking.'

'And why are they communists anyway?'

'They've got imagination. They're dreamers, creators, and they're romantics. Communism seems like an answer to a lot of problems.'

'And what made you join the Party?'

Aarons laughed. 'I don't think I ever did. The Party joined me. I got it from my father.'

'Was he an intellectual?'

'No. He was a very poorly paid worker. He worked at a glove factory before we moved to Paris.'

'Why did you move?'

'Because of the pogrom against the Jews.'

'They're dreamers too – the Jews. Dreamers and romantics.' He looked at his watch and then at Aarons. 'They looking after you all right – girls and . . .' he paused and grinned, '. . . and orange juice?'

'Yes, comrade.'

Aarons stood up as Khrushchev stood up, nodding to him as he headed for the door.

An official car took him back to Lensky's place and as he thought about his meeting with Khrushchev he wondered if Khrushchev had looked at his file. Did he already know the answers to his questions? Or more likely he wasn't important enough for a Minister to spend time checking on him.

Lensky had got him onto a plane to Amsterdam that left late in the evening of the same day. As they waited at the airport Lensky said, 'Don't answer if it's difficult – what did K want?'

'We just chatted. He asked me about things in the States. He didn't seem well informed. Most of what I told him could have been put together from the newspapers. Why doesn't our embassy do that?'

'Too busy protecting themselves. And even if they did it would never get to K unless it suited the plotters.'

'What the hell are they plotting?'

'God knows. It goes on all the time, like a permanent chess game. Moving the pieces and taking the pawns. Right now they've given up on K. They know he'll get the job but they're scared he'll start changing things. Letting a few cats out of the bag. You'd better go – they're calling your flight.'

Lensky patted Aarons' arm, turned, and walked away. Aarons turned to watch him. He looked like any old man, shoulders bent and a tendency to shuffle. But he was better dressed than most old men in Moscow. He wondered why Lensky had stuck it out for so long. He could have sneaked out long ago.

43

It was Bill Malloy who diffidently suggested that the
Aaronses should move to a better neighbourhood. They
were eating together, the two couples, at Aarons' place.

'What's wrong with this place?'

Malloy smiled, 'Tell him, Tania.'

'No. You tell him.'

'You haven't noticed how it's changed, Andrei. It
wasn't all that good when you first came here but it's quite
unsuitable for a decent bookshop now.'

'But it's near the library, it's central and most of our
trade now is not in the shop but by mail.'

Malloy shook his head. 'Andrei, you don't notice what's
going on around here. Beggars, hookers all along the
street, pimps, petty thieves and hoodlums on every corner.
It's not the Broadway Melody any more, people don't
even shuffle off to Buffalo any more let alone dance down
42nd Street at three in the morning, and Angelo's and
Maxim's have long gone.'

Aarons turned to Tania, 'What do you think, honey?'

She smiled, 'Well, I think some of the academics who
come to see you are a bit surprised at the location.'

Malloy chipped in, 'You'd make a good profit on the
lease, Andrei.'

'Why, if it's so undesirable?'

Malloy shrugged. 'Highly desirable to undesirables.'

'Where should we go?'

'There are apartments just off Union Square that have
been done up. I acted for the developers. There are two

or three still available if you'd like me to put you in touch.'

'Are they expensive?'

'Not beyond your means, Andrei. And plenty of room for your books and an office as well as good living space.'

Aarons looked at Tania, 'How about you handle it?'

She smiled. 'We don't have to move if you don't want to, my love.'

'I think it's a good idea. I just hadn't noticed what was happening round here.' He looked at the others. 'Bridge, five cents a hundred?'

They laughed and the girls stood up to clear the table. Aarons was a recent convert to the game, an assiduous follower of Ely Culbertson.

Despite Bill Malloy's influence it took three months before they had completed their move. Tania had always kept on her studio and her apartment but both businesses were now prosperous enough to allow her to furnish and decorate the new place to make sure that it was somewhere she could enjoy living in. One of the innovations was an RCA TV set, and she had bought a record player and a dozen LPs as a present for Aarons himself.

The Malloys had taken them to the Algonquin for dinner to celebrate the move. Malloy had smiled as he pointed out that it was May Day. Sunday, the first of May, 1960.

It was 3 a.m. in the morning when Aarons was awakened by the telephone and he made his way, half-asleep, into the living room, trying to remember where the phone was. He never gave a name when he answered the phone, just the number and he heard Malloy's voice say, 'That's not your number any more, fella.'

'Is something the matter?'

'Yeah, can I come across and see you?'

'When?'

'Right now. It's important.'

'OK. I'll wait for you.'

Malloy was wearing slacks, a thick heavy pullover and sneakers and he followed Aarons into the living room. Aarons had prepared a Thermos of coffee and as he poured Malloy said, 'I'm sorry to do this but I had a call about an hour ago from Harry Truman. He's back home in Independence but he'd been invited to some dinner at the White House last night by President Eisenhower, and he'd come up with Bess because it was something to do with the Veterans Administration.' He paused. 'Anyway, half-way through the dinner Ike was called away and about an hour later a message comes for Truman to join him. Seems he was put in a car and driven to the Pentagon. He sat in on a briefing for Ike about an urgent problem. When the briefing was over Ike took him to one side and asked him his views on how the problem should be dealt with. He gave his opinion and when he was back at the White House he phoned me and asked me to get your views because Ike doesn't agree with Truman's suggestion.'

'What's it all about?'

For a moment Malloy hesitated, then he said, 'Can I ask that this not be passed on elsewhere?'

'OK.'

'We've got special planes, called U-2s that do high-level reconnaissance. Some of their reconnaissance flights go right across the Soviet Union, photographing what they see on the ground. They fly so high that we reckoned that the Soviet gunners can't touch them. They're not only illegal flights but they could cause great friction between the Soviets and us.' He paused. 'The President was told at his Pentagon briefing that one of these planes had crashed somewhere in the Soviet Union. So far the Soviets haven't said anything. Maybe they haven't located it yet. But when they do they're bound to make a big thing of it, especially with a summit coming up in a few weeks.' He shrugged. 'So the problem is – what does Ike say when the balloon goes up?'

'What does he intend saying?'

336

'That we don't have spy planes and that it was a weather plane strayed off its course.'

'What does Truman suggest?'

'Tell the truth and apologise. Confirm that no such missions will be flown in future.'

'That would be tough to do. But it's the only way.'

'Why not Ike's way?'

'Because nobody in the world will believe him. Sooner or later someone will give the game away. Ike is admired because he is honest. People believe him. If they find that he lied to the world – then he's finished. The same feet of clay as all the others. And the United States is no better than Moscow and the rest of them.'

'So you agree with Truman. Bite the bullet and take your punishment but keep your reputation.'

'Exactly.'

Malloy stood up. 'Thanks. I'll pass it on to Truman and that will make him feel it's worthwhile trying to persuade Ike away from trying to cover up.' He stood up. 'I'd better get back, Andrei. Thanks for your help.' He smiled. 'You must have impressed the little man from Missouri way back. See you.'

It wasn't until the following Thursday that Khrushchev announced to the world that Russian gunners had shot down an American aircraft over Soviet territory. A not very inspired leak from the US Aeronautics and Space Administration said that a weather observation plane was missing over Turkey after the pilot reported having oxygen trouble. NASA hinted that the pilot might have strayed over the Russo–Turkish border.

The next day, Lincoln White, a State Department spokesman, said, 'There was no – repeat N-O – deliberate intention to violate Soviet air-space, and never had been.' The following day to its horror the White House learned that they were exposed to the world as liars when Khrushchev announced to the Supreme Soviet that a Russian rocket had brought down the plane and its pilot had been captured 'alive and kicking' and had made a full confession. A few days of desultory sparring went on before the State Department admitted that it had lied. Moscow said that the pilot would be tried.

Some relief was recorded in Washington when Khrushchev made no move to avoid the summit meeting in Paris at the Elysée Palace. And on May 16 the big four assembled, Eisenhower, Khrushchev, de Gaulle and Macmillan. Khrushchev demanded that he should open the summit and accused Eisenhower of 'treachery' and 'acting like a bandit'. And after delivering his diatribe he stalked out and drove to the Soviet Embassy, leaving the summit in total disarray. Two days later, still in Paris, Khrushchev held a chaotic press conference attended by 3,000 members of the world's media where he insulted the American president even more aggressively. And then announced that in the light of this offence against the Soviet Union he would now solve the Berlin problem by signing a separate treaty with Communist East Germany. Just one presidential lie had made possible the birth of the German Democratic Republic. The Cold War was closing in again, and it was election year.

44

Like a good many others Andrei Aarons was an admirer of Adlai Stevenson and hoped that he would get the Democratic nomination. It seemed odd that the Republican front runner, Richard Nixon, who had served as Vice-President, wasn't even supported by President Eisenhower. But it was Hubert Humphrey who seemed to be taking the Democratic support until the Wisconsin primaries when John Kennedy took 56 per cent of the vote. Kennedy was supposed to be disadvantaged on several counts. He came from a very wealthy background, his father was seen as an appeaser of the Nazis way back, and he was a Catholic. There had never been a Catholic President and the experts said there never would be. But it seemed that when Kennedy had a massive victory in supposedly anti-Catholic West Virginia the issue was settled. And as if to underline the difference between the two men Humphrey had to quit because he had run out of money.

Aarons had watched the Democratic convention on TV. It was now between Adlai Stevenson and John F. Kennedy. Kennedy was nominated on the first ballot and Aarons was impressed and moved by the man and his acceptance speech that spoke of 'the New Frontier'.

Richard Nixon was nominated at the Republican convention and the Gallup poll gave him a lead of 51 to 49 which became 53 to 47 in the following week.

The first opportunity that the public had to judge the characters and capabilities of the two rival candidates was the all-network coverage of their first public debate on September 26. It was a Kennedy triumph. Despite Nixon's high-office and debating experience the Republican candidate looked drab and uneasy compared with his handsome sun-tanned rival. Nixon had spent two weeks in hospital because of a knee injury and that was possibly responsible for his rather haggard appearance.

Despite Nixon's firm instructions one of his close supporters tried to stir up religious bias, but the most damaging incident came when Martin Luther King was arrested in an Atlanta store restaurant for refusing to leave the restaurant when he was barred from entering. King was sentenced to four months' hard labour. When reporters asked Nixon's opinion on the sentence he told them that he had no opinion, but privately he called the Attorney General and asked him to set up an inquiry. The Attorney General did as he was asked but Eisenhower made him drop the matter. Kennedy rang through to King's wife to express his sympathy and said he wanted to help. His brother Robert phoned the judge who had sentenced King and King was let out on bail the following day. King told the other black leaders of Kennedy's action and the word spread quickly through the black communities all over the States. The polls showed that the candidates had equal support. Communism, the high standard of living, the Cuban threat, Communist China were all proffered by the Republicans as reasons for getting the country's votes. Sneers at Kennedy's inexperience and Nixon's promise to start up atom bomb tests again played their parts. But somehow the Senator for Massachusetts seemed to draw people to him and his policy of a new start, a new look at America. He looked and sounded as if he meant it and could do it. A new word – 'charisma' – was creeping into the language of political commentators.

Malloy was surprised when he got the call from Truman's old friend, Abe Karney. And even more surprised when, at a meeting the next day, Karney asked him to work for

340

the Kennedy election team. Malloy was only marginally interested in politics and his own politics shared little with the Democrats. But old China-hands like Karney were shrewd pickers of people and a meeting with the top people at the Democrats' New York operation, followed by a couple of evenings with the bright young movers and shakers of the Kennedy circus were enough to make him realise that both he and Kathy would enjoy their time with such lively people.

There had been an organised visit to Washington for a brief meeting with the candidate and Malloy was impressed by the man. Not just the handsomeness, not just the obvious charm, but the words. They weren't a politician's words, they were poets' words, dreamers' words. They made you glad to be alive.

As election day drew nearer the charges and counter-charges became more and more virulent. Kennedy's aim to make a better America was dismissed as running America down. And Kennedy himself was not above gaining some affectionate female smiles by referring to his pregnant wife.

The day itself was unusually bright and the closeness of the contest led to the heaviest turnout in history. Nearly sixty-nine million people cast their votes that day. The candidates themselves relaxed in their own ways. Nixon drove a few friends down the California coast roads to Tijuana, and Kennedy played touch ball with the family at their compound in Hyannisport.

The TV news networks had to fill in the time between the closing of the polls and the counting of the votes, so they used a big IBM computer to forecast the results. By 7.15 p.m. the magic box predicted an overwhelming Nixon win: 459 electoral votes to Kennedy's 68. By 10.30 p.m. a lot of actual results had come in and now it looked like a disaster for the Republicans. Kennedy was well ahead of his rival.

All through the night Robert Kennedy had watched the teletypes and the television sets tuned to the different networks. Phone call after phone call to people of influence sent the Kennedy phone bill up to 10,000 dollars for that night alone. The candidates were still neck and neck but by 9.30 a.m. Michigan's Republicans threw in the towel and the Chief of the Secret Service put through a call from Washington to his team of agents holed up in Hyannis' Holiday Health Inn and they moved in on the Kennedy compound. Senator Kennedy was now President-elect Kennedy. But he had won by a margin of less than one per cent. In the euphoria of the campaign and the victory only politicians gave any thought to the Vice-President-elect, Lyndon B. Johnson. Because he was one of them – a real politician not a dreamer, and definitely not a poet. But a man who knew where the switches and buttons and levers of Capital Hill were located, and what you had to do to make them work.

45

Tania paid off the taxi and walked up the stone steps to the painted door. The small panel beside the door said 'Flat 3 – Sam and Anna'. No surname, and somehow it seemed right to be that way.

Anna was wearing a white blouse and a black skirt and the calm beautiful face was so smooth it could have been a young girl's face not the face of a woman in her late forties.

Anna had arranged a tray of drinks, coffee jug and cakes on a low coffee table and as Tania took her cup she smiled at Anna as she said, 'I came to ask a favour.'

Anna smiled back. 'Tell me.'

'Andrei said he wants to go to Brighton Beach on Friday, and he wants me to go with him.'

'What's he want to do there?'

'I think just look around, see how it is. Maybe remember other times. Better times.'

Anna shook her head slowly, 'They weren't better times, Tania. Perhaps better in some ways. His work was less involved then. Just finding out how to go about it.'

'But he loved Chantal a lot, didn't he?'

'Only the same way he loves you.'

'Does he love me? Or does he just put up with me?'

'You know better than that, don't you? Why this sudden loss of confidence?'

'Tell me about Chantal.'

'She was very young, her parents were well-off but she was involved with unions and that sort of thing. She was very beautiful and they fell in love with each other very quickly. They were just kids.' She shook her head slowly. 'A teenage boy whose mind was totally involved in Party affairs. A loving young girl who felt she had found a very special man.'

'Was she a good wife?'

Anna smiled. 'What makes a good wife? She was totally supportive. She asked for nothing. She did all she was asked to do, without question. She was a dear girl and I loved her very much. And sometimes I felt she deserved better than she got from my brother. Watching her cured me of any faith I had in the Party and its system. To me she was a victim of the system. The prisoner of a man she cared for instead of a prisoner in a labour camp.' She shrugged. 'There wasn't much difference.'

'You make him sound almost heartless.'

'In a way he was. But you have to think of the circumstances. How could he have learned what you should do as a husband? He had never seen how a man and a woman should live together. And he was intent on saving the world. His head was in the clouds.'

'And now?'

'What do you mean?'

'How do I fit into this picture?'

Anna smiled. 'It's a different picture. I could tell he was in love with you before I even met you. He talked about you so much. Your talent as a photographer. How assured you were. You had a mind that had worked things out. You were independent and yet rather mysterious.' She paused. 'I've seen you and Andrei together many times now. Your relationship with him is quite different. I know you care about him but you have a mind of your own. And that's what he needs. I've seen the changes you've made in his life. He's more alive. He was like a lost soul before you came along.' She shrugged. 'Poor Chantal didn't stand a chance. She didn't have a chance to be independent. She just had to tag along. And if I'm honest I have to say that he didn't make a good husband. He

344

didn't just sacrifice his own life to the Party but hers too. That's why I refused to go on with Party work. I hated that system and I hated the people who made it so.'

'Why do you think he wants to go to Brighton Beach?'

'I've no idea, honey. But if he's asked you to go with him then it isn't anything to do with Chantal.'

Tania had taken her camera with her, a 35mm Nikon with a dozen Kodachrome films and twenty loads of Ilford HP5 for black and white.

They went by subway and as they went down the stairs from the station platform to Brighton Beach Avenue she stopped him and took a picture of him on the stairs. She had no photograph of him, not even an old one, and then, as they went into the street she realised why. A photograph was identification. She looked up at his face. 'I'll scrap the shot, Andrei. I didn't think.'

He smiled faintly and nodded, and as they turned right she stood with the camera to her eye, the shutter clicking as she moved the lens from one view to another. After a dozen or so shots she turned to Aarons. 'This is fantastic, Andrei. It's like a foreign country. The people, the shops, the signs – everything's Russian. We could be in an old part of Moscow.'

He smiled. 'Or Israel.'

'Yes,' she nodded. 'Will they mind me taking pictures?'

'Of course not. They may look like Russians but they're Americans, hoping they'll see themselves in *Life* magazine.'

'Where are we going?'

'Let's carry on down the avenue.'

'Have you got something you have to do?'

'No. I just wanted to see it again. See how it's changed.'

'Has it changed much?'

'It hasn't changed at all. It's just the same.'

And as if to confirm the point at least half a dozen people had stopped him to shake hands and talk. People who had known him in the old days.

They ate lunch in Café Arbat and were joined by an old man with a beard who Andrei introduced as Rabbi Godlevsky. They spoke in English so that she could join in, but when either of them was intent on making a point she noticed that they lapsed into Yiddish. It amused her to see the old man treating Andrei as if he were still a very young man.

'This fellow of yours,' the Rabbi said, 'came in to put us all right. To tell us of the promised land. Not Jerusalem but Moscow. Worked all the hours the good Lord sends. Argued the devil's case better than the devil himself. All for one and one for all.' He laughed, 'Wonderful stuff. And a lot of people believed it, you know. He should have been a lawyer, defending the gangsters. Arguing that they were part of the economic system – Robin Hoods robbing the rich to feed the poor.' He turned to look at her, the red cheeks and the bright blue eyes making him look more like an out-of-season Father Christmas than a Rabbi. 'Can't you persuade him to come back here and keep us all alive again? We miss him, you know.'

She smiled, 'A wife must follow her husband wherever he goes.'

The old man laughed and nodded. 'And he says you take wonderful photographs. Of what, my dear?'

'To earn money, of fashion and cosmetics, for myself pictures of people. Poor people.'

'Ah yes. The winners and the losers. He says that your parents were Russian – do you feel Russian?'

'Only just before I go to sleep or when I see silver birches.'

The Rabbi nodded, looking at her intently. 'I can see why he fell in love with you, my dear. Not just that pretty face and those melting eyes.' He paused. 'Well, I'd better get on my way. Enjoy yourselves while the sun is shining.' He patted Andrei's arm as he stood up and was stopped to talk by two different people before he got to the street door.

* * *

Tania had photographed all afternoon, people, shop-fronts, fruit, salami hanging in rows from ceilings, shop signs in Yiddish, Russian and Polish, people from every part of Eastern Europe, mainly very old or very young – the others in-between were somewhere else, earning a living in Brooklyn or Manhattan, Queens and the Bronx.

As the sun went down they were strolling slowly along the boardwalk towards Coney and despite the warm air he shivered.

'Are you cold?'

'No. It was just one of those odd shivers.' He smiled. 'Somebody put his foot on my grave.'

'Let's go back home.'

He stopped and looked out at the ocean and then back towards the buildings of Brighton Beach. He sighed deeply and then said, without looking at her, 'Yes. You're right. Let's go home.'

They walked back along the boardwalk to the small park at Brighton Beach and took a cab back to Manhattan. They sat holding hands on the back seat and by the time they got to Prospect Park he was asleep. She looked at his face. He was fifty-three now, sixteen years older than her but sometimes he looked much older. His hair was greyer now than when she first knew him but the terrible way he had his hair cut gave him a kind of innocent boyish look. He wasn't handsome but he was definitely attractive. The hesitant way he spoke when he was intent on getting over some point made you listen more carefully and when he did smile, which wasn't often, it was a young man's smile.

She still had no idea why he had wanted to go to Brighton Beach. He hadn't shown her where the bookshop had been, he didn't seek out anyone, although a lot of people obviously remembered him. Maybe it was some kind of '*À la recherche du temps perdu*'. One of these days she would know what went on in that head.

They ate dinner at a small Italian restaurant on East 22nd Street, and then walked home together talking about the films that the restaurant owner had enthusiastically recommended they should see – *La Dolce Vita*, *L'Avventura*, and *Rocco and his Brothers*.

As they rode up to their apartment in the elevator Aarons said, 'It seems kind of strange not having a shop anymore.'

Tania laughed. 'You just can't get used to being a dealer in books instead of a bookseller.'

As he put the key in the lock they heard the phone ringing and when Tania answered it she turned to Aarons. 'It's for you – it's Bill.'

As he took the phone Aarons said, 'Hi.'

Malloy laughed. 'You've got more American now you've moved to Union Square.' He paused. 'You know that old thing we used to do with the guy from Kansas, I've been asked to contact you by the new guy. What d'you think?'

'How did he know about me?'

'The old guy told him. The new guy's very keen.'

'It's OK with me.'

'Can I contact you at your place tomorrow?'

'Yeah. I'll be here all day.'

The room Aarons had taken for his books and to use as an office was large, with a high ceiling. There was a roll-top desk and a small desk with an electric typewriter and a dictaphone that was used by a part-time secretary.

Down the centre of the room were two long tables of beautifully polished mahogany on which books were laid out, some single books, others four or five volumes together. Every wall had wooden shelves from floor to ceiling with an old-fashioned library ladder that Aarons had bought at an auction. And every shelf was full of books. In a bay window there were two armchairs at a low circular table.

Aarons stood at the window, the activity in Union Square always comforted him. All those people who were busy with their lives. Selling fruit or flowers at one of the

348

stalls or bustling along the streets to shop or work. None of them spending their days worrying about the rivalries of the super-powers or the state of the world in general. They didn't give a damn about the dialectic of materialism, they probably couldn't name the President of the Soviet Union. Their lives were bounded by their jobs and their families. They probably couldn't name the Secretary of State either, and many of them wouldn't even know the capital city of California. Maybe they were the wise ones, getting on with their lives oblivious of the fact that the political system of their country was permanently engaged in a grim struggle with a system that ruled a sixth of the world.

He called out as he heard the knock on the door and Malloy came in, shedding his coat as he headed for the chairs in the window. Tossing his coat over the back of a chair he sat down, 'I'm in a hurry, Andrei. Can we talk right now so that I can make a phone call?'

Aarons shrugged. 'Of course. Carry on.'

'Truman spoke to Kennedy about our arrangement with you, and Kennedy didn't hesitate. He wants to continue the arrangement and he's ready to start immediately. He's invited you and Tania to his place at Hyannisport this weekend.' He paused. 'Will you come?'

'Where is it?'

'In Massachusetts. He'll arrange for one of the family cars to pick you up.'

'What kind of man is he?'

'You'll like him.' He smiled. 'Like you he's a dreamer of dreams. He's a very shrewd politician but he wants to change things. Give it a try. He's quite a charmer.'

Aarons smiled. 'Seems to have charmed you anyway.'

'He has. I like him – a lot. I'll be on his staff.' He smiled. 'Unpaid, courtesy of Hancox.'

'Let me check that Tania doesn't need to be in town.'

He spoke to Tania on the internal phone without telling her what it was about. When he hung up he said, 'Yes, that's OK, Bill.'

'Can I use your phone?'

'Help yourself.'

Malloy dialled a number, said 'Yes,' and then just listened before saying 'OK' and hanging up.

'A car will come for you both 9 a.m. Friday morning. It's a longish journey but they'll make you comfortable. The driver isn't secure so far as this operation is concerned so don't talk about anything confidential. And don't talk about Kennedy or the family. OK? For the sake of your own security you'll have a different name and you'll be identified as looking over the Kennedy archives. We'll keep you out of sight as much as we can.'

'Will you be there?'

'Yes. So will Kathy.'

They arrived at the Kennedy compound mid-afternoon. There had been several security checks but the letter that had been given to the driver cleared them through. They were shown to a pleasant cottage where Kathy was already waiting for them.

Bill Malloy came over in the early evening as the three of them were eating and had taken Aarons to another cottage which seemed to be used as a communications centre. President Kennedy saw them in a small room that had a log fire burning against the cool spring evening.

Kennedy shook his hand and pointed to one of the leather armchairs. When Malloy had introduced them Kennedy grinned and said, 'They tell me I can't use names because we don't want them on the record. He tells me it's OK to call you Andy, is that OK?'

'Yes, sir.'

'Let's cut out the formalities. You're here as a friend who could help me to avoid mistakes with our friends in Moscow.' He paused. 'I want to ask you something. A favour. If you don't agree just say so and that'll be the end of it.'

'What's the favour?'

'It would help me a lot if we could expand our group.

I'd like my brother Robert to be part of it and I'd like to suggest that Bill Malloy here should be part of the group too. I'd like us to discuss things, kick 'em around a bit. It'd make it more useful.'

'I think you're right. Let's do that.'

Kennedy looked across at Malloy, 'Bobby's with Art over in the boat cottage. Can you bring him over?'

When Malloy had left Kennedy said, 'Bill tells me you got your interest in politics from your father just as I did.'

Aarons laughed. 'Well, not quite the same way. I didn't know there *was* anything other than Communism. It came as a surprise that you had to justify it.'

'They tell me that you were a great advocate for the Party when you were just a teenager.'

Aarons smiled. 'I defended its stupidities from time to time.'

'Do you see us as enemies?'

'Oh no.' Aarons shrugged. 'Just stupid like my lot in Moscow. The two biggest powers on earth who are so ignorant of the rest of the world and each other that it's almost unbelievable.'

'When you're in Moscow do you talk to them like this?'

'I talk like this to one man, he passes it on or uses it, and sometimes people take notice.'

'You ever meet Khrushchev?'

'A few times.'

'What's he like? As a man.'

'He's a peasant. Talks like a peasant and thinks like a peasant. Tough, shrewd and knows how to work the machinery.'

The door opened and Robert Kennedy came in with Bill Malloy. Aarons was introduced, there was some banter between the two brothers and then they settled down to talk.

They talked into the early hours of the morning and there was no apparent holding-back by either side. The President was eager to learn, particularly about how the seemingly ponderous machinery of Moscow worked. How

351

you got to the top and how you stayed there. When Aarons explained the convoluted system of favours done and influence brokered Robert Kennedy had grinned at his brother and said, 'Sounds just like Boston.' John Kennedy shook his head, 'More like Washington.' Aarons was surprised and flattered that the talk was so open, more like locker-room gossip than political discussion, and was pleased when Kennedy suggested that they should meet regularly.

They spent the next day with at least a dozen Kennedys, adults and children, playing games, eating from a barbecue and generally relaxing. Kennedy had walked with the four of them the following morning to the limousine that would take them back to New York and it was obvious that his charm had worked on Kathy and Tania.

46

Aarons and Malloy were sitting in the book-lined office drinking a mid-morning coffee.

Malloy smiled. 'How did you like John F?'

'I liked him a lot. I read his inauguration speech again – there were some thoughts of his that show how far-thinking he is.' He reached in his pocket, pulled out a card and read from it slowly '. . . to bear the burden of a long twilight struggle . . . against the common enemies of man: tyranny, poverty, disease, and war itself.' He looked up at Malloy. 'That man is something special. And because I've met him I know that they're *his* thoughts and *his* words, not those of a speechwriter.' He tucked the card back in his jacket pocket.

'He's got big problems at the moment.'

'What kind of problems?'

'I can't tell you. It's to do with Cuba. He's being pressured by powerful people to let something go ahead that he dislikes intensely.'

'Why doesn't he just stop it?'

'It was set up before he became President and it involves a very high-powered agency and cancelling would have a lot of political repercussions. You'll hear about it in the next few days.'

A week later Aarons heard the first radio reports of the Bay of Pigs disaster, and he read that the President had announced that the responsibility was his.

* * *

In the course of the following six weeks Aarons had three meetings with the Kennedy brothers, always at Hyannisport, and always he and Tania were treated as close family friends.

Aarons realised that the President was taking their meetings seriously when Malloy briefed him before the meetings on what Kennedy would like to discuss. Many of the questions were about the personalities of top Soviet leaders, their relationships with each other and their rivalries. Other questions were about the daily lives of Soviet citizens and their attitudes towards the government. But a lot of the time at their meetings was taken up with what the President called 'what-if' situations. What would be Khrushchev's reactions if the USA did this or that? What if the Soviets made an aggressive move in Berlin and the USA made a move against Soviet interests in the Far East, would the Soviets trade for a stand-off? If the Soviets made an aggressive move and the Americans threatened to take action against them was Khrushchev strong enough to back down if he wanted to?

The more Aarons saw of Kennedy the more he admired him. It was encouraging that the American people seemed enthusiastic about his plans for a new America in his speeches about the New Frontier. He didn't sound like a politician and he certainly didn't look like one. He wondered if some day there would be a man like that as President of the Soviet Union. But the men in the Kremlin weren't dreamers of dreams, they dealt in power not imagination, and their dour faces and their stony eyes were never going to charm anyone.

He was surprised when a few days later the Supreme Court decreed that the Communist Party in the USA had to register as an organisation under foreign domination. It seemed pointless, a thrust at Moscow that would anger them without achieving anything.

When Aarons picked up the phone the caller asked for Tania. It was a voice he'd heard somewhere before but he couldn't identify it. He was looking at the photographs that Tania had mounted for an exhibition at a new gallery in the Village but he was vaguely aware of concern in her voice as she talked on the telephone. When she hung up she hesitated for a moment and when he turned to look at her he saw that she was obviously upset about something.

'What's the matter, honey?'

'You didn't recognise the voice?'

'I'd heard it before but I couldn't place it. Who was it?'

'It was Jakob – my grandfather.'

'You mean Lensky?'

'Yes.'

He frowned. 'Phoning here? That's crazy.'

'He's here in New York. Wants to come over and talk with you. He's at the Plaza. I said I'd have to ask you.'

'Why didn't he speak to me? Why ask for you?'

She shrugged. 'I guess it's all part of the silly games you people play.'

'You people?'

'I'm sorry. I didn't mean it that way. It was a shock.'

'Where's he staying?'

'He wouldn't say. He just gave me a number. It's on the pad by the phone.'

'Did he say why he's over here? Is it something to do with me?'

'He didn't say but he was obviously worried about something.'

Aarons was silent for a moment, then he said, 'I'd better call him.'

Lensky arrived at their apartment an hour later, looking noticeably older but not obviously worried. When Tania had made him welcome and settled him down she went off with her portfolio of prints to her friends' gallery. She said she'd be back in a couple of hours.

They were sitting facing one another, Lensky with a vodka bottle and glass, Aarons with orange juice in a glass jug.

Aarons said quietly, 'What's it all about, Jakob?'

'It's a long story but what matters as far as you're concerned is that I'm pulling out of Moscow.' He paused and smiled, wryly, 'I'm going to live in Israel. As a private citizen.'

'When?'

Lensky shrugged.. 'Now. I'm going to stay in the States for a few weeks to get my affairs straightened out and to get my Israeli passport settled.'

'What made you decide to do this?'

It was quite a long time before Lensky answered, not looking at Aarons as he sat thinking, then turning to look at Aarons he said, 'Between you and me I've had enough of them. The rivalries, the vendettas, the sheer ignorance. At one time I thought I could influence them, show them a better way. A way that didn't have thousands of my compatriots in prisons and tens of thousands more in labour camps.'

'Did you say all this to them?'

'Of course not. I told them that I'm an old man, I need the sun and a quiet life. Still willing to be a consultant if they wish.'

'And what was the reaction?'

'At first suspicion and then after some discussion they suggested a deal. I send them reports on the Middle East. I said I couldn't abuse Israeli hospitality that way. They thought I was crazy but they agreed that I should only report on the Arab countries.' He shrugged. 'And that was it.'

'What made you choose this particular time?'

'I guess old age and the realisation that I had become no more than a kind of court jester. Tolerated but not taken seriously. Khrushchev listened to what I had to say, and I think he sometimes acted on it. But that only made them even more determined to keep me away from him.' He sighed. 'It was always like this I suppose but way back I thought I could help change things. If anything things have got worse. And now . . .' he shrugged, '. . . enough is enough.'

356

'Are you sure that they'll leave you in peace?'

'I shall take precautions but I'm not important enough to warrant any harassment. I asked them to pay me a modest pension and they'll see the threat of cutting that off as enough to keep me in line.'

'D'you need money, Jakob? We could help.'

Lensky smiled. 'No. I put all my money from way back in overseas banks. I've got all the money I need.' He paused. 'But I wanted to warn you of how things stand. I suggest that if they don't ask you to go to Moscow in the next couple of months you should go anyway. And if they talk about me just say I called on you and you were not only surprised but rather shocked. Don't whatever you do try and justify my actions.'

'Do they know about Tania?'

'Yes, but they don't know that she's related to me. They've got no records on her or her parents, I saw to that.'

'How long are you going to be in New York?'

'A few weeks – just for a rest and to get used to not looking over my shoulder.'

'What will be their attitude to me with you gone?'

'You were just a young man I spotted way back. You should be OK. You've got a first-class record and the information that you're getting for them now about this NSA surveillance organisation gives you all the insurance you need.' He stood up. 'I'll go now but we must meet again so that I can fill you in on all the current rivalries and who to latch onto and who to avoid.'

'Where are you staying?'

'At the Plaza.'

'I'll call you tomorrow. Let me ring for a cab.'

'I'd rather walk.'

47

The following weekend they were at Hyannisport but the Kennedy brothers' talk was of Vietnam. Their main concern was of the efficiency or otherwise of the two key Americans in Saigon. They were sending back optimistic reports. Ambassador Nolting and General Harkins were unknown quantities and the President had stuck to his plan of limiting US aid to advisers and money. They were now pressing for a build-up of the small contingent of American troops already in Vietnam to finish the job. But George Bull was a known factor, reliable and far-seeing. He had contacted the President and predicted that if the commitment was made it would not stay small. He had said that if the troops were sent the USA would be backing into a major Asian war. He went further and said that if more troops were sent there would be 300,000 US troops in Vietnam in five years' time. When they spoke the President had laughed and said, 'George, you're crazy.' But the prediction stayed in his mind. A nightmare scenario that haunted him.

Kennedy talked briefly with Aarons about the Berlin Wall going up. American and Soviet tanks had faced up to one another at the Brandenburger Tor but neither side had gone further. Aarons' view was that the real threat was that Moscow would sign a separate peace treaty with the East Germans and that would be an open challenge to the Americans.

* * *

Aarons had warned Tania not to let Lensky know about where they had been and never to mention any knowledge of the Kennedys.

He had made two journeys to Baltimore for meetings with Roger Cowley, who had supplied a considerable amount of the information asked for by Moscow but had pointed out the risks he was taking and had asked for a 'bonus' payment of 5000 dollars. Aarons reluctantly agreed the payment and when he had notified Moscow of the demand they had encouraged him to pay whatever was necessary. The information they were getting on the National Security Agency at Fort Meade was worth anything he had to pay. A week later he received a coded packet from Toronto with a list of further information they wanted. There was, however, a complaint from Moscow Centre that there had been a fall-off of general intelligence. They particularly urged him to find a source of information on the movement and deployment of US Navy ships and submarines. He had put Ivan to find out details of the locations of the main naval bases. Much of the information was available from reference books and newspaper files. There were people in the unions who could be used to provide leads to useful contacts, once they knew where the key bases were.

Lensky had decided to extend his stay in New York so that he could have his teeth fixed and a general medical check-up. They had taken him to see the usual New York sights but they had the feeling that Jakob Lensky was more knowledgeable about New York than he let on. But he had obviously enjoyed going to Sam's club and he got on well with both Sam and Anna, giving Sam a long lecture on that Russian boy named Israel Bailin, better known as Irving Berlin, son of Moses Bailin, who had come to the United States in 1893 to join the thousands of other Jews who became known as *farloyrene menshen*, the 'lost souls'. According to Lensky all the successful song writers were Russian Jews, not Americans.

Gershwin, Berlin and Hammerstein were favourite sons. Sam obviously loved the old man who seemed to know quite a lot about popular music and jazz.

48

The autumn of 1962 was exceptionally beautiful. It sent people to Vermont and it sold a lot of Kodachrome. October was a month to be remembered.

Sadly, for some, it was remembered for less pleasant reasons. For the White House the warnings of a tense October started way back in July, not that it was recognised as an ill-omen at the time. But on July 2nd it was routinely reported that Fidel Castro's brother, Raul, Cuba's War Minister, was in Moscow. US intelligence sources noted that large numbers of Soviet freighters from the Black Sea area were berthing at Mariel, a deep-water port on the northern coast of Cuba. There were no clues as to what their cargoes might be but there were large teams of Soviet technicians on board.

By the end of August there were more than five thousand Russians in Cuba and the CIA interrogator units in Florida concentrated on refugees' stories of convoys of flat-bed trucks carrying long tubular objects covered by tarpaulins. A CIA agent back from Cuba brought a sketch he had made of the tailpiece of one of the objects and the same week came an eye-witness report of a drunk in a Havana bar who boasted that Cuba now had long-range missiles with atomic warheads. The drunk had been positively identified as being Castro's personal pilot.

Much of this rag-bag of intelligence had come to the notice of Senator Keating of New York and he had made a number of public speeches in which he warned of a Soviet military build-up in Cuba. And on 10th October he publicly claimed that according to his informants six intermediate-range missile sites were being constructed in Cuba. A White House statement dismissed the comment as ill-informed and backed its judgment with a supporting statement from the CIA who confirmed that the sites were for standard SAM missiles only suitable for defence against air attacks. A couple of mischief-makers in the press pointed out that it was a Soviet SAM missile that had shot down Gary Powers' U-2 flying over Soviet air-space.

Aarons and Lensky sat drinking coffee in a small Italian coffee shop near the Flatiron Building. They had both seen the reports of Senator Keating's pronouncements on missiles in Cuba. And the White House's denials.

'What do you think, Jakob?'

'About what?'

'*Are* Moscow putting missiles in Cuba?'

Lensky shrugged. 'I'd think it's highly likely.'

'But why? It would be crazy to antagonise the Americans for such a useless gesture.'

Lensky stirred his coffee slowly, 'The key is Khrushchev. He's in a state of acute frustration. Blocked in Berlin, at odds with Peking, stalled in the Third World, and years behind the Americans in the build-up of missiles. He's desperate for something that makes him look significant.'

'All that risk for just a gesture?'

'He's got a lot of pressures on him inside the Soviet Union. Industrial growth stagnant, agriculture in a hopeless mess. Red Army generals demanding an even greater share of already limited resources and old-style Stalinists raising hell about K's tentative steps towards liberalisation. It took quite a lot of courage to make that speech to the Congress denouncing Stalin. A lot of those older Party members see Khrushchev as a traitor.'

'And how will this help him?'

362

Lensky shrugged. 'He challenges the Americans, that's always a good move.'

'And they challenge him back.'

Lensky shook his head. 'So what? There's talk of nuclear war, all sorts of denials mixed with threats from both sides. Moscow's view has always been that the Americans would back down rather than face the Soviet Union. Americans care about casualties, Moscow doesn't. Moscow will go to the brink.'

'All the way? To war with America?'

'Probably not, but they can scare the Americans with some deal that makes K look like he's won.'

'What kind of deal?'

'Who knows? The Americans agree to pull their missiles out of Turkey, or even out of NATO. Something like that would make it look like the Americans had sold out their allies because they were scared of a war. Every ally of the USA would know that they would be abandoned if it suited the Americans.'

'You mean you risk starting World War Three just to prove the USA would chicken out. I thought it was Moscow's official line that it was America that *wanted* World War Three and was planning for it.'

Lensky shook his head slowly. 'Andrei, I've known you for many years now.' He smiled. 'I can still remember you holding your father's hand outside the synagogue when I had to tell him that it was time he left Russia. He was holding Anna on his shoulder and Ivan was with your mother, poor soul. I can remember you when you came to Moscow from Paris, for training. You were so clever and yet so innocent. I wondered if perhaps I was doing the wrong thing. But they were days of such promise and for me you were part of it. Somebody who would help make it happen.

'I've watched you all these years and as time went by I felt guilty about you. Wondering if I hadn't robbed you of your life. I hope I haven't but there's one last piece of advice I'd like to give you.' Lensky smiled. 'It must seem

363

a long-winded diversion from answering your questions. And in a way it is a diversion. I think you've survived because you have had so little contact with Moscow and life in the Soviet Union. You wouldn't last a couple of months in Moscow.' He smiled. 'If it's any consolation Lenin wouldn't survive in today's Moscow either.'

'What are you trying to tell me?'

'I'm telling you to grow up. Being innocent is one thing. Being naive is something else. Apply that fine mind of yours to the facts of life.'

'What facts of life are you thinking of?'

Lensky shrugged and waved his hands. 'Stalin killed more Russians than the Germans. An economy that's falling to pieces. A society that's at the end of its tether but frightened to do anything about it. A society that's lost its way in a swamp of lies.' Lensky leaned forward. 'There were seven million abortions in the Soviet Union last year, if that doesn't mean that people have abandoned hope then I'd like to know what it does mean.'

'So what are you suggesting I should do?'

'Just use that analytical mind of yours. Look at the facts. You know more about American politics and policies than most Americans do. You've spent a life-time involved with Moscow and the Party. There's propaganda on both sides but you can ignore that. Both sides are selling a dream. The same dream actually. Maybe one of them really means it. Which one? If you can decide that then maybe you have to think about where you stand.'

'That sounds like you've already decided.'

'All I decided was that the side I was on, the side I understood, consisted mainly of ruthless, greedy men, whose lives had nothing to do with Leninism or Marxism.' Lensky smiled, a very Jewish smile. 'There's an old Jewish saying, Andrei – "Hoping and waiting turn wise men into fools".'

'Is what you said advice or a warning?'

'Both, my friend, both.'

* * *

364

Aarons took a cab down to Tania's studio. She was working with a large 8 x 10 camera. She pulled out from under the black cloth, smiling when she saw him.

'Just let me finish this. Just two more shots.' She waved him over. 'Come and look at this.'

This was a tape-recorder, a Grundig, placed on a red velvet cloth. As she switched on the studio lights they caught the surface of the spools of tape and the golden locks and fittings sparkled like jewels. The knobs and switches and the line of control tabs cast sharp-edged shadows across the plastic fascia.

'Why the red flannel?'

She laughed. 'It's not flannel, you idiot, it's velvet. Makes the product look valuable and distinguished. They aren't on sale yet but they're preparing the ads so that they can go to Germany for approval.'

'What do they do?'

'They'll record anything. Radio programmes, records, phone conversations, family stuff. They're very good. They demonstrated one for me.' She smiled. 'I'm hoping they'll let me keep this one as part of the deal.'

'How about we go out to dinner tonight?'

She looked pleasantly surprised. 'You bet. Where'll we go?'

'How about the Waldorf?'

'Great. Why don't you phone through a reservation while I finish this job.'

They had actually closed the door of the apartment behind them when they heard the phone ringing inside. Aarons went back reluctantly and lifted the phone.

'Yes.'

'Andrei, it's Bill. I've been asked to get you over here right away.'

'Over where?'

'Washington. He'll send a car for you if it'll help. Could be there in ten minutes.'

'I'm just taking Tania out to dinner. How about tomorrow morning?'

'You couldn't put it off, could you?'

'No. Definitely not.'

'What time will you be back?'

'Midnight, something like that.'

'How about I send a car at one and you could have a nap on the journey?'

'Why the rush, Bill?' He sounded on the edge of anger.

'I'm sorry. There's a crisis here, they need your help.'

'OK. Send the car.'

'It might take several days. Maybe you should warn Tania.' He paused. 'I'm afraid it's just you. This is for real, not just kicking ideas around.'

With his canvas hold-all on the seat beside him Aarons slept until the car stopped at a hotel. The driver said that his friend was waiting for him in the lobby.

Malloy was there, with a copy of *Newsweek* in his hand. He held out his free hand.

'Thanks for coming, Andy, they're very grateful. I've booked you a room here for today. I need to get you photographed for an identity card that will get you in the White House and other places we might have to go to.' He looked at his watch. 'The shops won't be open for another hour so let's have some breakfast.'

As they walked to the hotel's coffee-shop Aarons said, 'What's this all about, Bill?'

'I can't tell you now but when we've got your ID card fixed we'll be going to the White House.' He paused and looked at Aarons. 'It's serious, Andy, very serious.'

It was mid-day before Malloy drove Aarons to the White House. Their identity and status were checked four times before they were in a complex of underground offices. On his ID card Aarons was described as 'Interpreter/Translator – Presidential Level'. There was no name given but a typewritten note referred enquiries on a 'need-to-know' basis to contact someone with just a seven-figure numerical reference. Malloy showed him into a room whose door had a stencilled panel that said, 'Consultation Room 904'.

Inside the room the walls were white-painted concrete. There were no windows but the air was fresh and the ceiling lights gave a light that was like daylight. There was a long table with a continuous panel of electricity sockets on the wall behind it and a white screen on one wall surrounded by cork panels. A dozen or so folding chairs were stacked against a wall with two telephones on a panel above them. And in one corner were four leather armchairs set around a coffee table.

Malloy used one of the phones and then hung up and pointed to the armchair. 'He's coming down in a few minutes.'

'Who?'

'Bobby Kennedy. JFK is in his conference room with the intelligence people and the military. And people from State.'

'Is this Cuba?'

Malloy looked shocked. 'Have you heard something?'

'Only what I've read in the papers and heard on the radio and TV.'

The door opened and Robert Kennedy spoke to somebody outside before he closed the door. He walked over and sat himself down, sighing as he ran his fingers through his unruly mop of hair. He looked at Aarons.

'Sorry to drag you over but we'd value your opinion on this situation. Has Bill explained the problem?'

Malloy interjected. 'No. I haven't told him anything.'

Robert Kennedy nodded. 'OK. I'd better explain. You probably saw in the press the statements by Senator Keating that the Soviets were putting nuclear missiles with warheads in Cuba. The President denied it on advisement from the CIA. John McCone, the director of the CIA, was away at the time and when he got back he found that there had been no aerial reconnaissance of western Cuba, where the sites were supposed to be, for two months. The reconnaissance had to be by U-2s and after Powers' U-2 was shot down by Soviet SAM missiles in Soviet air-space the CIA were cagey about using U-2s over Cuba because it was known they had Soviet SAMs. But McCone sent two U-2s over Cuba, they photographed the whole of Cuba and when the films were developed and the enlargements evaluated by experts it was quite clear that Keating was right.

'The next morning October 16 they woke the President to tell him. He called a Cabinet meeting. They quizzed the experts who said that it looked as if the site at San Cristobal would be ready for firing in ten days' time. You can imagine that everyone was deeply shocked. It meant that we could be attacked almost anywhere in the States with no more than three minutes' warning.

'I've got to emphasise that these missiles are "first-strike" weapons. They have no defensive rôle. They are attack weapons. What is even worse is that both the military and the CIA agree that the weapons being set up in Cuba are half the total missiles available to the Soviet Union.

'Today's the 19th and the President is going on TV on Monday night to tell the American people what's going on. That gives us barely three days to decide what steps we are going to take. We have a number of choices. I'd like to explain what they are and the one that we have almost firmed up as our response.' He paused. 'Will you help us decide?'

Aarons said quietly, 'Have you had any recent contacts with Soviet officials in Washington?'

'Yesterday the President kept a long-standing arrangement to receive Andrei Gromyko. He made the meeting last as long as he could, two hours, to give Gromyko an opportunity of raising the missile business. He didn't say a word about them.'

'I'll help you, but when you've told me about the alternatives and your preferred action I'd like an hour or so to think about it on my own.'

368

'Where are you staying? What hotel?'

'I don't know.' Aarons looked at Malloy who smiled and said to Robert Kennedy, 'I've booked him in at the Dupont Plaza.'

'Look, the Ex Comm is still in session, how about you go back to the hotel and get some sleep and we'll meet here again mid-evening. Say nine and I'll lay on something for us to eat. Talk a couple of hours and then you've got all night to think about it.'

'Whatever suits you, sir.'

Kennedy smiled. 'I'm still Bobby. The President is having to keep to his usual schedule so that nobody can start getting ideas that there's some crisis. If people can see me around it'll help.' He stood up, straightening his loose tie as he looked at Malloy, 'Look after him, Bill, see that he gets all he wants.' Then he turned to Aarons. 'How's your lovely Tania?'

'She's OK,' Aarons said, and was touched by that genuine Kennedy concern, to remember his wife's name and ask after her in the middle of an international crisis.

Robert Kennedy joined them just after 9 p.m. and put a sheet of paper on the table in front of him.

'Let's get started. Jack's kept to his schedule and is campaigning for the Democratic candidates in Connecticut. Nobody outside the group seems to have picked up any idea that there's a crisis. I've been running the Ex Comm discussions so I'm right up to date on the alternatives. The medium-range missiles – that's with a range of a thousand miles – will be ready to fire in a week. The intermediates – two thousand two hundred miles – would be ready for early December.

'So – the alternatives. The majority opinion favours an air attack to take out the sites and the missiles. Snags – the Air Force say that would mean killing about twenty-five thousand Cubans and a number of Soviet technicians. Dead Russians would almost certainly lead to total war with the Soviet Union.

369

'Next we've got the blockade route. Cut Cuba off by sea and air from the rest of the world.' Bobby Kennedy looked at Aarons. 'Next option is we could do nothing. Next we could send a top man to Khrushchev and try to settle it just talking. No revelation, no publicity. Another alternative is to expose the Russians in the UN Security Council, photographs and all. But unfortunately the Soviets chair the Council this month – Zorin. Then we have the big one – we invade Cuba. Take it over lock, stock and barrel. Solve all the problems in one go.'

He looked at his notes. 'One last thing. Both bombing and blockading are technically acts of war.' He half smiled. 'That's the menu, Andy.'

'Can we talk about it a bit right now?'

'Sure.'

'Even if technically blockade is an act of war it sheds no blood. It keeps the stakes low.'

'So does doing nothing or trying out sweet reason at the Kremlin.'

'On the invasion – would the military really prefer this, using the missiles as an excuse – a reason for doing it?'

'No. But it has to be borne in mind. Not only is it an alternative but if we choose some other way and it doesn't work we have to come back to this.'

'Can I ask who supports doing nothing or a quiet talk with the Kremlin?'

'Sure. Nobody supports either. They are possibilities so they have to be considered.'

'Have you decided that you'd be ready to take military action if it came to it to take out the missiles?'

Robert Kennedy was silent for several moments before he said, 'I think you could say that we'll do anything that's necessary to remove those missiles.'

'Anything?'

'Yeah, anything.'

'What's your experts' analysis of why Moscow have put those missiles in Cuba?'

Kennedy shrugged. 'They haven't a clue. Every reason

put forward sounds crazy. The bottom line is that they know what they're doing and that means that either they're ready to risk a war with us – or maybe worse – that they actually *want* a war with us.' He paused. 'It's maybe outside our arrangement with you but can I ask you if you'd heard about this move from your people?'

'No. Not a word. All I know is what I've heard or read in the gossip and rumours in the media.'

'No gossip from your people?'

'Nothing. Absolutely nothing.'

'Why do *you* think they put the missiles there?'

'You know, Bobby, if we can answer that correctly we shall know what you have to do. For better or worse.'

'So tell us what your assessment is as to why they put the missiles in Cuba.' He paused. 'Or do you need time to think about it?'

'No. I don't think so. Maybe we should talk about it.'

'Go ahead, Andy. We need somebody who can see the other side of the coin.'

'Well, if you analyse the situation there can be only two reasons for them doing it. The first is that they really do want an excuse for a war. The second is that it's done out of weakness.'

'How could such an aggressive move be a sign of weakness?'

'In situations like this you have to sometimes ignore the deed because the motive is more important.'

'So what's the motive, Andy?'

His conversation with Lensky seemed almost designed to answer Kennedy's question. After a few moments to collect his thoughts he said, 'I think this episode is done for internal, domestic reasons.'

'I don't understand.'

'Put yourself in Khrushchev's place. The Soviet economy is crumbling, huge grain harvests are rotting on farms because there's no transport and no distribution system that works. There's a low standard of living and even if people save a few roubles there's nothing they can buy.

371

There's quite open bribery and corruption by Party officials at all levels. The armed forces raise hell for more money for themselves and point out that they are years behind the American build-up of arms. And on top of all that the old China-hands in the Party are accusing you of being a traitor.' Aarons paused. 'It took real courage for Khrushchev to denounce Stalin and what he had done. He has always had a genuine wish for reforming the system but it's too top-heavy. Nobody can change it. If you tried, the hard-liners would stop you.'

'Go on, Andy.'

'So what do you do to take people's attention away from your failures? How do you show that you are still a super-power? How do you please the military? You challenge the other super-power. You put nuclear warheads in its backyard. There are plenty of other places you could put them that threaten the United States. But they may not react to a threat a thousand miles away. But a threat from Cuba would be intolerable. And if the USA raises hell in the UN Security Council you point out that they have nuclear weapons in Turkey, the Soviet Union's backyard.'

'You think this is why they're doing this?'

Aarons shrugged. 'More or less.'

'All this just to get us to move our nuclear warheads out of Turkey?'

'It's not so small a victory. Every ally you have would know that when the chips were on the table the Americans would walk out on them if it was in their interest to do so. You could find that your position in NATO was very uncomfortable. The French would make much of it. They've always said that America was an unreliable ally.'

'And you would recommend that we pull the missiles out of Turkey?'

'Not at all. If I were President – which God forbid – I would do no deals at all. Neither open deals nor secret deals.'

'What would you do?'

'I'd threaten Khrushchev that unless the missiles were removed we would remove them ourselves.'

'Do you think he would back down?'

'He would be angry about having to do it but yes, he would do it. He's a gambler. The least he comes out with is that the world knows that the Soviet Union has to be reckoned with.'

'So which of our solutions do you go along with?'

'You're right to have the President tell the American people and the rest of the world what the Soviets are doing. That will shock Moscow. Tell of the assurances that Moscow has given you that there are no missiles in Cuba. You mount a naval blockade of Cuba and you give Khrushchev a date by which time the missiles have to leave Cuba for the Soviet Union.'

'Or?'

'Or you will remove them yourselves.'

'And if they call us on that?'

Aarons shrugged. 'I think you could deal with Cuba in a couple of days. Logistics would prevent the Soviet Union from doing anything.'

Kennedy sat looking at Aarons and then he said, 'Tell me, Andy, if your people in Moscow asked you what to do about something we had done, would you advise them too?'

'If what you were doing was aggressive and likely to lead to war then yes – I'd tell them how I felt they could stop you.'

Kennedy looked at Malloy, 'Anything else?'

'No. We'll be at the hotel if you want us.'

'I think the President might want to talk to you tomorrow before he finalises his decisions and drafts his TV address.'

'Whatever he wants, Bobby.'

Malloy had taken Aarons to dinner and then on to a late showing at a cinema of *Advise and Consent*. He had chatted on personal things to Tania on the phone and then gone to bed.

Malloy was called to the telephone as they ate a late breakfast. When he came back he said that John F wanted to see them at 4 p.m.

The hotel was in a street with Victorian row-houses and shops and foreign embassies. There were two bookshops and Aarons had bought a copy of Solzhenitsyn's *One day in the life of Ivan Denisovich* and Malloy had bought him the new volume of Pasternak's poems, *In the interlude*.

It was still a sunny October and they had coffee and a snack in a small café near the hotel. Back in the suite that Malloy had taken for them they listened to the radio and watched the TV but there was nothing about missiles or Cuba.

At 3.30 p.m. the car and driver came for them and they were in Conference Room 904 fifteen minutes later.

Robert Kennedy came down first.

'The media are beginning to start noticing things. Why so many lights on all through the night in unexpected places? People are checking on rumours, most of them in the wrong direction but we're getting very near to leaking. I don't know if we'll last through tomorrow, Sunday.'

He looked up as the door opened and the President came in, tie-less and still handsome despite the strain showing on his face.

'Hi, all of you. Andy, there's just one thing I have to go over with you. This question of Khrushchev backing off. People see that as a sign of weakness but I think that attitude is often a mistake. I'd say that if Nikita K is sure of himself and strong enough, he can afford to back off. If he's weak he'll just get carried along on the tiger, scared to get off in case his rivals eat him. What do you think?'

'You're right. I'm sure of that.'

'So which is he, tough or weak?'

'He's strong enough to back off. There are no rivals who would dare go for him at the moment.'

The President looked at Bobby. 'There's over a hun-

374

dred ships deployed now in the Caribbean. First Armoured Division are heading for embarkation points in Georgia right now. Five other divisions on full alert, and B-52s with atomic weapons are on permanent airborne patrol. When one lands another takes off. I think the *Trib* has a good idea of something going on. I'm sending a letter to Khrushchev which he'll get with a copy of my speech. He'll get both from our ambassador while I'm talking on TV.

'I'm warning all our embassies an hour before I go on air. There will be anti-American demonstrations and all the usual crap that starts up whenever we issue a threat.' He stopped and looked at the others, shaking his head slowly as he said softly, 'Outside it all goes on, Saturday night dates and dinner parties, the movies, the theatres, the cops, the crooks, the traffic, the hookers. None of them know that by this time tomorrow we will be in a flaming crisis. God help us.' As he walked to the door he stopped. 'If there's need for a meeting tomorrow I'll contact you, Bill. I think we'll just let it ride along. The decision's made, we've just got to wait for the reaction. Thanks for your help, Andy. We owe you.'

Sunday October 21 passed without any call from the White House but on the Monday morning a message came through that they were to be available from noon. A car came for them at 3 p.m. and they went straight to Conference Room 904.

Robert Kennedy was waiting for them, clip-board in hand.

'Just to put you in the picture. We've made arrangements for twenty congressional leaders to meet the President at 5 p.m. We've even sent Air Force planes for those who can't make it by commercial airlines. After that there are individual briefings by senior staff at State to forty-six ambassadors and other diplomats. At 6 p.m. Rusk is seeing Dobrynin, the Soviet Ambassador. Acheson is already on his way to brief NATO top brass and while the President is speaking Adlai Stevenson will deliver a formal request to Zorin at the United Nations to convene a special meeting of the Security Council.' He shrugged. 'That's about it. On the military side we've assembled more than enough resources to cope with anything likely to happen. There's all sorts of rumours flying around the town, some are near the mark but most of them are way out. But they've obviously all realised that something's going on.'

Malloy said, 'What's the President's attitude in his speech?'

'That this is a deliberate attempt by Moscow to upset the balance of power. He intends exposing the deliberate attempts at deception by them, and Cuba will be blockaded by the US Navy – the term he'll use is "quarantine" – and . . .' he glanced at his clip-board, '. . . it will be, I quote, our unswerving objective, unquote, to remove those missiles. Any ship attempting to run the blockade will be sunk by the US Navy and if a missile were launched from Cuba it would be regarded as an attack by the Soviet Union on the United States and the USA would respond immediately.'

Malloy nodded. 'Sounds pretty grim.'

Kennedy shrugged. 'It could have been worse if McCone hadn't insisted on risking those U-2 surveys.' He paused. 'Do you mind hanging around for a bit in case Jack wants some comment from you after his speech?'

Aarons shook his head. 'I'll stay as long as you want.'

At 5.40 the President and Bobby Kennedy came back to the room and it was obvious that he was very angry. It seemed that his meeting with the congressional leaders had been rough. The leaders claimed that the proposed response was too weak. They wanted action against Cuba immediately. Slowly, as Bobby talked with him he became calmer. Bobby had pointed out that when the President was first told about the missiles his reaction had been exactly the same. He had had time to work out the possible consequences of the various options and at least it was better that the politicians were so militant, they could have taken the view that his two-stage challenge to the Soviets was going too far too quickly.

Ten minutes later the President left to prepare for his broadcast and Bobby Kennedy took Aarons and Malloy to another room in the bunker where there was a radio and TV set and two rows of chairs. There were others already seated and a US Marine sergeant showed them to two empty seats before Bobby left the room to join his brother.

The room was silent as a meteorologist on the screen gave details of the weather all over the United States. Then the screen showed a still shot of the White House and a voice-over introduced the President. The screen cleared to show the President behind his desk in the Oval Office and then moved in to a head and shoulders shot. As the President spoke of the crisis his rather harsh Boston accent added a biting edge of scorn as he related the duplicity of the Soviet government and outlined what amounted to an ultimatum to Moscow to remove the missiles immediately or face the consequences. The rather square face was a young man's face but a young man who knew his way around. A young man who had served in the US Navy and who still felt the pain in his back but bore it philosophically. It was an impressive performance and Aarons wondered what Moscow's reaction would be. Despite their discussions they set great store on always maintaining the legal niceties when they went over the line. Being exposed to the world as lying to the President of the United States would shock them.

When the lights went on in the room there was almost no talking. It was obvious that the people there were well aware of the situation. Malloy and Aarons headed back to Conference Room 904 where Malloy made a telephone call and ten minutes later a US Marine came to tell them that their car was waiting.

When they got back to the hotel there was a call for

Malloy from the White House. They wanted them both to pack and go straight back to the White House where accommodation was available for them. What had become their car picked them up an hour later.

49

Bobby Kennedy had taken them personally to their accommodation which he said was officially designated the Green Room where screens had been erected around the portion they were to use. There were two single beds, several ornate chairs, a table and four upright chairs and several cabinets with appliances for making coffee and a line of cereal packets and silver containers of the usual condiments. On a desk in a corner was a large metal-cased Hallicrafter radio. Alongside the radio was a list of the frequencies of Radio Moscow for both internal and external broadcasts.

Kennedy stood hands on hips. 'The best we could do in a hurry.' He turned to Aarons. 'Andy, we want you to listen to Moscow radio round the clock. We've got people monitoring all their major frequencies but we want to have your impression of what they're up to. If they're aggressive do they really mean it? Are they scared or are they spoiling for a fight? Just your feelings about how they're responding to events. They've patched you in to a good aerial system that covers long, medium and short wave.' He smiled. 'There's top brass bedding down all over the place so you're in good company. Anything you need just dial nine. Food, drink, laundry, whatever. If you want to phone home dial zero and give the operator the number you want. OK?'

Aarons smiled. 'I'd like a Russian dictionary if you can find me one.'

Bobby Kennedy laughed, 'My God – what have we done to you, Andy?'

Aarons sat reading and listening to the radio the next day. There was no mention of the President's speech nor any trouble in Cuba until 6 p.m. EST when Radio Moscow announced that the American Ambassador had been summoned to the Kremlin and handed a note that accused the United States of piracy, and denying that the missiles were for military use. It was another hour before the Russians were told about the crisis and the American's blockade of Cuba.

Bobby Kennedy came to see them in the early evening.

'I went to see Ambassador Dobrynin personally today. He swore that there were no missiles in Cuba. You know – if I hadn't seen the U-2 photographs I'd have been inclined to believe him. I think those bastards in Moscow haven't told him what's going on.'

'There was very little on the radio. They sounded confused as if they haven't had time to decide what attitude to take.'

'There are twenty-five Russian merchant ships on their way to Cuba. They haven't changed course but our people at Fort Meade have monitored almost continuous coded messages to them from Russia. The President has modified the line of the quarantine interception from eight hundred miles to five hundred miles to give the Russians more time to make up their minds. All the merchant ships are being shadowed by our submarines.'

'What's happening at the missile sites?'

'The latest U-2 photographs show them still working on the sites. We've sent a Fleet Task Force at top speed to close off all five navigable channels that ships from mid-Atlantic have to use to approach Cuba. They should be in place tomorrow morning.'

Malloy asked, 'How's the President?'

Kennedy shrugged. 'He's pretty tense, and it's beginning to show, talks kind of staccato and his back's playing him up too. He's trying to look cool and calm but he ain't, that's for sure.'

'If it's any consolation there'll be worse panic in the Kremlin.'

'You reckon?'

'I'm sure. Khrushchev will be looking around for someone to blame and nobody's going to tell him that he's the one who's carrying the can right now.'

'But if they meant it?'

'OK. They meant to put the missiles there but they're now in a different game. This wasn't what they expected unless they've gone crazy.'

'I've heard people from the Pentagon hazarding guesses about where the first missiles will land on American cities.'

Aarons shrugged. 'Unless the President lets them launch an all-out attack on Cuba tomorrow, yes?'

Robert Kennedy half-smiled. 'Yeah.'

By 10 a.m. on Wednesday, October 24th the naval Task Force was in place in a wide arc 500 miles from the eastern tip of Cuba. Thirteen destroyers, six cruisers made up the forward picket line as twenty-five Soviet merchant vessels headed towards them, being shadowed by US Navy reconnaissance planes. They saw two Soviet ships ahead of the others and watched a Soviet submarine take up station between them.

The latest aerial photographs taken over Cuba gave a grim picture of feverish work on the missile sites. At least thirty missiles with warheads had been identified and at least twenty crated Ilyushin L-28s capable of delivering bombs on American cities.

The Secretary General of the United Nations, U Thant, sent identical letters to Khrushchev and Kennedy urging suspension of the blockade and Soviet arms shipments for a period of two to three weeks. President Kennedy refused to negotiate until all missiles and their bases had been removed from Cuba.

In Moscow, William Knox, an American businessman

known in Kremlin circles, was summoned to the Kremlin to deliver a message to Washington. He reported that at the interview Khrushchev looked exhausted and on the verge of collapse and was so incoherent that there was no message to pass on.

Then came the news that twenty of the Soviet ships had stopped dead in the water and further news that six ships had turned round and an hour later six more then turned back. The Ex Comm was well aware that this was only the first move in what was going to be a battle of wills. But one senior official did say, in confidence, to a colleague – '. . . I think the other fellow just blinked.'

The next day marked the first interception of Soviet ships. One was carrying petrol and the other a group of East German students. The President had given instructions to the Navy to allow time for the captains of intercepted vessels to contact Moscow. In both cases there was no resistance and after inspection they were allowed to carry on to Cuba.

But the highspot of the day was the clash on TV at the UN Security Council between Adlai Stevenson and the Soviet's Valerian Zorin. Zorin openly challenged Stevenson to prove that there were missiles in Cuba. Stevenson turned on him angrily, 'Do you deny that there are missiles there? Yes or no? Don't wait for the translation, answer – yes or no?'

Zorin said angrily that he was not in an American court-room and Stevenson seized on the statement.

'You are in the court-room of world opinion right now and you can answer yes or no.'

Zorin, backing off, said lamely, 'You will have your answer in due course.'

Stevenson said angrily, 'I'm prepared to wait for my answer until hell freezes over, if that's your decision. And right now I offer this evidence to the assembly.'

Whereupon Stevenson unveiled two easels which had previously been covered. They showed big blown-up photographs of the missile sites and missiles. Zorin swept angrily from his seat with the Soviet delegation. It was a public defeat for the Soviet Union.

All that day Malloy and Aarons had sat in an annexe to the large room where the Ex Comm was in permanent session.

The following day, Friday, October 26th was a day of conflicting episodes. Early in the morning the destroyer *Joseph P. Kennedy Jr* had stopped the *Maruda*, put on board an armed, naval search party who, finding nothing offensive, allowed her to go on her way. It seemed that Moscow had instructed Soviet captains not to resist search parties.

On Cuba it was now obvious that the missiles were within hours of being ready for firing and Robert Kennedy got in touch with Ambassador Dobrynin to tell him that the President could not hold off for longer than forty-eight hours.

At lunch-time John Scali, a TV journalist who covered the State Department for ABC, got a telephone call from an acquaintance at the Soviet embassy. The caller, Alex Fomin, was on the embassy staff but was almost certainly a colonel in the KGB. Fomin seemed to be in a highly agitated state and insisted that Scali met him in ten minutes time at a restaurant on Pennsylvania Avenue.

At the restaurant, the Occidental, Fomin wanted to know if the State Department would agree to a three-part deal. The removal of the missiles from Cuba, a promise from Castro to have no offensive weapons in future, and the United States' pledge not to invade Cuba. Scali left and the two met again at 7.30 p.m. at the coffee shop at the Statler Hilton. Scali had spoken to Rusk and told Fomin that the US government were definitely interested. Fomin left the hotel in a hurry.

Meanwhile, at 6 p.m., 1 a.m. Moscow time, a long, rambling letter from Khrushchev came through on the teletype machine that linked the US embassy in Moscow with the State Department. The letter proposed that no more missiles would be sent to Cuba, and the missiles already in Cuba would be removed or destroyed if President Kennedy agreed not to attack Cuba.

Late in the evening the Ex Comm after considering the proposal agreed to accept the proposal as if it were a formal diplomatic note. They would reply to that effect in the morning.

It was nearly midnight when the President and Robert Kennedy called in Malloy and Aarons. Robert outlined to them what had happened. Both Kennedys looked tired. It looked like a successful end to the crisis but the President seemed uneasy.

'Do you think they mean it, Andy?'

'To some extent they do.'

'What's that mean?'

'I don't think it was an accident or an administrative mistake that the proposal was in a teletype letter from Khrushchev.'

'Go on.'

'I think it was the first step of negotiations.'

'There's nothing to negotiate. We agree with his proposals.'

'Have you sent off a formal acceptance to Moscow?'

'No. We'll do that tomorrow morning.'

'I think that to delay the answer might be a mistake, Mr President.'

'Why?'

'Because they can claim that that was just a personal letter from Khrushchev. Not a proposal but just a sounding out of possible terms. Not with the backing of the Central Committee. Not even official, or it would have come by normal diplomatic means.'

'And when we've shown our hands they turn us down?'

'No. I think they'd just add in a few items that they would like themselves. They'll know that you're ready to do a deal. You aren't intent on invading Cuba. So maybe they can harden up the deal a little.'

'You really think they would do that?'

'Yes. That's how they think.'

'Well, they're making a big mistake, my friend. There'll be no changes to that proposal or the deal's off.'

'You'd really turn it down and leave only twenty-four hours before you went in to Cuba?'

'Yes. Congress would impeach me if I chickened out in these circumstances.'

'Then you must make that clear so that they can fall back on the original proposal.'

'Are you certain about that?'

'No. But it fits the pattern so far.' He paused. 'Unless I'm quite wrong and they really do want war.' He shook his head. 'If it had got to that stage they would have warned me and given me new tasks.'

'I hope you're right, Andy. I'd planned on sleeping tonight, and I'm gonna keep to it.'

Malloy and Aarons had made their way back to their accommodation in the Green Room and some instinct made Aarons switch on the radio. Radio Moscow was just beginning its day with weather reports state by state of the Soviet Union. These were followed by talks on Soviet agricultural experiments. There was a programme on various transport subjects and news of a new car being designed in conjunction with an unnamed European car manufacturer. Then came the news but there was no mention of Khrushchev's approach, not even of the missile crisis despite a mention of a record Cuban coffee crop.

There was an hour's programme from a running series on the history of the Revolution and then the broadcast stopped in mid-sentence. After a few seconds' silence the announcer said that there was a news-flash. Then followed the text of a letter from Khrushchev to President Kennedy. As a condition of removing the missiles from Cuba he demanded that the NATO missile bases in Turkey should be dismantled. And this letter was not in Khrushchev's own rather emotional style but the kind of letter that had obviously been put together by a committee.

Malloy was still asleep and Aarons walked over to the

telephone and dialled the internal operator's number and asked for Robert Kennedy. Kennedy was already reading a typed transcript of Khrushchev's letter. He said that he would speak to his brother and call Aarons back. He also mentioned that the President had reports from the FBI that Soviet diplomats were preparing to destroy embassy and consular documents.

He woke Malloy and told him the news and Malloy was still shaving when the President and Robert Kennedy came in.

'Your instincts were right, Andy. At least it doesn't come entirely as a surprise. To add to the scenario I've just been told that one of our U-2s has been shot down over Cuba. That means that they've got the SAM bases operational.' He paused. 'Any ideas?'

'Maybe you should reply to the first letter and ignore the second.'

Bobby Kennedy said urgently, 'That's it. That's it, Jack. Get them drafting a reply immediately.'

The President obviously wasn't happy with the idea but he went along with it. Several senior members of the executive composed draft replies but Robert Kennedy found fault with all of them. Finally the President said, 'If you disagree so violently with all the drafts then you do the draft.'

Robert Kennedy and Ted Sorensen picked the bits that suited them from both Khrushchev letters and the Fomin proposals. They were aware that they were confirming the US agreement to a set of proposals that the Kremlin had, formally, never made. The final letter was sent to Moscow just after 5 p.m. that evening and at the same time the White House announced that the United States had agreed to Moscow's conditions.

There was then nothing for any of the members of the Ex Comm to do. It was a time of extreme tension and several long-experienced members admitted later they had looked out at the October sunshine and wondered if it was the last time that they would do that. One had told his wife where to go with the children if Washington should be evacuated.

The two clocks that had been mounted on the wall showing local time and Moscow time only seemed to emphasise the distance between the two capitals.

Aarons went to bed early and set the small bed-side alarm that Bobby had lent him to 6 a.m. local time. But in fact he woke at 5 a.m. and washed, shaved and dressed for the new day. The radio had been on all night and he sat reading with the programmes as a permanent background.

Just before 9 a.m. there was an announcement that there was to be an important statement on the hour. Andrei woke Malloy who sat on the edge of his bed waiting for Andrei to translate what was going to be said.

The message was not long and it was the third paragraph that mattered. Aarons translated it slowly and carefully.

'In order to eliminate . . . as rapidly as possible . . . the conflict which . . . endangers the cause of peace . . . the Soviet government . . . has given a new order . . . to dismantle the arms which you consider . . . as offensive . . . and to crate them and . . . return them to the Soviet Union . . .'

Aarons smiled at Malloy. 'How about you phone through to Bobby in case he hasn't already been told.'

'What are you going to do?'

'Find another phone and call home.' He paused. 'Can we go back today?'

'I'm sure they'll arrange anything you want.'

'What day is it today?'

Malloy laughed. 'Sunday, October 28, 1962.'

Malloy and Aarons had packed their few belongings and the phone rang to say that their car was waiting. They were about to leave when the President came in looking tired but calm.

'I just wanted to say thanks for your help, Andy. It won't be forgotten.' He held out his hand. 'Have a good journey home.' He looked from one to the other. 'You don't need an invitation to Hyannisport, just come when you need some fresh air.'

50

In the list of telephone messages that Tania had noted down for him there was one telephone number with no name and no message. It wasn't, in fact, a genuine telephone number, just a signal for him to make contact.

He walked down to the deli just off Times Square and the old man nodded towards the bead curtains that separated the shop from the kitchens. Aarons walked through the curtains and the old man followed him wiping his hands on a greasy towel.

'He's gettin' scared because he couldn't contact you four, five days. So he ring me here to contact you.'

'D'you know what he wants?'

'He say he wants to see you urgent but got to be weekend time.'

'OK. Phone him. Tell him I'll see him next Saturday. Place number two, morning between ten and eleven. You got that?'

'I got it, chief.'

Aarons gave him an envelope and the old man squeezed it and then slid it into his back pocket.

Aarons took a taxi to the motel near the racetrack and booked in for two nights. There were photographs of the Preakness Stakes mounted in the lobby and a photograph of *Native Dancer* on the wall in his room. He unpacked and phoned Tania and looked at the titles of a dozen or so books on a shelf over a writing desk. He picked out Scott Fitzgerald's *Great Gatsby* and John O'Hara's

Butterfield 8 and laid them on the small table between the two single beds.

Settling down in an armchair by the window he reached over and switched on the radio, turning the knob to find a sweet music station. When he landed on Fred Astaire singing 'A Fine Romance' he left it on the station and turned to his briefcase. As he took out his note-book there was a soft knock on the door. When he called out Roger Cowley came in with a brown carrier bag which he tossed onto one of the beds.

He was wearing a cotton shirt with a yellow pullover and chinos. He had put on a lot of weight especially round his face.

'I got anxious about you, skipper. Couldn't contact you. Thought the FBI might have collared you at last.'

'I was busy.' He pointed at one of the beds. 'Sit down, Roger.' When Cowley was seated. 'Don't panic if you can't contact me. I've got a lot of work and some of it takes me out of town.' He shrugged and smiled, 'Like you today.'

'I got some stuff your people might find interesting. It's bulky and I don't like keeping it around at my place. They can search our houses without a warrant any time they like.'

'Have they ever checked you?'

'Not the apartment but I've had a couple of body searches at the guard-room.' He smiled and winked. 'Never found nothing.' He paused. 'They've just reorganised the two divisions that cover Soviet cryptanalysis. Made 'em into one with a new guy in charge. D'you reckon your people would be interested in the organisational plan for that?'

At first Aarons had thought that Cowley was teasing or joking and then he realised that he was actually too stupid to understand how important the material would be.

'Yes, they would be interested in that.'

'Would they pay a bonus d'you reckon?'

'What you got in mind?'

'Say five K.'

'When can I have it?'

'Tomorrow morning if you stay over.'

'OK. It's a deal. I'd like to be gone before noon.'

'No problem. I'll be here about ten.'

Aarons pointed at the bag on the bed. 'Do you want the bag?'

Cowley looked at the bag, frowning, then back at Aarons. 'Are you taking the piss?'

Aarons smiled. 'You're welcome if you want it. I don't need it. I'll use my own.' He pointed at the leather case on the bed beside him.

Cowley nodded, not entirely convinced. 'See you tomorrow. Ten.'

When Cowley had gone Aarons looked at the file. The photocopying wasn't good but everything was legible. The brief descriptions of the contents showed that all the reports were invaluable to Moscow. He wrote out a list of the items.

1. Report on patrols of Soviet ship *Shokal'skiy* used for hydrometeorological research in South Pacific.

2. Report on series of meetings to discuss building an NSA navy for ship-based electronic surveillance in coastal waters. (See Sinai report.)

3. Technical evaluation of current sleeve monopoles and parabolic reflectors.

4. Estimated budget of proposed monitoring facility in Manhattan to cover international communications from commercial carriers.

5. Current evaluation of Operation Shamrock.

6. Criteria for adding additional 'trigger words' to current list.

He had no idea of the real significance of the material but it was all headed 'Eyes-only'.

Aarons went into Baltimore and looked around the bookshops. After a meal at a Jewish restaurant he looked through the amusement guide in the local paper and went to the cinema to see David Lean's *Lawrence of Arabia*. Back at the motel he called Tania and heard that she'd been commissioned to do a book on the people of New York. She was still arguing about editorial control but she expected to get what she wanted.

Cowley came punctually at ten the next morning, he handed over the additional report and Aarons paid him the $5,000. Aarons decided to take the plane back to New York and Tania picked him up at the airport. Later that evening he put the parcel of documents in a locker at Grand Central Station. At the Post Office he sent the telegram to Toronto.

The reply came back three days later and he packed a bag, booked a flight to Toronto and told Tania that he would be back in five days.

There was a two hour wait at Toronto for the Stockholm plane and a four hour wait at Bromma for the SAS flight to Moscow.

51

As the plane came in to Sheremetyevo Aarons could see that the snowploughs were still clearing one of the runways. He wondered who would meet him in now that Lensky was no longer in Moscow. It was nearly half an hour before the aircraft steps were in place and the passengers allowed off. On his way to the terminal building he stopped for a moment to look at the big Aeroflot Ilyushin. It was a beautiful plane and with its newly-painted livery it showed that Soviet technology was catching up fast.

Inside the terminal he walked towards the passport check, his solitary bag in his hand. He had the special tag that ensured that inside the Soviet Union it had the same status as a diplomatic bag. As he approached the bench he saw Yakov beside the KGB document man who lifted a flap and waved Aarons inside.

Yakov shook hands and nodded. 'Let me take your bag.'

'It's OK. I've got security material in it for Beletsky and Denikin.'

'We have to check everything. Let's go in the office.'

Yakov took Aarons' arm quite firmly and led him to a corridor. At the far end was a door that said, simply, 'State Security'. Yakov leaned forward, opened the door and waved Aarons inside. Aarons saw with surprise that it wasn't an office, it was an interrogation room with the standard solid table, facing chairs and ceiling lights behind a metal cage. He stopped and looked at Yakov.

'What's going on?'

'Sit down, comrade.' Yakov pointed at one of the heavy chairs at the interrogation table.

'Are you crazy?' Aarons' voice was raised and Yakov tried to calm him.

'Sit down for God's sake. Let me talk to you. Let me explain.'

'You do that, my friend. Right now.'

'Some problems have arisen concerning you. We just have to straighten things out.' He paused. 'It's a question of your relationship with a defector.'

'And who might that be?'

'Lensky.'

'Jakob Lensky?'

'Yes.'

'And you claim that he's a defector?'

'There are people who say that.'

'More fools them.'

Yakov shrugged. 'Let me check your bag and then we'll go into Moscow.'

Aarons handed over the cheap metal keys to his case and stood watching as Yakov took everything out. A couple of paperback novels, a change of underwear, two shirts, toilet and shaving kit and a large bar of chocolate. And at the bottom the fat manilla envelope and its bulging contents. Yakov took out each file, checked the title, looked at a few pages and then put them back in the envelope. He packed everything back into the case, snapped the locks and took hold of the case, looking at Aarons as he said, 'Let's go.'

He led Aarons out to a parking lot at the rear of the offices. A uniformed driver opened the rear door of a black Zil. Twenty minutes later as they went over the bridge Aarons realised that they were heading for Dzherdzhinski Square and the headquarters of the KGB. It seemed crazy. He was a colonel in the KGB but he had only once been to the HQ building before. Yakov had not spoken on the journey but as they walked up the stone steps of the headquarters building Yakov said, 'Have you met Petrenko before?'

'Yes. Only once.'

'And Noskov? The red-haired fellow.'

'Yes, I've met him once some time back.'

'Those two are waiting to talk to you.'

Aarons had had time enough to collect himself and he said, 'Let's go then, comrade Yakov. Let's go.'

Yakov took his arm and they walked along a corridor and down two flights of stone steps to another corridor. At the far end was a steel door. Yakov pushed the bell button beside the door and a red light flashed momentarily as Yakov pushed open the door.

It was a rectangular room about twenty feet by ten feet, heavy carpets and panelled walls. The only furniture was a quite long table with chairs on either side. There were no windows and the lights were behind circular metal fittings. Petrenko and Noskov sat side by side at the far end of the table. Yakov pushed him forward towards them and turning, left the room, closing the door behind him.

Noskov pointed to a chair opposite the two of them. 'Sit down, Aarons.' For a moment Aarons was angry enough to refuse but he decided to go along with the farce.

'You know that Lensky has defected?'

'No. I didn't know that. When did it happen?'

'He visited you in New York recently and you deny that he was a defector?'

'He was passing through and we met briefly a couple of times. But there was no indication that he was a defector. And I don't believe he is.'

'We're not interested in your opinion, comrade.' Noskov paused. 'Why do you think he contacted you in New York?'

'I've known him since I was a child. He was always my contact when I came to Moscow. I admired him.'

'What did he tell you when he contacted you in New York?'

'He told me that he was very, very tired because of his

age. He needed a rest. He was going to Israel and he would do work for the Party from time to time if it was needed.'

'And you would supply him with information.'

Aarons leaned forward, elbows on the table. 'You're wasting your time. And you're wasting my time too. I came over to talk about the material I'm getting for Beletsky and Denikin. This talk of Lensky being a defector is ridiculous. An old man who's worked all his life for the Party and in his seventies he needs a rest – and idiots like you accuse him of being a defector.'

Noskov's face flushed in anger. 'Watch your words, comrade Aarons. Watch your words.' Petrenko touched Noskov's arm as if to calm him down and Noskov jerked his arm away in irritation. 'Maybe it is time you were brought back to Moscow. Maybe you need reminding what loyalty to the Party really means.' He paused for a moment. 'And of course you will deny that your friend Maria was also a defector.'

'I don't know who you are talking about.'

'Of course not – Maria Consuela Garcia. You've never heard of her?'

'No. I haven't.'

'She was on the same Comintern training course as you. You and she had special KGB training together after the course. You remember her now?'

Aarons nodded, 'That was years ago, long before the war and . . .'

'And you were with her much later in Mexico City – yes?'

'Yes. I'd forgotten about that.'

'And your meeting there was with Lensky, was it not?'

'Yes.'

'And six months later Maria Consuela Garcia resigns from the Party and marries a Mexican capitalist.'

Aarons smiled in disbelief. 'And what's that got to do with me?'

'That's what we want to find out.'

'On what authority are you questioning me? Who authorised it?'

'It's routine. When people defect we look at their contacts.' Petrenko shrugged. 'Do you think that you're too important to be questioned?'

Aarons hesitated for a moment and then he said, 'Yes, too important to be questioned by you two. If the Directorate wants to question me then I want it to be a proper enquiry and authorised by somebody above my rank.' He paused. 'You'd better pass the material in my bag to Beletsky or Denikin or you could find them raising questions about what authority you have for holding up urgent documentation.'

Noskov stood up and walked to a telephone on the far wall. He spoke too quietly for Aarons to hear what he said. When he turned to look at Aarons Noskov said, 'We'll see how you feel tomorrow.'

A KGB sergeant came in and Noskov pointed at Aarons. 'That's him.'

The sergeant walked over and grabbed Aarons' hands, pulling them behind his back. As Aarons realised that the man was hand-cuffing him he turned to protest and the man's fist hit him squarely in the face. He staggered back and felt the gush of warm blood from his nose and mouth, then the manacles clamped on his flesh. He was fleetingly aware of a look of triumph on Noskov's face before the sergeant shoved him clumsily through the open door. They seemed to walk a long way down the corridor before he was stopped, a steel door unlocked and he was pushed inside. The manacles were unlocked and slid off then the door clanged to behind the sergeant.

Inside the cell, for that was plainly what it was, there was a concrete block covered by a straw palliasse with two grey blankets neatly folded at one end. The walls were of some metallic finish that Aarons realised was to ensure that messages or other information scrawled on them could be wiped away with just a damp cloth. There was no sound from outside, just the rushing sound inside his head.

He put his hand up to his mouth to wipe away the blood but it was caked on his lips and chin and his lips were too swollen and too painful to touch. He had always accepted that some day he might get caught but not with this scenario. At least he'd assumed that he would be caught by the other side, the FBI or the CIA. And he'd known exactly how he would react. He was a bookseller, a law-abiding citizen. They wouldn't be able to prove a thing. But it had never entered his mind that the blow would fall from his own people. With such stupidity and with such an unlikely confrontation. Jakob Lensky, who for years had pushed his own judgement aside to serve the Party. They'd worn him out and when he finally had to take refuge in Israel he was suddenly a defector. And because he had been a kind of protégé of Lensky he was suspect too. Even that pretty Spanish girl was a traitor to the cause for marrying a rich foreigner. They were like monks in some ancient order who saw sin everywhere and treason in every relationship. He had heard about the fanaticism of some of them but surely the material he'd been sending them for years and the risks he had taken added up to more than guilt by association with a man who was guiltless anyway. Did they really think that having a thug punch him in the mouth would frighten him? Was this really what it was all about? Not a dream but a nightmare.

He wondered what Tania would think of it all. She wouldn't be surprised. She never wanted to know what went on. He was like a man who had some secret vice, some furtive unmentionable hobby or pastime, tolerated but not shared.

He heard the rattle of keys on a ring and then the door opened and a woman walked in wearing a pale blue KGB woman officer's uniform. She leaned back, arms folded, against the wall facing him. She wasn't pretty but she was attractive. And she knew it.

'And how is Comrade Aarons? A little ruffled I hear.'

398

Aarons said nothing and the young woman smiled. 'You don't remember me?'

Instinctively he looked at her but she was right, he didn't recognise her.

'When you first met Beletsky and Denikin. I was there. Glazkova. Aleksandra. I look after them. See that they don't get into trouble. All they care about is that stuff you send them. Mathematics, cryptanalysis, computers.' She paused. 'People like Noskov and Petrenko aren't important. But they can cause a lot of trouble. They were always jealous of Lensky. He was rich and highly intelligent, he'd travelled outside the Soviet Union and he had Khrushchev's ear. What was more he'd had Stalin's ear before that.' She smiled. 'He was covered either way. So they had to wait until he'd retired before they dare attack him.' She paused. 'That bloody mouth of yours is his really. But don't worry. Things will change tomorrow morning.'

'In what way?'

'Beletsky and Denikin are with Khrushchev right now. Telling him about the treasure trove you've brought over for them. And, of course, landing Yakov and the other two in the shit for what they did.'

'So why do I have to stay here until the morning?'

'Oh, come now, Comrade Aarons. You may be useful – but you aren't important. What's a thick lip and a night in the Lubyanka in the great tapestry of life.' She smiled. 'You'll get a state visit from the Deputy-director. Of course he won't notice your cracked lip but he'll apologise for a bureaucratic error and he'll give you Famous Saying Number Two.'

'What's that?'

'All Famous Sayings inside this building are by our great founder – Feliks Edmundovich Dzerzhinsky. And Famous Saying Number Two is – I quote – I would like to embrace all mankind with my love, to warm it and to cleanse it of the dirt of modern life – unquote.'

'What was Famous Saying Number One?'

'Ah yes – Famous Saying Number One – I quote – We

399

represent in ourselves organised terror. This must be said very clearly – unquote.'

'Do people really see Lensky as some sort of traitor?'

She frowned. 'Let's say they never really understood him. So for the likes of Petrenko and Noskov he was a bit of a mystery. The rank and file don't understand or like any kind of mystery. But Lensky had that final insurance policy – direct access to Khrushchev. Nikita trusted him because he never wanted anything. Asked no favours, sought no privileges. Pretty rare stuff these days, comrade.'

'Why did you come here to tell me this?'

'I didn't come. I was sent. To smooth the way. To apologise without apologising. My grandmother used to say – "Spots on the character can be removed – with a little gold".'

Aarons smiled. 'Was your grandmother Jewish?'

'No. She just borrowed their wisdom.'

'Do I really have to stay here all night?'

'Yes. Once the wheels have started turning they just have to grind away.' She paused. 'How long since you've had real *piroshkys* and *kluykva*?'

'*Piroshkys* I often get – what are *kluykva* – they're some kind of fruit, aren't they?'

'Cranberry. I'll arrange for you to get a good meal and a bottle of wine.'

'The wine would be wasted but I'd be glad of something to eat.'

She nodded. 'About an hour. I'll be back.'

It was nearer two hours when she came back with a young guard, two trolleys and a chair. When the guard had left she sat down facing him across one of the trolleys.

She pointed. 'Help yourself. The meat is Siberian deer or wild boar, there's quail's eggs and several different breads. Mineral water and orange juice for you and a glass of genuine Tokay for me.'

They ate more or less in silence but when later they

picked at a bunch of seedless grapes she said, 'You know part of what annoys people like Noskov and Peretsky is that you're so American. Just like a lot of people don't like Lensky because he was so European. The Viennese charm and the French logic.'

'Did you know him well?'

'Over the last four or five years I saw him most days.'

'Did you like him?'

'I loved him but it was a waste of time.' She smiled. 'Not just the vast difference in age but he saw us all as children. Young men were sons and young girls were daughters. But he had a good eye for those who were going to be useful to the Party some day.' She smiled. 'It was Lensky who spotted you, wasn't it?'

'I guess it was. When did you learn your good English?'

'Moscow University and then four years in Australia and two in Canada. Ciphers and then cultural attaché.' She paused. 'You left Moscow when you were just a kid, didn't you?'

'Yes.'

'And now you're completely American.'

'Me?' He frowned in disbelief. 'How do you make that out?'

'You look healthy. You're in jail but you look confident that you'll soon be out. You're sure of yourself. You don't give a shit for the likes of Noskov and Peretsky.' She wagged a finger at him. 'And that, Comrade Colonel, is a big mistake.'

'Tell me why?'

'Because in this city when you get shoved in jail you're scared. You offer bribes. Cash, goods or favours.'

'Even colonels in the KGB?'

She shrugged. 'Doesn't mean a thing when the chips are on the table. Especially with guys like you who get made up to colonels to make you feel important. If you get thrown into this place you don't behave like your attorney's coming along and you ain't answering questions till he gets here. Because he ain't ever coming. If you were going to get a lawyer you'd be in the Public Prosecutor's Office, not here.'

'Interesting. If they suspect me of being a defector why the hell do they think I came here? And why don't they just talk? Why all this schoolboy scenario?'

'They can't help it. They've been doing it so long it gets to be a habit.' She smiled. 'I've got some good news for you.'

'Tell me.'

'They'll be taking you to a very nice *dacha* in Peredelkino tomorrow morning. Red carpet.' She shrugged. 'Red everything. That stuff you brought over for Beletsky and Denikin must have been something very special.' She looked at her watch and pointed at the trolleys. 'They can clean those away tomorrow morning. Have a good sleep.'

'Thanks for the food. And thanks for your help.'

For long moments she stood looking at Aarons and then she said, 'You're welcome,' and she walked to the door and let herself out. He heard her say something to the guard outside before he heard the key turn in the lock.

He pushed the trolleys away from the concrete slab that was to be his bed, undressed slowly and covered himself with the two blankets, his jacket folded under his head for a pillow.

He wondered how much of what the girl had said was true. She seemed unusually frank in her views and she must have been aware of the near certainty that any conversation in the cells was recorded. The building housed the control centre of an intelligence organisation that covered the whole world. And a separate security force that policed every living soul in every state of the Soviet Union. And yet they could suspect poor Lensky of being a traitor because in his seventies he needed a rest from the world of revolution. And he could be suspect too by association. And if he had been a traitor then the crude amateurish approach of Noskov and Peretsky was not likely to unmask him. He could remember Lensky saying that Moscow Centre could never really bring themselves

402

to trust even a Soviet who lived outside the Soviet Union. Something that stuck in his mind was how they knew that Lensky had contacted him in New York. Knowing Lensky he had probably told them that he would make contact. He was too valuable for the Centre to put one of their routine agents onto a surveillance of his movements. If the FBI spotted the agent they would have let him run until they had a picture of his work and his contacts before they put him inside.

Aarons had slept for just over two hours when the girl woke him, waited for him to dress and took him up to the sixth floor and a luxurious suite of rooms that were obviously used as an office and meeting area with living accommodation for some very senior officer. He bathed, shaved and changed his shirt and underwear which had been laid out in the marble bathroom from his travel bag.

There was fruit and coffee laid out for them on a side table and as she poured the coffee she said, 'The man you're going to meet is nothing to do with your Chief Directorate. The material you have been producing recently is being handled by 8th Chief Directorate who cover communications and cryptography. His name is Rabinovich. Lev Rabinovich. Very civilised. Going to the top. Too good at his job to need to be political.' She smiled. 'A bit like you.' She walked to the door and stopped. 'Tell him what travel arrangements you want and I'll put them in hand.'

He nodded. 'Thanks.'

A few minutes after the girl had left the door opened and a man came in. He was in his mid-fifties but he looked younger. Well-dressed, he could have easily been a top manager in some New York company. He held out his hand, 'Rabinovich. Lev. We owe you an apology. Two little bureaucrats who don't know what they're doing can cause a lot of trouble. One is already on his way to the KGB office in Yerevan and the other will soon be on his way to one of our frontier units on the Chinese border. Again our apologies.' He paused, smiling. 'I've arranged for us to do our talking at my place in Peredelkino. You'll like it. Right on the edge of the forest.' He paused. 'Is that agreeable to you?'

Aarons nodded. 'Whatever you want.'

The *dacha* could have fitted happily into any New England rural setting. Outside it was painted a pale pink with blue surrounds to the windows. Inside it was all polished and waxed wood and the well-designed furniture looked as if it was either Czech or Swedish.

A young woman had poured them coffee and then left them alone.

They talked for two hours about the material that Aarons had brought over, with Rabinovich explaining carefully which parts were particularly important. He also talked about other areas on which information would be of vital importance in planning their anti-surveillance systems.

Rabinovich had suggested a walk before lunch and had found Aarons a thick jacket and a pair of fur gloves against the cold.

They walked as far as the edge of the frozen lake, their breath hanging in the cold air, their cheeks stinging from the cold as they turned back to the *dacha*.

'Do you own the *dacha*?'

'It's on permanent loan but I can buy it at a fixed price when I retire. If I want to.'

'Are you married?'

'Yes. My wife works for Sovfilm as a director. She's away in Cuba at the moment, doing a film about Castro.'

'My wife is a photographer. Still photography.'

'Who does she work for?'

'She's independent. She doesn't work for anyone. She's a freelance.'

'How much can she earn in a year that way?'

'It varies. I guess last year she made about thirty thousand dollars.'

Rabinovich stopped as they got to the garden's picket

fence, his gloved hand resting on the gate. 'You mean just one woman earned that money in one year?'

'Yes. It's quite good but there will be photographers earning more.'

Rabinovich shook his head as if in wonderment and Aarons followed him into the *dacha*.

The girl had laid out a tray of sandwiches and fresh fruit and as they ate Rabinovich said, 'Do you like living in New York?'

Aarons shrugged. 'It's OK. I get by.'

Rabinovich smiled. 'The place isn't bugged. None of the *dachas* here are bugged. It's one of our privileges.' He laughed. 'And just as a precaution my men sweep it every day.'

'Do you have to get involved in politics?'

'It would help if I did but it isn't essential. And I would find it terribly boring.'

'You're very fortunate in a way.'

Rabinovich laughed. 'How?'

'All your work is passive – listening – keeping surveillance – nobody gets killed, nobody gets hurt even. There's no way you can be aggressive.'

'The same applies to what you do.'

'Do you think that what we are doing is justified?'

Rabinovich smiled and said quietly, 'Who knows? I have asked myself that question a hundred times.'

'You must have some views.'

For a long time Rabinovich was silent, and then he said, 'I console myself that the work I do gives power to those who still want to make the dream work. A balance against the so-called men of action who could lead us into war.'

'Who will win – the dreamers or the missile-men?'

'I don't know – I'm not sure that I want either of them to win.'

'What's that mean?'

'It means that I think – perhaps – that nuclear weapons on both sides do more to prevent war than anything else. But nuclear weapons and dreams don't go together and

405

it's the dreamers that really matter.' He hesitated. 'For me, that is.'

Aarons smiled. 'How soon can you get me back to New York?'

Rabinovich stood up. 'Are you prepared to fly all night if there are suitable connections?'

'Yes.'

It was no more than ten minutes later when Rabinovich came back. 'We leave in ten minutes. I'll drive you to Sheremetyevo. Oslo, Reykjavik, Ottawa, Newark. That's the best I could do.'

'That's OK.'

'Is there anything you want to take back with you? Vodka, caviar, books?'

'No. I never buy anything on my journeys.'

'What do you do about passports and visas?'

Aaron smiled. 'I get by. That's my business. All those Russian Jews in Brooklyn got the rules worked out long ago.'

As the plane came into land at Oslo Aarons looked at his watch, and then realised that he had lost track of time zones. At the transfer desk they told him that there was a seat on a direct flight to Ottawa if he wanted it. He took it and went straight to the boarding gate and an hour later he was asleep. When he awoke the other passengers were already reaching up for their coats and hand luggage. He had slept all the way to Ottawa. The last leg to Newark was uneventful and he took the airport bus to the New York terminal.

52

Tania heard the phone ring, tied the belt on her towelling bathrobe and picked up the phone.

'Yes.'

'It's Bill, Tania. Are you on your own?'

'Yes. Andrei's gone down-town somewhere.'

'What happened – his mouth I mean?'

'Did you ask him?'

'Of course. But he just changed the subject.'

'I don't know what happened, Bill. I asked him again and again but he wouldn't tell me.'

'It looks like somebody hit him in the mouth.'

'Yeah. But whatever it was he isn't saying.'

'How long was he away?'

'I can't say, Bill.'

'You mean you don't know or that it's not my business.'

'It's his life, Bill. I don't get mixed up in it. He doesn't want me to be part of it.'

'Do you mind?'

'Yeah. But I knew that was how it was going to be, right from the start. I've no cause to complain.' She paused. 'He keeps me out from that part of his life so that if anything goes wrong I'm not involved.'

'I feel uneasy for him. I wish I could help him.'

'You can't, Bill. Nobody can. Maybe one day but not yet.'

'What do you mean – maybe one day?'

'One day he's going to run out of road and he'll need help – but until then he has to do it his way.'

'Are we still meeting at Sam's place tonight?'

'Yes, so far as I know.'

'Good. See you then. Love from us both.'

Tania replaced the phone and walked over to the window. It was three days before Christmas and the square was busy with last-minute shoppers. There would be shops open on Monday but the commuters were finishing today. Such things as Christmas and Thanksgiving meant nothing to Andrei. He went along with the present giving and the small rituals but for him a day was just a day. Whether it was a Monday or a Wednesday or Labour Day was no matter.

She realised that if she didn't have an independent life and career of her own she might have been less tolerant of her husband's life. But there had never been any deception or dissembling on his part, he was all of a piece. A believer in something that she found not only spurious but evil. But she found religions too to be evil and deceptive. Who could really believe that an unbaptised baby that died would spend an eternity in Purgatory? Or who could believe that if you died killing an infidel you would go to an Islamic paradise that sounded like a cross between Vermont and Madam Claude's? What mattered to her right from the beginning was that his thoughts were for humanity. There was no drive to gain benefit for himself. His only failing was that he had never realised that it was humanity itself that made it impossible. Christians did not follow Christ's teachings. Communists didn't live by the manifesto. They behaved like men. Fallible, primitive, two-legged animals who killed and savaged for power and conquest, not for food. She wondered what he would have been like if his father had believed in some other creed or religion. Andrei was no more a Russian than she was. He wasn't an American either. And then she smiled to herself – maybe he was more American than she thought. One of those fanatic TV evangelists who preached absolution in return for belief. And you didn't even have to send him money.

Aarons had a meeting with Cowley in the last week in January. They met at the usual motel and Aarons had briefed him on the information that Moscow wanted. Cowley had brought specimen test papers used for testing potential recruits to Fort Meade and a test designed to highlight potential operatives capable of becoming experts on communications traffic analysis. There was also a report on the use of polygraph machines on both recruits and regular employees, together with a check-list used by clinical psychologists to check out staff who might eventually have access to highly classified material. There was a brief criticism of the use of EPQs, embarrassing personal questions, querying the relevance of a person's sex life to his honesty and patriotism. The criticism noted that a congressional investigation was being carried out on the EPQ tests.

He had sent the new material to the new address in Quebec the same night. Ten days later there was a message from Moscow congratulating him and reminding him of the other material that they wanted.

They had both had a pleasant weekend with the Malloys at Hyannisport. Robert Kennedy had told them of the President's rising concern over the integration of blacks in the southern States. They were trying desperately to avoid confrontation but it seemed that there were powerful people like George Wallace who were determined to defy the law to the bitter end.

He had two meetings with Cowley in February and March and the second meeting worried him. It covered so much material and a lot of anecdotal information that it meant staying at the motel overnight. The material that Cowley brought was of very high quality but what worried Aarons were the signs of a change in Cowley's life-style. He arrived in a bright red Mustang convertible that looked brand new and it attracted a lot of attention outside Cowley's cabin at the motel. What was more disturbing was that later that evening as they sat in Cowley's cabin there was a knock on the door and when Cowley opened the door there was a young girl there who Cowley introduced as his girl-friend. She was very pretty and Aarons guessed that at the most she was fifteen. He collected up his papers and left and arranged to meet Cowley the following morning.

Aarons had a meal alone at a kosher restaurant in town and then took a taxi back to the motel where he went through the material from Cowley and slid it into the false bottom of his case.

The next morning he knocked on Cowley's door and the girl opened it. She was naked and she smiled at his surprise.

'He said for you to wait. He won't be long, he's just gone to the bank. Come on in.'

She closed the door behind him and pointed at a chair. 'Help yourself. You like a drink? We got Scotch or Bourbon, whatever you fancy.'

He shook his head. 'No thanks.'

She sat on the edge of the bed, smiling, and obviously used to the effect that her young body had on men.

'What d'you do last night?'

'I had a meal and then went to bed.'

'That's crazy, you should have come to the club.' She shrugged. 'I could have shown you the girls. Why sleep on your own?'

'What club is that?'

'It's where I work at nights. It's called the Green Cockatoo.' She laughed. 'Calls itself a night-club but it's just a girlie club really. There's two other girls from my school work there at night.'

'You're still at school?'

'Yeah. It's a waste of time.' She grinned. 'I earn more in a night than the teachers make in a month.'

'How long have you known him?'

'About six months. He wants me to move in with him but I'd get bored with just one guy. And I want to make enough dough to have my own set-up.' She smiled. 'I got

410

a real nice place in town if you'd like to party with me some time. No need to tell old Roger.'

Aarons looked at his watch and stood up. 'Would you ask him to come to my cabin when he gets back.'

'Sure.' She smiled. 'Don't forget. The Green Cockatoo. I'm there from six every day including Sundays.'

It was nearly an hour before Cowley came and as he sat down he grinned at Aarons. 'She thinks you're real cute.'

'You're taking unnecessary risks, Roger.'

'She doesn't even know where I work, chief.'

'It's not just the girl. That car cost a lot more than your job would allow.'

'I'm a single man. If I choose to treat myself sometimes I'm entitled.'

'What do you do with the money I pay you?'

'I got two separate bank accounts for that money and some I keep in cash at my place.'

'What name are the bank accounts in?'

'My name of course.'

'Are these banks in Baltimore?'

'One in Baltimore and one in Washington.'

'How old is the girl?'

'No idea, chief.' He grinned. 'Let's just say old enough.'

'She's under-age.'

'She told me she was sixteen but I didn't ask for a birth-certificate.'

'The security people at places like Fort Meade are always on the look-out for people living above their earnings.'

'They aren't interested in bums like me. I'm just a repairman.'

'My dear Roger. When intelligence agents want information out of some installation or a company they go for the women who clear out the waste-paper baskets not the top men. You'll be as suspect as anybody.'

'So what d'you want me to do? Drive around in an old wreck and screw old ladies?'

'You'd be wise to sell that car. It's just drawing attention

411

to you. And everybody who looks at it is going to wonder how you can afford it. Did you pay cash for it or monthly payments?'

'I paid cash.'

'You're crazy.'

'OK. I'll sell it.'

'When?'

'Soon as I can. But I'll lose on it if I have to sell in a hurry. How about you pay me what I lose.'

Aarons shook his head. 'No, mister. I pay for the risks you take. I don't pay for stupidity.'

'You're real het up about this stuff, aren't you?'

'Yes. It worries me.'

'Don't worry, boss. Even if they picked me up they wouldn't be able to pin anything on me.' He smiled. 'And I wouldn't send you down the river, I promise.'

'I'll see you here in two weeks' time. OK. We'll talk about something else I've got in mind for you.'

'Does it make more money for me than this game?'

'Yes. A lot more.'

'I'm your man, chief. You can rely on me.'

At the next meeting Cowley showed Aarons the sales document for the car and Aarons felt that he had brought Cowley into line. He'd lost $500 on the sale of the car and Aarons paid him in cash despite what he had said. Cowley was too valuable a source to want to risk offending him unnecessarily. He had brought the report of an internal enquiry into the shooting down in September 1958 of an EC-130 ELINT aircraft 'ferreting' for NSA. It had been shot down by three MIGs in Soviet airspace near the Turkish border thirty-five miles north-west of Yerevan. His other contribution was a report on the first year's work of a section called Stochastic Math Unit. Aarons didn't understand what it was about but it had a top security rating.

She came in smiling and excited, clutching the big black folio with its ribbons tied in bows.

'It's been my lucky day, Andrei.'

He kissed her and smiled. 'Tell me.'

'First of all I had a call to say that one of my photographs had been chosen for a special exhibition called *The Family of Man*. It's going all round the world and it'll be a book as well.'

'That's wonderful. Which picture was it?'

'It's one you liked, two little boys, one black, one white, sitting on the edge of the gutter with the white boy's arm round the other's shoulders. And they're looking at each other smiling.' She paused. 'And that's not all. Five minutes later there was a call from *Life* magazine. They want me to do a six-pager on Harlem Today.'

'Let's go to Sam's and celebrate.'

She laughed. 'Why not? I'm so pleased, Andrei. I can't believe it. All in one day.'

She came back from the bedroom fluffing out her hair with one hand, the other holding a piece of paper.

'I'm terribly sorry. I forgot in all the excitement. There was a telephone call for you at the studio. A woman – sounded very sexy. She said would you phone this number and said would you phone from the jazz place. I suppose she means Sam's.'

'Did she say who she was?'

'No. I asked her and she just said that the message was from Jay.' She held out the paper. 'Anyway here's the number. I must go and get ready.'

Aarons looked at the number. He didn't recognise it and it wasn't a New York number. He wondered who Jay was. He folded the paper and slid it into his pocket. There was something odd about it. He had never given Tania's studio number to anyone. He didn't want her to be involved. And who was it who knew them well enough to know about Sam's club?

Although it was only early March it was a mild evening and they walked down to Sam's club. When they had ordered something to eat Anna showed him to the small back office where he could use the phone. He checked the code with the White Plains operator who told him that it was an Israeli number for Tel Aviv. And then he guessed that the mysterious 'Jay' was probably Jakob. Jakob Lensky.

He dialled the number and after the usual clicks and buzzes he was through. The voice that answered was a man's who stated the number without identifying himself.

'Is that Jakob?'

'Who is that calling?'

'It's Andrei.'

'Hold on a moment.'

A few seconds later Lensky took over. 'Hello Andrei. You're using the phone I suggested, yes?'

'Yes.'

'I want to warn you, Andrei. I want you to take notice of what I say. Will you do that?'

'Of course.'

'You were in Moscow recently?'

'Yes.'

'And you spent time with a man named Rabinovich. Lev Rabinovich?'

'Yes.'

'How did you get on with him?'

'Very well, I thought.'

'But you had some trouble before you met him.'

'Yes. I guess I was arrested. They took me to the Lubyanka.'

'On what grounds?'

'They never really said.'

'You don't need to cover up, Andrei. They said you associated with a defector. Me?'

'More or less.'

'And you defended me?'

'Of course.'

'Where did you do your talking with Rabinovich?'

'In his office in the Lubyanka and at his *dacha* at Peredelkino.'

'All his time with you was taped. He's in a labour camp now. Got fifteen years for association with enemies of the State. And that means you.'

'But they congratulated me, the technical people, on what I was getting for them. They've sent me congratulations in the last month or so.'

'Doesn't mean a thing. Mark my words. Carry on if you have to for some reason but never repeat never go to the Soviet Union or to any Warsaw Pact country.'

'But why this attitude?'

'The people who were the hard-liners hated my guts. They still do. Don't fall for any story that takes you back there. You won't come back if you do.'

'How do you know all this, Jakob?'

'I've got my sources.'

'What are you doing out there?'

'Thinking, resting, sitting in the sun and enjoying the privilege of talking with people who can think for themselves.' He paused. 'You should try it some time.'

'Thanks for the warning, Jakob.'

'And you'll heed my warning?'

'You bet.'

'*Shalom.*'

Aarons said '*Shalom*' softly and hung up.

When Anna found him he was sitting there on the stool by the phone with his head in his hands. She knelt down and put a hand on each of his shoulders.

'What is it, Andrei? What's the matter?'

He looked up slowly, his eyes closed and he said gently, 'I'll be all right, Anna.' He sighed. 'Don't say anything to Tania, please.'

'Whatever you say. But you worry me, my brother.' She paused. 'Bill Malloy and Kathy came in, they're with Tania now. Do you want an aspirin?'

He laughed despite himself. 'No. An aspirin won't cure my problems.'

'What do you need? Tell me. Maybe I can help.'

'Tell me you're happy with Sam.'

'Of course I am. I love him and he loves me. Why do you ask?'

He shook his head. 'I knew you were happy with him. I just wanted to hear someone say something good came out of my life.'

'Don't talk like that, Andrei. You've spent all your life trying to help people achieve a place in the world.'

He shook his head, stood up, helped her to her feet and kissed her brow.

'Come back with me, Anna.'

When he was with the others she went over to Sam and whispered to him as he played 'Mood Indigo'. He moved on into Andrei's favourites, 'Manhattan', 'Love Walked In' and 'Love is the Sweetest Thing'.

He left with Tania just after midnight. She had been aware of the pale, drawn face and the flatness of his voice. But she said nothing.

He lay awake beside her through the night, for once the sound of police sirens and the noise of traffic were a comfort. He knew that his life had changed or was going to change. He didn't know how and he wasn't even sure why it would change. It wasn't a time for rushing into decisions. Sooner or later there would be a sign and he'd know what to do.

53

It was at a weekend at Hyannisport with the Kennedys that Aarons became aware of the efforts they were making, and the political risks they were prepared to take to enforce the laws on integration of blacks into the communities of the southern States.

The daily conflicts were the task of Robert Kennedy and some of his sharpest disputes were with the Vice-President, Lyndon Johnson. The on-going dispute was the charge by Willard Wirtz, the Secretary of Labour, that two thirds of companies holding government contracts didn't employ blacks, and Johnson was defending the companies' attitude. They had been playing with the family children and had come back into the President's study so that he could see the statistics that Wirtz had passed to Bobby and when the President had looked through them he looked at Bobby and said, 'That man can't run this committee. Can you think of anything more deplorable than him trying to run the United States? That's why he can't ever be President.'

By June it was obvious that Governor Wallace was prepared to go to any lengths to prevent black students being registered at the University of Alabama. The earlier violence in Birmingham was there as a reminder to all concerned as to what could happen, but only the White House seemed to care about avoiding an even greater division of opinion in the country as a whole. For Governor Wallace every blustering confrontation was an electoral advantage.

When the President was finally shown figures that confirmed that only fifteen of the 2000 federal employees in Birmingham were black – less than 1 per cent in a city that was 37 per cent black, he had had enough. He was ready to make heads roll to get some action. Bobby Kennedy had told Aarons of meetings where top men, including the Vice-President, had been deliberately humiliated by the President.

Back in New York Aarons watched day after day the battle against Governor Wallace on TV. Orchestrated defiance at the doors of the university, theatrical harangues in front of the cameras. Finally, after every attempt at reason had failed the President federalised the National Guard and Wallace retreated and the battle was over. The two black students were registered.

Aarons was impressed that despite all the stresses and strains, he and Tania had still been invited regularly every two or three weeks to Hyannisport, and had been treated almost as part of the family. And for months there had been no reference to Moscow or Soviet affairs.

He and Tania had watched the President on TV after the crisis was over. It was a more passionate declaration on racial justice than any American President had ever made before. Aarons was moved particularly by the final sentence – *'Who among us would be content to have the colour of his skin changed and stand in his place? Who among us would be content with the counsels of patience and delay? The time has come for this Nation to fulfil its promise of freedom.'*

He turned to Tania. 'He's something special, that man.'

She smiled. 'I agree, but why do you think so?'

For a moment he hesitated and then he said, 'He's my idea of what Communism is all about.'

She laughed. 'Only you could see it like that. But I know what you mean.' She paused. 'So why haven't there been any communists like him?'

He shook his head slowly, 'I don't know.'

'There have been communists like him. You're one. But

in Russia they don't end up in the Kremlin, they end up in a Gulag labour camp.'

The coded letter had been posted in Paris. Moscow wanted him to go back there for a discussion on re-organisation of agents in Europe and South America. There was an address in London for his confirmation and travel schedule. He replied two days later that he would be unable to attend as he was booked into a New York hospital for an examination for a possible stomach ulcer.

The reply came back ten days later instructing him to cancel any arrangements he had made and proceed to Moscow immediately. This time it was an order not an invitation. He had been waiting for a sign as to what to do and this was it. After his warning from Lensky it would be foolish to ignore his advice.

That evening he told Tania what had happened on his last visit to Moscow and about Lensky's warning. When he had finished she said quietly, 'Why are you telling me this?'

'I've decided to break with Moscow. I'm going to close down my network.'

'What will they do when you tell them?'

'I shan't tell them until it's done.'

'Won't you be in danger?'

'I shall tell them that I have lodged copies of a confidential report on my work from the first day to now. They will be lodged in two different hands and if there is any harassment the reports will be handed over to the FBI and the press.'

'What has made you decide to do this? Was it what happened in Moscow?'

'Not just that. Maybe that was the last straw. But I've been worried for a long time about what I was doing.'

'What worried you?'

'I came to realise that I was on the wrong side. Knowing the Kennedys made me realise that the contrast between them and the men in Moscow was too obvious to ignore.'

419

'Will they make any attempt to harm you?'

'I'm in a different position to most KGB officers. I'm not defecting to the other side.' He smiled. 'And the men in Moscow will know that if they do play games that I only have to go to the FBI and offer to cooperate and they'll give me all the protection they can.'

She shook her head. 'It sounds so strange when you refer to yourself as a KGB officer. I never see you that way.'

He smiled. 'I'm glad. I don't either.'

'Maybe we should move.'

'It wouldn't be difficult to trace where we had moved to.' He paused. 'I was thinking of talking it over with Bill Malloy, what do you think?'

'Do you trust him?'

'I've no reason not to. I've helped them all I could and he knows that.'

'Why did they let you go on running the network?'

'It was part of the deal. I was trying to help both sides understand one another better.'

'Did you succeed?'

He smiled. 'Lensky was my mouthpiece in Moscow. I don't think I ever changed their minds on fundamental things. It's hard to tell. I think I helped Truman a little and the Kennedys rather more.'

'Did you meet Truman himself?'

'Yes. It started with him.'

'Who did you meet in Moscow?'

'I met Khrushchev a few times. I think he took some notice of what I said but the pressures in the Kremlin are more vicious than in the White House.'

She shook her head. 'It's crazy. Here you are, a quiet respectable bookseller in New York, who has actually given advice to people like Jack Kennedy and Khrushchev.'

'Not advice, my love. Just comment.'

'And if you do this you'll be content just to be a bookseller.'

'Yes.' He shrugged. 'To me I always was a bookseller.'
He smiled. 'A bookseller with a dream. A dream that
could have worked. But didn't.'

'Does it anger you that it doesn't work?'

'Oddly enough it doesn't depress me.'

'Why not?'

'Because there are people here in America, people with
power, who believe in the same dream and are going to
make it work.' He paused. 'The Kennedys have all the
money they could possibly want but they give up their
lives to making Americans care about one another. They
don't need the power or the money or the status.'

'Will you go on helping them?'

'Yes. If they want me to.'

'Who was it said – "No man is an island . . ."?'

'John Donne in *Devotions*. Why do you ask?'

'Because he was wrong. *You* are an island. I am your
wife and I know so little of your life. Nobody does. Anna
and Ivan don't, not even the people in Moscow know you.'

'We'll make up for lost time,' he said quietly, and she
knew that he meant it.

He had spent two hours with Malloy, telling him of what
he intended doing.

'Can I tell the Kennedys?'

'If you think they would be interested.'

'Of course they will. They value your advice. Will you
still advise them?'

'If they want me to.'

'Will you be able to live off the bookselling business?'

'Yes. And we have Tania's income too. We'll be OK.'

'Is there anything I could do to make things easier?'

'Could it be fixed so that I'm an American citizen?'

'But you are already, aren't you?'

Aarons smiled. 'I've got two American passports and
supporting documents. And a Canadian passport, a German one, a French one and a Spanish one. All of them
are false. I'd like the genuine thing.'

421

Malloy smiled. 'At least your Soviet passport's for real.'

Aarons shook his head. 'I've never had a Soviet passport.'

'The President's going to Berlin. Can it wait until he gets back or do you need it right away?'

'I can wait. It will take me some weeks to close down my operation.'

The Aarons and the Malloys had watched on TV the President's official visit to West Berlin. Taking a look at the Wall and Check-Point Charlie and afterwards on the balcony of the Rathaus draped with a huge American flag and the short speech that brought the thunderous applause from 150,000 West Berliners packed into the square facing the City Hall. *'All free men, wherever they may live, are citizens of Berlin. And therefore as a free man, I take pride in the words,* "Ich bin ein Berliner".'

It was a speech that sent a message to the world about America's support for freedom of passage and drew attention to a regime that had to build walls with barbed wire, guard dogs, armed guards and minefields to keep its citizens from voting with their feet for freedom and prosperity. The speech re-emphasised the Russian repression and bloody-mindedness that caused the Allies to mount the Berlin Air-lift to prevent the Russians from starving the West Berliners into submission.

Malloy had talked to Bobby Kennedy about the documentation for Aarons. It would take some time but both Kennedys were delighted with the news. It would be a longer process than usual because such things would normally be dealt with by either the FBI or the CIA. Those agencies were used to creating new identities and backgrounds for defectors, but Aarons was not a defector, neither must his identity be revealed to any government agency. But Aarons was in no hurry. He had to close down his network without arousing anyone's suspicion that that was what he was doing.

Then in August there was tragedy in the Kennedy family. Jackie Kennedy gave birth to a premature baby. It was a son, five weeks premature and born with a lung ailment. The baby lived for less than two days and the President was grief-stricken.

54

Tania looked up from the copy of *Life* that she was reading and watched Aarons as he sat at the small desk by the window. A shaft of pale November sunlight slashed across his face, emphasising the furrows and lines that made it look as if it were a piece of sculpture. The deep-set eyes, the full lips and the aquiline nose made it look like the head of some Aztec god or a Sioux warrior.

He was going over his check-list of things that had been done to close down the network. There was little more to be done before he finally notified Moscow that he was no longer a player. She had never seen him so relaxed. As convinced as any college-boy that the White House was a new Camelot, swept along by the charm and energy and good intentions of the Kennedy brothers. Impressed by their determination to make America in the image that those old men had worked out all those years ago when they drew up the Constitution. And now he was no longer a hanger-on but part of it, eager to help in any way they wanted. Already she could discern a change in his outlook, a touch of optimism about the human race and where it was heading. Old habits die hard but Andrei Aarons was well on the way to being an American.

She put aside the magazine and went into the kitchen, switching on the coffee percolator and putting two slices of bread in the toaster. Almost without thinking she switched on the radio for the 3 p.m. news. At first she assumed that it was a hoax like Orson Welles and *The War of the Worlds*. But as the announcer went on with comments from the Dallas priest who had administered the last rites and the confirmation that Lyndon Johnson was now the President of the United States of America she knew that it was no hoax. She was stunned and disbelieving. Why were they in Dallas anyway? Tania Aarons had never fainted in her life but she reached for the kitchen stool and sat down slowly. Poor Jackie and little John. It didn't bear thinking about and she put her head in her hands and sobbed. And that was how Aarons found her.

As his hand touched her shoulder she looked up at him, her face tear-stained. 'They've killed him, Andrei.'

'Killed who, honey?'

'They killed Jack Kennedy in Dallas. They shot him.'

For a moment he was silent, then he said softly, 'Are you sure?'

'It was on the radio. They've stopped all the normal programmes.'

He took her arm and led her into the living room, easing her onto the couch as he turned and switched on the TV. He sat down beside her, his arm around her shoulders as he saw the pictures that they would see a hundred times again. The motorcade in Dallas, the Texas School Book Depository building, Jackie cradling her husband's bloody head in her arms. The hospital entrance with police, doctors and people from the President's team. A newsman giving the latest details and the news that a Dallas policeman had been gunned down by a man he had stopped for questioning. Finally, the sad group mounting the steps of Air Force One and Lyndon Johnson, now President Johnson, making a brief statement at Andrews Field. And still they couldn't believe that it had really happened.

The next few days passed like a bad dream that didn't end despite the coffin on Pennsylvania Avenue with its horse-drawn caisson led by a riderless horse with reversed boots in the stirrups. A commentator, David Brinkley, came near to summarising an assassination that was beyond understanding when he said, 'The events of those days don't fit, you can't place them anywhere, they don't go in the intellectual luggage of our time. It was too big, too sudden, too overwhelming, and it meant too much. It has to be separate and apart.' With the news of Lee Harvey Oswald's murder by a Dallas night-club owner named Jack Ruby it seemed only to add a bizarre twist to the already unbearable tragedy.

Sad as she was herself at the killing of John F. Kennedy, Tania was aware that its effect on her husband was disturbing. He seldom left the apartment and he seemed to have lost all his energy. When she spoke to him he often didn't answer. Not out of rudeness but because his mind was a long way away. Never a communicative man, he now seemed mentally cut off from the world. And from her.

Finally she talked to Bill Malloy on the phone and suggested it might help if he casually called in and talked with Andrei.

Malloy came after lunch, ostensibly to talk about the position in the White House now that Johnson was President. He sat facing Aarons whose eyes avoided him and who seemed not to be listening as he talked.

'Johnson has always disliked Bobby and there's going to be no close relationship there. I don't see much chance of Johnson wanting to know about you and me.'

Aarons looked at him, taking a deep breath. 'How could they do it, Bill? What kind of people are they?'

'You mean Oswald?'

'Yes. But there must have been others. How could they bring it all to an end?'

'Lots of people hated him, Andrei. And hated what he was doing. Some people would talk openly of wishing him dead.'

'What kind of people? They must have been sick.'

'People like Jimmy Hoffa. Some Republicans. There were even people who swore he was a communist in the pay of Moscow. The powerful people who fought against racial integration. The same kind of people who hated Roosevelt.'

'But why? Why did they hate him?'

'Because they wanted to preserve their power, or hated all Negroes. The people who want Martin Luther King dead. Union people who were being investigated about corruption. The Mafia. Hoover kept a personal file on Jack and his relationships with various women. Hoping that he could use it to control the President of the USA.'

'Hate him enough to kill him?'

'Yes. I'm afraid they would.' He half-smiled. 'And although Lyndon Johnson is almost the opposite on everything to Jack there are just as many people who hate *him*.'

'So why the thousands of letters they say that Jackie gets every day sympathising with her?'

'They're just ordinary people, Andrei. They loved the dream. But they don't have power or wealth to lose.'

'And they didn't care about the man and the dream?'

'Oh yes. They cared all right. But like I said, they don't count except every four years. And when the chips are on the table with the big boys you're playing Texas hold-'em and the stakes are mighty high. Killing someone who gets in the way is just a way to make sure that you keep whatever it is you have. Or whatever it is you covet.' Malloy shrugged. 'The Mafia kill people every day who get in the way. Politics and Cosa Nostra are very alike.'

'So Jack Kennedy was an indication that what America needs is an aristocracy.'

Malloy smiled. 'I don't see how you get that far.'

'Because Kennedy was a politician but he had all that he wanted. Great wealth, power, a good mind, a family. He had no axe to grind in politics for himself. What he did, he did for other people. Citizens who were being despoiled by the barons.'

'That's going too far. They, the two brothers, are human beings. They have their faults. They make mistakes. All Presidents do.' He laughed. 'Someone asked Truman what it was like to be President and he said, "It's great. For the first two minutes".'

Tania was pleased to see that as the two men talked Andrei seemed to be coming out of his shell but once Malloy had left Aarons walked over to the window and stared out across the square. As if to wash out any memory of what had happened Aarons no longer watched TV or listened to the radio.

In the week before Christmas Aarons seemed even more disturbed than before.

She walked over to him and looked up at the sad, drawn face. 'Let's go to Sam's place this evening.'

'Is that what you'd like to do?'

'Yes. I'll phone Anna so that she'll be there too.'

They had been at the club just over an hour when the barman whispered to Anna that she was wanted on the phone. She excused herself and went into the back-room that served as a primitive office and a store-room for the cases of drinks.

It was Bill Malloy. 'Thank God you're there, Anna. I'm coming over to the club. Be there in about fifteen minutes. Will you warn Tania that I've got some bad news to pass on to Andrei.'

'What is it, Bill?'

'Don't ask. Just leave it to Andy to tell you. And warn Tania.'

'My God, he doesn't need more bad news. He's already consumed with doubts.'

'I know, I was with him a few days ago. I'll be there as soon as I can. Will it be OK with Sam if I take Andy into your office there?'

'Of course it will. I'll warn him so that you're not disturbed.'

It was almost half an hour before Malloy arrived at the club and there was snow melting on the shoulders of his coat. He didn't sit down as they said their hellos and he turned to Aarons.

428

'Can I have a word with you, Andy?'

'Sure.'

'Let's go in Sam's office.'

Looking puzzled Aarons followed Malloy to the back of the bar and into the small office. Malloy pointed at the solitary chair by the desk, and when Aarons was sitting Malloy took a deep breath. 'I've got some bad news, Andy. Serov's dead. Murdered. And it's political. The KGB or one of those hit-squads they run.'

'What happened?' Aarons said very quietly.

'Angie had gone to visit her parents. When she got back their apartment door had been broken open and Serov was lying there in a pool of blood. She rang for the police and an ambulance but he was already dead. His head smashed in.'

Aarons closed his eyes and was silent for several moments before he looked at Malloy.

'What makes you think it was political?'

'When the police checked his identity and saw he was employed by the CIA they contacted them and they in turn contacted the FBI. It was the FBI who said it was political.'

'How did you hear about it?'

'Angie phoned me and I got in touch with Abe Carney. He phoned me back with the details.'

'Why are the FBI so sure it's political?'

'First of all, nothing was taken. The place had been searched professionally they said. And then the way they killed him. They smashed his head in with an ice-pick. The FBI said it was the same way they killed Trotsky in Mexico, way back. They reckon it's a message, or a statement.' He paused. 'If they've been tailing Serov it means you could be in danger too, Andy. I took the liberty of contacting Bobby Kennedy. He says that they'll cooperate in any way you want. Somewhere to move to. A pension. New identities for you and Tania. Whatever you want.' He paused. 'How about you move in with us for a few days while you work out what to do?'

'Let me talk it over with Tania first.'

'Bobby said that he would arrange FBI protection for you but that would mean explanations and draw their attention to you.'

'We'll go to a hotel for a couple of days.'

'Bobby said if you moved in with us he could get us protection on the grounds that it was for me because I knew Serov from the war and I work on confidential legal work for Defence. And that's fact.'

'If Serov's murder was a message and they know he had contact with me then the message was for me. They don't send messages if they're going to kill you. They just do it.' He shrugged. 'And they're desperate for me to go on feeding them my current stuff.'

'How can you be so sure?'

Aarons looked at him. 'Because I know the bastards. I know how their minds work. I've continued to keep them supplied with what they want. If they write me off they'd have to start from scratch. They daren't stop the flow.'

For the first time since he'd met Aarons Malloy realised that Aarons really was a spy. Behind that mild, reasoning, rational man was a man who took risks and who worked for people who used ice-picks in a man's skull as no more than a message. He had always imagined Aarons as a man who researched information on technology and the politics of America and posted them by some route to Moscow. He was aware that Aarons could have been trapped by the FBI and tried as a spy but it had seemed no more than a merely theoretical possibility – not reality. All those years aware that that day could be his last day of freedom. No wonder he went out of his way to have no friends. It must have taken great courage to go along with their deal advising the White House. He had seen it as praiseworthy conviction but it was much more than that.

'I'll be worried about the two of you until I know what you've decided to do. And you've got to take it for granted that anything I can do will be done. Just ask and I'll do it.'

430

'We'll go home tonight, Bill, and I'll sort things out and contact you tomorrow.' He shook his head. 'Poor Serov. And poor Angie. Will you be able to help her?'

'Abe Carney's already taken her under his wing.'

Aarons stood up. 'Let's go back to the girls. I won't mention anything to Tania until we're back home.'

'I phoned Anna before I came here and asked her to warn Tania that I was bringing bad news. But she doesn't know what it's about.'

Aarons saw the concern on Tania's face as they got back to the table and she made no comment as he suggested that it was time for them to go home.

They held hands in silence in the taxi and when they were inside the apartment she said, 'What was the bad news?'

He led her into the living room and when she had sat down he sat facing her. He told her the news about Serov and she shook her head slowly in disbelief as she listened. When he had finished she said quietly, 'What do we do now?'

'Have you got any views?'

She shook her head. 'I'm out of my depth, Andrei. You know best what we should do.' She sighed. 'You are in danger, you must know that.'

'Would you mind leaving New York?'

'Not if it makes you safe.' She paused. 'Where should we go?'

He sighed. 'I feel that I've been a fool. A reckless fool too.'

'Why?'

'Thinking that all Americans were like Jack Kennedy. Or at least that they wanted what he wanted. I could never have believed that Americans could kill a man for his politics. I could understand people disagreeing with his policies – but not killing him. That's obscene. That's what the people in Moscow do.' He paused and looked at her. 'I don't want to be part of it. So what am I – an American or a Russian?'

She smiled. 'Have you ever noticed that Russians are never called immigrants, they're always *émigrés*. It implies that they didn't come here because they wanted to but because they were forced to, driven out of their own countries.'

'So I'm an *émigré* . . .' he shrugged, '. . . so what?'

'You know, my love, it's taken you a long time to learn the facts of life.'

'What does that mean?'

'You were never a Russian and you're not an American.'

'So what am I?'

'You're a Jew, my love. And despite everything you always were. And you still are.'

For a long time he was silent and then he smiled. 'So what do we do?'

'We do what Jakob did. We leave it all and we go to Israel and forget the KGB and the White House. You go on selling books and I take photographs.' She smiled. 'And we live happily ever after.'

'How long have you thought this?'

'Almost from when I first knew you.'

'Why didn't you say so?'

'Because just telling you wouldn't have been enough. You had to do it your way. You had to learn.'

'Learn what?'

'That all over the world people behave like people. The human race is the most terrible animal that the good Lord created. They don't just kill for food. They kill because they like it.'

'And Israelis don't kill people?'

'Only in self-defence. But I'm not suggesting we go there for that reason. But because it's a small country. It's not a world power like the Soviet Union or America.'

'And what about you? You are an American.'

'One half Jewish, my friend, and I don't give a damn for politics or politicians. You do. You've got to forget them. You should never have been involved in the first place. You didn't choose to be a communist, you just absorbed it from your father. And he was conned like the rest of the Russians. And you did the same. You defended something that didn't exist.' She smiled and said softly, 'And the White House was never really Camelot. Except for your background you and Jack Kennedy were very much alike. Both dreamers, and both ready to ignore the facts of life. That's why he was killed. And now Serov. And that's why we should move to Israel.'

'Maybe I should take photographs and you should look after the philosophising.'

She smiled. 'There ain't gonna be no philosophising, honey. And taking photographs in Harlem might bring you down to earth.' She paused. 'Anyway. What do you think about my idea?'

'First of all I think you are much wiser than I am. Just hearing you talk is an incredible relief. I feel like a man who's just been let out of prison.' He looked at her fondly. 'When do we go?'

'In days not weeks. You can clean up your mess. I can deal with my assignments. And my agent can start looking for work for me in Israel.'

Aarons went to his office in the Flatiron Building and sat for two days working out the state of his resources and separated KGB assets from his own. He was pleasantly surprised to find that his own account stood at 75,000 dollars excluding the profits that he would make on the sale of the lease of the apartment and a small profit on the lease of the office in the Flatiron Building. He had no idea what assets Tania had. But it was obvious that even if it took some time for him to establish his business in Israel they would live quite comfortably.

He arranged a meeting with Cowley at their usual place and Cowley handed over an envelope which Aarons didn't open.

'I'm going to close down the operation for a while, Roger.'

Cowley looked stunned. 'But why? I thought we were doing well.'

'We were. But I need to let things cool down for a bit. A question of security.'

'Nobody knows a damn thing.' He frowned. 'Are you telling me they're onto us?'

'No I'm not. I just want to make sure that we don't take any risks.' He paused and reached into his jacket pocket and brought out an envelope. 'There's three thousand dollars in there.'

'Thanks. I'm gonna need that. How long before we can get going again?'

'At least six months, Roger. Maybe longer. In this business it pays to be patient. Just carry on with your job and your own life and I'll be in touch when it's safe again.'

'Is this from Moscow?'

'Partly.'

'Do they know something we don't?'

'No. They're just playing it safe. It's quite a usual procedure when an operation has gone on for a long time.'

'And what are you going to do? Are they closing you down too?'

'It's possible.'

Cowley looked relieved by Aarons' answer.

'I'd like to thank you for all the good work you've done, Roger.' He stood up. 'I'll be in touch.' He put out his hand and Cowley stood up and took it.

'Well. Back to the grindstone. Be seein' you – I hope.'

Ivan had acted as a courier for Aarons and had spent a lot of time liaising with the four people in Brighton Beach who were still connected to the network. Aarons used them frequently but except for the radio ham it took very little of their time. Ivan had moved in with Sam and Anna at their apartment near Prospect Park for just over a year but for the last two years he had a small apartment of his own in Brighton Beach, over a shop that was not far from the old bookshop which was now used by some Jewish women's organisation. Ivan made up his income with a series of jobs none of which lasted very long. When Aarons phoned him to come up to see him he arranged a date for late afternoon the next day.

Tania was at the studio and they sat in the kitchen. Ivan had a Coors from the fridge and Aarons made himself a cup of tea.

'I'm going to close down the network, Ivan.'

Ivan showed no surprise. 'Is this beer for your guests?'

'Yes.'

'You should be able to provide better than this.' He smiled. 'Trouble with Moscow?'

'What makes you think that?'

Ivan shrugged. 'Just a question of time, old buddy.'

'Why?'

'Someday you were going to see through them. I'm surprised it took so long.'

'I didn't say why I was closing down.'

Ivan grinned. 'I may not be as brainy as you are, fella. But I've got more common sense. They ain't gonna get rid of a guy like you. So if you're closing down it means you've had enough.'

'What do you think about it?'

'You should have done it years ago. You were a sucker to carry on after the war and after what they did when you wanted to borrow the money for Chantal when she was in hospital. They gave you the finger, kiddo. You should have given it 'em back.' He paused. 'What you gonna do?'

'Tania and I are moving to Israel. Do you want to come with us?'

Ivan smiled. 'I got some news for you. Rachel and I are getting married next week.'

'I thought she married that fellow from the restaurant in the Bronx.'

'She did but she divorced him about six months ago.'

'What went wrong?'

He shrugged. 'She found out he was screwing all over

435

the place, including the waitresses at the restaurant.' He paused. 'We're going to open a haberdashery and notions shop on the Avenue. Old man Henschel's putting up the dough. A no-interest loan.'

'How much is he putting up?'

'Six thousand bucks.'

'So you're not interested in moving to Israel?'

'No. I belong here. I always have.' He smiled. 'I wouldn't mind a holiday there some time.'

'You'd be welcome any time. Both of you. How is she, Rachel?'

'Much the same. Older, a bit fatter, cheerful despite what she's gone through.'

Aarons smiled. 'Anna was always sure you two would get married.' He paused. 'I owe you a lot of money from over the years. You've never had a fair deal from me. I've put aside fifteen thousand dollars from my Moscow budget for you. I was going to give it to you next week on your birthday but I'll give it to you now before you go.'

'What about those bastards in Moscow? They'll go crazy when they know you've finished with them.'

'I'm giving you a packet and I'll be giving Bill Malloy the same material. If anything happens to me or Tania there are instructions in the packet as to what to do with the contents.'

'Do you think they'll come after you?'

'No. We'll be gone before they know and they won't want what's in that packet to go to the FBI and the press.'

'You think you've got a stand-off?'

'I'm sure I have.'

'What's Tania say?'

'She's delighted. I guess it's her idea more than mine.'

'But you're happy yourself about it?'

'Yes. Like you said, I ought to have done it long ago.'

'You'll be around for the wedding?'

Aarons smiled. 'You bet.'

'You know something, kiddo?'

'What?'

'I ain't seen you smile so much in the last twenty years. It suits you.'

Apart from Roger Cowley Aarons didn't inform any of the other people in his network. They weren't dependent on him for their livelihoods and if there were no more contacts from him or the cut-outs they would just accept it as part of the game.

A few days later Malloy phoned and said that 'the man from Kansas' would like to meet him before he left and a meeting had been arranged in Washington. It seemed that Truman had been kept informed about the help that Aarons had given to the Kennedys and he'd asked Aarons if he would give advice in the future if there was some really vital decision to be made concerning the Soviet Union. The old man was very persuasive and he understood why Aarons had had enough and in the end Aarons had agreed that if such an occasion occurred he would be willing to help but not on a regular basis, only in a time of crisis.

It was obvious when he and Tania had gone for one last weekend with the Kennedys at Hyannisport that it was Bobby Kennedy who had asked Truman to persuade him to be available if it was really crucial.

The lease of the apartment and the Flatiron Building office had been sold profitably and Tania had two prospective buyers for her studio building and apartment. And it was Tania who would spend ten days in Israel finding somewhere for them to live. She would be staying with Lensky while she was there.

They had talked about whether they should live in Tel Aviv or Jerusalem but they knew that they were talking in ignorance. Neither of them had any more than a superficial knowledge of Israel. They would have to take Lensky's advice and the decision would be Tania's.

Lensky met her in at Ben Gurion, obviously delighted to see her and at their decision to move. Lensky lived in central Tel Aviv in an area that was almost solely residential. His was a small apartment with a living room, two bedrooms, kitchen and bathroom.

But by the end of the third day Tania knew exactly what she wanted for them. She had fallen in love with Jaffa as soon as she saw it. It was so alive and so obviously receptive to artists. Galleries, jewellers, restaurants and simple eating places and a mixture of Jews and Arabs.

As soon as she saw the house that was for sale she knew that it was just what they wanted. It was in walking distance of the Flea Market and not far from the beach. It had obviously once been a traditional Arab house with high ceilings and archways. But it had been discreetly and lovingly modernised by its present owner, an architect who was moving back to America. It was approached from a narrow alley and the arched entrance gave onto a courtyard with a pond, the house itself occupying three sides of the courtyard. Inside there was room for ample living quarters and for a studio and darkroom and rooms to spare for Aarons' books. The architect was one of Lensky's friends and he had haggled about the price on Tania's behalf while she walked around the small walled garden at the rear of the house. The asking price had been reduced by 10 per cent and she had shaken hands on the deal before she left. She also made an offer for most of the furniture which the owner said he would consider.

She had phoned Aarons that night, elated with what she had found for them. He seemed pleased and told her that all the books that he would be taking with them were packed already. Fourteen large wooden crates. She left two days later having photographed their new house and signed the transfer of ownership. The house would be available in two weeks' time and her offer for the furnishings had been accepted.

On the flight back she hoped that Andrei wouldn't feel that she had been wildly extravagant. She knew she had been. She'd been carried away by its beauty and its rightness for both of them. She wouldn't mention the price until he'd seen the Polaroids. The palms in the garden and the bougainvillea everywhere would make him fall in love with it too. It made all that had happened worthwhile just to spend their lives in that house, with the sun and the volatile Israelis she had met. Wall to wall intellectuals, artists, actors, writers and musicians. And of course *felafels* and wonderful ice-cream. Anyway she had enough money in her own account to pay for the house.

When she got back she was surprised that Andrei made no comment on the cost of the house and it was obvious that from the photographs of the house he was delighted. Not without veiled wonderings about whether they weren't being self-indulgent. She'd laughed and said that he was probably right but that it was a just reward for a lifetime's caution and penny-pinching. For his part he had done all that he had to apart from a last get-together with the Malloys, Ivan and Rachel, and Anna and Sam. It was to be at Sam's club. Sam was now the sole owner and they had moved from Prospect Park to an apartment over the club that was spacious and central but not easy to let because of the club itself.

The party was to be on a Sunday night when the club was normally closed.

When Ivan was talking to Sam about the get-together he said that he wasn't sure whether it was going to turn out to be a party or a wake. But ten minutes after they were all sitting around the table there was no doubt that it was a party. A farewell party maybe but with Aarons so obviously happy with the change in his life.

They reminisced about the days at Brighton Beach but it was Anna and Ivan who talked of those days, and about their own lives, not Aarons'. But they had all laughed at Aarons' reconstruction of his first encounter with old man Henschel on Ivan's behalf. Much blushing from Rachel. But as the time went by Aarons relaxed. It seemed unbelievable. These people seemed quite genuine when they said they would miss him. They were sorry that he was leaving.

Malloy said, 'Andrei, you've got three countries in your life – Russia, France and America. What do they mean to you?'

Aarons smiled. 'Russia for me is Tolstoy and Dostoevsky . . . Rachmaninoff and Tchaikowsky. France is . . .' he hesitated 'God knows. It means nothing for me except dear Chantal. And America? America is John Steinbeck, Scott Fitzgerald, Irving Berlin, Jerome Kern and . . .' he looked from one to the other and said softly, '. . . no. America for me is all you people.'

It was Ivan who put up his hand and said, 'And what have you learned from the three countries?'

For several moments Aarons was silent, thinking. And then he said, 'I learned what Shakespeare meant in *Henry V* when he said –

> *'Trust none,*
> *For oaths are straw, men's faiths are wafer-cakes,*
> *and hold-fast is the only dog, my duck.'*

And he looked, smiling, at Tania who smiled back but said nothing.

Sam had made a tape of half an hour of Andrei's favourite tunes and they danced until it was over and they were suddenly quiet as they got into their street clothes. There was Ivan's wedding the next day and after that Andrei Aarons would no longer be around. It was the first time that they had realised how much that strange, solitary man had been the centre of their lives.

55

It was night when they landed and the faithful Lensky was waiting for them. They could see him waiting at the reception windows as they stood in line at immigration. Being met in by Lensky gave Aarons an odd reminder of the life he had left behind. It seemed strange too to be holding a genuine passport, stamped and issued by the Israeli embassy in Washington. An immigrant's passport so it took a little longer for them to be processed than for the tourists. A young woman took them to the New Immigrants Terminal and waited with them while their documents were checked. When they were waved through she asked them if they had relatives meeting them or if they needed some help. They told her that they were being met. Lensky had guessed that as they couldn't read Hebrew they would go to the wrong terminal but he had walked across to their terminal. It was a warm greeting for both of them. Arms around them and kisses on their cheeks.

Lensky had a car waiting for them with a driver and half an hour later they were at their new home. There were lights on in the courtyard and over the arched entrance and the house itself was ablaze with lights. A middle-aged woman, one of Lensky's friends, was waiting at the open door. She greeted them in Hebrew and Aarons smiled and thanked her in Yiddish.

When Aarons had been shown around the house the four of them went to a small restaurant for a meal. The streets were still busy with shoppers but the shops were beginning to close.

When they were alone Tania said, 'Do you like the house?'

He smiled. 'I can't believe it. We did it all in such a rush. It's a beautiful house. I think we're going to be very happy here.'

By the end of the first month New York seemed a long way away. They had friends, some of them they had met through Lensky, others Tania had met through photographic contacts. Already she had two local assignments and one from a New York magazine.

Setting up the book business was taking longer. Andrei had a lot of introductions to academics but it was wealthy immigrants who were more interested in his books. But he made enough on his sales of rare and antique books to keep the business going. They had been in Israel just over six months when Aarons was invited to give a talk at the university on the history of the Revolution. He did it reluctantly but it was obviously a great success with the students. It was the Revolution seen by a contemporary with a perceptive eye that now had the benefit of hindsight.

It was Yehuda Cohn, head of the History Faculty, who asked him the following spring if he would care to lecture two days a week at the university. Although Aarons had said that he didn't feel he was qualified to teach at any level, Cohn had smiled and said that he was too modest and that was part of the reason why the students liked him so much. That and his lack of bias.

The Malloys came to stay with them the following Christmas and a month later they had a visitor who came unannounced to the house.

He was in his forties, a handsome man who spoke good English and introduced himself as Amos Frankel. Could he have a private word with Aarons?

Andrei took him to his library and offered him a coffee which he smilingly declined. When they were both seated Aarons said, 'What do you want to talk about?'

Frankel smiled. 'You.'

'Me? Is this something to do with books or is it the university?'

'Neither. I wanted to ask for your help.'

'What kind of help?'

'I suppose that vaguely it's to do with the subject you lecture on at the university.'

The dark eyes were watching Aarons' face and Frankel smiled. 'It's not an official approach, my friend. Just a . . . let's say . . . a look at one another.'

'I don't understand.'

'I think you do, but I understand your response.' He shrugged. 'We think you have experience that would help us in our relationships with Moscow and we wonder if you might help.'

'You say – "we think" – who are we?'

'A government organisation.'

'Mossad?'

Frankel shrugged. 'In that area, but not Mossad. Solely concerned with politics and diplomacy.' He smiled. 'Not doers, more thinkers.'

'What makes you think that I could help?'

Frankel smiled. 'An old friend thought you might be willing.'

'I think your old friend was mistaken.'

'Our information is that you helped others to keep the peace, why not your own country – Israel?'

'Where does your information come from?'

'It's a long story.'

'So tell me.'

For a few seconds Frankel was silent, then he said, 'Four weeks ago colleagues of mine in another organisation came across a man. A Soviet. Here as a tourist with a Canadian passport. Let us say he was taken into custody and was interrogated for many days.' Frankel looked at Aarons' face. 'If I say that he confessed to being on a mission for Directorate D – Active Measures – of the First Chief Directorate you'll know what I'm talking about.'

'And who was the target?'

'Let's just say it was an old friend of yours. And of mine too. And because of the reasons the Soviet gave as to why our friend was the target we briefed him and had a long talk with him. He was worried about you being a target too. He told us a little of your background.' He smiled. 'Just enough to make us look after you.'

'What happened to the Active Measures man?'

Stony-faced Frankel said, 'My colleagues in the other organisation assure me that he'll not be a problem in the future.'

'Tell me your friend's name.'

'You want me to say it?'

'Yes.'

'It's Lensky. Jakob Lensky.'

'Why was he a target?'

'He was classified as an enemy of the State.'

'That's ridiculous.'

Frankel shrugged. 'They don't have to produce evidence, those people. I'm sure you know that.'

'So what has this to do with me?'

'Nothing. You asked me how I knew about you.'

'I left all those things behind when I left New York. I'm happy here. For the first time in my life. We came here to live simple lives, my wife and I.'

'You're a Jew, Andrei Grigorovich. And an Israeli.'

'So?'

'We are a small country surrounded by enemies. Jordan, Egypt, Iraq, Iran, Syria, the Palestinians. We need all the help we can get.'

'I know virtually nothing about the Middle East.'

'We know that.'

'So what help am I?'

'You know how the machinery works in the Kremlin and in Dzerdzhinski Square. You could maybe save lives.'

'Does Lensky know about this?'

'No.'

'He knows more about those things than I do.'

'D'you know how old he is?'

'No.'

'Eighty-two. He's an old man, my friend. He's had more than he can take. He hasn't got long to live. He's a sick man.'

'And if I don't help you?'

'We shall be disappointed but we shall understand. It happens to our people as well.'

'What happens?'

'They get worn out by men's evil. They don't just read about it in newspapers. They see it, they experience it. Day after day. If they are wise they do what you did. They call it a day.'

'And if they don't?'

'We send them to nice quiet embassies overseas. New Zealand's got great healing powers for an over-active mind. Nice people, nice country.'

'So why disturb *my* peace of mind?'

'We won't, I assure you.' He smiled. 'How about we do a deal?'

'What deal?'

'Come and have dinner with my wife and me once a month.'

'And?'

'And nothing.' He smiled. 'I had a duty to ask you. But we aren't a press-gang. We're volunteers. Most of our people are escaping from something. Some want to fight on. Some don't.'

He stood up, still smiling and held out his hand. As Aarons took it Frankel said, 'Except for our deal, forget our talk.'

Despite his refusal to help, Aarons had been impressed by Amos Frankel. He was perceptive and understanding without much explaining of Aarons' feelings. He seemed to understand by experience or instinct that he was asking too much. He was a likeable man too, easy to talk to and a vibrant, alert personality. Sophisticated in the true meaning of the word.

Two months later came the first invitation to dinner and the Aaronses took instantly to Rebecca Frankel and her husband. The two couples met every month at one house or another and they became occasions to look forward to.

Six months later Jakob Lensky died after a fall that broke a leg and turned to pneumonia. Both couples attended his funeral. By then Aarons and Frankel were close friends. Meeting two or three times a week for coffee and a game of chess. Frankel had never again raised the question of Aarons cooperating in some way, nor did he ever bring international politics into their talk.

The sunshine and the lively Israelis had made a real difference to Aarons. For the first time in his life he felt that he belonged. Most Israelis were like him, having left something that they had found oppressive. But he gradually became aware that he had left behind something that he disliked whereas most others had left in the wake of a ruthlessness and cruelty that was sickening to think about. Lives that were best forgotten but could never be forgotten. Faded photographs, those tattooed numbers on wrists, the faraway look in old people's eyes, the constant awareness of the precariousness of the small country in which they lived, surrounded by enemies who had sworn to sweep them into the sea. That sparkling, blue sea where he and Tania walked along the beach.

It was the third year anniversary of their arrival in Israel when he phoned Amos Frankel and arranged to meet him at the coffee shop on Kiryat Yam.

'I've changed my mind, Amos. About helping.'

'Why?'

'This is the country I came to to find some peace. I've found it, and I'm grateful. I guess it's time I paid my dues.'

Frankel smiled and shook his head slowly, 'It's not necessary, Andrei.'

'But I want to help.'

'It's some years now since you were involved with Moscow. Things have moved on since then. People too.' He paused. 'How about we leave it that when we would like a second opinion on some policy matter we could call on you?'

'Anything you want.'

'That's fine. There are some people I'd like you to meet but there's no hurry.'

It's not easy to be a loner in Israel. Doggedly loyal to their communities and their country, Israeli men were not too concerned with the niceties. As Ben-Gurion said to Truman, 'There are three million presidents in Israel.' It wasn't just the background of concentration camps but the harsh conditions of the early years of the State that bred a loyalty to one's fellows in times of peace as well as war. Casual dress and a lack of inhibitions were the outward uniform of people whose homes were sanctuaries for even the least observant of Jews, with its *mezuza* attached to the door-frame to remind all who entered that it was a Jewish home.

As the years went by Aarons' old life seemed so far away as to be unreal. He seldom thought about it and when he did it was with amazement that he had let it go on for so long.

Their income was not much more than half what they had earned in New York but their living was less expensive too despite the fact that their personal lives were more active. He had no regrets about leaving their old life in New York. Looking back on it it seemed a narrow, broken-backed existence. But he sensed that there were New York things that Tanya missed, and when her old New York agent wrote offering an assignment for a photographic book on the ethnic minorities of New York he noticed that she didn't hurry to reply. When he asked her how long it would take she had said she would need three months' hard work. But he had seen her eyes light up when he suggested that she took the assignment to keep up her New York contacts.

They had been Israeli citizens for just over ten years when he saw her off at Ben-Gurion. Sad that she was going, hating being on his own but loving her too much not to let her go. She was going to stay with the Malloys. Bill Malloy was now senior partner at his law firm and wealthy enough to retire in a couple of years' time. It was from Tania that he learned that Ivan's stormy relationship with Rachel had finally ended in divorce despite the fact that 'little 'van' was now a wealthy man.

Tania's assignment stretched out to four months but when she got back he had his reward. She had loved the work but had hated New York, and was desperately glad to be back in their old routine.

Aarons had been co-opted onto a committee working on a Constitution for the State of Israel. His old skills of analysis, quiet argument and diplomacy were much respected and valued. He taught full-time now at the university but the journey to Ramat Gan was beginning to be a strain. Approaching his late seventies and suffering from the onset of arthritis, Aarons retired and Tania took on fewer assignments so that she could be with him. Still mentally alert, he suffered from time to time enough pain in his hands to make normal life difficult.

The Malloys visited them most years for a few weeks and Aarons heard the gossip of New York and Washington and was glad that he was not involved.

Malloy had phoned Tania first, to ask her if Aarons was well enough to travel.

'He never goes anywhere these days, Bill. His arthritis gives him almost continuous pain. And he's an old man. Why do you ask?'

'The new man heard about what happened about the Cuba thing. He's desperate to have a talk with Andrei.'

'He left all that sort of thing decades ago, Bill.'

448

'There's no crisis. He just wants Andrei's opinion about Gorbachev and *perestroika*. Nothing more. I promise.'

'I don't think he'll want to come. Where would it be?'

'At Camp David. Just for a weekend. You too of course. VIP travel all the way.'

'Are you phoning because you want me to ask him?'

'No. Just to find out what you thought, before I raised it with him.'

'I think he should be left in peace.'

'It's a personal request from the President, Tania.'

'We're Israelis, Bill. He doesn't even involve himself in those old games over here.'

'This country is a very good friend to Israel, my love, you know that.'

For several seconds she was silent and then she said, 'All right. Speak to him. He's asleep now. Call him in a couple of hours, OK?'

'Bless you, honey. And thanks.'

She had said nothing about the call from Malloy and she made sure that Andrei took the call himself. And two minutes later she realised that she'd been suckered. Andrei was listening intently and his replies were laced with 'Mr Presidents'. Nobody was going to refuse a personal request from George Bush.

56

They stopped Malloy's car outside the gate at Camp David and made him get out. It was an official car and they had seen Malloy around the place dozens of times but they stuck strictly to the book. That's what the Secret Service men were there for. They were both young, as soberly dressed as any IBM salesman and Malloy stood patiently as they checked his ID. One of them standing a few paces away, shining a torch on his face, the other man with his torch on the ID card. The young man handed back the card and unhooked a small transceiver from inside the pocket of his jacket. He pressed a rocker switch and then several numbers on the key-pad. He was intent on what he was doing and turned slightly away from Malloy as he listened. Malloy heard him say 'Cactus to Royal Crown' and he waited. Cactus was the radio code for Camp David and Royal Crown the code for High Priority White House Communications. With the radio to his ear he waited, his face lit by the beam of the other man's torch. They looked so young and earnest, Dan Quayle lookalikes. Then the man said 'Yes' and nodded as if the listener could see the nod. He closed down the aerial and slid the transceiver back into his pocket. He nodded to Malloy. 'The Chief wants to see you. I'll take you over, sir,' and he touched Malloy's arm and guided him along the gravel path, shining his torch in front of them despite the fact that inside the grounds were well-lit.

It was quite a long walk to the President's quarters where he was handed over to an older Secret Service man watched by a US Marine. He was taken inside and led down a short corridor to the private room next to the general living room where the door was ajar and he could hear Ella Fitzgerald singing 'Manhattan' – '. . . *we'll go to Coney and eat baloney on a roll – in Central Park we'll stroll . . .'*

The music stopped, the door opened and the President waved him inside, a glass in his hand, smiling as he said, 'I love that song and nobody does it like she does . . . anyway, take a seat.' He paused, still smiling. 'A Coke, white wine or would you rather have a whisky?'

'A malt if you've got it.'

Bush grinned. 'We've got everything. How about a Glen Livet?'

'Fine, thank you, sir.'

When he had poured Malloy's drink and handed it to him Bush said, 'How's Kathy?'

'She's OK, thank you.'

'You got time for a chat?'

'Sure.'

'Did he get off OK?'

'Yeah. He was flying back via Toronto.'

'Why Toronto? Why not direct?'

Malloy shrugged. 'I guess old habits die hard.'

'He's a strange man. Not easy to understand. But we could have made a lot of silly blunders without his advice.'

'Was he useful on this trip?'

'Yes. He's got an instinct for what matters and what doesn't.'

'What don't you understand about him?'

'How can a man with a brain like his choose to be a communist? I don't get it.'

Malloy put down his glass and leaned back in his chair. 'He didn't choose Communism. He heard it all from his father when he was a kid and growing up. Like some American kid in Brooklyn going to see the Yankees with his old man. They're his team for the rest of his life even if he moves to LA. You don't make a choice, you just absorb it. A kind of osmosis.' He paused. 'And of course with that kind of man there's a flaw.'

'What's the flaw?'

'You have to find explanations for the inexplicable. And they have to be the truth or very near it.'

'Give me a for instance.'

'I asked him about his reaction to Moscow's pact with the Nazis. He said it was to buy time and the Brits had done the same when they sold the Czechs down the river. Moscow's line was very different but when Aarons talked to his people he told them the truth, because he understood their revulsion.' Malloy shrugged. 'He saw both sides. And if you do that you end up in an ivory tower – or a psychiatric ward.'

'So why did he decide to help us? Way back.'

Malloy smiled and shook his head. 'He didn't – he helped humanity. You've only got to look at his personal life – he loved humanity, but he didn't love individual people. He barely noticed that they existed.'

'What about his wives and his family? You told me they're very fond of him.'

'They are. But it's a one-way traffic. I think his women loved him like they would love some deprived child. He was responsible for his family when his father died and in practical terms he did a good job. But it was from the head, not the heart.'

'You make him sound like a pretty cold fish.'

'I think he was. He got stuck with Communism because of his old man. The Party ruled his life. He went wherever they sent him. He did whatever they asked – and did it well.'

'But how could he believe in it – Communism?'

'I'm not sure he did believe in it – he cared about humanity but you could say that about Christians. They go to church out of habit but I doubt if they believe in it. If they do they don't make much effort to put it into practice. They don't turn the other cheek and they don't love their neighbours.' Malloy smiled. 'I once told him

452

that there was really no difference between Communism and Christianity. Both would work if it weren't for people.' He paused. 'That's why he went to Israel. Moscow couldn't live up to his ideals, neither could we – no country could. So he escaped to Israel with all its tensions and problems. But they're not his problems. And it's worked for him. He has friends there which he never dared have here. I've even seen signs of affection for his wife.'

'But he was so shrewd in his judgments of people.'

'No, sir. He wasn't. He made assessments of people but he never made judgments. He accepted people as what they were – frail, flawed – all the vices – to be observed, not judged.'

'I always thought you liked him.'

For a few moments Malloy was silent, then he said, 'I did. Maybe on reflection it was more admiration than liking. I admired his sharp mind. He would have made a great lawyer but I also admired his courage. He ran an espionage network for years without getting caught. If he had been caught it could have been a life sentence or even the electric chair. He fitted so well into his cover as a bookseller that it's hard to believe that in fact he was a spy.' Malloy smiled. 'Were you ever tempted to look at the FBI files to see if they had spotted him?'

Bush grinned, the blue eyes twinkling. 'I'm not saying.' He paused. 'I think they were looking at the wrong member of the family. The brother – Ivan, wasn't it?'

'Anyway, even when he was helping us he didn't ask for any protection if he got caught spying. Just think what a deal he could have done with us if he'd chosen to defect. And I'd swear it never entered his mind. He was all of a piece, that man, and he took what the fates handed out to him and got on with it.' Malloy shrugged. 'But to answer your question I guess I liked his mind. And his innocence.'

'Innocence? How come?'

'Just think of what he knew. About Moscow, about us.

And despite that he never played Machiavelli. He played no games and ground no axes. He could be a rich man but he lives in Jaffa, just getting by comfortably because of Tania's photography.'

'What about a pension?'

'No. He'd never accept it and he wouldn't even be grateful for the kind thought.'

Bush smiled. 'What are we talking about – a saint or a hero?'

Malloy shook his head slowly. 'I don't know. I really don't know.'